A Dawn Like Thunder

"Strap yourself in as Robert J. Mrazek takes you on a heroic flight into history."
—James Bradley, author of
Flyboys and *Flags of Our Fathers*

"A spectacular achievement."
—Hon. Charles Wilson of *Charlie Wilson's War*

"A remarkably vivid tale . . . [an] epic story."
—Rick Atkinson, author of *The Guns at Last Light*
and *The Day of Battle*

"Destined to become a classic."
—Alex Kershaw, author of *The Liberator*
and *The Longest Winter*

"Fast-paced. . . . [Mrazek] melds a good story with solid and skeptical research." —*The Washington Post*

"A must read . . . gripping."
—Curled Up with a Good Book

"Robert J. Mrazek has, with a raw, unsparing telling, given grace and life to so many who died so young . . . so gallantly." —Frank Deford, author of *Over Time*

"Compelling." —*The Columbus Dispatch*

continued . . .

"A first-rate World War II adventure."
—Susan Isaacs, *New York Times* bestselling author of
Goldberg Variations

"Tautly gripping, with vividly malevolent characters and some excellent historical color." —*Kirkus Reviews*

"[An] exciting thriller." —Historical Novel Society

"Full of dark twists and turns, this brooding drama underscores the brutal nature of both the physical and the psychological casualties associated with war." —*Booklist*

Praise for Robert J. Mrazek's Nonfiction

To Kingdom Come

"Riveting." —*Library Journal*

"A great book with 'hold on to your seat' suspense."
—Donald Miller, author of *Masters of the Air:
America's Bombers Who Fought the Air War
Against Nazi Germany*

"Rendered . . . in vivid clarity."
—Hugh Ambrose, *New York Times* bestselling
author of *The Pacific*

"[A] work of cinematic sweep and pace."
—Richard Frank, author of *Downfall* and *Guadalcanal*

"Superb historical research and powerful narrative writing."
—Tami Biddle, professor, U.S. Army War College,
and author of *Rhetoric and Reality in Air Warfare*

VALHALLA

ROBERT J. MRAZEK

A SIGNET BOOK

SIGNET
Published by the Penguin Group
Penguin Group (USA) LLC, 375 Hudson Street,
New York, New York 10014

USA | Canada | UK | Ireland | Australia | New Zealand | India | South Africa | China
penguin.com
A Penguin Random House Company

First published by Signet, an imprint of New American Library,
a division of Penguin Group (USA) LLC

First Printing, October 2014

ISBN 978-0-451-46872-7

Printed in the United States of America
10 9 8 7 6 5 4 3 2 1

To Martin Andrews

"Lo there do I see my father. Lo there do I see my mother, my sisters, and my brothers. Lo there do I see the line of my people, back to the beginning. Lo they do call me. They bid me take my place among them in the Halls of Valhalla. Where the brave, may live forever."

The Vikings, *The 13th Warrior*

PROEM

He could no longer endure the agonizing cold.

The eternal darkness.

The ever-howling wind.

He was the last one left.

Ice particles peppered his cheeks as his bruised and aching fingers labored at their final task. He imagined the rest of them celebrating with bowls of honey-soaked mead in the halls of Valhalla. Where he would soon join them.

The rescue party would come in the spring. They would see what he had done in these last hours of mortal life. They would bring the tale back home and share it with the others. Grindl would learn of what he had done. She would always be proud.

And they would know of the hallowed place.

And go there.

THE RUNES OF
THE GODS

ONE

"A toast to the crew of *March Hare*," John Lee Hancock shouted above the shrieking wind as he raised his pewter Air Force Academy goblet and downed three inches of vintage 1942 Dom Pérignon champagne. "Tonight we will unearth her secrets."

Hap Arnold, Hancock's one-hundred-twenty-pound white Alsatian, stirred at his master's feet as the twelve other men in the expedition joined him in the toast. Outside the operations tent, the wind was blowing forty miles an hour and the unfastened flaps were making snapping sounds like pistol shots.

"Steve and I will be the only ones going into the ship, but you'll be able to see everything we do on the television monitors up here," said John Lee.

In December 1942, *March Hare*, a newly christened B-17 Flying Fortress with a ten-man crew, had been flying from Goose Bay, Labrador, to join the Eighth Air Force Bomber Command in England when it had disappeared in a blizzard over the Greenland ice cap.

Due to Greenland's violent weather patterns, dozens of warplanes had gone down there during the war, but *March Hare* was unique. Instead of bombs, it had been carrying ten wooden crates of Christmas gifts from President Franklin D. Roosevelt to his European admirers, including King George VI, British prime minister Winston Churchill, the exiled monarchs of Europe, and the top Allied war commanders.

The manifest included personally inscribed books and handwritten letters from the president, a slew of commemorative gold coins and stamps from his personal collection, "New Deal" oil paintings by Thomas Hart Benton and Grant Wood, ancient Navajo turquoise jewelry, hand-carved wooden puzzles, and a dozen cases of Old Forester Kentucky Straight Bourbon Whisky.

March Hare captured Hancock's interest and he immediately committed five hundred thousand dollars to locate the lost war bird. The founder of Anschutz International, a technology pioneer in the field of oil and gas exploration, Hancock was reputed to be the eighty-second richest man in the world. He found his personal pleasure in the pursuit of high adventure.

In the plane's last radio transmission, its radio operator had reported severe blizzard conditions and that the pilot was attempting to land somewhere along Greenland's rugged and unforgiving eastern coast.

His message had been picked up by a weather-monitoring station near Kulusuk. Based on the strength and direction of the signal, a search party set out from Comanche Bay to an area near the coastal settlement of Angmagssalik. Battling hundred-mile-per-hour winds, they discovered no trace of *March Hare* or its ten-man crew. The plane was never found.

Hancock's expedition team needed just four days to locate it.

Knowing the aircraft's original flight plan, as well as the strength and direction of the radio operator's last transmission, they decided to start the hunt for the plane on the Helheim Glacier, to the west of Angmagssalik.

Hancock's expedition was equipped with two Bell 206L4 LongRanger IV jet helicopters, and they began the search patterns along twenty-kilometer parallel lines at one-kilometer intervals. After completing a search pattern, the birds would then fly the same grid quadrants perpendicular to the first one.

A QUESTON (V) ice-penetrating radar system was deployed under each helicopter, its antenna clusters capable of sending and receiving an ultrawide spectrum of RF energy pulses through more than a thousand feet of glacial ice, and producing clear virtual imagery.

Four days into the search, recognition signals on one of the helicopters began registering a target in the glacier. It was less than ten miles from the coast. The second helicopter converged on the location and both landed on the ice cap to take more definitive readings.

The virtual images revealed that *March Hare*'s pilot had made an almost miraculous landing between two jagged peaks. The Fortress was sitting primly on its wheel struts where it had rolled to a stop, but it was now encased in a solid tomb of ice one hundred forty feet beneath the surface of the cap.

"We're going down after her," said Hancock to his expedition leaders.

TWO

It was a calculated risk to attempt the recovery in November, but Hancock had spent his life taking risks, from the air battles he had fought as a fighter pilot in Desert Storm to the founding of Anschutz International with fifty thousand dollars he had won in a Kilgore, Texas, poker game.

They were down to six hours of sunlight each day. By November 22, it would be only three hours. By December 1, the cap would be cloaked in total darkness, and the sun would not appear again for forty-five days.

Hancock wasn't about to wait six months to recover the plane. His men and equipment were ready to go. Worst case, they would have to abandon the recovery effort and return in the spring. He told Steve Macaulay, his second-in-command, to do whatever it took, regardless of the cost.

A day later, Base Hancock One took shape on the ice.

Two de Havilland DHC-6 Twin Otters had been modified to carry freight, and they began flying in supplies and equipment the following day, including two thermal meltdown generators, pumps, drilling equipment, diesel generators, spare parts, a satellite communications system, a fully equipped camp kitchen, two bulldozers, and storage containers crammed with meat, vegetables, and other food supplies.

The men quickly constructed a small complex of insulated arctic tents in a rough circle around the proposed drilling site. A helicopter pad was laid out with landing lights. A thousand-gallon tank of diesel fuel was flown in from Kulusuk, and fuel lines were run to all the tents and the modular washroom/latrine.

The effort to recover *March Hare* began the second day. A steel platform rig was set down over the site of the drilling shaft, followed by a thermal meltdown generator. Nicknamed the BADGER, it was twelve feet in diameter, and would melt a circular shaft until they reached the plane. At a melting rate of two feet per hour, the team members extrapolated they would reach *March Hare* in about three days.

Heavy snow and driving winds from the Arctic Circle hit them hard as soon as they were under way. The tents were nearly buried in the first blizzard, but the snow provided good insulation, and the expedition's bulldozers kept the pathways open between the complex and the helicopter pad.

The temperature fell to well below zero degrees Fahrenheit and stayed there. Off duty, the men wriggled into their arctic mummy bags to keep warm. Four days after they commenced drilling, the BADGER reached the targeted depth of one hundred forty feet.

Hancock and Macaulay made plans to enter *March Hare* through the underbelly hatch in the forward compartment. Knowing that human remains might still be on the plane, Macaulay had arranged to have an honor guard flown up from the Mortuary Affairs Center at Dover Air Force Base to accompany the bodies home.

The BADGER was removed from the shaft and replaced with a steel elevator cage operated by a power hoist. Two men equipped with high-pressure steam hoses were lowered down the shaft. At the bottom, they began burrowing toward the forward hatch, melting a tunnel as they went.

As soon as they reached the Fortress, the men were brought back to the surface, where Hancock and Macaulay, both wearing waterproof thermal suits and insulated rubber boots, were waiting to go down.

Macaulay planned to operate a lightweight, high-definition color zoom camera designed for use in confined spaces. Hancock carried a portable floodlight. Two transceivers with voice-activated microphones were incorporated into their headgear.

"Hey . . . take a look at this," shouted one of the engineers at the entrance to the platform rig.

Outside, the snow had stopped and the dark sky was filled with pulsating ripples of violet, red, and brilliant green.

"The goddess Aurora is trying to tell us something," Macaulay said with a laugh.

In Desert Storm, Macaulay had been Hancock's air squadron commander. Now their roles were reversed. In some ways, they couldn't have been more different. Quick to laugh, Macaulay was tall and slender with an easygoing personality. Hancock was short, stocky, and intense.

"Let's get going," said Hancock.

When they reached the bottom of the shaft, he led the way into the tunnel to *March Hare*. A steady drip of melting ice wept from the frozen concave roof above them. When they reached the polished steel hatch beneath the forward compartment, Hancock reached up to turn its handle.

"Okay . . . we're going in," Hancock radioed to the surface.

THREE

Hancock's breath condensed like cigarette smoke in the frigid air as he directed the floodlights toward the bombardier's station in the nose of the plane. Macaulay followed the lights with his camera. The compartment was empty. The bombardier's leather data case rested against one of the anchored legs of his chair. A Red Sox baseball cap hung from the bombsight harness.

"No bombsight," said Hancock.

"The Norden was top secret back then," said Macaulay. "The bombardier wouldn't have been assigned one until they got to England."

The plane's navigator had also worked in the forward compartment, and his metal desk was covered by a topographical map of Greenland. He had penciled in the plane's route all the way from Goose Bay. The line ended over Greenland.

There was no corrosion anywhere, no decay of any kind. The machine guns lying on the deck were oiled and ready to fire, along with the bright copper casings of ammunition.

They climbed up to the cockpit, where the pilot and copilot had commanded the plane. It was empty too. Maybe they had all gotten out, Macaulay thought. But where could they have gone?

Macaulay eased himself into the pilot's seat. An open pack of Lucky Strike cigarettes rested on the edge of the console by the throttle controls. The instrument gauges looked like they were waiting to be turned on. It struck him that the restoration team back in Lubbock wouldn't have much work to do on this plane.

He and Hancock headed aft past the top-turret machine gun to the bomb bay compartment. Aside from the scrape of their ice cleats on the steel deck, it was as silent as a tomb.

The bomb bay was crammed with unmarked wooden crates still strapped into position with thick cordage. Inside were President Roosevelt's Christmas presents to the European elite. Hancock pointed to another stack at the rear of the compartment. Each crate was labeled *Old Forester Kentucky Straight Bourbon Whisky*. One of them had been cracked open.

The radio compartment was next and it was as empty as the others. The aircraft's BC-348 radio receiver was mounted to the tabletop. A *Dick Tracy* comic book sat on top of it. The BC-375 transmitter on the opposite bulkhead was turned to the ON position.

In the waist gunners' compartment, they found the answer to the riddle.

The crew hadn't gotten out after all. Nine of them lay sprawled out in the compartment, which had clearly been organized as a last redoubt against the agonizing cold.

The men had sealed the hatches of the waist guns and gathered all their clothing and blankets together to stay warm. Most were wearing their sheepskin-lined flying suits with lined bunny boots. They had all frozen to death.

Hancock directed the lights at their faces one by one, and Macaulay recorded them on his video camera. Their faces reflected a mixture of sadness, resignation, perplexity, and despair.

"Not the worst way to go, Steve."

"Buried alive wouldn't be my choice."

Dick Slezak, the turret gunner, looked impossibly young for a man who would now be approaching ninety if he had survived the war. He would always be eighteen.

"Ted Morgan is missing," said Macaulay after they examined the nine bodies.

Morgan was the pilot who had made the miraculous landing in the middle of the blizzard. He had been twenty-three years old and hailed from Macaulay's hometown of Lexington, Virginia.

Shortly after Pearl Harbor, Morgan had married an army nurse named Cherie Carter. A year later, she had given birth to a baby girl. Cherie was still alive, now a ninety-year-old grandmother. She had remarried seven years after Ted had disappeared.

They found him in the tail gunner's compartment. He was lying on his back and staring up toward the surface of the ice cap as if visually attempting to escape from their tomb.

Macaulay remembered his face from Morgan's personnel file. It had reminded Macaulay of himself, lean and square-jawed, with a hint of cockiness. A hot flier who had wanted to be a fighter pilot and had instead been assigned to bombers.

The cockiness was gone now.

The opened bottle of Old Forester stood next to him on the floor of the compartment. Three inches remained in the bottom. Near his outstretched hand was a leather-bound diary. Macaulay unzipped it and thumbed through the last few pages. Morgan had survived almost two weeks. He had been the last to die.

28 December '42. Did a good job landing the plane in snow and darkness. Everyone safe. Radio not working, but Jeff hopes to fix it soon and send out our approximate position. Can't be more than ten miles from the coast.

5 January '43. Snow hasn't stopped since we landed. Slezak dug his way up from the waist door and broke through the snow layer about eight feet above the top turret. Men now take turns going up with a flare gun. If one hears an airplane, he is to shoot off a flare. Brutal up there. No one can stay outside more than thirty minutes.

8 January '43. Jacobs fired all our flares off when he said he heard aircraft.

Morgan's handwriting began to deteriorate.

9 January '43. Can no longer get to the surface. Slezak tried to break through but gave up at twenty-five feet. We are trapped. . . . Emergency food gone. No gas left in tanks. Flashlights dead. Total darkness.

The heat from the floodlight Hancock was holding began to melt the patina of ice on Morgan's face. Some of it pooled in the corners of his eyes, and he looked as if he were crying.

11 January '43. Last one left. If anyone ever finds us, please contact Cherie and tell her I loved her to the end. Forgive me.

Macaulay handed the diary to Hancock.

"Poor bastard," he said after reading the last entries.

Morgan had shot himself in the heart with his army-issue .45.

Macaulay lifted up the opened bottle of Old Forester, took a long swig, and passed it to Hancock.

"Like you said up top, J.L. . . . to the crew of *March Hare*."

They finished the bottle.

FOUR

14 November
Helheim Glacier
Greenland Ice Cap

After *March Hare*'s crew members were brought to the surface, their bodies were temporarily interred in an ice cairn, and the expedition team gathered for a brief memorial service.

Macaulay couldn't help wondering how Ted Morgan's wife would react after gazing down again at his twenty-three-year-old face. He had already relayed the names to the Mortuary Affairs Center at Dover Air Force Base. They would be sending an honor guard to escort them home.

"I need Melissa," Hancock said to Macaulay when it was over.

"Sure, J.L.," he replied with a grin.

An hour later, a slim, busty young woman wearing a jaunty ski cap, gold-trimmed sunglasses, and a form-fitting ski suit arrived on the Bell helicopter from the airfield at Kulusuk. Macaulay met her at the edge of the landing zone. She was fuming.

"I've been living for a week in a tar paper shack back at what they call an airport in this godforsaken country," she pouted.

A Dallas Cowboys cheerleader, she was one of John Lee's flavors of the month. As he had for the others, he had bought her a new Porsche 911 Carrera. The dealership in Fort Worth now gave him a fleet rate. He let each girl pick her own color. Melissa's was neon pink.

"From those to whom much is given, much is expected," Macaulay said to her with a straight face.

"What's that's supposed to mean?" she demanded.

"The parable of the faithful servant, Melissa," he said. "Luke 12:48."

She looked at him as if he had lost his mind.

"Where is he?" she demanded.

Macaulay pointed to Hancock's sleeping tent, and she headed over to it, carrying a small leather briefcase. A few moments after she entered the tent, Hap Arnold, Hancock's white Alsatian, came lumbering out.

An hour later, Melissa reemerged, got back aboard the helicopter, and flew off. When she was gone, Hap stuck his head back inside Hancock's tent to see if he was welcome, and joined his master inside.

Over the next two days, men using steam hoses melted a massive cavern above and around the fortress. One of the team's mechanics concluded that if *March Hare* had been on the surface, they would have only had to replace the batteries and add fuel to the tanks to fly it off the cap. Instead, the bomber would have to be brought up in sections.

Macaulay was in the operations tent, going over the logistical plan to fly out the components, when Noah Hastings, one of the helicopter pilots, came inside with a puzzled look on his face.

"Steve, I happened to turn on the QUESTON (V) in the bird this morning and it's really weird. . . . We have another strong metallic signal below *March Hare*."

"How far below it?" asked Macaulay.

"I'm not sure. George is doing an equipment recalibration of the radar equipment to make sure I wasn't seeing things. He ought to have pictures soon."

George Cabot was a former air force intelligence officer and the team's technical expert. He arrived a few minutes later with the virtual scans, his carrot red hair standing straight up. Hancock joined them.

"This is definitely interesting," he said.

"Could it be an ore deposit?" asked Hancock.

"Too small," said Cabot. "And there's a pattern to it." He laid the scans on the table.

"Look here. You see these dots? They're almost exactly a foot apart from one another and run in almost straight lines. . . . These four intersect."

"So what could that mean?" asked Hancock.

"If I had to make a wild guess, I'd say it looks like four long rows of iron rivets," said Cabot.

"A ship?" asked Macaulay.

"Possibly . . . Whatever it is, the thing is nearly a hundred feet long and fifteen feet wide at the center. The rivets look like they taper at each end. These ones down the center line could be a keel, these others the ribs and thwarts."

Macaulay stared down at the images.

"Incidentally," added Cabot, "there's another metallic pulse coming from the bedrock underneath that thing. . . . No idea what it could be."

"What would a ship be doing this far from the coast?" asked Macaulay.

"Who knows? They've recorded two-hundred-foot seas in the North Atlantic . . . or maybe it was portaged there. All I know is that it's sitting on original bedrock, so it's been down there a long time."

"How far?" asked Hancock.

Cabot looked at the second scan.

"More than five hundred feet," he said.

"That's three times the depth of *March Hare*," said Macaulay.

"Yeah, too far," agreed Cabot.

Hancock was still gazing at the possible rivet lines.

"Well, we're already down a hundred forty," he said, "and it will take us at least four more days to bring up *March Hare* and get it shipped out of here. The BADGER is definitely too slow. Let's put the WEASEL to work."

"You're going after it?" asked Cabot, scratching his red hair.

"We're here anyway. . . . Hell, it could be fun," said Hancock.

The WEASEL was the smaller of the two thermal meltdown units designed and built by his engineers. Only three feet in diameter, it could melt ice at five feet per hour, almost triple the rate of the BADGER. Another three hundred sixty feet would only take about three days.

An hour later, it was operational.

FIVE

16 November
Helheim Glacier
Greenland Ice Cap

They were down to little more than three hours of watery sunlight each day, or at least on those days the sun actually emerged through the leaden clouds. In two weeks, they would be in total darkness.

One of the recovery teams, equipped with acetylene torches, began cutting *March Hare* into sections that would fit into the twelve-foot shaft. A second team loaded the retrieved components into the de Havilland Twin Otters, which flew them to a former United States Air Force base at Narsassuaq. A third team drilled the WEASEL ever deeper toward the mysterious target.

When an air force honor guard arrived to remove the bodies of *March Hare*'s crew, work was briefly suspended while the expedition team stood in falling snow to participate in a flag service.

A day later, the last sections of *March Hare* were

brought to the surface. Another winter storm struck without warning that afternoon. Six feet of dense snow buried the tent complex, and flights in and out had to be canceled while the airstrip was cleared with the bulldozer.

Shortly after midnight, Macaulay was napping on his cot in the operations tent, when an engineer woke him to say that the WEASEL had reached bedrock more than five hundred feet beneath the ice cap.

"Let's go," said Macaulay, heading over to wake Hancock.

George Cabot was waiting for them at the edge of the new shaft a hundred forty feet below the surface. A power winch had been rigged to allow one man at a time to stand on stirrups attached to a steel cable and ride slowly to the bottom.

"I sent two men down there with the steam hoses an hour ago," said Cabot.

"You still don't want to go, George?" said Macaulay, smiling.

"I may be small, but I'm not stupid, Steve," said Cabot, puffing on his meerschaum pipe. "I don't fancy climbing down a fifty-story building inside a three-foot sewer line."

"You don't have to climb down, George," Hancock added. "Just close your eyes and the power hoist will have you at the bottom in twenty minutes. Besides, it's only about forty stories more. We're already fourteen down."

"No, thanks," said Cabot. "I'll stick to the instrument readings."

Macaulay stared down into the hole. It was no larger than a manhole cover.

"No lights along the way?" asked Hancock.

"With the steam hoses, there isn't enough room to string floods," said Cabot. "You'll have to use flashlights."

The radio receivers suddenly crackled.

"My God, you've got to see this," yelled one of the men at the bottom of the shaft.

Cabot turned on the power hoist and Hancock stepped into the stirrups. He was gone a few moments later. Macaulay quickly followed him down the hole. Watching them disappear into the blackness, Cabot crossed himself.

Inside the narrow shaft, Macaulay couldn't move his arms without grazing the ice walls. In spite of the thermal suit, he felt a profound coldness penetrating him as they went deeper.

It wasn't physical fear. As a child, he had walked away from the horrific automobile accident that had killed his parents. He had also survived a ditching in the Persian Gulf after shooting down his second Iraqi MiG during Desert Storm. This was different. It was something unreasoned. Whatever was down there filled him with dread.

Reaching the bottom, they stepped out of the stirrups and turned in the direction of the light. The two other men were shining their powerful flashlights at an object less than twenty feet away.

Macaulay almost gasped aloud. The steam hoses had exposed the front section of an ancient ship. The bowsprit swept up and away from the lap-straked hull in an arcing swirl that looked like the coiled head of a sea snake. Intricate carvings of weapons and battle scenes were engraved on the outer gunwales.

Stepping onto an ice shelf, Macaulay looked down inside the hull. Nestled in the bow section was a sea chest, studded with what looked like silver or pewter fittings. Three rowing benches were exposed behind it.

"I've seen paintings of craft like these that the Phoenicians used about a thousand years ago," he said.

"The Norsemen adapted their ship-building designs from the Phoenicians," said Hancock. "Their ships were propelled by either sail or oars, just like this one."

He pulled out his jackknife.

"I'm going to take a wood chip for carbon dating," he said.

"George said there was another metallic impulse beneath the ship," said Macaulay.

The two other men aimed their steam hoses at the ice shelf below it.

A few minutes later, a rock-edged wall hole materialized in the bedrock, and then a small black opening. Hancock ordered them to shut off the hoses. He shined his flashlight through the opening.

"It looks like a cave," he said.

Using his gloved hand to expand the hole, Hancock crawled inside. Watching from the ice tunnel, Macaulay could see Hancock's flashlight beam gyrating in all directions. Less than a minute later, he crawled back out.

His stunned face said it all.

"Seal it up again," he ordered. "No one comes down here."

SIX

Alexandra Vaughan had just experienced the most thrilling day of her life.

Its genesis was three years earlier when an old farmer plowing a rocky field near Solem discovered a broken axe blade by the marshy headwaters of Ostlund Lake. It had odd carvings along the edges, and the farmer had sent it to the Minnesota Historical Society in St. Paul for analysis.

Alexandra had recently completed her doctorate in Norse archaeology at Harvard. Now thirty, she was working in a staff position within the society's archaeological unit. The axe blade ended up on her desk.

Simply holding it in her hands had sent a thrill of excitement through her. She had seen identical blades in the collection of Norse weaponry at the Danish National Museum in Copenhagen.

Although St. Paul was being battered by a winter gale, she got in her old Land Rover and drove up to Solem. After interviewing the farmer, she was sure he was telling the truth about how and where he had found it. A week later, carbon dating confirmed that the axe blade had been fabricated more than seven hundred years ago.

She took her findings to Dr. Benchley, the head of the archaeology unit, and recommended they undertake a comprehensive dig at the Solem site. After briefly reviewing the folder of material, he laughed at her.

"Lexy, it's another Kensington stone," he said, "a complete hoax. The Norsemen never reached Minnesota. This farmer probably bought the axe from a cousin in Norway. He's looking for his fifteen minutes of fame."

"The jury is still out on the Kensington stone," Lexy replied hotly. "And I happen to believe the rune markings on it are genuine. That's what brought me out here."

"Fine," he said. "Why not go out and find Sasquatch while you're at it."

Undeterred, she spent her two-week vacation camping in the fields and rock-strewn slopes near the spot where the farmer had discovered it. The place was very remote and she had to ford two streams in the Land Rover to get there.

Her first efforts yielded nothing. It might have been sheer stubbornness, but her instincts told her there was something important to be found there if she searched long and hard enough.

Using most of her personal time, Lexy returned to Ostlund Lake six times over the next two years, eventually combing the area with probes and a metal detector. On the sixth trip, she expanded her search to include a nearby rocky slope dotted with aspen trees and thick undergrowth.

While crossing a spiny ridge, she noticed a depression in the earth that covered a vein of the rock ledge. Running her metal detector over the ledge, she received a positive hit.

She began to dig. When the excavated defile reached a depth of six feet, she was rewarded with the discovery of a cleft in the otherwise solid rock. After removing nearly a foot of soil and detritus from inside it, she uncovered her first find.

It was a flattened section of beaded metal, possibly part of a battle shield. She brought the object back to the historical society and subjected it to radioisotope dating. It was seven hundred years old.

She was now sure it was a Norse burial site, and that whoever was entombed there had been buried with his weapons for the journey to Valhalla, the mythical home of the Norse gods. She hit pay dirt on her next visit, unearthing another axe blade, and then the hilt of a sword with a cocked-hat-style iron pommel. A Norseman's sword. She had seen one identical to it at the Wikinger Museum in Hedeby, the largest Nordic city during the Viking age.

The discovery was why she had taken the job in Minnesota in the first place, passing up prestigious fellowships in London and Istanbul. She was descended from the ancient Norsemen on her mother's side. Some of her earliest memories were the Viking tales told to her by her Norwegian grandparents. The Vikings were in her blood.

During her trip back to St. Paul, the Land Rover

stalled out in one of the streams, and she had to rig a pulley hoist from a tree on the opposite shore to hand-winch it into the shallows. By then, her boots, corduroys, and anorak were caked in mud.

An hour out of St. Paul, the brakes began to fail. As she drove through the gate of the historical society, the brake pedal went all the way to the floor, and she had to use the emergency brake to bring the vehicle to a stop in the employees' lot.

Grabbing her specimen case, she used her electronic key to enter the labs in the subbasement, taking a short-cut through the suite in which the society was restoring Minnesota's Civil War flags.

A tall man was standing in front of the display case holding the battle flag of the 28th Virginia that had been captured during Pickett's Charge at Gettysburg. He was unshaven and dressed in rumpled khakis and a navy blazer.

"Dr. Vaughan?" asked Macaulay as she kept walking toward the archaeology lab.

"This is a restricted area," she said. "The public exhibits are upstairs."

She looked back and saw that he was following her.

"What do you want?" she said, turning to face him.

The girl's violet eyes made Macaulay regret he hadn't shaved in three days. She reminded him of his late wife, Diana. . . . She had the same intelligent good looks and, despite her mud-caked clothes, more than a hint of sexuality.

"Can we talk for a few minutes?" he said.

"I don't have time right now," she said without slowing down.

"Dr. Benchley told me he thought you would be able to give me a little time," he said.

She paused in her tracks, not wanting to tick off Marvin Benchley any more than she already had.

He handed her a card and she glanced down at it. A colorful logo surrounded the words ANSCHUTZ INTERNATIONAL. The name underneath it was BRIG. GENERAL STEVEN MACAULAY, UNITED STATES AIR FORCE (RETIRED).

She looked up at him again. His thick brown hair was just beginning to gray, and his face had a square-jawed leanness along with brown eyes and a dimpled chin.

"You look too young to be a general," she said skeptically.

"I've got a painting up in my attic that does all the aging. Have you ever heard of a man named John Lee Hancock?"

"The billionaire oilman whose core philosophy in life is to drill for oil and gas in every wildlife refuge?" she said.

"Let's just say he's a strong advocate for energy independence."

"I'm sure he's for truth, justice, and the American way, but right now I'm busy," she said, using her other electronic key to open her lab door.

"Five minutes," said Macaulay.

She thought of Benchley again.

"Come into the lab," she said.

The big high-ceilinged room was antiseptically clean. Wooden cabinets with glass doors lined three of the walls, each holding dozens of objects on the shelves. Lexy placed her specimen case on a square table centered under a bank of surgical lamps, and motioned him over to the chair near her desk.

"We have made an interesting discovery that would benefit from your knowledge and expertise," he began.

"Where?" she asked.

"The Greenland ice cap."

He saw the first hint of interest in her eyes.

"We were up there to recover a Second World War bomber. J.L.—Mr. Hancock—is the founder of the Cactus Legion, which has recovered and preserved rare war birds all over the world."

"I'm glad he believes in preserving something."

Macaulay ignored her sarcasm.

"While we were recovering the plane, we found something else a lot deeper down in the ice. It appears to be a Viking ship."

"Is it rigged?"

"I don't know," said Macaulay. "Most of it is still encased in ice."

"No one has ever found a fully rigged Viking ship. The Gokstad ship discovered in 1880 was almost intact, but it had only the barest remnants of its sail and rigging. So you may have made a good find."

"Will you come up and help us determine its significance?"

"I've recently made my own find, and I believe it's of far greater value to archaeological history. It will prove that the Norsemen came to this country two hundred years before Columbus."

"Only two hundred years?" asked Macaulay with mock innocence.

"We'll never know now."

"We carbon dated a wood chip from the ship yesterday, and the trees that were felled to build it were cut down more than a thousand years ago," he said.

"That's not surprising," she said. "Erik the Red, Leif Eriksson's father, established his first settlement on the southwest coast of Greenland in 982. Your ship might have been part of one of his supply vessels."

"What if I told you that we made another discovery aside from the ship?"

"What is it?"

"I'm afraid I can't tell you that until you get there."

"Sorry," she said with finality. "Is that all?"

"Time is of the essence, Dr. Vaughan. Winter is about to set in up there and the weather is deteriorating. We only have about three hours of sunlight each day."

"I told you I can't come."

"We're bringing in three other archaeologists on this," said Macaulay. "Maybe you've heard of them—Professor Hjalmar Jensen from Norway, Sir Dorian St. George Bond from England, and Rob Falconer from Berkeley."

"Sir Dorian wrote the canon on Norse navigation techniques," she said. "Jensen is the leading authority on Norse genealogy. Falconer is brilliant if a bit ruthless. You're in good hands."

She didn't mention that Falconer had once been her lover. He had almost cured her of men.

"We would like you to come too."

"Why?"

"Professor Finchem, your mentor at Harvard, told me yesterday that when it comes to runology, no one in the field has more instinctive ability to translate early Norse markings than you do. He referred to you as 'the code breaker.'"

She laughed.

"Barnaby knows more than I'll ever know about rune markings. You should get him to go."

"Actually, he was our first choice," said Macaulay. "Unfortunately, he's recovering from open-heart surgery and is not up to the rigors of the ice cap. He recommended you."

"That's very flattering, but it's still no," she said. "I have a job here, General Macaulay, and I've used all my personal and vacation time."

"Your Dr. Benchley is all for your going," he replied. "He's very grateful for the contribution Mr. Hancock has just made to the historical society's capital fund. I have one other inducement to offer. If you go with me, I'll transfer fifty thousand dollars into account number one-one-four-five-six-three at the Pilot Grove Savings Bank before we leave this room."

It was her checking account number.

"How can you do that?"

He held up his smart phone.

"Your bank information is already registered in here."

Money had never been important to her. It wasn't now, although the thought of her Land Rover sitting outside with no brakes, along with her graduate school loan payments being six months overdue, made her pause.

"I have a Learjet waiting for us at the airport, Dr. Vaughan, and I'll have you back here in four days to continue your own work."

"This is crazy."

"Let me tell you about the very rich. They are different from you and me," he said.

"So you also have time to read Fitzgerald."

"Long time ago."

She hoped she wouldn't regret her decision.

"I'll need to go to my apartment," she said, "to shower and gather my gear."

"No problem."

"My car is not functioning right now."

"I have a rental right outside."

SEVEN

Hancock's Learjet had barely leveled off at twenty-five thousand feet above St. Paul when a young Eurasian woman dressed in a blue silk wrap arrived at Lexy's club chair and handed her a hand-inscribed parchment menu.

She remembered that the last thing she had eaten was a cardboard snack pack of cheese and crackers in the back of the Land Rover the previous night. She was suddenly ravenous.

After a glass of Pinot Grigio, she savored a plate of sautéed sea scallops with shallots in cream sauce, and a side dish of asparagus vinaigrette. Macaulay joined her at the polished teak inlaid table as she was finishing her crème brûlée. He had shaved and showered after boarding the plane, and changed into jeans and a blue work shirt.

Cleaned up, he looked even younger. There were

laugh or stress lines etched into the corners of his weary brown eyes. He had nicked himself shaving.

"How did you get the permission for us to take off?" she asked him.

"The world works in mysterious ways," he said, ordering a dry martini.

It had been snowing hard when they arrived at the Minneapolis airport, and the flight manager at the private aviation terminal told Macaulay that all landings and take-offs had been canceled until visibility improved. Flights weren't expected to resume until the following day.

The waiting room in the small terminal was packed with newly stranded travelers, all trying to rent cars and find accommodations. Macaulay had told her to wait there until he returned.

As the minutes passed, she began to wonder if the whole episode was some kind of ludicrous practical joke. On impulse, she used her cell phone to call her branch of the Pilot Grove Savings Bank in St. Paul. After she provided her personal data, the teller said, "Your current checking balance is $50,082.36."

Twenty minutes later, Macaulay was back.

"Let's go," he said.

"Back to St. Paul?"

"Out to the airplane," he said. "I had to make sure it was de-iced before we take off."

"But the flight manager said all flights were canceled," she began, but he was already leading her outside.

The Learjet was airborne less than ten minutes later.

"Will they come after us?" she asked as Macaulay began chewing his first bite of rare prime rib.

"Who?"

"The sky police . . . How the hell do I know? You broke the law."

"All in a good cause," he said.

They landed in Quebec to clear customs.

"What do I say is the purpose of my visit?" she whispered as they approached the counter.

"Pleasure," he said. "Pure pleasure."

They were back in the air fifteen minutes later. When the plane reached cruising altitude, Macaulay asked the Eurasian girl to bring two snifters of Hancock's hundred-year-old Armagnac. Lexy found the first taste sublime.

"I'm going to make an assumption about why you're bringing me along on this escapade," she said.

"Go ahead," said Macaulay.

"In addition to the Viking ship you found up there, I'm guessing you found a tablet, or vellum scroll, or something else with rune markings on it."

"Good assumption," he said, savoring the brandy.

"So, what do you know about runology?" she asked.

"The same as you probably know about the Eighth Air Force missions to Schweinfurt in 1943," he said with a lazy grin.

"August and October," she said. "Sixty forts were lost on the first one and seventy-seven went down on the second. They creamed the ball bearing works the second time, but Speer had already diversified production."

He stared intently at her for several seconds.

"Will you marry me?" he said.

She laughed.

"My grandfather was a B-17 pilot. He was lost over Berlin in 1944. Have you ever heard of the Kensington stone?"

"Your Dr. Benchley told me that it's a two-hundred-pound slab of rock covered in alleged Viking markings and that you're fixated on it. He said it was an elaborate hoax and that it would be a big mistake to bring you on our little lark. He volunteered to come himself."

"I'm going to prove it's genuine," she said, pulling several sheets of paper out of an old leather satchel case. She laid the first one on the table in front of him.

"This is the inscription on the Kensington stone," she said.

Macaulay gazed down at a mass of odd-looking symbols, letters, characters, and what appeared to be stick figures, all bunched together in what might have been separate lines of possible text. He hadn't slept in two nights and was having difficulty concentrating. His weariness was compounded by the brandy and by this unsettling young woman.

"It looks a little like hieroglyphics," he said.

"Very good, General," she said, smiling. "The Norsemen used the same principle in creating the runic alphabet. Runic inscriptions date back almost two thousand years, and until Christian monks introduced Latin to Scandinavia in the eleventh century, the runic alphabet was used to record all their important events. It's fairly simple, with these sixteen characters being the most frequently used. Later on, the basic characters were augmented with what are called dotted runes."

Macaulay looked up to see the big violet eyes focused on him. In the light from the bulkhead lamp behind her, he could see glints of old gold in her thick auburn mane of hair. She was undeniably attractive, but the last thing he needed at this point in his life was another woman. Not after Diana.

"Most of the runic stones from the eleventh century are either memorials to the departed, family sagas, or accounts of famous expeditions. They were carved by skilled stonecutters. Two years ago, I translated a rune stone dating from 1050 that was unearthed in Norway. It recounts the discovery of Vinland the Good by Leif Eriksson fifty years earlier."

"Where is Vinland?" asked Macaulay.

"Theories have ranged from Nova Scotia to Cape Cod, but no one has ever found archaeological evidence to prove it."

"So what happened to Eriksson?"

"No one knows."

She placed another piece of paper in front of him.

"This is an interlinear transliteration of the rune markings on the Kensington stone," she said excitedly. "Would you like me to translate them into English for you?"

Macaulay looked down at the confusing jumble of letters. It was the last thing he wanted her to do.

8 : göter : ok : 22 : norrmen : po :
. . . o : oppagelsefärd : fro :
vinland : of : vest : vi :
hade : läger : ved : 2 : skLär : en :
dags : rise : norr : fro : þeno : sten :
vi : var : ok : fiske : en : dagh : äptir :
vi : kom : hem : fan : 10 : man : röde :
af : blod : og : ded : AVM :
frälse : äf : illü.

"How did you get interested in all this?" he asked.

"I'm half Norwegian," she said. "My maternal grandmother was an amateur archaeologist and my first inspiration."

Macaulay couldn't help yawning.

"Let's get some rest," he said. "We'll land in Goose Bay in a few hours to refuel, and then it's four more to Kulusuk Island on the east coast of Greenland. Fortunately, we won't need to check in with customs there. They assume that if people are crazy enough to want to come, why bother."

"Sleep would be good right now," she agreed.

"You're welcome to J.L.'s cabin," he said. "It has the most comfortable bed you'll ever find at thirty thousand feet."

He was right.

EIGHT

Dawn was creeping past the curtains of her compartment porthole when Lexy heard a light knock at the door. It slowly opened, and the Eurasian girl's face appeared around the edge.

"We'll be landing in thirty minutes. Do you wish to have breakfast with General Macaulay?"

She could smell fresh coffee brewing and discovered she was hungry again.

"I'll be right there."

She dressed in the same combination of clothing she always wore in the field, loose-fitting corduroys, a Scotch plaid flannel shirt, and rubber-soled leather hunting boots.

"You're going to need to ramp up your winter gear when we get there," said Macaulay when she joined him at the breakfast table. He was enjoying a western omelet with coffee and orange juice, and she ordered the same.

"I've checked in by radio with our base camp on the ice cap. Your three colleagues have already arrived," he told her. "It's blowing a gale there, but I'm hoping we can make it over in one of the team helicopters."

Gazing through the windows at the endless landscape of ice and rock, Lexy felt a deep sense of isolation at the enormity of it all. Some of her ancestors had come here more than a thousand years ago.

Macaulay had followed her eyes.

"In some places the ice is two miles deep," he said. "Who knows how many secrets it holds?"

Toward the horizon, she saw the jagged edge of a gigantic iceberg floating calmly on a slate gray sea. It almost looked big enough to land on. As the Learjet slowly descended toward the desolate coast, they passed over a small Inuit settlement. The simple huts were gaily painted in red, blue, and yellow. Near the settlement, a man was running behind a dogsled.

A few minutes later, they landed on a long, ice-bordered runway.

"Welcome to Kulusuk," said Macaulay. "In its glory days, this place was part of the old DEW Line radar defense system for providing an early warning of a Soviet attack. It's fallen on hard times since we pulled out."

A small cluster of ramshackle old buildings flanked the landing strip. A Bell 412EP jet transport helicopter was parked on one apron near two twin-engine planes, all of them bearing the logo of Anschutz International. As soon as the engines were turned off, she could hear the howling wind.

"The weather may look rugged to you, but I can fly

the Bell in this," said Macaulay. "Before we leave, you'll need to put on some warmer gear. There's plenty of it inside the Kulusuk Four Seasons over there."

They stepped off the plane into fierce, gusting wind. Ice particles lashed Lexy's face as Macaulay led her to the largest of the frame buildings. Inside the foyer, the moan of the wind was barely diminished. The waiting room smelled of frying bacon.

"Steve!" came an anguished cry from the small barroom across the lobby.

"Oh no," groaned Macaulay as Melissa came rushing toward him.

"Thank God," she said, wrapping herself in his arms in a cloud of bourbon. "I've got to get out of here, Steve. The sun barely rises in this place and then it is night again. You have to tell J.L. that if he doesn't want me here anymore, I need the Lear to fly me back to Dallas."

"I'll tell him," said Macaulay.

"Seriously, I think I'm going to die here, honey," she said, tears beginning to stream down her milkmaid cheeks. "He loves that goddamn dog of his more than me."

Melissa's eyes focused on Lexy.

"Who is she?" she demanded.

"Dr. Vaughan is an archaeologist," said Macaulay. "I'm flying her out to the base camp."

"Why does she get to go and not me?"

"It's important, Melissa."

"She's J.L.'s new one, isn't she?"

"No," he said firmly.

"Don't leave me here, Steve. I swear I can't take it anymore."

"I told you I'll talk to J.L.," he said. "Just hang on a bit longer."

He led Lexy up the stairs to find the winter gear.

"What was that all about?" she asked while putting on a thermal suit over her clothes.

"How would you like a brand-new Porsche Carrera 911?"

"I don't understand."

"Inside joke," he said. "John Lee enjoys the company of beautiful women and he appreciates having them available, which isn't that often when he's feeling the high adventure like this one. Anyway, he usually treats them to a new Porsche."

"I see."

Ten minutes later, they were outside again and heading for the Bell 412EP jet helicopter. It was the team's principal transport chopper. Hancock's ground crew had completed its flight inspection and warmed up the two Pratt & Whitney engines for him.

It was a dual-control ship and Macaulay motioned Lexy into the copilot's seat. She could already feel it rocking back and forth from heavy wind gusts before they were even off the ground.

"Don't worry," he reassured her. "It's going to be bumpy, but the trip will only take about fifteen minutes unless we run into a serious snow squall."

It ended up taking thirty, and she was airsick most of the way. The combination of updrafts and downdrafts was vicious. One moment they were rocketing upward and the next careening wildly down. For the first time in her life, she understood the meaning of having her heart in her throat.

She felt her first tremor of actual fear when they hit the snow squall. It was a total whiteout, and she lost all sense of their position in relation to the mountain range they were approaching. It was bad enough to be flying through milk, but then they would hit another wind gust and be plunging down again. She clutched the steel frame of her cushioned seat and held on.

Whenever she glanced at Macaulay, he appeared oblivious to it all, remaining calm and seemingly relaxed as he maneuvered the big helicopter through the treacherous air.

When they finally emerged from the squall, she saw that they were approaching a small tent city on the ice cap. Macaulay brought them down onto a helicopter pad ringed with landing lights.

"You did well," he said after shutting down the engines. "Not a fun ride in that soup."

Lexy didn't say anything. She was grateful that she hadn't thrown up all over the cockpit. Still queasy, she climbed out of the helicopter and followed him to the largest tent in the complex.

Inside, a dozen men were scattered around tables full of electronic equipment. One was standing in front of a briefing board. The others sat at tables deployed in a rough circle around two diesel space heaters. They all turned to look at the new arrivals.

"The code breaker is here," one of them called out.

It was Rob Falconer.

NINE

John Lee Hancock stood up from the head table and walked toward her.

"I'm John Lee," he said, shaking her hand.

Lexy hadn't known what to expect, but she was mildly surprised to discover he was shorter than she was, with salt-and-pepper hair brushed straight back above his blunt, clean-shaven face. His dark brown eyes were hooded and intense.

"Forgive me for saying so, but you look a bit under the weather," he said without releasing her hand. "Can I offer you a bracer?"

"I'm all right . . . really," she said, "but yes, I'd welcome one."

Still not letting go of her hand, he led her over to one of the tables, where an open bottle sat beside a tray of glasses. It had an old-style label, and she could read the

words *Old Forester* above his fingers as he poured an inch
of it into a glass. She took the dark, smoky elixir down in
one long swallow. It had an astonishingly mellow taste.

"Very restorative," she said, smiling.

A man approached her from the other side.

"I believe we met in London three years ago," he said.

She turned to see Sir Dorian St. George Bond, his
distinguished face still crowned by the familiar shock of
unruly silver hair. At eighty, he was still a giant in the archaeological field, the man who had followed Howard
Carter into Egypt's Valley of the Kings, and had then
blazed a new archaeological trail with his treatises on the
secrets of early Norse navigation methods.

"Thank you for remembering me," she said.

"You delivered a brilliant paper that day."

When she had last seen him, Sir Dorian had been strong
and erect. His gray eyes still glinted with intelligence, but
the dark patches under them looked like bruises. He had
shed at least fifty pounds and become gaunt. She wondered why he would risk his health to be there.

Hjalmar Jensen replaced Sir Dorian in the small queue
that had formed to greet her. The fifty-year-old Norwegian anthropologist had studied at Oxford and been part
of the team that discovered the Homeric location of Troy,
south of the Dardanelles. Now a leading expert in Nean-
derthal biology as well as European evolution, he had
been the first to extract DNA from ancient Scandinavian
human fossils.

"I'm pleased to meet you, Dr. Vaughan," he said, welcoming her with an engaging smile and a clipped Norwegian accent. "Like Sir Dorian, I have been quite impressed
with your work."

With rimless metal spectacles perched on his little nose, he reminded her of Mr. Rogers from the TV program she had enjoyed as a child. The Norwegian gave way to Rob Falconer.

Strong and compact, with the build of a downhill racer, Rob still had the same shoulder-length raven hair, black-bearded face, and striking eyes the color of pale amber. They were as arrogant as she remembered.

"I need no introduction to this archaeologist," he said with the familiar South Carolina drawl.

After getting his doctorate at Berkeley, Rob had specialized in underwater archaeology and earned international fame after finding the remains of the Ottawa River encampment of Henry Hudson, whose mutinous crew had set him adrift on his final voyage.

Lexy had fallen in love with him after they met in Mesopotamia during the summer of her senior year at Harvard. He was very different from the often humorless archaeologists she had known. Rob was wildly irreverent, confiding in her that he was pursuing "the Indiana Jones branch of archaeology."

"We were a great team," said Falconer to the others. "I still don't know why she chose to abandon me."

They had lived together for two months. She practically worshipped him until he hacked into her computer one night and stole her thesis on twelfth-century dotted runes to complete his own doctoral work. She had wanted to expose him, but her mentor, Barnaby Finchem, advised her to let it go.

"It would only be ugly and inconclusive," he had told her. "Don't worry. You'll make your mark."

"We shared a very small tent," Falconer went on. "Maybe I snored."

Lexy watched Macaulay's eyes harden as Hancock asked everyone to take a chair, and then stood facing them in front of the banks of computers and communications equipment.

When they were settled near the space heaters, Hancock's white Alsatian wandered over to Jensen. Turning in an ever-tightening circle, the dog curled up at his feet. The Norwegian reached down to stroke him behind the ears.

"You have a way with dogs, Professor Jensen," said Hancock, clearly impressed. "Old Hap rarely cottons to anyone except me."

Jensen smiled as he continued petting him.

"I only wish I had the same power with the opposite sex," he said.

"Now that you have all arrived," said Hancock, "we're ready to make our first descent to the Viking ship and the cave below it. You should know that you are here for one purpose, and that is to provide me with your insights and conclusions after viewing what I've discovered down there. There will be ample rewards for all of you, both professionally and financially. I'm well aware that archaeology does not generate the same returns as oil and gas drilling."

He was trying his best to sound self-deprecating.

"Here are your ground rules," he continued. "Security is paramount at this stage. You will understand why when you see what's down there. There will be no note taking, no journals, no pens and pencils. You will not bring a camera or a cell phone or an electronic device of any kind. You will touch nothing after we're down there unless I give you permission to do so."

"What are we allowed to do?" asked Falconer.

"Observe," replied Hancock caustically. "You're being paid to observe."

Looking around the operations tent, Lexy could see that the members of Hancock's expedition team were almost out on their feet. The strain of whatever they had undertaken in the previous days and weeks could be read in the gray pallor of their faces and reddened eyes.

"You will each have to agree to a brief body search before we put on the thermal suits to go down," said Hancock. "If you are not comfortable with that, tell me now and we'll fly you out of here right away."

No one said anything.

"We'll spend about thirty minutes down there after making the descent. We're concerned about the infusion of too much heat into one of the discovery sites, so instead of floodlighting, you will be restricted to high-powered flashlights."

He turned to a briefing board and pointed at a sketch of the two ice shafts.

"The first part of the descent will be in an elevator cage. There's room for all of us in it. The second shaft is nearly four hundred feet deeper and we'll be going down one at a time using a power hoist. You'll stand in foot stirrups and just hold on to the chain until you hit bottom. The second shaft is only three feet in diameter. I hope none of you is claustrophobic."

Lexy felt her stomach lurch. She thought about speaking up, to say that she was sick with apprehension at the thought of ever being confined in a small space. At the age of ten, she had fallen through the rotting boards that covered an abandoned well at her grandparents' farm. It had taken them ten hours to find her, and she had spent an excruciating night floating in the slimy water at the bottom, getting through it only by shutting her eyes and pretending she was in their bathtub at home.

She opened her mouth to speak, but saw that the others had accepted the news with calmness, if not excitement. As the only woman, she didn't want to be conspicuous in admitting her fears.

"I'll be going down first," said Hancock. "The rest of you will follow at intervals of ten feet. The order of descent will be me, Sir Dorian, then Falconer, Professor Jensen, Dr. Vaughan, and last General Macaulay."

Macaulay met the archaeologists in the mess tent one by one to conduct a brief body search, after which they put on thermal clothing and rejoined Hancock. Falconer was the only one who gave him a problem. He insisted on bringing his pocket journal with him, claiming he was worried the others would steal it. When Macaulay gave him the option of staying behind, he turned the journal over.

Lexy was the last one.

"Just go ahead and get dressed," said Macaulay when she arrived. "I've got to trust somebody around here."

It was snowing again as they entered the elevator cage and began their first descent. This won't be too hard after all, Lexy thought as they dropped slowly through the large well-lit shaft.

Thirty minutes later, they reached the *March Hare* cavern.

The huge, empty ice cavity remained brilliantly lit, like a movie set of Santa's workshop in a Disney movie. The gnomish George Cabot was waiting for them at the power rig over the smaller shaft.

Macaulay ordered him to start the power winch, and it began making a loud clanking noise, like a ship's anchor chain dropping to a seabed. Wasting no time, Hancock stepped into the first set of stirrups. A few moments later, he disappeared down the hole.

Cabot halted the movement of the chain after ten feet and attached the second set of stirrups. Sir Dorian got into them without a problem, but his hands were too weak to maintain his hold on the chain. He gave up after two tries.

"Strap me to the bloody thing," he said urgently.

Cabot found a length of towline and ran it around Sir Dorian's chest twice before securing the line with a sailor's hitch. He started the winch again, and the octogenarian slid down into the darkness, barely fitting through the hole. Falconer and Jensen assumed the next two positions on the chain without further problem.

Then it was Lexy's turn. She felt the first bolt of terror when she walked over to stand above the little hole. Closing her eyes, she forced herself to remember that something incredibly important was waiting for her down there, something she had waited most of her life to see. When she opened her eyes again, the hole seemed to have shrunk even farther.

"I'm not sure . . . ," she began.

"What the hell is going on up there?" Hancock shouted from fifty feet below them.

Macaulay saw her distress.

"Don't worry about it," he said reassuringly. "Just envision yourself going down a dark well."

"That's . . . the problem," she said.

"All right, we'll go down together," he said.

He had Cabot attach a second set of stirrups just below the first one, and Macaulay stepped into them.

"Come here," he said.

"Odin save us," said Lexy, stepping into the upper stirrups. Hancock reached out to wrap her in his arms and motioned to Cabot to start the winch. The clanking began again and they dropped downward.

"Sweet move, General," Cabot called out to Macaulay as they disappeared from view.

Twenty minutes into the descent, she began imagining that the black wall of ice was closing in on them, and started shivering uncontrollably. Putting her arms around his back, she drew Macaulay closer.

"Forgive me," she said.

"You're forgiven," he replied.

TEN

When Lexy and Macaulay touched bottom, the other four were standing in the concave tunnel that had been hollowed out with steam hoses at the foot of the shaft. Their flashlight beams were all pointed in the same direction. Jensen was gaping at something, openmouthed.

She turned to look. In the glare of the powerful flashlights, it appeared that the ancient Viking ship was sailing straight toward her out of an icy fog. It was the living embodiment of something she had seen only in eleventh-century drawings.

Stepping closer, she marveled at the intricacy of the carvings along the tip of the bowsprit, which was coiled into the head of a sea snake. Familiar with its design, she was sure that the stern of the ship, still encased in the ice, was tapered into a similar carving.

"As the almighty bard once put it," said Sir Dorian in

his imposing voice, " 'I could a tale unfold whose lightest word would harrow up thy soul, freeze thy young blood, and make thy two eyes, like stars, start from their spheres.' "

Lexy was examining the engravings on the carved sea chest that was tucked inside the bow section, when Hancock spoke for the first time.

"There will be ample opportunity to explore the secrets of the ship. Right now, we have a more important discovery to show you. Go ahead, Steve."

Approaching a section of the ice beneath the keel of the ship, Macaulay began chipping away at it in a circular pattern with a hatchet. Within minutes, he had opened a hole large enough for them to get through.

Lexy crawled into the mouth of the cave on her hands and knees. Inside, she waited a few moments for her eyes to adjust to the gloom. To her left was the ice-covered surface of a smooth basalt rock wall. Twenty feet in, the cave began to widen and grew progressively higher.

All of them except Macaulay were able to stand up straight. After another ten feet, Hancock stopped and dipped his flashlight beam to the rock floor at the edge of the wall.

"It's not possible," said Sir Dorian.

It was the perfectly preserved body of a man. He was lying on his back with his arms crossed at his chest in the ceremonial pose of the dead. Beyond him lay another man, his boots a few inches from the first man's head. He had been posed in the same manner. She saw that the line of bodies continued all along the edge of the wall.

"How many are there?" asked Falconer, bringing up the rear.

"Ten," said Macaulay.

Sir Dorian reached the ninth body in the line.

"Look at this man," he said.

The Viking's mane of thick blond hair was nearly three feet long, and carefully arranged under his two massive arms. His head was resting on a rolled-up sheepskin sleeping bag. Lexy could see that his ice-covered skin had been fair. The open eyes were a startling blue.

"Note the dolichocephalic skull," said Jensen almost reverently. "Pure Nordic. In his time, a young Teutonic god."

The man's outer cloak was trimmed in red and gold braid.

"And one of the leaders," said Lexy.

"Are we allowed to examine their clothing?" asked Falconer. "It will give us clues to who they were and when they arrived here. We can't do that without touching them."

"Go ahead," said Hancock.

Falconer knelt by the second man in line. His head and upper shoulders were covered by a hooded leather helmet that protected his ears and cheeks. A thin leather belt was cinched around the waist of his outer cloak. Hanging from it on one side were a long knife and a leather pouch. Falconer struggled to open the pouch and pulled out a fire starter.

"Not much good, I guess, after you've run out of fuel," he said.

The Norseman's outer cloak was frozen stiff. It covered his torso from the shoulders to the knees. The dense woolen material was trimmed off at his right shoulder blade.

"The weapon arm was always left free for sword work," said Falconer.

Uncinching the man's belt, Falconer pulled apart the frozen cloak. Beneath it, he was wearing a linen tunic with a button and loop at the neck opening, and two pockets at the waist. Under it, he wore loose-fitting leather trousers with straps under the heels. Cloth wrappings protected his legs from his knees down to his leather boots.

Falconer dug his fingers into the man's waist pockets and came up empty.

"There's one more body farther into the cave," said Hancock.

The tenth Norseman was lying on his side near the back wall. He was clutching a chisel in his left hand. A double-headed hammer lay next to him on the cave floor.

"This one was a stonecutter," said Sir Dorian, kneeling next to him. "Look at the condition of his hands."

In the beam of her flashlight, Lexy saw a stone tablet leaning against the inner basalt wall, which was covered with ice. About three feet square, the face of the stone tablet was covered with faint markings, most of them also encrusted in ice.

"And this must be his saga of their expedition," she said.

There were twelve horizontal lines of markings, each incorporating dozens of symbols. The top seven lines ran straight from left to right. The three at the bottom began to curve lower, reflecting the stonecutter's weakening strength. The last one went almost straight downward.

"Maybe your stonecutter was drunk," said Falconer.

"He was dying," said Lexy. "His hands could barely hold the hammer and chisel."

"And he was working in total darkness," said Sir Dorian, picking up the closest firepot. Like the others on the cave floor, it was lying on its side.

Macaulay remembered the last words in Ted Morgan's diary after his group of fliers ran out of fuel and became entombed in the same ice a thousand years after these men. Both Morgan and this stonecutter had left their final thoughts for rescuers who never came.

"Can you decipher any of it?" asked Hancock as Lexy knelt in front of the markings.

More than an inch of ice coated most of the face, making it impossible to read any of the markings behind it, although a few areas at the edges were clear and legible.

"It is written in the old futhork," she said, "which presumably makes it pre–twelfth century."

The first symbols on the top line were clear. To a layman, they would have looked like incomprehensible stick figures, but she translated them easily. Reading them made her shiver with excitement.

The numbers were 1016.

Training her flashlight beam at the other exposed markings along the edges, she translated another word at the beginning of the fifth line. The stonecutter had written *Vinland*. At the end of the following line, she read the word *Leifr*. The final set of symbols on one of the last erratic lines translated to *the hallowed place*. The rest of the saga was cloaked behind the ice.

"How much can you translate?" asked Falconer, his vision obscured by the others.

She was about to respond, when a drop of water

splashed the top of her hood. It was quickly followed by two more. Jensen shined his flashlight up at the cave's ceiling. It was starting to drizzle ice melt.

"If we don't leave now, these men will begin to decompose," he said, his Norwegian accent more pronounced, "and that would be a great loss to science."

Hancock led them back out of the cave. In the tunnel near the foot of the shaft, he told Steve Macaulay to reseal the entrance with a large block of ice that had already been cut for the purpose.

When they reached the surface, Hancock turned to George Cabot and said, "Cut all the juice to the elevator cage and to the power winch down below. And make sure it stays off."

"Check, Boss."

ELEVEN

They emerged from the elevator rig into the violent grasp of another storm.

"Temperature's dropping again," shouted Macaulay to Hancock above the blast of arctic wind that forced them to bend over almost double as they crossed the small snow-packed compound.

Inside the operations tent, two members of the communications team were slumped asleep in front of the bank of radio and telecommunications equipment. Another was watching a download of *The Shawshank Redemption* on his laptop while he waited for messages.

Lexy went straight to the stainless steel coffeemaker. Macaulay joined her there.

"You deciphered some of it, didn't you?" he said. "I can see the excitement in your face."

"Is it that obvious?" she asked.

The others joined them for coffee. Hancock laced his mug with a big dollop of Armagnac. Sir Dorian poured only the brandy into his own. Above them, the roof of the tent shuddered and swayed from the power of the wind.

"So, what have we learned so far?" asked Hancock as they all moved closer to the tent's space heaters.

Sir Dorian spoke first. It was clear to Lexy that the trip to the cave had severely sapped his strength. She could see the pain behind his eyes as he took a long swig of brandy.

"I'm confident that carbon dating will confirm that the men in that cave have lain there since the early eleventh century," he said.

"Were you able to read any of the markings?" Hancock asked Lexy.

"The first rune symbols in the saga recorded a date," she responded. "The year 1016."

Her statement was met with stunned silence.

"I was also able to translate two other small sections at the edges of the text. They included the words, *Leifr*, *Vinland*, and *the hallowed place*."

A look of astonishment registered on Jensen's face.

"If that's true . . . ," he began, and then stopped.

"If what's true?" asked Hancock.

"Perhaps a little history is in order," said Sir Dorian, looking at Hancock. "In the year of our Lord 982, the Viking Erik the Red, who was looked upon by many as a deity and who had been banished from Iceland over a blood feud, came to this desolate place and called it

Greenland. The year 982 is the first indisputable date of European arrival in American history."

"You mean the far north," said Hancock.

"Call it what you will," said Sir Dorian. "It's no farther from here to the American mainland than the Bahamas archipelago was when Columbus arrived there on his way to America five hundred years later."

"But Columbus got to our mainland first," asserted Hancock.

"Perhaps," said Jensen.

"After Erik the Red explored these waters," resumed Sir Dorian, "he built a settlement on the southwest coast of Greenland near Cape Farewell. Then he went back to Iceland and organized a fleet of ships to bring hundreds more settlers to his new paradise."

"But that was thirty years before our stonecutter made those markings down there," said Hancock.

"Correct," said Sir Dorian. "My point is that those first settlers, and the thousands who followed, quickly discovered there was no timber to build homes for their families or shelters for their livestock. The winters were fearsome, as you will discover if we stay here much longer. They yearned to explore farther south to warmer climes."

As if to confirm his argument, one of the tent poles buttressing the roof suddenly snapped off with a loud crack. In now-obvious pain, Sir Dorian winced as he tried to settle comfortably in his chair. Another swallow of Armagnac temporarily restored his spirits.

"Which brings us to Leif the Lucky, Leif Eriksson, the son of Erik the Red," he continued. "Dr. Vaughan told us that she found the letters L-E-I-F-R among the rune markings in the cave. *Leifr* is the old Norse spelling of the anglicized Leif."

"Maybe there was more than one Leif," said Hancock. "The name had to be pretty common in Norway and Iceland."

"No," said Sir Dorian. "In conjunction with the date of 1016 and the few other words Dr. Vaughan translated, we're dealing with a Norse deity here, possibly his last expedition."

"What do we really know about him?" asked Macaulay. "The truth—not the legend."

"He was born in 980," said Sir Dorian. "At just nineteen, he sailed across the North Atlantic from Greenland to Norway, almost two thousand miles, in a small open boat. No one had ever done it. He was the finest navigator of his age."

"How did they navigate a thousand years ago?"

"The early Norse explorers had no way to plot longitude," said Sir Dorian, "but they learned how to determine latitude by using primitive sun shadow boards that had a pin in the center surrounded by concentric circles. It was crude but effective. I wouldn't be surprised if we found one in the ship down there."

"It doesn't sound very exact," said Hancock.

"It was exact enough for them to make it all the way to the Volga River in Russia and the Nile in Egypt," said Falconer.

"Eriksson was twenty-three years old when he led a sailing expedition south of Greenland and discovered a place that he called Vinland," said Sir Dorian. "According to the Flateyjarbock . . ."

"The what?" asked Hancock.

"The Flateyjarbock or Flatey book," said Sir Dorian, "is a medieval manuscript in which the most significant Norse events are recorded, like the discoveries of new lands. It includes descriptions of Vinland."

"So where is it?" asked Hancock.

"No one knows for sure," said Lexy. "In the sagas, it was described as a place where salmon teemed in the rivers and there were many species of wild game. Grapes grew there in great abundance. The Norsemen were fond of wine."

Sir Dorian's eyes momentarily flashed.

"The natural grapevine was quite rare in Nova Scotia and even as far south as Maine and New Hampshire," he added. "However, it did grow in abundance along the shoreline of Massachusetts."

"You're saying you believe that Vinland was Massachusetts?" asked Hancock.

"There is no proof of it," said Sir Dorian, "or you Americans would be celebrating Leif Eriksson Day every year. What we do have is a good idea of Eriksson's sailing course, which is described twice in the sagas. It records that he was traveling southwest for two days from Markland, or Nova Scotia as we now know it, before he sighted land. He could easily have traveled three hundred miles in those two days and nights. At that point, he recorded sailing westward between a large island and a cape to reach the place where he spent the winter. Only two places fit that description—the Cape Cod Peninsula and Nantucket."

"Hell, he might have run into a storm over those two days. It could have been a hundred miles," said Hancock, unconvinced, as two members of the expedition team made temporary repairs to the roof of the tent.

"One more point," said Sir Dorian. "Eriksson and his men spent a winter in Vinland. They cut down trees to build houses, and stacked a large number of cut logs to bring back to Greenland, where there were no trees. But when spring came, Eriksson left without them. We can only assume that he expected to return."

"Then why didn't he?" asked Hancock.

"When he returned to Greenland, his father, Erik the Red, had died," said Jensen. "Fever broke out in the settlements. Leif became their leader. In any event, there is no record of him ever going back."

"That's all you've got?" asked Hancock, obviously disappointed.

"Unfortunately, there is no hard evidence," concluded Lexy.

"Unless it's five hundred feet below us," said Rob Falconer.

In the ensuing silence, another brutal gust of wind split open the northern end of the tent wall and knocked over the metal stand holding the coffeemaker. One of the team members grabbed a canvas tarp and headed out into the darkness.

"Do we know when Eriksson died?" asked Macaulay.

"We know that he was still alive in 1015," said Jensen, the expert in Norse genealogy. "There is no mention of his death in the sagas."

"What do you think the stonecutter meant when he wrote about the hallowed place?" asked Hancock. "Could it be Valhalla . . . the home of the Norse gods?"

"I think the saga will tell us that he is in the hallowed place," said Lexy.

"Who is there?" asked Hancock.

"Leif Eriksson," she said.

"On what basis do you assume that?" he asked.

She hadn't really thought about it up to that moment. It had simply occurred to her. Perhaps it was something she had absorbed down there without even noticing it. There was no reasonable basis for the conclusion.

"Call it instinct," she said.

"We will hopefully find the answer to that and many other questions when we have translated the rest of the stonecutter's markings," said Sir Dorian.

"All right," said Hancock. "We're going to have to move fast. Tonight, we'll bring the Norsemen up in body bags and put them in cold storage to prevent further decomposition until we arrange for a transport with freezer units. After that, we'll collect their tools, weapons, and other personal belongings, cataloguing everything we find before crating it all to ship back to Texas. While that's being done, Dr. Vaughan will go down to the cave and begin translating the rest of the rune markings on the stone. We need to bring that up with special care. Another team can clear the ice away from the Viking ship. We obviously can't raise it right now, but it may have valuable items in the hold."

"Mr. Hancock," Sir Dorian interrupted, his voice rising, "I must protest. . . ."

"I'll also need recommendations on the laboratories that are best equipped to do scientific and medical research on a fully preserved thousand-year-old man," went on Hancock. "The Texas Aggies will kiss my ass to get one of those guys."

Macaulay stood up from his chair.

"J.L.," he said, "take a minute to think this through. Our team is exhausted. Just look around. They're out on their feet."

Hancock glanced at the men napping in front of the communications bank.

"A week from now, we'll be in total darkness, Steve," said Hancock.

"The United States Air Force ran a war up here for four years in the dead of winter," said Macaulay. "We can work up here for as long as it takes. If we push the guys too hard, there's going to be an accident or worse."

"Okay," Hancock finally conceded. "We'll all get a good night's sleep and get started in the morning."

Sir Dorian wasn't finished. He stood over Hancock, his mottled cheeks flushed with anger.

"I must strongly advocate that you do not take these precipitous actions," he said. "This could be one of the most important archaeological and scientific finds in history. It deserves far more careful planning than you have suggested."

"Thank you for your opinion, Sir Dorian," said Hancock, "but we're quite experienced in these matters."

"But you can return with your team in a few months and do these things in the spring with all the necessary protocols," came back the old man.

Hancock laughed. "Do you think we'll be able to keep this discovery a secret for the next four months? Half the countries in the world will find a way to claim ownership of everything we discovered down there. Just be grateful it was the Hancock team that found it. We know what to do."

"You must not do this," said Sir Dorian, looking to the other archaeologists for support.

"Mr. Hancock," began Jensen, "I must confess that Sir Dorian makes a reasonable point. Depending on what's written in those rune markings, this could be a find worthy of Howard Carter in the Valley of the Kings. You just can't pack it all up and cart it off to Texas."

"Why not Texas?" said Hancock. "Do I need to remind you and Sir Dorian that the British Museum in London is crammed with artifacts looted from ancient civilizations all over the world? Dallas will make just as good a destination for this find."

Privately, Lexy supported Sir Dorian. To ransack the cave was almost sacrilegious to her, but the reality of modern archaeology was that there were no longer any sacred canons. On most of the major digs in which she had participated, there had been brutal rivalries between archaeologists over who would win the glory and where the objects would go.

She was about to speak, when Hancock stood up and said, "We're done here. I'm going to bed."

Returning to her own tent, Lexy saw that the temperature was still dropping. Although the space heater was turned to its highest setting, her breath was condensing in the light of the gas lantern. The bottle of water she had left on the stand next to her cot was frozen solid.

It took her ten minutes to thaw the moisture inside her mummy bag by drying it over the space heater. Before she crawled in to get warm, she placed her flashlight inside it, clipped her doeskin-lined gloves to the leather cord strung above the cot, and turned off the lantern.

She slowly fell asleep to the wail of the wind and the constant hum of the diesel generator that powered most of the camp complex. Later, she dreamed she was in the belly of a great spacecraft sailing through the trackless universe.

TWELVE

21 November
Schloss Falkenberg
Koblenz, Germany

After he finished listening to the voice message recorded on the secure phone in his private study, Johannes Prinz Karl Erich Maria von Falkenberg, the ninth prince in the succession of the royal house of Falkenberg, was overcome with emotion.

As he gazed out the arched window facing the north parapet of his castle above the Rhine River, tears of unalloyed joy slowly began coursing down his pale cheeks. For several minutes, he continued to watch the soft, wet snow falling gently on the outer battlements, the scene illuminated by floodlights emplaced along the gorge that surrounded the shield walls.

The neo-Romanesque castle, rising majestically above the great river, stood at the pinnacle of a deep gorge. Through the centuries, it had withstood sieges and attacks by the French, the Italians, and most recently the

Americans at the end of the Second World War. Since 1215, it had been the ancestral home of the royal house of Falkenberg.

Prince von Falkenberg's personal staff had retired many hours earlier, and the private study was silent except for the crackling of the log fire in the immense stone grate. Above the marble mantelpiece, his late wife, Ingrid, gazed down at him from an oil painting commissioned shortly after their wedding.

He shook his head again in wonder. The news was simply astonishing, and he made a silent prayer in gratitude for still being alive to witness its potential impact on the world.

Holder of the Knight's Cross of the Iron Cross for his heroism as a young panzer group commander on the Russian front, he had survived the war's horrors only to come home to the destruction by Allied bombers of most of his family's industrial holdings, and the rape and murder of his wife, Ingrid, and their three daughters at his estate in Koenigsberg by marauding Russian troops in 1945.

Only his fervent unwavering faith had sustained him through those times. It had been the root of his being since he was a boy, and the only true cause he had ever worshipped. He and his family had shared only contempt for Hitler and his henchmen.

Never remarrying, he had spent many decades restoring his family fortune before regaining his place as one of the richest men in Germany. At ninety-five, he was still slender and fit, with a full head of pomaded white hair and a thin aquiline nose.

Putting on a blue Chinese silk brocade robe over his

silk pajamas, he sat down at his desk and recorded the key elements of the telephone message on a sheet of monogrammed notepaper, before adding a complete set of instructions. When finished, he rang for his personal manservant, Steiger.

"Please awaken Ernst," he said to Steiger when he appeared a few minutes later. "I want this message encrypted and sent to Sorensen in Reykjavik immediately. Mark it urgent."

"At once, Herr Hauptmann," he said, referring to von Falkenberg's wartime rank.

During the Battles of Kursk in Russia in 1943, Steiger had saved the prince's life during a machine gun attack, and come back to Germany minus his right leg and left hand. Unable to work, he had been reduced to begging on the bomb-ravaged streets of Berlin. Von Falkenberg had tracked him down after the war and offered him a place in his personal household as long as he lived.

Leaving the prince's private study with the handwritten message, Steiger wondered what could have possibly happened to restore such a beatific smile to the Hauptmann's face after so many years of total impassivity.

THIRTEEN

Lexy bolted awake. The battery-powered digital clock on the stand next to her cot read 02:07. The wailing of the wind and the hum of the generator were exactly the same, but she sensed another person was with her.

Slowly unzipping the top of the sleeping bag, she pointed her flashlight across the tent and switched it on. Rob Falconer stared back at her, his long mane of raven hair covered with snow. Little icicles were frozen into his beard.

He was kneeling at the end of her cot with one of her boots clutched in his left hand. Her small leather-bound archaeological journal, which she always placed in one of the boots before going to bed, was in his right.

His grin shattered the tiny icicles around his chin. Raising the journal in the air like a magician conjuring a familiar trick, he carefully inserted it back into her boot, and placed it next to the other one by the space heater.

"All safe and sound," he said.

"Your latest larceny won't bring you any reward, Rob," she said. "I haven't made any notes yet in my journal."

"I couldn't be sure you were holding out on me," he said, moving closer to sit on the edge of her cot.

"Only you would think that way," she said.

"My sweet, sexy Lexy," he said, leaning down toward her. "Is there room for me in there with you?"

In the glare of the flashlight beam, his pale amber eyes were glowing with exhilaration.

"What have you done?" she asked.

"I haven't done anything—yet," he said.

"I know you," she said. "You had the same look after you hacked into my computer and stole my thesis."

He laughed.

"I'm going to rewrite history," he said, "and I could be persuaded to allow you a place in the sun."

There was a faint petroleum smell on him, and she noticed an oily smudge on the chest of his thermal suit.

"Where have you been?"

"Can I trust you?" he said.

"You've never trusted anyone," she said.

"Let me show you," he said, leaning down to kiss her.

She slammed him in the head with her flashlight, and he fell back on the floor.

"Goddamn you," he hissed.

"Get out of my tent or I'll scream all the way to Valhalla, and then you can explain what you're doing here to John Lee Hancock."

He got up from the floor and began backing away,

rubbing his temple. She kept him in the beam of her flashlight until he slipped through the tent's inner and outer flaps into the wind-driven snow.

Lexy thought about getting dressed and going over to wake Steve Macaulay, but she was bone weary from the long air trip and everything that had happened since. She decided to wait until morning. Zipping up her mummy bag again, she fell back into a deep sleep.

Shrill noises began insinuating themselves into her brain. A few moments later, she came up out of the fog of sleep, fully awake. She could hear voices shouting outside in the darkness.

The air in the tent was frigid, and she could no longer hear the hum of the generator. Unzipping the mummy bag, she slipped on an additional layer of long johns, followed by her thermal suit, gloves, and boots.

Stepping outside, she saw several members of the expedition team running across the compound with flashlights. She walked over to the operations tent, where she found Hancock, Cabot, and Macaulay standing in front of the now-dark communications array. The tent's space heaters were as cold as the one in her tent. Two small gas lanterns provided minimal illumination.

"Someone sabotaged the main generator," said Macaulay. "We're trying to patch in power from two of the smaller backups."

Hancock's manner remained calm and assured.

"Right now, heat and communications are the top priority, even if we have to suspend the recovery operation. If we can't get the heat restored, Steve, you'll have to ferry the team back to Kulusuk in the transport chopper."

"What the hell is going on here?" said Cabot as he left to find the cause of the problem.

"I don't know," said Hancock, "but I'd say we need reinforcements."

"Obviously, there is someone here attempting to sabotage what we're doing," said Macaulay. "The question is who."

Lexy quickly told them about Falconer's visit to her tent, and how she had caught him trying to steal her journal.

"What time was that?" asked Macaulay.

"About three hours ago."

"Why didn't you wake one of us up?"

"I'm sorry. . . . I didn't think it was all that important."

"It was," said Hancock. "If he was the one who wrecked the satellite phone, he could have used it to arrange a rendezvous. He might even be on his way to the coast right now."

Macaulay sent Doc Callaghan over to search Falconer's tent. He returned a few minutes later to say that the archaeologist's personal gear was gone.

"One of the snowmobiles is also missing," he added.

"This has to be related to the Viking discovery," said Hancock. "Someone needs to go down there—one of the people who's seen everything."

Looking at Lexy, Macaulay said, "I'll do it."

"I need you here, Steve. You may be flying people out soon, and the transport chopper will have to be checked for more sabotage. As for the others . . ."

"I'll go," said Lexy, hoping the first jolt of fear she had just felt wasn't registering on her face.

FOURTEEN

"Maybe we could send Doc Callaghan down with her," said Macaulay, knowing John Lee wasn't aware of her claustrophobia.

"I'll be all right," she said.

"Good," said Hancock, turning to a member of his communications team. "As soon as we get power back, I want you to get Dallas on the horn. Tell them I want a fully equipped security team up here in the next twelve hours. I don't care how they have to do it."

"Use the walkie-talkie if you get into trouble," Macaulay whispered to Lexy. "I'll come right down."

"Aye, aye, General," she said with a mock salute.

"Wrong branch," he said to her departing back.

She rode down the bigger of the two shafts with George Cabot. When they reached the first cavern, he used his security code to activate power to the second winch and then attached a set of metal stirrups to the cable for her next descent.

Staring down into the small black hole, Lexy realized she was no longer afraid of the descent. Maybe it was because she had already been down there, or because she was so excited to see more of the discovery. Whatever the reason, she was grateful for the emotional reprieve.

She was about to step into the stirrups when she looked up and noticed an oily substance dripping from the power winch onto the cable.

"Not to worry," said Cabot, following her eyes. "These things leak oil all the time.

As the cable slowly began cranking her downward through the shaft, Lexy kept her flashlight beam trained on the ice wall in front of her. She began to notice a re-curring pattern of furrows, interspersed with small round fissures in the ice every forty or fifty feet.

She had done some rock climbing over the years, and the tiny fissures resembled those left by a piton. She then remembered that Rob was an experienced climber. It would have been easy for him to rig up a chest harness. The only thing he would have needed to rappel down the shaft was enough stout line.

In the glare of the flashlight beam, the base of the shaft finally arrived beneath her. Stepping off the rig into the black tunnel, she turned on her flashlight.

The Viking ship looked untouched to her, but she saw that someone had been there since their last visit. The block of ice that Steve Macaulay had placed in front of the cave opening had been shoved to one side, and the hole was now uncovered.

Inside the cave, ice melt was drizzling from the ceiling,

although the bodies of the Norsemen appeared to still be free of decomposition. When she looked down at the flaxen-haired Viking whose outer garment had been trimmed in red and gold braid, she saw that his cloak had been ripped open and the side pockets of his tunic torn out. Whatever he had possessed was gone.

At the back of the cave, the stonecutter was still lying where they had left him, but when she raised her flashlight to the rune stone, she saw that the ice shield that had covered it was no longer there.

She saw how Rob had done it. On their first visit, the Norsemen's iron firepots had been lying on their sides, empty. Now, two of them sat upright at the base of the stone. An empty plastic Coke bottle lay next to them. She sniffed its remaining contents. It was diesel fuel.

Her hands were trembling as she knelt in front of the stone and examined the top row of the inscription in the beam of the flashlight. Some of the symbols had been so crudely etched that she could not immediately interpret the individual characters, and thus their meaning. A few of the other symbols were unfamiliar to her, reflecting an idiom she had never encountered in translating other ancient texts.

She quickly concluded that a full translation of the saga would require hours of research, including an analysis of all the early Norse phrases and symbols she had catalogued back in St. Paul.

There were enough legible characters for her to conclude that if the stonecutter was recording true events, it was the most important archaeological discovery since the finding of the Dead Sea Scrolls.

We have come through the storm and survived, she read.

Her instincts had been correct. They had been part of Leif Eriksson's final expedition to Vinland in 1016. On their way back to Greenland, they had encountered something fearsome and powerful on an island where they had been forced to seek shelter. In battling it, Eriksson had been killed and was buried there.

He lies in the hallowed place. . . .

A voice suddenly startled her. It came through the earphones of her radio transceiver.

"Lexy, you need to get up here right away," said Steve Macaulay.

"All right," she said, her mind involuntarily continuing to translate the remaining symbols in the next row.

The next markings were meant to be a set of signposts for a new expedition of Norsemen to find Eriksson's burial place and whatever was buried there with him. The stonecutter had recorded descriptions of landmarks to help them find their way back there, places that had existed a thousand years earlier.

Under the tail, she read from the next line.

"George says you're not in the stirrups yet," called out Macaulay over the radio in a worried tone. "Is anything wrong?"

"I'm coming," she said, reluctantly retracing her path through the cave and out into the tunnel.

After restoring the block of ice to the mouth of the cave, she radioed George Cabot that she was ready to come up. In a few moments, the power winch began cranking and she was on her way.

Although it was past seven in the morning, there was no hint of daylight on the surface. Since her descent, the wind had died to a low moan, but it was still snowing.

She heard a dog barking in the distance as she made her way to the operations tent. The cries were deep and cadenced, and repeated every few seconds. It had to be Hancock's Alsatian.

Inside the tent, Sir Dorian was slumped next to the bank of space heaters, almost hidden under a mound of thermal blankets. His eyes were dull and unfocused. Jensen was helping him swallow some pills with a mug of water. Macaulay and Hancock were standing at the communications array, sipping coffee.

"Hap found something a little while ago," said Hancock. "You may be able to help us identify it."

He started to lead her out of the tent, when Hjalmar Jensen and Doc Callaghan stepped into his path. Jensen had an anxious look on his face.

"Sir Dorian has had some kind of heart attack or stroke. I believe he needs to be hospitalized as soon as possible."

"I agree," said Doc Callaghan. "His symptoms are consistent with an ischemic stroke in which an artery to the brain is blocked. With a blocked artery, the neurons can't make enough energy. At some point, the brain will stop working."

"We'll fly him out on the Bell transport as soon as we get back," said Hancock.

Outside the tent, he climbed onto a snowmobile and motioned for Lexy to join him. Macaulay followed on a separate machine as they crossed the compound and traveled out onto the dark ice field. Lexy noticed they were following the path of the heavy-duty fire hose that was used to pump meltwater out of the shafts.

Reaching the ice crevasse where the hose terminated, Hancock stopped his machine and got off. Someone had mounted a battery-powered floodlight on a steel tripod that faced down into it. A member of the expedition team was standing at the edge, holding the excited Alsatian at the end of a leash.

"Hap smelled it and came out here to investigate," said Hancock.

Stepping forward, Lexy looked over the edge of the crevasse. The body of a man was lying facedown about halfway down the slope. He had been stripped naked and his body had a bluish tint from the subzero cold. His head was frozen into the surface of the ice. She couldn't recognize it through the milky glaze.

"In another hour, the corpse would have been covered by snow and ice melt," said Hancock.

"We think the hose pump was still running when they got him out here," said Macaulay. "It froze around his head after they were finished."

"There is only one identifiable mark on his body," said Hancock. "It's a tattoo."

Lexy stepped closer to the body. The torso looked like a male manikin in a department store window. There was a tattoo on the right cheek of the man's buttocks.

"It's Rob Falconer," she said.

"How do you know for sure?" asked Macaulay.

"The tattoo . . . is in Sanskrit."

"What does it mean?"

"It's not important," she said, her teeth beginning to chatter.

"Let me be the judge of that," said Hancock.

She hesitated a few moments before glancing up at Macaulay.

"It's Sanskrit for the name Alexandra."

FIFTEEN

The lights in the operations tent suddenly came on, and Lexy heard a ragged cheer from the men at the other end of the compound. A few minutes later, George Cabot came in to report that they had patched enough power together from the two smaller generators to operate the space heaters.

"It was meant to look like an accident, but someone purposely turned the big Kohler generator into junk," he said. "Pretty ingenious, actually. He used the oil-overflow valve to empty a gallon of engine oil out of the machine into a plastic container and then poured a gallon or so of kerosene into the oil reservoir to replace it. It probably took a half hour or so for the bearings to burn up and the engine to seize. By then he was well enough away. I found the container of engine oil behind the tent."

Macaulay was staring at the array of communications

equipment on the far wall. The two fixed radio ground stations, high modularity units with frequency-hopping waveforms designed for use in warships and armed service installations, had provided them with a direct link to any receiving station in the world. They were still dark.

"Don't tell me . . . ," groaned Hancock as Cabot went over to the array.

After examining the switching controls and interface modules on the two rigs, he said, "Everything looks fine here."

Kneeling down, he crawled behind the heavy gauge steel table that supported the units, and disappeared behind it. A minute later, he crawled back out and climbed to his feet, holding what looked like a large plastic hypodermic syringe.

"Two hundred thousand dollars of radio circuitry went shit to bed from this thing," he said disgustedly in his down-east twang. "Take a sniff."

Macaulay held it up to his nose.

"Acid?"

"Exactly," said Cabot. "He used this syringe to remove the sulfuric acid from one of our deep cycle batteries and then injected it through the ventilators into the backs of the radios. It fried all the circuits."

"What is that thing?" asked Macaulay.

"I think it's a cake decorator," said Lexy, "for putting on icing."

"Where's the cook?" demanded Hancock.

When he arrived a few minutes later, Thorwald, the Norwegian cook, was shown what had been used to destroy the radio array.

"We have this in the kitchen equipment . . . of course,"

he said, seemingly perplexed. "I don't know how it got here."

Hancock made his next decisions without delay.

"George, I want every inch of that Bell transport helicopter checked for possible sabotage. Put a guard on it when you're finished."

"Done," said Cabot, heading across the ops tent.

Turning to Macaulay, he said, "It will be light soon, Steve—at least for a couple hours. That should give you time to fly up to Kulusuk and bring back the spare radio unit. While you're there, call the Anschutz security director in Dallas and tell him we need a fully armed security team up here right away. Contract it out to whoever can get here the fastest. I don't care what the price quote is."

"What about Falconer?" asked Macaulay.

"I'm tempted to send his body back with you," said Hancock, "but I'm not going to tamper with a crime scene. The police authority in Greenland is up in Nuuk. Radio them what happened. I'm sure they'll want to send an investigator and a forensic team down here. In the meantime, we won't touch anything."

"His body will be covered with a foot or two of ice by then," said Doc Callaghan.

"That's their problem."

Thirty minutes later, the transport helicopter had been thoroughly checked by the ground crew and warmed up on the landing pad. The wind had temporarily died, and there was a hint of dawn in the eastern sky.

"The ship is clean," said Cabot to Macaulay. "I personally checked every square inch."

"Thanks, George," said Macaulay.

"Bring back the cavalry, Steve," said Hancock with a wry grin.

Shaking hands, they watched as Sir Dorian was carried on a makeshift litter from the operations tent to the landing pad. Hjalmar Jensen, Lexy, and Callaghan walked together behind him.

When they arrived at the helicopter pad, Sir Dorian was still conscious.

"Sorry to be a bloody bother," he said to Hancock with a parting attempt at a grin. "Please do the responsible thing with this discovery, Mr. Hancock. It deserves no less."

"After what's happened, I now share your view," said Hancock as the archaeologist was carried into the chopper and his litter was strapped to the steel deck beneath the rotor and transmission housing. Lexy and Hjalmar Jensen went aboard to give him a brief final farewell, and Jensen set Sir Dorian's kit bag next to his litter on the deck.

"I look forward to seeing you again in London, Sir Dorian," said Lexy as Doc Callaghan administered a sedative to relax him during the flight.

Hancock and the others stood at the edge of the landing pad as Steve Macaulay gently lifted the big chopper into the air. Lexy was waving at him cheerily, and he raised his hand to acknowledge her before heading north toward Kulusuk.

SIXTEEN

23 November
Greenland Ice Cap

Macaulay leveled off at an altitude of one thousand feet and advanced the speed to one hundred twenty miles per hour. The two Pratt & Whitney Twin-Pac turboshaft engines were running with their familiar, throaty roar. With no air turbulence ahead of him and nearly two miles of visibility, he would see the runway lights at Kulusuk in about fifteen minutes.

He was grateful to Cabot for thoroughly checking the bird. Macaulay had never fully trusted helicopters. He was a fighter pilot. He trusted wings. He had survived several crashes in the air force because the wings had allowed him to glide long enough to safely eject from the stricken planes.

When he was assembling Hancock's fleet of corporate aircraft a few years earlier, Macaulay had made sure all the company helicopters were modified with crash-attenuating seats that would compress downward under any serious impact. It limited the potential g loads on the crew and would protect their vulnerable necks and backs. He had also insisted on the installation of doors and windows that could be jettisoned, as well as self-sealing fuel tanks to reduce the chances of fire after a crash.

As he flew on across the desolate ice cap, his mind kept wandering back to all the events that had taken place over the previous twenty-four hours. Obviously, someone was desperate enough to kill in order to bring the recovery effort to a halt.

It was impossible to believe that one of the twelve original members of the expedition could be responsible for murder and sabotage, but a few of them were new to the team, including Thorwald, the Norwegian cook, and two native Inuit who were part of the maintenance crew.

If it wasn't a member of the expedition team, that left the four archaeologists as suspects. But Falconer was dead, and Macaulay refused to believe that Lexy could be involved. That left Hjalmar Jensen and Sir Dorian Bond.

He remembered Sir Dorian's passionate appeal to John Lee that he must halt his plans to remove the Norsemen from the deep cave. It struck him that the old Englishman could be feigning illness, and might be heading back to alert someone in the outside world to what they had found.

Macaulay turned to look back at him.

His eyes were closed and he appeared to be asleep. In any event, the straps that secured the litter to the steel deck would keep him immobilized until they reached Kulusuk.

He was checking the instrument gauges a few moments later when the explosion suddenly detonated behind him. He felt the first wave of searing heat as it ripped through the cockpit, walloping the back of his flight helmet with shards of metal and plastic, and smashing the windshield. Only the steel-reinforced pilot's seat saved him from the deadly blast.

He turned to glance back at the source of the explosion. The blast area appeared to be centered underneath the rotors and the transmission housing. With the transmission housing immobilized, the rotor blades no longer received the power to rotate.

They were going in.

He watched in horror as Sir Dorian, still strapped to the litter, burst into flames. His shock of gray hair was on fire, along with the blankets covering his body. There was no way to save him.

None of the safety features he had added would make any difference if the rate of descent was unsurvivable. He was dropping at nearly forty feet per second, and he had to slow the rate down by getting the rotors turning in auto rotation. If he could stabilize the bird for a few seconds, natural airflow alone would provide enough energy to turn the rotors and allow a relatively controlled descent. The minimum altitude threshold for auto rotation was about four hundred feet, and he hoped he was still above it.

He had about ten seconds to prepare for the crash. The flames were licking close to the cockpit, and he could feel the intensity of the heat through his boots on the steel flight deck. He put on his thermal gloves to protect his hands.

Looking up, he saw that the rotors had stopped and the ship was now in free fall.

Reaching to his left, he pulled the handle that jettisoned the cabin window next to the pilot's seat. The pilot's seat was also equipped with a five-point safety harness that had a single-release mechanism. When he felt the helicopter skids first begin to impact the ice, he would pull the release on the safety harness and attempt his escape.

When the helicopter slammed into the frozen ice cap, Macaulay was blinded by an eruption of brilliant magnesium-white light. Surrounded by a geyser of flames, he could hear the agonizing shriek of tortured metal as the ship began to rupture around him. Ten seconds later, the flames found one of the perforated gas tanks and the Bell 412EP jet helicopter exploded in a fiery ball.

SEVENTEEN

From inside the modular fiberglass latrine at the far edge of the compound, Lexy paused while brushing her teeth as the rumbling roar of an approaching helicopter grew ever louder.

Her first thought was that it might be Steve returning from Kulusuk. But he had left the camp only an hour earlier. It seemed unlikely he could be returning so quickly unless he had run into a problem.

Sitting at the desk in his sleeping tent, John Lee Hancock knew from the pitch of the jet engines that it wasn't Steve. As the rumble grew louder, he quickly realized there was more than one helicopter. His initial thought was that they might be the police officials dispatched from Nuuk.

George Cabot watched them coming in low above the ice, not more than fifty feet up in the air, and flying from due east. In the pale morning light, he couldn't see any markings on the ships. Cabot was thinking about turning on the landing lights until he saw that one of them looked like a military attack helicopter. The other two were transports.

With radio communications out, there was no way to contact them as they flew a direct course to the base camp. When they arrived over the team's landing pad, the pilots of the transports turned on the four powerful searchlights that were mounted to the bellies of each ship, lighting up the whole compound. While the smaller attack helicopter continued circling the camp, the two transports began their descent.

Hancock stood with his Alsatian at the opening of his tent to observe their arrival. He saw that the ships were painted gloss white to blend in with the icy landscape. He recognized all three as military aircraft manufactured by Eurocopter. None of them displayed the internationally required markings and numbers.

Who are these bastards? he wondered, his mind racing. What are they doing here? Had they come to rob him of his discovery? He watched five members of his expedition team, including Doc Callaghan, approach the edge of the landing pad as the two transports touched down.

The first man to step out of the helicopters was the mission commander. Tall and slender with coarse-grained blond hair, he had luminescent, reflective blue eyes and a trained, always-serious face. His name was Joachim Halvorsen, but they called him the Lynx.

A former veteran of the elite Norwegian Special

Forces, he took infinite care with each and every detail of an operation. Preliminary intelligence for this mission had been minimal, and his roving eyes were already taking in the configuration of the camp, each tent and outbuilding, every man in sight.

He was always planning for the unexpected, the steps he would immediately take if anyone offered resistance or threatened the success of the mission. Two hundred feet above him, the third helicopter continued to circle the camp, ready to intercept anyone who escaped the cordon.

Like the fourteen commandos who emerged from the two transports behind him, the Lynx was dressed in a white thermal winter suit and lightweight, bulletproof armor. He carried a Czech-made Skorpion Evo III submachine gun, a 9 mm Glock 19 semiautomatic pistol, and a belt with extra magazines for both.

The rotor blades slowly came to a stop.

"Raise your hands and you will not be harmed," he shouted over the dying whine of the helicopter engines.

Four of the five men at the landing pad raised their hands. The fifth, Doc Callaghan, demanded angrily, "You have no right to threaten us with weapons. We are here at the invitation of . . ."

The Lynx shot him in the head. He fell to the ice.

Thorwald, the Norwegian chef, had come out of the cook tent to see what was happening. Seeing Doc Callaghan fall, he knew he had to defend himself. In the cook tent, he had a selection of lethal knives. He had become an expert with them during his own military service.

The Lynx saw him move out of the corner of his eye, and estimated the distance at twenty meters. In one smooth motion, the submachine gun was at his shoulder, and he squeezed off a single round. It took Thorwald in the chest, killing him instantly.

Hearing the first shot, Lexy had gone to the door of the latrine and cracked it open in time to see Thorwald killed. As she watched, the blond killer issued orders to the other men in the unit. One of them began herding the first four prisoners toward the elevator cage at the top of the ice shaft. The others began fanning out across the compound.

George Cabot had known they were trouble from the moment he saw the three ships coming in. Before they landed, he had headed straight to the open-ended shelter that housed the expedition's snowmobiles.

After hearing the first two shots, he ran to the Arctic Cats. They were the fastest snowmobiles in camp and could reach a speed of a hundred miles per hour. That wouldn't be enough to outrun an attack helicopter, but there were plenty of ice fissures and natural caves out on the ice cap where it might be possible to hide. Anything was better than dying like a trapped animal. He started the engine on the white one, hoping it might blend in better with the pallid landscape in the feeble morning light.

A moment later, he was racing out of the tent at the edge of the compound, heading east toward the coast. For more than a minute, the attack helicopter appeared to take no notice of him. By then, he was streaking across the ice toward exactly the kind of depression that could provide him with a temporary hiding place. A snow squall was coming in the distance that would make it even harder to find him. He was home free.

Racing up the ascending ice shelf at breakneck speed, he reached the top and launched the snowmobile over the wide depression, sailing out for ten meters before the Arctic Cat came down with a heavy thud on the ice floor.

He could hear the attack helicopter coming as he slowly braked the snowmobile to a halt under the concave wall above the depression. It was just the kind of protective barrier he needed until visibility disappeared under the snow squall.

He suddenly felt the ice floor begin to shift underneath him.

With mounting awareness, he realized that he wasn't in a natural depression at all. He had landed on an unstable ice bridge. A few moments later, the tenuous bridge began to give way under the weight of the Arctic Cat.

"Oh shit," Cabot muttered as he plummeted soundlessly down through space into a chasm that seemed to have no bottom.

EIGHTEEN

23 November
Base Hancock One
Greenland Ice Cap

When Lexy saw the phalanx of commandos fanning out across the compound, she shut the outer door of the washroom and searched for a possible place to hide. The small outbuilding was modular fiberglass. It had two shower stalls, four sinks, and two small built-in cupboards on the far wall. A squirrel couldn't find a hiding place there.

The latrine end of the building had been positioned over a bulldozed ice pit that was lined with a heavy-duty 20 mil polyethylene tarpaulin to contain excrement and effluent from the toilets.

She knew they would search every stall in the latrine. The only possible hiding place was the ice pit beneath it. She stepped into the last stall of the latrine, raised the back of the toilet seat, and hurled the leather satchel holding her toilet articles down the open hole.

Stepping up onto the fiberglass deck that surrounded the opening, she looked down through the hole. Six feet below it, she saw the accumulated mounds of frozen excrement covering the plastic lining.

The hole appeared too small to get through, but it was her only chance. She heard shouting outside as the attackers continued rounding up the expedition team members in the compound. They would be coming through the door at any moment.

Putting her feet together, she slid down the hole, stopping short when her hips came to a halt halfway down. If she tried to force her way farther down, she knew she would only remain stuck.

Another gunshot rang out.

Terrified at the thought of being captured, she pulled herself back up from the opening, unzipped her thermal suit, and stepped out of it. A moment later, she heard the outside door of the washroom slam open and then the guttural voices of two of the attackers as they stepped inside.

She dropped the thermal suit through the hole and slid down into the opening again. Although her hips quickly jammed again, she grasped the back of the toilet seat in both hands and forced herself downward. A moment later she was through the opening, landing on all fours on top of the frozen mound.

Glancing upward, she could see the face of the attacker as he entered her stall, the barrel of his machine gun pointed ahead of him. If he looked down through the hole, he couldn't help but see her.

His face disappeared. She heard the outer door of the washroom slam shut again as they went outside to continue their search of the compound. Without the heat protection of the thermal suit, her body was already going numb from the agonizing cold. Sitting up, she quickly put it back on.

There was a small vent at each end of the fiberglass housing a few inches above the edge of the pit. Climbing across the frozen excrement, she looked through the vent facing the compound.

Two of the expedition team members were being herded toward the elevator cage at the top of the first ice shaft. Six more were already waiting there under guard. She heard the power winch begin its familiar clanking noise, and the elevator slowly descended out of sight.

NINETEEN

At the other end of the compound, John Lee Hancock stood waiting behind the inner flap of his sleeping tent. The Alsatian sensed his tension and began growling at the sound of a man approaching the tent.

Hancock was holding the Louisville Slugger baseball bat given him by the owner of the Texas Rangers baseball team after they had won the American League Championship Series.

After seeing Doc Callaghan and Thorwald murdered, he had no doubt what they would do to him if he was caught. But why? He understood that the find in the Viking cave had significant financial value, and that there were plenty of bragging rights to be had if the secrets of the cave were as important as Sir Dorian had suggested. But who would slaughter two men for that? It made no sense.

He saw that the morning sky was already darkening. It

would be almost pitch-black again in less than an hour. He just needed to avoid capture until he could make his way out of the camp in the darkness.

The inner flap of the sleeping tent swept open and the nose of a submachine gun preceded one of the commandos into the tent. Momentarily stunned at seeing the snarling dog about to lunge for him, the commando lowered his weapon to fire at Hap.

Hancock swung the heavy bat with all his strength at the back of the man's head. When he dropped to the floor, Hancock swung again, crushing his neck below the helmet.

Now there was a chance. The commando was about his own size. Wearing the man's thermal suit and helmet, he might be able to pass for him outside and then make his escape. He quickly removed his own thermal suit with the Anschutz International logo.

While stripping off the man's body armor, Hancock noticed a red emblem stitched over the heart of his tunic. It looked like a small upright ship's anchor with the ends of the two flukes trimmed off. Maybe they were part of some nautical unit, he thought as he removed the man's thermal suit and began putting it on.

A small gold pendant was dangling from the dead man's neck. It was the same shape as the red emblem. After putting on the man's upper-body armor and helmet, Hancock picked up the submachine gun and stepped outside.

Three of his expedition team members were being taken at gunpoint to the elevator cage at the top of the shaft. After what had already happened, Hancock presumed it would be a one-way trip.

He thought about what he could possibly do to help them survive.

One of Hancock's strengths throughout his adult life was his innate capacity to recognize an opportunity and exploit it when it arrived. When he saw that the pilot of one of the transport helicopters had started his engines again, he resolved an immediate plan of action.

The ship was ready to fly. It had a radio transceiver in the cockpit. All he needed to do was get airborne long enough to radio for help and give his position. The transport couldn't outrun the attack helicopter, but once word of their attack was out, the intruders would have to head for cover.

Like Steve Macaulay, Hancock had plenty of experience flying helicopters. The German Eurocopter couldn't be all that much different from American military models. He just had to get aboard the ship, disable the pilot, and take off. He would deal with the attack helicopter once he was in the air.

Carrying the Czech submachine gun, he began walking toward the landing pad. The helicopter pilot saw him coming and waved. He waved back. The passenger hatch was wide-open.

Stepping inside the fuselage, he moved toward the cockpit. Glancing outside, Hancock saw that Hap had followed him from the tent. A moment later, the dog leaped through the hatch to join him.

In the cockpit, the pilot was eating a sandwich while he adjusted the pitch on the jet engines. Hancock brought the stock of the machine gun down on the back of his neck, and he slumped forward.

Dragging him out of the seat, Hancock took his place

at the controls. His eyes scanned the gauges. It would be easier than he thought, slowly moving the throttle forward to takeoff speed.

A moment later, he felt the barrel of a machine pistol at the back of his neck.

"They say that a dog is a man's best friend," said Jensen. "In this case, I'm afraid yours has cost you your freedom."

TWENTY

The Lynx surveyed the tent encampment in the garish glare of the helicopter floodlights. Everything had gone smoothly so far, even though he had received orders to conduct this operation less than twelve hours earlier.

His mission was to secure the expedition site on the ice cap and to recover everything that Jensen considered important enough to bring back with them.

Jensen told him he had already eliminated two of the targets by placing a bomb aboard their helicopter.

Hancock, the expedition leader, was now being held in the larger cavern along with all but two of the other targets. One had tried to escape in a snowmobile, but the gunner in the attack helicopter radioed that he had disappeared down a thousand-foot chasm. The other missing target was a woman. Jensen told him he wanted her taken unharmed.

"She may prove to be of important value to us in the future," he had said.

The Lynx wondered if Jensen's motives were personal or professional. The Lynx had already killed two women, both sanctioned executions, and he had found a particular thrill in observing their final moves and reactions, the two of them unaware of what he planned to do until the moment he ended their lives.

In hunting for this woman, his men had searched every tent and outbuilding in the small complex several times. Jensen told him she had definitely been there. The one remaining possibility was that she had been working down in one of the caverns when they had arrived, and had hidden in an ice pocket. His commandos were now scouring the walls of the ice shafts and the caverns.

The Lynx had no idea what these people had done to deserve elimination, and he did not care. He had already informed his men that he would personally carry out all the executions, telling them he didn't want them to feel guilt over these people being unarmed and defenseless. From their reactions, it was clear they now admired him even more for making the supposed sacrifice.

In truth, he was looking forward to each one. He knew he was unlike other men. His urge to kill was deep and primal. Once again, he would bestow the God power to himself, the excitement of standing close to a person who was full of life and sending him into the everlasting void.

Where was the woman? he wondered again.

Through the tiny vent under the latrine, Lexy had watched the last members of Hancock's expedition team being captured one by one. They were all taken to the elevator rig and then sent below.

At one point, she was shocked to see Hjalmar Jensen, now dressed in the same kind of thermal suit the attackers wore, personally deliver John Lee Hancock into their hands at gunpoint. The Norwegian archaeologist no longer resembled the Mr. Rogers character she remembered from her childhood. His eyes were cold and pitiless.

Soon after the prisoners were taken below, a new round of activity commenced as the marauders began to bring to the surface a stream of objects that were quickly stowed aboard the transport helicopters.

With no physical threat remaining, the attackers had removed their body armor. She now noticed the red emblem that was stitched over the hearts of their thermal suits. From a distance, it looked anchorlike and vaguely familiar.

The first objects that went into the transports were black plastic body bags, each one carried by two men. She counted ten of them, concluding they contained the Vikings from the deep cave.

The next load of items consisted of large metal bins, more than a dozen of them, each heavy enough to require two men to carry them. A second load of bins followed the first as darkness fell over the compound. The pilots of the helicopters turned on their searchlights to illuminate the compound as work continued.

Her view of their actions was interrupted several times by the commandos' use of the latrines. In order to avoid detection, she had built a pillar of excrement near the vented end of the pit. It blocked any view of her through the latrine holes.

Less than two hours after they arrived, the procession of metal bins ended and things became quiet for a few minutes. Then she heard one of the bulldozers being started, quickly followed by the second one.

As she watched, the larger of the two began rumbling toward the latrine.

TWENTY-ONE

23 November
Base Hancock One
Greenland Ice Cap

Hancock stood with the other captives in the *March Hare* cavern one hundred forty feet beneath the surface of the ice cap. Their wrists had been bound behind their backs with fiberglass handcuffs, and they were guarded by two commandos with machine guns.

In the previous two hours, he had witnessed the looting of the deeper cave by Jensen and the others. They had brought up the ten Norsemen and reverently placed them in body bags to be transported to the surface. Several ornately carved sea chests, including the one he had seen in the bow of the longship, came next. Their weapons, personal regalia, and equipment were brought up and stowed carefully in solid metal bins before being sent up in the elevator cage.

The last thing to be hauled up was the large flat stone engraved with rune markings. Two men wrapped it in several layers of padded blankets and hand-carried it to the elevator cage.

Still outwardly calm, Hancock remembered his own excitement when he and Steve Macaulay had stood in almost the same place and were about to enter the nose compartment of *March Hare*. In hindsight, he wished that he had never given the order to go after the second discovery. He realized that decision was about to cost him his life.

With everything of importance removed from the cave, the Lynx ordered all but four of his commandos to return to the surface. As Hancock watched impassively, the blond-haired killer fed a round into his 9 mm Glock 19 semiautomatic pistol.

Hancock hated the thought that his time on Earth had to end here. He had always lived on the edge, and he had taken enough risks to know the slender thread of life. That was why he had eventually come to savor every day of it.

A fatalist, he was sure that there was no afterlife, no spending of eternity in one of the mansions of heaven. If there were a heaven and hell, they were right here on Earth. He had sampled both.

Two of the soldiers forced the first captive to his knees. The blond-haired killer stepped quickly behind him, grabbed him by the hair, placed the barrel of the silenced pistol to the back of his head, and fired. The man fell forward and they moved on to the next captive. Trying to escape their grasp, he began shouting for help.

Hancock had two principal regrets.

There was so much more he wanted to do in his life, women he hoped to meet, places he wanted to explore, mysteries he wanted to solve. Now, there would never be the chance. His only other regret was that he wouldn't be alive to see these bastards destroyed. He would have enjoyed doing it himself.

Two of the commandos forced him to his knees. He felt the cold muzzle of the pistol against the back of his head as the Lynx moved behind him.

"Why?" he called out to Jensen, who stood off to the side near the elevator rig.

He didn't expect an answer. None was given.

Hancock could hear Hap Arnold howling madly at the top of the ice shaft. His last conscious thought before the bullet tore through his brain was the hope that Jensen would let the old Alsatian live.

TWENTY-TWO

23 November
Base Hancock One
Greenland Ice Cap

The final stage of the operation was under way. The two hours of light left in the subarctic region had disappeared, and the last part of the mission had to be performed under the powerful searchlights mounted on the transport helicopters.

Returning to the surface after executing his prisoners, the Lynx ordered his commando team to eliminate every trace of Hancock's expedition that remained on the ice cap.

The smaller bulldozer began grinding its way through the tent complex, driving everything in its path toward the ice shaft and shoving it over the edge, then returning to cut another broad swath of destruction through what remained, including the operations tent, snowmobiles, the kitchen and mess tents, and the flagpole that was still flying the American flag and Hancock's family coat of arms.

The larger bulldozer, a Caterpillar D10R, focused on flattening the more significant structures in the compound, and plowing the wreckage into the same shaft. In ten minutes, the massive generator housing was reduced to rubble and had disappeared down the twelve-foot passage.

As Lexy watched with horror from her hiding place in the pit, the rumbling snarl of the Caterpillar grew to a bedlam as its treads rolled toward the modular fiberglass latrine.

She could see the vague outline of a man in the insulated cab above the steel blade as it slammed into the front wall, crumpling the fiberglass structure as if it were made of cardboard.

Then it was rearing over her like a colossal monster, its treads grinding down through several feet into the frozen muck as it thundered past her hiding place with an ear-splitting roar, its right tread missing her by less than a foot.

Terrified, she thought for a moment about climbing out of the hole and running toward the darkness, but the compound was bathed in the glare of the lights, and she would have been captured immediately.

After driving the shattered wreckage of the flattened latrine building into the mouth of the ice shaft, the driver quickly pivoted and began plowing a mound of snow and ice ahead of it to fill the latrine pit and eliminate any trace of human activity there.

Lying on her stomach, Lexy could only press herself

down in the pit, pulling the edge of the black plastic liner over her upper body to hide it from view. Seconds later, the bulldozer dumped a small avalanche of ice into the hole, burying her under it before moving on to the next objective.

Hjalmar Jensen watched the eradication of Hancock's camp impassively. It gave him no pleasure to take human life, but in this case it was for the most important cause in his life.

A search party would be sent out within days, and it would find the remains of Hancock and his men one hundred forty feet below the surface. It would raise innumerable questions, but there would be no one alive who knew about the deeper cave and its importance.

The Lynx approached him as the last remaining structures in the camp were being destroyed. He noticed that the white dog had attached itself to Jensen for some reason and was now following him. He didn't know or like dogs, but it struck him as curious that the animal would be drawn to the man who had his master killed.

"The woman is still missing," said the Lynx.

"It's unfortunate, but we can search for her no longer," replied Jensen. "It is already past our scheduled departure time. You have assured me there was no place for her to hide up here. If she is not up here, then she must obviously be down there. If she isn't already dead, then she soon will be."

As if in confirmation, they heard the muffled crump of a loud explosion far below the surface. It was the explosive charge set by the demolition team in the deep cave that had been home to the ten Norsemen for a thousand years. There would be no trace of it left.

A few minutes later, a massive secondary explosion signified the collapse and destruction of the cavern that had housed *March Hare*, sealing all the debris from the base camp and the bodies of the original expedition team.

It would take a well-equipped search effort to locate them and then try to figure out what had happened. By then, there would be numerous red herrings placed in the path of the investigations, including the first one, suggesting an international terrorist organization.

After the smaller bulldozer was shoved into the shaft by the larger one, the Lynx ordered the last cache of explosives to be detonated near the top of the ice shaft, collapsing it inward. The Caterpillar then leveled the remaining depression with the surrounding landscape.

Jensen took a last brief walk across what had once been the compound. Although it was scarred with the tracks of the bulldozers, nothing remained on the surface to indicate human activity. It was starting to snow again. Within hours, the surface of the cap would be pristine.

Everything had gone well, considering how little time there had been after the discovery was made. He had caught and killed Falconer, the archaeologist who had attempted to defile the tomb. He had successfully sabotaged the communications equipment and fashioned the crude explosive device that had brought down Macaulay and Sir Dorian Bond.

He had also ordered their attack helicopter to follow the course Macaulay would have flown from the base camp to Kulusuk. The pilot had reported back that they had found the Bell transport helicopter on the ice cap and it was a burned-out shell.

Only two members of the commando team had been killed—the young Swede who had foolishly entered Hancock's tent without backup and the Danish pilot Hancock had killed in his escape attempt.

Most important, the discovery in the deep cave was safe. Once he had a chance to decipher the clues in the stonecutter's saga, he was confident they could accomplish the ultimate goal.

His thoughts briefly went back to the missing woman, Dr. Vaughan. She could have been very helpful in translating the tablet. Next to Barnaby Finchem, she was the most gifted runologist he had ever met.

It was snowing hard as the commandos hitched harness cables from the belly of one of the transport helicopters to the Caterpillar. It would be flown back to the coast and jettisoned into the ocean near the ship that was waiting off Kap Lovenorn for their safe return.

The Lynx shook hands with each member of the team as they boarded the helicopters. The first to step off at the start of the mission, he was the last man to get back aboard.

As he was about to enter the passenger hatch, he turned and saw the white Alsatian. The dog was waiting expectantly in the snow, whimpering for the chance to follow Jensen. He pulled the Glock from his belt and aimed it at the dog's head.

"Ikke skyte ham," shouted Jensen through the open bay.

The Lynx put the pistol back in its holster, climbed into the passenger compartment of the helicopter, and closed the hatch behind him. It didn't matter to him one way or the other. He was still thinking about the woman.

Jensen watched the dog through the port as the ship rose above it.

"Gå tilbake til vill, min venn," he said quietly.

Return to the wild, my friend.

TWENTY-THREE

Macaulay crouched in the darkness, galvanic with fury. At the same time, he knew he had to overcome it in order to survive, and to help the others make it through too.

The seemingly mild-mannered Jensen had tried to murder him. Of this he was certain. There was no other possibility after Cabot checked the bird and pronounced it clean. Jensen had put the explosive device in Sir Dorian's kit bag.

It was only through a minor miracle that he hadn't joined the Englishman in becoming part of the melted wreckage of the helicopter. As it plummeted in free fall toward the ice cap, he doubted the crash would be survivable.

After pulling the handle that jettisoned the cabin window next to the pilot's seat, he had waited until he felt the first hint of an impact of the bird's skids on the ice, and then released the five-point safety harness.

The flames seemed to be pursuing him as he dove sideways through the open window housing and away from the burning ship. He was almost through, when the vast bulk of the helicopter slammed into the ice, trapping his legs and feet inside. If the ship collapsed on the pilot's side of the cockpit, he was dead. If it went the other way, he had a chance.

When he felt the twisting wreckage carrying him upward, he dragged his legs free and began to scramble on his hands and knees away from the fiery wreckage. Ten seconds later, the fuel tanks blew up. The force of the blast carried him another twenty feet through the air, but he wasn't hit by any shards of the flying metal.

As the ship continued to burn, Macaulay took stock of his situation. Both his knees were in pain and there was a bleeding laceration on his forehead, but otherwise he had come out of the inferno whole.

He knew he needed to move out right away. The flaming wreckage could be seen for a mile, and he had no idea who else might be in the plot aside from Jensen. He got up to test his knees and spied a metal spar. It was about six feet long, and had also been blown clear of the wreckage. It would relieve some of the pressure on his knees.

Should he try for Kulusuk or return to the base camp? He decided to head back, if nothing else to get his hands on Jensen and prevent him from any further sabotage. He had flown about six miles on the northerly route after taking off. He set a goal of walking back to the base camp within two hours.

In the glare of the flames, he glanced down at his Suunto Core military wristwatch. Along with an accurate altimeter and thermometer, it was equipped with a digital compass. Recalling the course he had been flying to reach Kulusuk, he simply reversed it for the correct heading back to the camp.

He started walking. According to his watch, the temperature was five degrees below zero Fahrenheit, almost balmy for that time of the year. With his thermal suit, gloves, and insulated hood, he would have no trouble staying warm.

Night fell shortly after the noon hour. He was in almost complete darkness after the first two miles. A cold keening wind bore down from the north, and the temperature started dropping again. Light snow began to fall.

An hour later, he heard the low, growing snarl of a helicopter engine. Checking his compass, he saw it was coming from the direction of the base camp. Since there were no friendly helicopters at the camp, he flattened himself on the ice.

Gazing upward, he saw that it had the configuration of a military attack helicopter with a searchlight rigged under its belly. His white thermal suit melded with the surface ice and the searchlight passed over him.

The ship disappeared to the north, and he continued walking. Twenty minutes later, the helicopter returned on the same compass heading with the searchlight switched off and passed over him on its way toward the base camp.

He walked at a brisk pace, periodically checking the compass bearing on his watch. He estimated he was less than a mile from the base camp, when the glare of more searchlights brought him up short.

There were four of them, and they were sweeping back and forth over what he assumed was the camp complex.

The falling snow prevented him from seeing exactly what was happening. He slowly went forward, careful to stay out of the reflected glare of the lights.

If it had been in his earthly power to attack them, he would have tried, but his current armament consisted of a pewter flask full of Jack Daniel's, two Hershey's bars with almonds, his wristwatch, and the Stockman jackknife his father had given him on his twelfth birthday.

Crouched in a shallow ice crevasse, he watched as the three helicopters took off one by one and headed east toward the coast. One of the transports was hauling the expedition team's Caterpillar tractor.

He tried to make sense of it all as he walked forward in the darkness. They obviously hadn't come to steal a bulldozer. He knew it had to be related to the Viking discovery. Everything had started going wrong after that, the sabotage and then the two murders.

When he arrived at the area the helicopters had taken off from, there didn't appear to be any familiar elements to the landscape. He knew where the tent complex was in relation to the landing area, but there didn't seem to be any trace of it left.

He began walking in ever-widening circles in the snowy darkness. The realization slowly dawned on him that everything was gone. He tried to take in the enormity of that conclusion. Where could they have taken everything? Only a fraction of the camp facilities would have fit on the three helicopters.

It seemed impossible they could have buried it all with the two camp bulldozers in the short time he had been gone. The notion struck him that the upper ice shaft might be large enough for it all, but with the landscape scoured clean, he lost all perspective on where the shaft had been located.

His thoughts were interrupted by a low howl, different from the moaning of the wind. In the darkness, he had no idea what it could be, and no sense of where it was coming from. He sensed rather than saw something charging at him from across the ice, and he braced himself for the attack.

A moment later, Hap Arnold leaped onto his chest, knocking him onto his back. The big Alsatian seemed overjoyed to find him alive, fiercely nuzzling him while yelping with excitement.

Macaulay stroked his back as he rose gingerly to his feet.

If only the Alsatian could talk, he thought. A cliché, but damnably true. He could only assume the intruders had taken Lexy, John Lee, and the rest of the expedition members away with them in the helicopters.

His Suunto watch began throbbing on his wrist. It was equipped with a storm-warning sensor, and the sensor was registering an incoming storm. The temperature had fallen to fifteen degrees below zero, and the wind was strengthening by the minute.

He decided to strike out for the coast. The nearest point of shoreline along the Denmark Strait was probably less than ten miles southeast of where he was standing. A few small Inuit settlements dotted the strait and he knew the Danish government maintained a string of survival huts for stranded mariners along the coast. Maybe he would be lucky enough to find help at one of them.

He was ready to start when he realized that the dog had taken off somewhere in the darkness.

"Hap," he called out over the rising wind.

There was no response. With a storm coming, Macaulay couldn't afford to wait any longer. The dog would have to find him again whenever he decided to follow his scent. He made a final check of the bearing on his digital compass and headed into the darkness.

He hadn't gone fifty feet when he heard the dog again. This time he wasn't wailing or yelping. It was full-throated barking, the same yowling that accompanied the Alsatian's discovery of the corpse of the archaeologist Falconer.

Macaulay followed the sound until he was close enough to see the dog's shadowy outline against the ice. The Alsatian was digging for something with his front paws. Dropping to his knees, Macaulay reached down to feel the edges of the small hole that the dog had already burrowed out. Unlike the surrounding ice, it wasn't hard-packed; it was more like ice chips and snow that had been spread across the area.

They began digging together, Macaulay using the base of his pewter flask to sweep away the layers of ice detritus. The dog began barking louder as the hole slowly deepened and widened.

They had reached a depth of nearly two feet and still hadn't found anything. Macaulay was ready to quit. The dog had probably returned to the place where they had interred Falconer. There was no point in digging up a dead man.

Then he felt something firm and smooth under his right glove. He swept away more snow and ice chips. Now he could feel the edge of it. It was the corner of a thick plastic tarpaulin.

Dragging the edge clear, he reached down into the

narrow cavity below it and felt the hood of a thermal suit. A body was lying prone and motionless on its stomach under the tarp. He swept away the ice that covered the back and legs and turned the body over.

A heavy woolen scarf was wrapped around the hood, covering the face. He gently tugged away the scarf. In the faint illumination from his wristwatch, he recognized Lexy. Removing his right glove, he touched her forehead. It was ice-cold.

He felt tears flooding his eyes, certain she had to be dead.

Raising her up, he held her in his arms while turning his body against the wind to protect her. Reaching into his pocket, he unscrewed the cap of his flask of Jack Daniel's. Parting her rigid mouth, he gently opened her throat passage by suppressing her tongue with his finger, and poured a small dollop of whiskey into her mouth.

There was no response. He poured a second dollop, and a moment later, her body spasmed and she retched some of the whiskey up. He hugged her close to him, feeling a surge of joy at the thought she was still alive. The dog nestled close on the other side.

Putting his glove back on to protect his fingers, Macaulay started rubbing her arms and legs to restore circulation. She was obviously suffering from hypothermia, but the thick plastic tarp, along with her thermal suit, hood, and gloves, had provided enough insulation to preserve life.

There was nothing to do now but try to keep her as warm as possible. He poured one more mouthful of whiskey into her throat as a stimulant, and she swallowed it. This time it stayed down.

A minute later, she spoke for the first time.

"Who are you?" she asked, unable to see him in the darkness.

"Steve Macaulay," he said.

"Steve," she repeated dully, still disoriented.

Another minute passed as he held her close and continued stroking her legs with his free hand.

"Oh God, Steve," she cried out. "They're all dead."

TOTENSONNTAG

TWENTY-FOUR

24 November
Greenland Ice Cap

As Macaulay cradled her in his arms, Lexy haltingly recounted what she had seen from the latrine after the helicopters landed, and how the expedition members were rounded up and sent down the ice shaft, the explosions, and the destruction of the camp by the commandos.

"Hjalmar Jensen is one of them," she said finally.

"I know," said Macaulay.

There was only time to tell her about the bomb Jensen had put aboard his helicopter before the storm alarm on his watch began throbbing again on his wrist. It was registering the imminent arrival of another major gale.

"When the wreckage of my helicopter is found with only one body, they'll come back to search for me," he said. "We're going to head for the coast. If we're lucky, we'll come out near one of the Inuit settlements and I can get through to our security division in Dallas to arrange for protection."

"I'm not sure I can walk," she said.

When Lexy tried to stand up, she began swaying. It was obvious to Macaulay that she was in no condition to hike nine or ten miles to the coast or any part of it. Her core body temperature was probably less than ninety degrees, and she was clearly disoriented.

"I hope this might help you," she said, removing her small flashlight from the side pocket of her thermal suit.

"Invaluable," he said, taking it.

He held her close again before lowering her back on the plastic tarp. If she was to survive, it was vital to keep her as warm as possible during the journey ahead of them. He made her eat half of one of his Hershey's bars and take another swallow of whiskey before he rewrapped her face with the heavy woolen scarf.

His mind raced to come up with a plan.

He would have to haul her, which meant fashioning a crude litter. He looked down at Hap. The Alsatian sure looked the part of a sled dog. Hopefully, he was still a product of his ancient lineage. Together, they might be able to pull Lexy a long way.

He trained the flashlight across what had once been the base camp. There was nothing to be seen above the scarred ice. He would have to make the litter out of the plastic tarpaulin.

In the beam of the flashlight, he glimpsed the end of a length of the nylon rope that had been used to stake the top edges of the tarp to the surface ice. Scraping away more ice chips and snow, he used his jackknife to cut off several lengths of rope.

It took him ten minutes to splice the lengths into two crude harness lines, one for the dog's chest and one for his own. After that, he freed up a section of the tarp that was about six feet square, and cut it loose.

By then, Lexy had lost consciousness again. She finally responded to the sound of his voice after he briefly uncovered her face and shouted to her above the rising wind.

"I'm going to wrap you in a kind of blanket. If you need anything, just call out."

He thought about giving her his woolen head mask. It covered everything but the eyes and mouth, but he knew he would need it on the journey. He made her swallow another pull of Jack Daniel's before strapping her thermal hood close to her cheeks and shielding her exposed face again with the scarf. Placing her arms on her chest, he wrapped her twice in the plastic tarp, using lengths of nylon cord to secure her inside it.

He planned to tow her on her back, with her head and upper body raised toward him. He would take the lead with the longer harness line, and the dog would hopefully follow in tandem with the shorter line. If they could find a good rhythm, their combined strength might give them a chance to make it.

After placing one of the harnesses loosely around the dog's chest, he attached the end of the rope to one of the metal grommets on the top edge of the tarp. Because Hap's body was so much closer to the ground, Macaulay cut the dog's harness line shorter. Macaulay brought his own line up tight against his armpits and then connected the end of it to a second grommet on the tarp.

They were ready to go. Before leaving, he took a few moments to stand silent in tribute to John Lee Hancock and the rest of them. He had seen death in many forms, but it had always been in combat. This was different. This was a massacre. He silently vowed that when it was all over, he would come back to this desolate place.

Macaulay checked his proposed compass heading on the wristwatch and took his first few steps forward. Without a hint of any verbal command, the Alsatian moved out behind him.

A problem quickly developed when Hap kept lunging forward to pass Macaulay, his ancestry apparently demanding that he be allowed to break trail. Macaulay considered allowing the dog to haul the litter by himself, but he was sure it would be too heavy a strain for the long haul. After a few minutes, the dog seemed to understand that they were a team and slowed to a steady walk beside him.

They had gone no more than a few hundred yards when the gale hit with a vengeance, slashing down from the north and hitting them from the left side as they slowly moved southeast. Every few minutes, Macaulay had to check the compass heading to make sure they were still moving in the right direction.

He tried to take his mind off their desperate situation by focusing on everything that had happened. It was hard to imagine John Lee dead. He had been a force of nature, larger than life in every way, capable of cutting corners to get what he wanted, but with a deep capacity for kindness and generosity in so many other ways. With John Lee, the loyalty went both ways. Macaulay would miss him like a brother. He would make Jensen and the others pay for what they had done. But first he had to survive.

After an hour, he stopped to rest, sitting down on the edge of an ice shelf and turning his back to the wind. The dog nestled close to him. He removed the flask of Jack Daniel's from his thermal suit and took a small slug to revive himself.

Taking off his right glove, he slid his fingers through the layers of plastic and found Lexy's carotid artery under her left jaw. Her skin was still unnaturally cold, but he could feel a pulse.

He checked the time. It was five in the morning. They would see the first hint of dawn in about four hours. After that, there would be an hour or so of light to find a settlement—if they made it that far.

The temperature had risen to five below zero, which at least gave them a chance. Typically, it fell to thirty below at night, which they never could have survived in combination with the merciless wind.

They moved out again. The landscape slowly changed. What had been a relatively flat shelf gave way to irregular ridges and ripples in the ice. Macaulay recognized the new terrain as sastrugi, a phenomenon caused by wind erosion and deposition that created stark and often-jagged irregularities in the ice.

It made for much harder going, with the surface now undulating between sharp depressions and overhanging masses like frozen sand dunes. It felt like being on an alien planet a million miles from Earth.

At six o'clock, the wind shifted and began blowing from the east, directly into his face, biting his eyes and lips. He could only lower his head and keep going, his senses now reduced to small numb signals as he listened to the many moods of the wind. It was like a living creature, one moment issuing a shriek, then a lament of agony.

Stung by the ice particles, he closed his eyes. A fleeting

image of Diana flashed across his mind. It was one from the good years, the early years, when every day they spent together was one of discovery and deepening love. More images followed. Diana in her stunning maillot at the officers' club pool at Travis. Standing proudly at the entrance hall to her first exhibition at the Art Students League in Manhattan. The glorious night of lovemaking in which they conceived their baby.

Trudging forward, he couldn't erase the next images: the memory of being at Walter Reed when she was diagnosed with primary progressive multiple sclerosis; the searing image of her face after losing their unborn child; and the day she went permanently blind. His final mental image was of John Lee when he took Macaulay aside at Al Kharj during the lull before Desert Storm to tell him that Diana had taken her life at the assisted living facility where they had put her.

He felt the familiar surge of crushing guilt at not having been there for her. With her. Guilt for all the times he had made her cry. The birthdays he had missed because he was overseas. If he had been more sensitive, he could have resigned his commission. He could have found a way to avoid going overseas. He could have done a lot of things. But he didn't. And she had died alone.

Later on, he found his comfort in the hope that she had forgiven him, and that she was watching over him like some kind of guardian angel, protecting him from harm. He sent up a silent prayer that she was at peace in heaven.

"I'm still here, Diana," he said out loud, the sound carried away by the wind.

On and on they went, Macaulay bent over, one step at

a time on his trembling legs. Each breath was like a torch in his throat, as if he were strangling. He no longer thought of anything else, not of Diana or John Lee or home or warmth or food or lovemaking, nothing but the next step, the next depression, the next rise in the ice.

He now had an all-consuming desire to sleep, the fervent urge to rest his aching muscles by simply lying down in the soft and inviting snow. But to lie down was to fall asleep. To fall asleep was to die. In an hour, the ice surface above them would become a hard shield. A few hours after that, there would be no trace of them left.

At one point, his feet went out from under him on a frozen dune and he fell hard on his back. Rolling over, he found himself sobbing in frustration, the tears freezing on his cheeks.

Stay here and rest, an inner voice began singing out to him. It was a sultry and welcoming voice. Stay here and rest. You've done enough. Only the dog's persistent nuzzling at his head forced him to get up again.

They moved on.

Wrapped inside the plastic tarp, Lexy was largely oblivious to their desperate journey. Her brain seemed anesthetized, a relief actually, the spark of reason slowly diminishing, her eyes shut behind the woolen scarf wrapped around her face.

She found herself dreaming of the nine worlds of the Norse gods, Asgard, the home of Odin's Valhalla, and Einherjar, where the souls of the greatest warriors lay in paradise, each of them selected by the Valkyries. And Yggdrasil, the world tree, with its roots being eaten by the serpent Nidhogg. The form of Nidhogg took shape in her fevered mind. He was the blond killer.

Ice began crystallizing on Macaulay's eyelids, and he feared he could go snow-blind. If he did, even temporarily, there would be no way to find a settlement along the coast. He could only keep moving like a staggering drunk. Each minute seemed like an hour. An hour became like an interminable day.

Macaulay periodically checked the big Alsatian. The magnificent animal hadn't flagged once as they struggled on for mile after mile, but when he started making low whimpering noises, Macaulay stopped to examine him.

In the glow of the flashlight, he saw that the rope had lacerated the dog's chest, and he was bleeding through his white fur in several places. Macaulay cut a section of the plastic tarp away from the base of the litter and wrapped it several times around the dog's chest to cushion the impact of the rope.

They moved on.

The wind-driven snow particles had felt like bee stings, finding tiny paths to penetrate the apertures around the eyes and mouth of his woolen face mask, pricking the exposed skin like tiny needles until it finally went numb. There was no way to know how close he was to frostbite, with the possibility of losing his nose or lips. He needed to massage the affected skin to get the blood flowing again, but that was impossible.

He began to notice fissures in the crust of the rippled ice. Although he didn't want to exhaust the batteries in the pocket flashlight, he needed its feeble illumination to pick his way through them.

By eight o'clock, he was reduced to counting steps in the unrelenting darkness. He would lurch forward a few, stagger a few more, count off twenty, and then start again. He wasn't sure he was even counting properly, but it kept him going.

At eight thirty, the snow suddenly stopped and the wind began to die. One moment it was driving hard into his face; the next it had disappeared. He checked the temperature gauge on his watch. Plus five degrees Fahrenheit. Almost a sauna.

In thirty minutes there would be light.

He was sure they had to be somewhere near the coast. With the arrival of dawn, they would have an hour or so of daylight to find help before the darkness descended again.

His first awareness of the new threat began when the Alsatian began to growl menacingly. Groggy with exhaustion, Macaulay wondered what might have caused it, when he heard a yelping cry come out of the gloom ahead of them. It was quickly followed by another one off to the left. Macaulay stopped.

Hap continued to growl, staring forward into the darkness. When Macaulay tracked the flashlight beam from left to right, he saw a momentary glimpse of movement that disappeared in the shadows.

It was a wolf. He knew that wolves often traveled the ice cap in packs. In winter, they usually stayed near the coast, where they could prey on pets and small livestock near the Inuit settlements. It struck him that they might be near a settlement.

There were at least two of them, maybe three, and they were circling closer as the yelping continued. As soon as Macaulay released Hap from his harness, the dog adopted a rigid stance, his nose twitching with anticipation.

A moment later, he bolted off. Macaulay tried to track his flight with the flashlight, but the Alsatian quickly out-distanced its range. Macaulay counted to fifteen before the first raucous sounds of the fight reached him across the ice.

He could hear the ferocity of Hap's savage howling, punctuated by the enraged cries of animals engaged in deadly battle, the low, guttural snarls from Hap and the higher-pitched cries from one of the wolves.

Macaulay removed the harness from his chest, pulled out his jackknife, and jogged through the murky gloom to the sounds of the struggle. Drawing closer, he heard a loud snapping of jaws, followed by a cry of pain. The yelping became frenzied, then frantic.

He could see the shadowy forms of three animals thrashing about together, separating briefly before charging at one another again, and baring their teeth as they sought to inflict a fatal wound.

One of the wolves had been hurt. Macaulay watched as it sought to escape, finally dropping to the ground in the midst of its flight, its throat torn open, but still alive, glaring up at him, fangs exposed.

Ahead, the bitter struggle continued, with the Alsatian and the second wolf each seeking advantage as they alternately charged and withdrew. Macaulay staggered toward them, hoping he could get there in time to help.

Hap suddenly dropped to the ice, continuing to fight from his back as the other wolf loomed over him, his jaws slashing at the dog's throat. Macaulay was about to strike the wolf with his knife, when Hap cried out in agony. Sensing Macaulay's presence, the wolf released the dog's throat from its jaws and loped off.

Hap was lying on his side, the blood flowing from wounds at his throat, chest, and legs slowly turning the snow red beneath his body. Macaulay began stroking his ears, remembering the first time he had ever seen him.

They had been driving across Elmendorf Air Force Base in Anchorage, when Hancock had seen the dog run out of the darkness into the road, where a car hit him.

One of his front legs was broken, and the Alsatian was trying to drag himself away. Hancock stopped the car, picked him up in his arms, and drove him to a veterinarian's office to have the leg set. After that, they had become inseparable.

Hap stopped breathing.

Dawn slowly rose in the east, illuminating the landscape around him. In the distance, Macaulay could see the ocean, dark and forbidding. He scanned the shoreline from north to south. Black rock formations covered the vista as far as he could see.

He had only an hour or so to find help before darkness fell again. Plodding back to the litter, he picked up the rope harness and placed it around his chest. He could go north or south along the shoreline. The decision was easy.

In his near delirium, he decided to walk south toward the warmth of the Florida Keys. As he dragged the litter over the new snow, he remembered visiting Hemingway's home, remembered the cats, dozens of them.

There was no indication that humans had ever visited this part of the world. His initial optimism gave way to despair as he saw the light begin to fade in the western sky.

That was when he saw their salvation, a small shack, not much larger than an outhouse, sitting back on a stone promontory above a shale beach, its weather-beaten clapboards scarred from endless battering of the wind.

It was one of the survival huts sprinkled along the rugged coast for lost mariners. Well, he was lost all right, even if he wasn't a mariner. Cutting open the plastic tarp, he picked Lexy up in his arms and carried her to the shack.

The door was unlocked. He shoved it open and lurched inside.

TWENTY-FIVE

Jessica Birdwell, the deputy Homeland Security adviser assigned to the White House, held up her access pass to the security camera mounted above the faux walnut steel security door, and listened for the signal that unlocked it.

Stepping through the doorway, she followed the underground passage leading to the smallest of the three soundproof situation rooms in the intelligence management center beneath the West Wing.

Her boss, Ira Dusenberry, the deputy assistant national security adviser to the president, was already there, talking to one of the duty officers on the watch team. A copy of the president's morning book, which contained the latest compendium of incidents with potential national security implications, was spread out on the conference table next to Dusenberry's ever-present mug of black coffee.

"Morning, Jess," he said as she opened her briefcase, removed her Apple MacBook Pro, and turned it on.

At thirty-six, Dusenberry had thinning brown hair and a blunt, good-humored face. Short and thickset, he had the shoulders of a sumo wrestler and an even broader expanse of waist.

He had just participated in the morning briefing of the president, and was giving the duty officer an update on the priority issues that needed careful monitoring. His eyes remained focused on Jessica.

Tall and slender with dark gold hair, she was wearing a white blouse and charcoal skirt that enhanced her wide-set blue eyes. As always, she seemed serious and intent, not unfriendly, but polite and reserved. Not for the first time, he wondered if she had a lover.

"Addison just called to say he is on the way," he said after dismissing the duty officer.

"What's the emergency?" she asked.

"I think we should wait for Ad," he said, sipping his coffee.

"Anything new in the morning book?" she asked.

"The same tired litany of iniquity, peccancy, and evil-doing," he said with his familiar sarcasm. "The Russians are tracking a rogue army colonel with access to fission-able material who's on his way to Iran. There's another bombing threat in Jakarta, a fledgling shoe bomber in Greece, a shadowy group that is working to isolate the autoimmune gene and wipe out the African race, Chinese hackers who have created an invasive virus to wreck our most secret codes, a scheme to poison the water supply in Southern California, and a terrorist plot to kidnap both a liberal and a conservative television talk show host and hold them for ransom."

"Let's hope the last one pans out," pronounced Addison Kingship, the executive assistant director for national security at the FBI, as he walked into the room and dropped his suitcase-sized satchel on the conference table.

Classically good-looking with dark brown hair and a thin aquiline nose, the Princeton-educated Kingship had been rewarded with his current post after leading a celebrated FBI task force that had prevented at least a dozen serious attacks against American installations around the world.

Jessica saw the deep wrinkles at the corners of his gray eyes. The cynical side of Washington was obviously wearing him down, she thought, wondering how long he would remain in the cauldron.

Ira Dusenberry closed the morning book and said, "Sorry about the short notice, but we have a breaking event here. You would have already been briefed on it, Ad, if you hadn't been up on the hill. It's too soon to know all the implications, but I need your input. . . . I should first point out that this issue is not strictly within our purview."

Kingship began shaking his head.

"It's nothing illegal, Ad," said Dusenberry. "Just politically sensitive."

"Right," said Kingship skeptically.

"It involves a group of American nationals who are currently in a friendly nation," said Dusenberry, "but who may have become the targets of a terrorist organization."

"It's up to that friendly power to investigate the incident if it's on their sovereign soil," said Jessica. "Protocol requires that we only help if we are asked."

"Yes . . . well, one of the American nationals is John Lee Hancock," said Dusenberry.

The revelation registered on their faces. Hancock was a close friend of the president, and his most active supporter within the energy industry. Probably his only one.

"Has the president been informed?" asked Jessica.

"He has," said Dusenberry with a pause. "Unofficially."

"And now?" demanded Kingship.

"Unofficially, he is hoping that we might take a look at the situation and possibly provide some assets and logistical assistance," said Dusenberry.

"Was he kidnapped?"

"We don't know."

"That could be a good pretext for our getting more actively involved," said Kingship.

"No one is sure exactly what happened yet," said Dusenberry. "This has occurred in a very remote area of Greenland, which is as you know still part of the Royal Danish Commonwealth. Although the Greenlanders have home rule, functions like defense and security are provided by the Danes. Suffice it to say, with a million square miles of ice and rock, there isn't a significant security apparatus up there on the ground."

"So what do we actually know?" asked Jessica, beginning to type notes into her laptop.

"At oh six twelve this morning, Mark Devlin, the head of corporate security at Anschutz International, called the local FBI office in Dallas to state they had lost communication with Hancock and it couldn't be restored," said Dusenberry. "Then he called here."

He refilled his empty coffee mug from the insulated pitcher on the table.

"By way of background," he went on, "one of Hancock's vanity foundations is called the Cactus Legion, and it travels around the world recovering lost Second World War military aircraft. According to Devlin, Hancock and his team had successfully recovered a B-17 Flying Fortress that was buried beneath the ice cap, and then shipped the plane in sections back to Texas. For some reason, Hancock then decided to stay at the expedition site with his team. Now they've lost all contact."

"The weather at this time of year must be horrendous up there," said Jessica. "Maybe it knocked out his radios."

"That was already explored, Jess," said Dusenberry. "Devlin said Hancock has the latest satellite and VHF equipment with full redundancy, and it was running perfectly."

Ira passed them each a copy of another verbatim communication.

"At oh nine twenty this morning," Dusenberry went on, "an RAF air-sea rescue plane coming in to land at an old DEW Line installation called Kulusuk on Greenland's eastern coast reported flying over the wreckage of a large helicopter that had crashed and burned. After the plane landed, a rescue party went out in a snow tractor and found a badly burned body in the passenger section of the helicopter. It was a Bell 412EP. Hancock had one in his corporate fleet."

"No sign of the pilot?" asked Kingship.

Ira shook his head. "Only one body."

"Where is Hancock's expedition site?" asked Jessica.

"About six miles from the helicopter crash," said Dusenberry. "After searching the wreckage, the search party used its GPS to try to reach Hancock's team, but it couldn't find a trace of his base camp."

"Maybe the search party had the wrong coordinates," said Kingship.

"Possibly," said Ira. "There was also an arctic gale blowing and visibility was limited in the darkness."

Ira handed them the second verbatim communication.

"So here is the latest piece of news, and it's wild," he said. "That's a transcription of the call I received about thirty minutes ago from Devlin, along with the e-mail message he received from an organization claiming responsibility for taking Hancock and his team hostage."

"An exploiter of Islam?" said Kingship, reading from the transcript.

"I gather Hancock's company was one of the consortia that got the oil and gas wells up and running in Iraq after the war," said Dusenberry. "I don't know what his interests are in the Persian Gulf now."

"An Arab commando team operating in Greenland?" said Jessica. "That sounds a little far-fetched, but these days anything is possible."

"It's also possible Hancock made some serious enemies in the Gulf," said Kingship. "Maybe they're settling old scores. If they had in fact been targeting him, maybe this was where they thought he would be most vulnerable."

"It's too early to answer those questions," said Dusenberry. "Our first job is to try to locate Hancock and determine if he is safe, and so far, the response from the

Greenland government has not exactly been robust. In reply to our request for an emergency response team to be dispatched to the area right away, the government security office in Nuuk has agreed to send a police detective to the area once they can arrange transportation for him."

Addison Kingship rose from the table and picked up his satchel.

"I'm due back on the hill," he said sourly.

"I would strongly recommend that we put a special mission unit from the Joint Special Operations Command on immediate standby and try to deploy an MH-60 as close to the mission area as possible, maybe Halifax, where they won't be so noticeable," said Jessica. "The cover legend can be that we're preparing an emergency mission to provide necessary medical care to one of the members of Hancock's expedition team."

"Agreed," said Kingship.

"Good," agreed Dusenberry. "I'll ask State to make a high-level call to the Danish foreign ministry in Copenhagen requesting their cooperation in our sending in a medical team. Within the next couple hours, we'll also have a surveillance satellite with infrared capabilities trained on the coordinates that Devlin gave me to pinpoint Hancock's expedition site. It should hopefully provide some kind of picture of what's there."

"I'll give you both an update this afternoon," said Dusenberry, following the other two out of the situation room.

An hour later, the Lynx was awakened in his stateroom aboard the ship by one of the master's mates and was told he was needed in the ship's command center. Jensen was waiting for him with the decoded message he had just received.

"General Macaulay did not perish in the helicopter crash," he said. "Presumably, he is still alive and on the run somewhere on the ice cap."

TWENTY-SIX

25 November
Eastern Coast
Greenland

Macaulay awoke to the roar of the sea outside the windows of the survivor's hut. Checking his watch, he saw that it was nine o'clock. In the darkness, it was easy to lose track of time, but it had to be night. He had slept for twelve hours.

After stumbling into the hut for the first time, he had taken a few moments to train his flashlight around the single room. A bunk bed was built into the rear wall, and he laid Lexy down on the lower of the two straw-filled mattresses.

In a quick look around the room, he saw an old cast-iron stove near the side wall. The wood box next to it was empty. He was too numb with exhaustion to go outside to replenish it.

Macaulay had only one thought before succumbing to sleep, and that was to begin restoring Lexy's body temperature before she sustained lasting damage from hypothermia. Unzipping the front of her thermal suit, he placed his hand over her heart. The beat seemed irregular and her body unnaturally cold.

He scoured the room to find a means of warming her. Aside from the blankets on the bunk bed, there was nothing. He spread them over her and then pulled the thin mattress off the upper bunk and laid that on top of the blankets. He slipped under the covers beside her.

As he listened to the surf pounding the shoreline, he vaguely recalled the air force studies he had reviewed during his last stint in the Pentagon on methods for improving the survival rate of pilots downed in the sea.

He remembered that skin-to-skin contact was considered the most efficient method of heat transfer using the principle of conduction, if not the fastest way to restore a person's body temperature. The technique was to place the hypothermic person together with a rescuer who was not hypothermic after removing both individuals' clothes.

Pushing aside the covers, he removed her boots, thermal suit, flannel shirt and trousers, all the while conjuring lame excuses for how to explain himself when she woke up. He was too numb with fatigue to feel any sense of conscious virtue.

After she was stripped to her underwear, he shed his own clothes and crawled under the blankets with her. Spooning the back of her icy body with his own, he began rubbing her arms and back to help restore circulation. She was still unconscious when he finally dropped off into oblivion.

Now fully awake, Macaulay pondered what to do next. His body ached from head to toe, and he was in no condition to continue their journey on foot. Lexy was still unconscious or in deep sleep, and obviously could not walk either. Gently touching her carotid artery, he found her pulse stronger and steadier. Her body was warm to the touch.

He climbed out of the bunk and put on his shirt, pants, and thermal suit before lacing up his boots. Using the flashlight, he found a kerosene lamp on the table near the kitchen alcove, along with a tin of lamp oil. He filled the reservoir, lit the wick, and replaced the chimney.

In the comforting glow of the lamp, he could see his breath in the air, but estimated that the temperature was above freezing inside the hut. He began a thorough search of the cabin.

It was one of the survival huts the Danish government had built along the Denmark Strait, consisting of one large room, with clapboard walls on unmilled studs, rough pine flooring, and four small windows. The kitchen alcove had a Primus stove and rough shelving that held a small assortment of pots, pans, and plates. A metal pitcher and washbasin served as the lavatory.

No one had been there for a long time. A thick layer of undisturbed dust covered every surface. He noticed a shortwave radio sitting on a table set against the far wall. It was a Danish model, probably fifty years old. The battery sitting next to it was as large as a loaf of bread. When he connected the wires, it was dead.

He found the cabin's meager food supply in a cupboard beneath the kitchen shelves. It consisted of a few cans with the labels long reduced to dust and some tightly sealed metal canisters that contained hard-packed flour, dried tea leaves, and salt.

His first task was to build a fire, for warmth as well as for meltwater to drink. He glanced through one of the windows facing the sea. Although it was still dark outside and the window was fogged with salt spray, he could see the heaving white-capped sea lashing the rock formations that surrounded the narrow stony beach.

He stepped outside into the rising wind that foreshadowed another storm. Shining the flashlight in both directions, he glimpsed a wooden lean-to attached to one of the side walls, which probably held the hut's firewood.

It was empty of firewood but contained something else. The object was covered by a large swatch of rotting canvas. When Macaulay pulled the edge away, he saw that it was an old kayak.

He began combing the edge of the beach for firewood. Here and there were shards of driftwood, the ends frozen into the ice. He wasn't about to spend time breaking them free. He went back to the lean-to and began ripping off the roofing boards.

The snow was falling more heavily as he returned to the hut.

After stoking the stove, he looked around for a fire starter. Next to one of the chairs, he found a Swedish pulp magazine from 1952 with a photograph of a young boxer named Ingemar Johannson on the cover. The crumpled pages burned well.

Once the fire was going, he grabbed an iron poker and a large pot from the kitchen shelf and went outside to break up enough ice chunks to fill it. The new snow had already obliterated his tracks from the morning. Returning to the cabin, he placed the pot on top of the stove.

Lexy still hadn't stirred from under the blankets in the

bunk. Careful not to wake her, he checked her vital signs. She was breathing normally and her color was much better.

Twenty minutes later, he had meltwater. Drinking down three mugs of it, he set aside another two quarts for drinking, and let the rest continue to heat on the stove.

There was a six-inch-square metal mirror on the kitchen wall. In the glow of the lamp, he saw a gaunt stranger with a week-old beard staring back at him. His unruly brown hair was filthy and matted to the sides of his head. There was a long, jagged gash on his forehead where he had hit the instrument panel after the helicopter crashed. It was still seeping blood. His thin nose was fish-belly white. Rubbing it, he could feel sensation, which meant he had somehow avoided frostbite. All in all, he had been very lucky.

He found an ancient bar of gray soap in the kitchen, along with a straight razor and leather strop. Taking off his clothes, he washed his body in the rest of the hot water, and then shaved. With no towel or rag handy, he could only dry himself next to the hot stove.

He almost jumped when he heard her voice.

"I appear to be almost naked myself," she said, her face peeking out at him from the edge of the covers.

Embarrassed, Macaulay put on his underwear, and then his shirt and pants without saying anything. As he dressed, Lexy saw that his lean body was covered with bruises. Then she noticed the gash on his forehead.

"Are you all right?" she asked.

"Sure," he said, "can lick my weight in polar bears."

"Where are we?" she asked.

"In a survivor's hut on the Denmark Strait," he said.

Putting tea leaves into a kettle, he added hot water and waited for it to steep before pouring the tea into two mugs and adding a spoonful of sugar. He carried the mugs over to the bunk and handed one of them to her, sitting down on the edge of the mattress.

"I seem to recall your hauling me a long way," she said, feeling the hot strong tea warm her inside. "I was a little delirious most of the time."

Macaulay told her of their journey across the cap, of the attack by the wolves that had killed the Alsatian, and the small miracle of finding the survivor's hut in the brief window of natural light before darkness fell again. He was attempting to explain the theory behind skin-to-skin contact as a means to help someone recover from hypothermia, when she interrupted him.

"I understand. . . . You were serving the interest of science," she said, smiling.

"Something like that," he said.

"Well . . . it worked, Steve. Thank you for my life."

He felt an almost-desperate urge to wrap her in his arms. Embarrassed at his thoughts, he got up from the lower bunk and went over to the kitchen alcove.

"The next stage in your recovery is to get some hot food into you," he said, picking up one of the unmarked cans.

When he opened it with his jackknife, he saw that it was cured bacon and still edible. The second tin yielded what looked and tasted like stewed prunes. Lighting the spirit stove, he began frying the bacon in a skillet while making a thick batter of flour and water in a mixing bowl.

Clad in her underwear, Lexy got out of the bed and slowly walked on trembling legs to the woodstove. After luxuriating in its heat for a few minutes, she used the remaining hot water in the iron pot to bathe as Macaulay had done. After allowing herself to dry next to the fire, she put on her flannel shirt, corduroys, and leather boots.

By then, the meal was done.

"Camp cakes with bacon and stewed prunes," said Macaulay, serving it out on the table next to the stove. "Julia Child gave me the recipe."

"Delicious," she said, wolfing down the first bite.

"You're an easy date. Remind me to take you to a place I know in Antarctica," Macaulay said as the rising wind moaned through the cracks in the clapboard walls.

"How did you wind up a general?" she asked.

"Long story."

"I mean why did you decide to spend most of your life in the military?"

"That's even more boring," he said.

"I'm listening."

He took a long time before he answered.

"I guess it comes down to my being a life, liberty, and pursuit of happiness kind of guy—all of us equal and all that. Not just some of us. All of us. I think that's worth fighting for."

"I agree," she said, smiling at him. "Not very eloquent, but I get the point. Thank you for that."

"Maybe we'll get there in another thousand years," he said.

After they finished the meal, Macaulay went back out to replenish the firewood supply. When he returned, they sat together in front of the open stove, absorbing the life-giving heat.

Removing the pewter flask containing his Jack Daniel's, Macaulay divided the last inch of it between their two mugs.

"You're trying to get me drunk," she said.

"Not on this supply," said Macaulay. "I just wish I had a bottle of that whiskey we found in *March Hare.*"

His words brought back the enormity of everything that had happened.

"Why did they have to kill them all?" asked Lexy.

"Probably so that no one would be left to tell about the discovery of the Viking cave," he said.

"Then why did they destroy the cave?"

"Because they had everything they needed from it," he said. "You told me you saw big bins coming out of the shaft along with body bags. They must have taken the rune tablet as well."

"Then they have what they want," said Lexy.

"Which is?"

"The clues to the greatest archaeological discovery of modern times," she responded. "If I'm right, the saga depicted in those rune markings pinpoints the location of the tomb of Leif Eriksson, and it's probably somewhere along the New England coast . . . Massachusetts, New Hampshire, or Maine."

"And that would be worth the lives of a dozen men?" said Macaulay bitterly.

"You obviously don't know much about the archaeological world."

"You don't systematically massacre all those people over a discovery like this, even if it changes history as we know it," said Macaulay. "This was a well-trained commando force conducting a complicated military mission.

They weren't rogue archaeologists. There has to be more to it. . . . The question is what."

"I guess we'll never know. They have it all now."

"I'm going to find out," said Macaulay with menace in his voice. "Did you recognize any of the men aside from Jensen?"

"No. They were all wearing helmets except the leader, the blond one. He murdered Doc Callaghan and the cook."

"What else do you remember?"

"Two of them were Norwegians."

"How can you be sure?" asked Macaulay.

"I told you my maternal grandparents were Norwegian and I learned the language as a little girl," said Lexy. "The two men spoke to each other when they were using the latrine."

"What were they saying?"

"Only that the mission had been ordered with almost no notice. They had no idea it was coming until a few minutes before they left the ship."

"What ship?"

"I don't know that."

Macaulay added boards to the fire. It briefly flamed out through the stove's iron door.

"Tell me about Falconer," said Macaulay.

She shuddered involuntarily.

"A past mistake," she said.

"I don't mean that," he said. "Tell me about his visit to your tent before all hell broke loose."

Lexy repeated the sequence of events, beginning with her sensing that someone was in the tent and switching on her flashlight. She described Falconer holding her notebook in the air after removing it from her boot.

"Rob knew that I always kept my journal in one of my boots at a dig."

"Why would he try to steal your journal if he had already been down to the cave and had seen the rune markings?"

"I don't know."

Macaulay was still staring at the fire when his eyes came alive with excitement.

"Maybe he was bringing something to you," he said. "After he photographed the rune tablet, he had to assume there was a chance he might get caught, and if he did, he would be thoroughly searched. He may have decided you were the one person he could use to hide what he had, something as small as a digital memory card."

"If that was the case, it's gone," said Lexy. "The journal was in my sleeping tent, which was bulldozed down the ice shaft with everything else."

"That's why Jensen removed his clothes," said Macaulay.

"I'm not following you," she said.

"Jensen murdered him," said Macaulay, "almost certainly because he discovered that Falconer had breached the secrets of the cave. After killing him, he stripped his clothes off because he thought there might be something hidden in them, and he had no time to make a careful search."

Lexy was having trouble keeping her eyes open.

"You need to rest," said Macaulay. "I'll bring in enough wood to last the night. We should probably pull out early in the morning."

Putting on his thermal suit, he went back out to the lean-to. The snow was coming down in a dense white curtain. A wild and mountainous sea was slamming into the shoreline. No one could find them in this weather, he concluded.

She was already in bed when he returned to the hut, her eyes gazing up at him like twin violet moons. After restoking the fire, he shut the stove's iron door and partially closed the damper.

By the time he went to the table to turn down the kerosene lamp, she was asleep.

TWENTY-SEVEN

26 November
RV *Leitstern*
North Atlantic Ocean
Yarmouth, Nova Scotia

The rain was coming diagonally, slashing at the Perspex windows of the pilot's cockpit as the AgustaWestland AW139 jet helicopter slowly descended through the windswept darkness toward the brilliantly lit landing deck.

The ship was pitching and rolling in a heaving black sea, but the helicopter pilot was a veteran of North Atlantic air-sea rescue missions and an expert in contending with aberrational winter weather.

It was the last stage of a long journey for His Royal Highness Johannes Prinz Karl Erich Maria von Falkenberg, who had left his castle on the Rhine River one day earlier to fly by private jet across the Atlantic to Halifax, Nova Scotia, and then had boarded the Italian-made helicopter that took him the rest of the way.

The helicopter's sumptuous leather VIP seats were designed for ultimate comfort, but they couldn't eradicate the searing pain that was raging unabated through the prince's lower abdomen.

Steiger sat beside him, an ampoule of morphine resting in his hand; he was ready to administer it if the pain became too great to endure. When the helicopter touched down, the Lynx rushed across the landing deck to the passenger compartment to help the prince disembark.

Determined to emerge by himself, von Falkenberg stepped out into the earsplitting roar of the icy wind and was almost carried away. The Lynx scooped him up in his powerful arms, crossed the deck to the nearest hatchway, and carried him inside.

"Danke, mein Sohn," said the prince.

Out of the wind and fierce rain, he revived quickly, regaining his feet and his composure. Bowing his head for a moment, he silently prayed. Wodan give me the strength to see this through and grant me the chance to cast my eyes on my god.

A bearded man in a trim blue naval uniform and the distinctive white cap denoting his rank as captain joined them in the passageway. Peter Bjorklund was forty-seven and a former captain in the Norwegian navy. He had first met the prince prior to the refitting of the vessel in Stockholm a year earlier.

"Would you like to take a few moments to rest, Your Grace?" asked Bjorklund.

"There is no time," said the prince. "Please lead the way to the Marquess de Villiers."

As they walked along the passageway, the prince glanced into a succession of well-appointed compartments, each decorated with warm and inviting pastel colors. Steiger followed him, carrying his emergency medical kit in a leather satchel. The Lynx led the way, his eyes taking in every new movement ahead of them.

"No expense was spared to meet the challenges you outlined," said Captain Bjorklund. "The *Leitstern* is prepared for any eventuality."

Originally designed as a research vessel by the Ludendorff Institute for Marine Research in Bremerhaven, the four-hundred-foot-long *Leitstern*, or *Lodestar*, had been built for service in Antarctica. It was double-hulled and capable of breaking through a five-foot-thick belt of ice. The ship's lower decks now contained a satellite communications center, a small hospital, and three fully equipped laboratories devoted to biological, genetic, and chemical research.

After *Leitstern* had been acquired by a holding company controlled by Prince von Falkenberg, the research ship had also been modified in other ways. It was now equipped with an advanced command-and-control weapons system that included a bank of concealed cruise missile launchers, an array of antiship and antisubmarine missiles, and modern Gatling guns.

Along with its weapons arsenal, the ship had become the operational headquarters for a full company of the elite commando unit known as Thor's Hammer, along with its complement of six attack and transport military helicopters.

Captain Bjorklund led him into a gleaming white compartment. A woman sitting at the polished oak conference table was typing a message into a mobile operating system. She stood up and bowed when she saw it was von Falkenberg.

Cherubically plump, with bushy white eyebrows and a spray of purplish hair surrounding her head like a victory wreath, the sixty-five-year-old Frenchwoman may have resembled a female version of Dickens's Mr. Pickwick, but she was one of the most brilliant and influential diplomats in Europe.

The Marquess Antoinette Celeste de Villiers was the European Union's current secretary-general of health. She and von Falkenberg had been friends and colleagues for forty years.

"Is everything in place?" asked von Falkenberg breathlessly.

"Phase one will begin on schedule," said de Villiers. "And we are thrilled to have you here to witness its implementation."

TWENTY-EIGHT

Macaulay awoke to an unnerving silence. The ghostly light of early morning suffused the room. Outside, the wind had died. He slipped out of bed and went to the front windows. What he could see of the ocean was black and tranquil, with gentle waves rolling toward the stony beach.

He looked at his watch. It was almost nine o'clock. They had slept another ten hours. He could feel his strength slowly returning as he thought about the next steps in their journey.

Once it was discovered that only Sir Dorian had died in the helicopter crash, they would be coming after him, whoever they were. They might already be on their way. The snowstorm would have obliterated his tracks across the ice cap, but the pursuers would certainly have sophisticated tracking tools aboard their helicopters, and they would know he couldn't have traveled far on foot.

It was time to go.

Macaulay wasn't sure exactly where they were along the coast, but from the compass headings he had followed in the blizzard, he knew they were south of Kulusuk, the closest destination that had satellite radio communications. Once there, he could contact Anschutz in Dallas and they could alert the FBI. After he and Lexy were able to tell their story to the authorities, their lives would no longer be at risk.

By walking north, it might also be possible to reach an Inuit settlement where one of the natives had a snowmobile or some other means of transportation to carry them the rest of the way. But if the surrounding rock-strewn landscape was any example, they would have serious problems making good headway on foot.

He thought about the kayak out in the lean-to. If it didn't leak, they might be able to make it to Kulusuk by sea. He didn't want to think about what would happen if they were caught in open water by the attack helicopter.

After stoking the fire again, he put on his thermal suit and went outside to the lean-to. Pulling away the remainder of the canvas cover from the kayak, he dragged it out for closer examination.

Most kayaks he had seen were flat-bottomed, but this one was V-shaped, with gunwales that rose to a point at the bow and stern. It was about twelve feet long with three cockpit openings. The fabric on the deck and hull appeared to be made of stretched animal skin. He went over every inch of it with his flashlight but couldn't find any fissures or cracks. In the lean-to, he found two long paddles.

If the old kayak proved seaworthy and the ocean remained calm, they could probably cover three or four miles an hour. He decided the kayak gave them the best chance to make it. Returning to the hut, he found Lexy standing at the Primus stove.

"Camp cakes in bacon grease," she said, smiling at him. "James Beard."

"They'd better be good," he said.

The cabin was now warm, and she was wearing only her long flannel shirt, its tails barely covering her panties. Her feet were shoved into her boots. He reluctantly repressed the idea of helping her remove the shirt and steering her back to the bunk.

As they ate, he told her his plan to launch the kayak. In response, she crossed her legs and began to remove one of her boots. He stared down at it as if seeing them for the first time.

"Your boots," he said.

"L.L. Bean," she said. "I've had them for years."

"No," said Macaulay, shaking his head. "Falconer knew you always placed your journal in one of your boots. What if he had planned to hide the memory disc or whatever it was in your journal and you surprised him before he could do it. It's possible he just slid it inside the boot he was holding. What if he put the memory card or whatever it was into a boot instead of the journal?"

He grabbed the one she was holding and began removing the laces while she pulled off the second boot. Spreading the leather uppers, he searched its interior down to the sole for a slit or opening in the insulated lining, but found nothing unusual. The sole was covered by a rubber insole. Removing it, he checked the underside, and then shined the flashlight into the toe area.

"Damn," he said. "It's not here."

"No, it's here," said Lexy, her fingers emerging from the insole and holding a tiny plastic-and-metal chip. They both stared at it for a few moments.

"Now we're back in the hunt," said Macaulay.

Outside, he found the plastic tarp he had used to haul Lexy across the ice cap and cut away three circular patches, each about three feet in diameter. In the rapidly waning light, he and Lexy hauled the kayak down to the water's edge.

"I'll take it out far enough to make sure the seams are holding," he said.

He inserted his legs into the rear cockpit and Lexy gave the kayak a shove out into open water. Using one of the paddles to gain headway, Macaulay went across the cove and back. As Lexy watched nervously, he brought it ashore and stepped out.

"The seams are okay," he said. "We'll stay close to shore. If it starts leaking, we can head straight in."

He took one of the plastic patches he had cut and used it to seal the circular middle cockpit opening. Then he cut intersecting slits in the other two, showing Lexy how to slide it up and around her waist to cover the opening when she got into the front cockpit.

"If the sea gets rougher, the patches will help prevent waves from filling the kayak," he said, getting into the rear cockpit.

Glancing into the darkness that was settling over the sea, he saw that fog was rolling in. He felt it slowly envelop them, cold, dense, almost impenetrable. The perfect cover if it lasted.

When they had paddled out fifty yards, Macaulay used

his compass to steer due north. A slight wind was coming from the south, which helped to propel them along.

They quickly settled into a slow, steady rhythm.

Through occasional breaks in the fog, Lexy glimpsed the unending rock formations along the forbidding coast. At one point, they had to steer around an ice floe, its bluish core menacing them from just under the surface.

Macaulay estimated they had gone a mile or more, when he heard the slowly mounting roar of a jet helicopter engine. It was coming from the north and moving slowly down the coast.

He stared up to see the reflected glow of powerful searchlight beams trying to penetrate the fog bank as it came toward them. It flew directly over, the thunderous din of the jet engine assaulting their eardrums. The noise slowly receded as the big helicopter continued south.

"They're searching for me," said Macaulay. "They couldn't know you're still alive."

The sea became turbulent. Lexy was alarmed when chunks of ice began coursing across the narrow deck. She could feel seawater seeping down around the plastic patches and soaking her legs.

A moment later, they were in a maelstrom of converging currents and the kayak was spinning. They could only sit helplessly as it swung around, almost broaching under the force of the waves. After glancing off a partially submerged black rock, they plunged onward.

Lexy was forced to stop paddling after three hours. The deck of the kayak was coated with ice, and an unnatural coldness had seeped back inside her. She felt her mind going numb again, when she thought she heard a bell ringing. To her torpid brain it sounded like a demented volunteer for the Salvation Army ferociously ringing a Christmas bell.

"It's a bell buoy," said Macaulay, staring into the distance.

The fog began to dissipate as he slowly paddled toward the sound. The clanging was getting louder, when the noise was suddenly drowned out by the mounting crescendo of another helicopter. It was coming from the south. Macaulay thought it was probably the same one that had passed over earlier.

Its powerful searchlights were turning a forty-foot-wide swath ahead of them into virtual daylight as the helicopter came on. Macaulay paddled furiously toward the nearest bank of curling fog, but the kayak remained fully exposed as the helicopter arrived overhead. Lexy averted her eyes from its blinding intensity until the kayak finally skidded inside the fog bank.

There was no way for Macaulay to know how many eyes aboard the helicopter were still scanning the sea. He waited in the darkness, expecting with each passing moment to hear the change in engine pitch that signaled the helicopter was turning around to come back.

Instead, it continued on along the same northerly track until nearly out of sight. Macaulay was still watching its trajectory when the search beams went out, replaced a moment later by the helicopter's green landing lights.

As it began to descend, the landscape erupted in parallel lines of high-intensity white, yellow, and red lights. Macaulay immediately recognized them as the runway lights of an airport.

"It's Kulusuk," he called out as Lexy slumped over in her cockpit.

He paddled the kayak into the inlet next to the Kulu-suk Four Seasons, and ran it up onto the gravelly shoreline. Easing Lexy out of the front cockpit, he cradled her in his arms and helped walk her to the hotel.

The front entrance was garishly lit with strings of multicolored Christmas lights. From inside, he could hear voices raised in laughter. Through one of the lobby windows, he saw a small crowd of drinkers at the bar, a few of them in uniform.

The first-floor windows were dark at the rear of the building. The back entrance door was unlocked and led into the hotel kitchen. In the shadowy glow of a bare lightbulb hanging over the dishwasher, Macaulay found the service stairs that led up to the guest rooms on the second floor.

Hancock had booked four rooms for the duration of the expedition, and the first one Macaulay came to was unlocked. He helped Lexy inside and onto the bed. He covered her with blankets and went to the window overlooking the airfield.

An air-sea rescue plane with Royal Air Force markings was the only aircraft parked on the apron near the hotel. He looked for the helicopter, and finally saw it at the other end of the runway. It was inside a fenced compound. A group of men was moving in and around it.

Lexy was already asleep. He decided to head downstairs to try to set up a satellite call to Anschutz headquarters in Dallas. Locking the door behind him, he began walking toward the front stairs.

"Fancy seeing a general bloke in a squalid place like this," came a voice from behind him with a clipped British accent.

Macaulay turned to look at the man who had just come out of one of the rooms. He was wearing a one-piece flying suit with the Union Jack patch on his chest and colonel's bars at the collar. Recognizing his imperial mustache and flaming red hair, Macaulay shook his head and gave him a weary smile.

"It's good to see you, Harry," he said.

"Let's not get mawkish, General Sir," said the Englishman. "A handshake would suffice."

Like Macaulay, Harry Tubshawe had been an air squadron commander in Desert Storm. The two men had come to respect each other in the workup to the air battle. Tubshawe had been shot down over Baghdad and spent time in an Iraqi prison. Macaulay hadn't seen him in twenty years.

"You're as ugly as ever," said Macaulay.

"I take that as a compliment from a pillicock like you," said Tubshawe.

"That air/sea rescue crate out there yours?" asked Macaulay.

Tubshawe nodded.

"Some plonkers from the Royal Geographical Society got themselves trapped above the Arctic Circle. We pulled them out but were then forced down here two days ago with a poxy engine. Had to wait for spare parts to be flown up from Narsassuaq. You ready for a piss-up downstairs?"

"Can't right now," said Macaulay. "I need to make a satellite call to the States."

Tubshawe shook his head.

"No long-distance communications here," said Tubshawe. "Some arsehole cocked up the whole works the night we got here."

"Any idea who those guys are at the other end of the field?" asked Macaulay.

"Haven't a clue," said Tubshawe. "These days, every minor potentate and oligarch sports his own cavalry. Have guns, will travel. They have at least three birds over there. . . . In and out all the time. Probably some winter training exercise."

"Any of their guys staying over here?"

"They don't mix with low society," he said as they descended the stairs. "What we do have here is one sweet pukka. Laid up here for weeks . . . very accommodating . . . a Texas lass."

Macaulay looked across the lobby into the hotel bar. One of Tubshawe's crewmen was sitting on a pub stool, downing a pint of beer. Melissa was curled up in his lap like a big cat.

"She deserves some comfort from the Queen's Own," said Macaulay.

"The dog's bollocks," said Tubshawe.

"When are you pulling out, Harry?" he asked.

"We're taking off for Narsassuaq in three hours, weather permitting. The RGS plonkers are eager to get back to the sunny isles."

"Can you take two more passengers as far as Narsassuaq?" asked Macaulay.

Tubshawe looked at him closely.

"Highly irregular, old man," he said. "Totally against regulations."

Macaulay nodded.

"Where is your cock-up friend?" asked Tubshawe. "I thought bloody Hancock had his own air force."

"He's dead," said Macaulay. "He was murdered by those people over there."

Tubshawe saw the pain in his eyes. He didn't ask for details.

"I have two extra flight suits . . . just in case they're watching," he said.

TWENTY-NINE

28 November
West Wing
White House
Washington, DC

Cold rain was spattering the windows of his office when Ira Dusenberry got back from the Redskins game in Landover. He was in a sour mood after watching them get punched out again by the Cowboys after their new quarterback threw five interceptions.

Removing his wet loafers and socks, the deputy assistant national security adviser to the president rubbed his frigid toes into the deep-pile carpet and loosened his pants to help relieve his bloated stomach.

In spite of his vow to maintain a healthier diet, he had assuaged his frustrations at the game by devouring three Italian sausage subs with peppers and onions, and washing them down with a half dozen beers.

There was a loud knock on his door. It swung open to

reveal Addison Kingship, his Bogart-styled trench coat saturated with rain.

"This had better be important," he growled.

Taking off his trench coat, Kingship hung it on the rack behind the door and sat down in one of the leather club chairs. Through the windows behind Dusenberry's desk, the needle of the Washington Monument was bathed in floodlights.

Jessica Birdwell arrived a few moments later, somehow looking impervious to the rain. Cool and imperturbable as always, she was wearing an ivory cocktail dress cut just above the knees.

"Did you see the goddamn Skins game?" Dusenberry asked as Jessica took the other club chair.

"I couldn't care less, Ira," growled Kingship, a former tailback at Princeton. "Just tell us what's going on."

Dusenberry furtively lowered his left hand behind his massive desk and began massaging his aching stomach.

"I need to bring you up to speed on the John Lee Hancock situation," he said. "On my way back from Landover, I received another call from Mark Devlin, the head of security at Anschutz in Dallas. He had just gotten off the phone with Steven Macaulay, who was Hancock's number two at the company and a member of the Greenland expedition. Macaulay told him that Hancock had been murdered along with most of the other members by some kind of elite military unit equipped with attack helicopters."

"Where was he calling from?" asked Kingship.

"Right now he's at a former U.S. air base in southern Greenland at Narsassuaq," said Dusenberry. "Macaulay claims that Hancock discovered something on the ice cap that set off the massacre of his team. The only other survivor is an archaeologist they brought up there to document the findings. Macaulay asked to have the FBI or Homeland Security waiting for him when he lands in Bangor."

"We should call off the special mission unit we've deployed to Halifax from Joint Special Operations Command," said Jess. "They've been on immediate standby."

"Agreed," said Dusenberry.

"What is this discovery?' asked Kingship.

Dusenberry shook his head wearily.

"Don't laugh," he said. "It's something involving ancient Vikings."

Jess looked at him as if he had lost his mind.

"Yesterday it was an Arab commando team," said Kingship. "Today it's the goddamn Vikings. This whole thing sounds like a hoax, with Hancock looking for his fifteen minutes."

"That's not his style," said Dusenberry, "and we have to treat it as a legitimate threat. Whatever happened up there, it has apparently cost a lot of people their lives, and the president will want to know why."

"How is Macaulay getting to Bangor?" asked Kingship.

"One of the small jets in Hancock's air fleet was left in Narsassuaq to bring out the expedition team. Macaulay is a retired air force brigadier. He'll be flying it to Bangor as soon as the weather clears. According to Devlin, he and the archaeologist have no papers or passports. Everything they had was lost. He wants federal protection for himself and the archaeologist as soon as they arrive."

"How do we know Macaulay didn't go rogue?" asked Jess. "It's happened before."

"I have no idea," said Dusenberry.

"We have an FBI satellite office in Portland," said the still-skeptical Kingship.

"If any of Macaulay's claims are true, I think we need more horsepower than regional field staff," said Jess.

"I agree," said Dusenberry.

"What about a senior agent from our new domestic antiterrorism task force?" suggested Jess. "Maybe Jim Langdon."

"I had him in my shop for two years," said Kingship. "Top-notch."

The task force had recently been put together to synchronize the counterterrorsim activities of nine different federal agencies, including the FBI, the Defense Intelligence Agency, and Homeland Security. Langdon was a former combat infantry officer who had joined the FBI under Kingship and had later gone on to Homeland Security.

"That's fine," said Dusenberry. "And, Ad, you'll probably want to give a heads-up to the satellite office in Portland. They can provide backup."

THIRTY

Special Agent Eamon Gallagher, Jr., surveyed the Portland skyline through the picture window of the bureau conference room, and felt the first pure jolt of excitement he had ever experienced in his four-year FBI career.

Eamon was the only special agent left in the office that day, which was why he was given the high-priority classified dispatch just received from FBI headquarters in Washington.

The dispatch confirmed that James Langdon, a member of the president's domestic antiterrorism task force, would be arriving at the Portland airport in less than an hour and required backup assistance from the regional FBI office to conduct an interview with two Americans arriving from Greenland who had uncovered a possible terrorist plot.

Eamon quickly downloaded Langdon's background credentials from the Home Security personnel database. Langdon was a West Point graduate and had retired from the army as a major after serving three tours of duty in Iraq. He had been awarded two Silver Stars.

At five feet six, the twenty-nine-year-old Eamon struck no heroic figure, at least to himself. Nevertheless, he yearned to be a hero. It was why he had joined the FBI. On September 11, 2001, he had been working as an accountant for a tax preparer when the World Trade Center was attacked. His father had been one of the first responders who disappeared into the red dust. The loss changed Eamon's life. After considering what he could do to honor his father's memory, he found his future on the FBI Web site.

Become a special agent, the Internet banner read. *It is challenging. It is exciting. It is rewarding. And every day you have a chance to serve your country.*

"Eamon, we need you in accounting," the placement coordinator told him after he graduated near the top of his class at the FBI Academy.

For the next three years, he sat in Washington, reviewing expense files. Every time he applied for an operational assignment, his supervisor took him aside to say he was accomplishing far more with his spreadsheets. He had finally been transferred to the Portland regional office.

Eamon checked the pistol in his hip holster. With his small hands, he had never been comfortable with the full-sized Glock 21. Instead, he carried the baby Glock 26 subcompact 9 mm. He had fired it only on the shooting range.

At the Portland airport, Eamon presented his FBI credentials to the guard at the charter terminal. He was walking toward the flight desk when a voice called out, "Special Agent Gaskins?"

Eamon recognized him from the photo in the personnel database.

"Don was called away on another assignment," he said, reaching up to shake the man's hand. "I'm Eamon Gallagher."

"Jim Langdon," said the big man.

He looked like a combat soldier, rugged and deeply tanned, with a full head of prematurely gray hair.

"We got an early start out of Andrews," said Langdon. "I wanted to make sure we have security in place at Bangor when General Macaulay arrives."

"We'll give you our full cooperation and support," said Eamon as they walked to the plane.

"I assume you know why I'm here," said Langdon.

"I read the briefing memo," said Eamon.

"It's pretty muddled," said Langdon. "One report suggests that an Arab terrorist group unleashed an attack on John Lee Hancock's Greenland expedition, and another indicates there is some sort of Viking connection. We're here to learn what happened."

During the short hop from Portland up to Bangor, Eamon found it hard to contain his excitement. At one point, he closed his eyes and focused on breathing calmly. When he opened them again, Langdon was staring at him. Eamon kept wondering what he had done to earn the Silver Stars, but he didn't want to ask him directly.

"What was Iraq like?" he said instead.

A full minute passed.

"Betrayal," said Langdon.

A fleeting image of Jake Nash's ruined face stampeded through Langdon's brain as it had every day since the moment he had caught up to the caravan of abandoned vehicles in his Humvee and shined his flashlight into the backseat.

Langdon had been a company commander when the request came in from the governor general of their province to provide protection for a Shiite religious celebration. He and Jake Nash were sent down in a rotating combat team to provide the security presence. Their headquarters, inside an Iraqi police complex next to the governor's office, was protected by an electronic security cordon.

Langdon had just handed off command to Jake and left the headquarters, when a convoy of eight SUVs filled with men wearing American uniforms was waved through the gates by Iraqi police. The intruders exited the SUVs, firing automatic weapons. Five Americans were killed. Four more, including Jake, were taken away alive as the Iraqi police stood by.

A frantic chase ensued as the vehicles headed north into the night. It ended an hour later on a deserted road. Jake and two of the other soldiers were already dead, their hands tied behind their backs. Langdon hoped the fourth man would die quickly. Like the others, his eyes had been gouged out with knives. The attackers had cut off the men's balls and stuffed their penises in their mouths.

In the following days, the battalion's S2 staff built a case that the governor general had been complicit in the attack. One of the vehicles was registered to his wife and forensic evidence placed one of his bodyguards in the vehicle Jake had died in.

Langdon asked when the killers would be arrested.

"My hands are tied, Jim," said the battalion commander. "The governor is part of the prime minister's inner circle. I had to apologize to him for disrupting the religious celebration. Forget about it and do your job."

After the last American military unit left Iraq in 2011, Langdon had returned to Baghdad as a member of the president's new antiterrorism task force. The visit was designed to provide him with an update on the continued presence of Al Qaeda operatives in the region. He spent four days in the country.

On the day of his return to Washington, Langdon picked up the daily CIA briefing summary. It reported that the former governor general had been found dead early that morning on a deserted road north of the city, his body showing signs of horrific torture before he was killed.

Langdon looked out the window of the passenger jet and saw it was snowing as they descended toward Bangor. He said a silent prayer for both forgiveness and deliverance.

THIRTY-ONE

Flying on instruments, Macaulay dropped through a dense snow ceiling until the de Havilland finally broke into the clear at five hundred feet. Sitting next to him in the copilot's seat, Lexy awoke from a deep sleep and watched the curtain of wet snow lashing the windshield as they came in to land.

"Are we back in Greenland?" she asked.

"We're almost back in the good old USA," said Macaulay wearily.

"I'm glad we're still alive to see it," Lexy said.

"I spoke to Mark Devlin at Anschutz before we took off," said Macaulay, "and he assured me the FBI would be here waiting for us. We're to be placed under immediate federal protection."

As he taxied the plane off the runway, Bangor tower control radioed him with directions to deplane at a security gate near the general aviation terminal. They taxied past the brightly lit main terminal, some dark hangars, and the long-term parking facility.

A dozen small planes, all deeply covered by snow, were parked on the apron. At the security gate, Macaulay brought the de Havilland to a stop and shut down the engines. He and Lexy climbed out of the cockpit.

She began shivering again as soon as they were on the ice-coated tarmac. In the distance, Lexy saw four Bangor police cars, their strobe lights flashing, deployed at the front and rear entrances to the terminal. At the rear entrance, two men in overcoats were waiting for them under the concrete portico. One was tall; the other quite short.

"Welcome home," the short one called out.

Inside, the terminal was deserted, its overhead lights revealing a large waiting room with old leather chairs and couches surrounding an empty flight desk.

"All the charter flights have been canceled because of the weather," said Langdon. "I had the Bangor police stake out the terminal in case news of your arrival somehow reached the wrong people."

Macaulay asked to see their credentials. The taller man, Langdon, was a member of the White House domestic antiterrorism task force. He looked ex-military. The smaller one, Eamon Gallagher, Jr., was a regional FBI agent. He looked like an accountant.

"I've arranged for us to talk in a secure office on the second floor," said Langdon.

The second-floor corridor was as empty as the first. A bulletin board on the painted concrete block wall proclaimed that Carlos Lugo, a member of the lavatory staff from Orono, was the terminal's employee of the month.

Langdon led them into a well-lit conference room surrounded by leather armchairs. When Langdon removed
his overcoat, Macaulay noticed the Silver Star ribbon on
the lapel of his suit jacket.

"Second Gulf War?" asked Macaulay.

Langdon nodded. "Operation Iraqi Freedom, they
called it."

"I was there for the first one," said Macaulay.

"I'm sure we both lost friends over there, General,"
said Langdon.

He asked them to take the two seats opposite the video
camera mounted on one side of the conference table.

"I know you both must be tired, but we need your
statements as soon as possible," he said, opening his briefcase and removing an iPad. "A transcript of the interview
will go out electronically as soon as we're finished. These
days, nothing is hoarded. Fifty agents from different
shops will be working this case by tomorrow morning.
For now, we just need to know everything that happened
so we can go after the people who did this."

As Lexy sat down, the little agent set a plastic tray in
front of her and then delivered a second one to Macaulay.

"Maine's finest," he said, smiling.

She gazed down at a lobster roll stuffed with big
chunks of meat surrounded by a heaping mound of onion
rings and French fries. A hand-baked chocolate chip
cookie flanked the plate.

"We thought you might be hungry," said Eamon.

"I'm ravenous," said Lexy as he brought over two
mugs of coffee.

While they ate, Langdon turned on the video equipment and adjusted the settings.

"The fragmentary reports we've received about what happened up there sound pretty ridiculous," he said. "The first one involved an Arab commando team and the second concerned a group of Vikings."

"There weren't any Arabs up there," said Macaulay as he finished his coffee. "Someone sent you a red herring there."

"Fine," said Langdon. "Let's get started."

Lexy began first, describing her arrival at the expedition site, the discovery of the Vikings in the deep cave, the existence of the rune tablet, and the events that followed, including the arrival of the attackers, the removal of the artifacts, and the destruction of the camp.

"So you're saying that every member of the expedition, with the exception of Professor Jensen and General Macaulay, is dead," said Langdon.

"Yes," responded Lexy.

Macaulay took over at that point and described what had occurred in the wake of Falconer's murder, the sabotaging of his helicopter by Jensen, the return to the destroyed base camp, and the trek across the ice cap to the coast.

"I'm sure they are still looking for us," he concluded.

"Without a doubt," agreed Langdon. "You're incredibly fortunate to be here."

In spite of the harrowing nature of the events the pair described, Eamon was riveted by each new revelation. This was why he had joined the FBI, to bring a band of vicious terrorists like this to justice.

"Well, I guess that does it," said Langdon, turning off the video recorder and pulling a large brown envelope out of his briefcase. Opening it, he sorted through a sheaf of photographs that were inside, and handed one to Lexy.

"Do you recognize this man?" he asked.

"Yes, that's Hjalmar Jensen."

"And this one?"

"Sir Dorian Bond," she said.

"How about this man?" he asked, handing her a third photograph.

It was the blond leader of the commando team.

"How did you . . . ?"

"His name is Joachim Halvorsen. They call him the Lynx," said Langdon. "He is a former commando in the Norwegian Special Forces."

"Then you already know who they are," said Lexy. "That's a relief."

Langdon nodded and said, "Could you recognize any of the attackers aside from those two if you saw them again?"

"I'm sure I could," said Lexy.

As Langdon took back the photographs, she noticed the lower rim of a small tattoo on the back of his wrist. Most of it was hidden by his watch, but it somehow looked familiar.

"You said this other archaeologist, Mr. Falconer, was murdered by Professor Jensen because he acquired valuable information about the discovery, is that correct?" asked Langdon.

"It's a memory card from his Nikon camera," said Macaulay. "Our assumption is that Falconer photographed the rune tablet containing the saga of Leif Eriksson's last voyage, including his burial place somewhere on the East Coast."

"That would change history," said Eamon.

"Where is the memory card now?" asked Langdon.

Lexy felt a growing sense of alarm. She tried to get Macaulay's attention by prodding him in the knee, but he was already answering the agent's question.

"We have it here with us," said Macaulay.

"Good," said Langdon. "Then we have everything we need. The sooner we get the memory card to Washington, the sooner we can begin to decipher its secrets and get a better understanding of why it was important enough to massacre fourteen men."

"I can't think of any reason to send it into the bureaucratic maze," said Lexy, looking to buy time. "There is no one there more capable than I am of deciphering those markings. I would be one of the first people they called to make the translation."

Macaulay sensed the change in attitude.

"That may be true," said Langdon, "but there are national security implications involved here, and the card needs to be put in the hands of people who can measure its overall importance."

"I've already measured its importance," she said. "As long as General Macaulay and I are receiving federal protection, these issues will resolve themselves."

"Please give me the memory card," said Langdon.

"No," said Lexy as Macaulay continued staring at her.

Langdon reached back into his leather briefcase. His right hand emerged from it holding a Heckler & Koch P2000 semiautomatic pistol. A silencer was screwed into the barrel.

"I'm sorry about this, Eamon," said Langdon.

He pointed the pistol at the FBI agent and fired a

single shot into his chest. Eamon's eyes registered shock and pain as he collapsed to the floor behind the conference table. Lexy stared down at his lifeless body. A dense stream of blood began spreading across the polished linoleum floor.

"I need that memory card," said Langdon, aiming the pistol at Macaulay.

"Why should we make it easy for you?" said Macaulay. "You're going to kill us anyway."

"My orders are to kill only one of you," said Langdon, his eyes filling. "I take no pleasure in murder, particularly people like Eamon who did not deserve to die, but I am on a mission and it's a sacred one. I must do what is required of me. Each one of us is expected to fight, to sacrifice ourselves, to die if necessary."

"Why did you have to kill him?" asked Lexy.

"No one must be allowed to learn of this discovery, at least right now," said Langdon, training the pistol on them. "The future of the world is at stake. I know this will give you no solace, but I am part of a movement committed to saving it. I must have the memory card."

"No," repeated Lexy firmly.

"Since one of you obviously has it and I don't know which, I have to ask you to remove your clothing and pass it across the table."

"You are sick," said Macaulay.

"The world is sick," said Langdon. "No more delay."

Lexy knew their only hope was to buy more time. The memory card was still in her boot, and it was the last thing she planned to hand over. By then, someone, maybe one of the police officers outside, would come to investigate where they had gone and end the nightmare.

Macaulay handed over his shirt. Langdon spread it on the table and used his left hand to examine the pockets and lining while keeping the gun aimed at them with his right. Lexy's flannel shirt came next. Removing her bra, she tossed it across the table.

"Would you like to examine these too?" she said, trying to sound provocative.

"No," said Langdon, watching Macaulay.

As Lexy reached down to unlace her boots, she saw a hint of movement out of the corner of her eye. The little agent was lying on his side, facing away from her, but his right-hand fingers were moving through the expanding pool of blood. His fingers paused for a few moments and then started moving again as his consciousness came and went.

She left her boots on the floor and stood up to remove her corduroy pants. After dropping them on the table, she glanced down again. Eamon's hand was now at the hip holster on his slacks.

Langdon finished searching Macaulay's trousers and said, "Let's have your boots."

Macaulay handed them over.

The gun was now in the little agent's hand. She gently prodded Macaulay in the ribs, trying to signal that something was about to happen. He glanced back, trying to divine her thoughts.

Eamon was close to losing consciousness for the last time. God, there was so much of his blood on the floor. He didn't know he had that much inside him. There couldn't be much left. There was only the chance to save the others.

Through the dizziness and pain, he could see Langdon's legs on the far side of the table. He considered shooting upward through the table and trying to hit him in the chest. But what if he missed? His knees were less than five feet away. It would be hard to miss at that range. But first he needed to raise the gun off the floor.

"And now your boots, Dr. Vaughan," he heard Langdon say.

The handgrip of the baby Glock was slippery with blood and felt like it weighed a thousand pounds. It took all his strength to raise the barrel a few inches off the floor. Langdon's legs were swimming in and out of focus as wave after wave of nausea swept over him.

"Thank you, Dr. Vaughan," said Langdon as he pulled the memory card from her boot. "We're done here. Now if you promise me . . ."

When the shot roared out, Macaulay saw Langdon's face contort with pain before he staggered to his feet and fired the silenced pistol three times through the tabletop. The third round ripped through Eamon's forehead, blowing his brains out. By then, Macaulay had launched himself across the table, grabbing Langdon's gun hand and wrestling him to the floor.

Grunting with desperate effort, they fought for the gun. Even with a bullet in his knee, Langdon was stronger and far more experienced in hand-to-hand combat. Trapped in a headlock, Macaulay watched as the barrel of the pistol turned inward toward his belly.

Another shot rang out, and Langdon went limp in his arms. Macaulay wrenched the pistol from his hand and shoved him away. He looked up to see Lexy standing above them and holding the other agent's gun in her hand.

Langdon rolled over on his back. The bullet had torn through the side of his chest and punctured his lungs.

They watched as he spit out bloody foam. His breathing was reduced to brief spasmodic gasps as he stared up at them.

"Valhalla," he cried out before his eyes rolled up inside his head.

Macaulay felt his carotid artery.

"He's dead," he said.

Lexy knelt next to Langdon and raised his left arm. Unstrapping the wristwatch, she examined the tattoo in the harsh overhead lights. It wasn't the flukes of an anchor. She recognized the symbol immediately.

"I doubt the police outside could have heard your shot over the noise of the wind," said Macaulay while he dressed. "We'll know soon enough."

He stepped out into the corridor and listened for movement from the first floor. Apart from the wail of the wind, there was none. When he returned to the conference room, Lexy was dressed and gazing down at the body of the little agent.

"Thank you, Eamon," she said.

Macaulay's mind raced. By now he had hoped to be lying in a Jacuzzi with a Jack Daniel's in his hand and looking forward to a good night's sleep. Instead, there were two federal agents lying dead at their feet. It was all too big, too complicated to begin to figure it out.

He opened Langdon's briefcase and pulled out his federal credentials.

"If these aren't forged," he said, "and I doubt they are, this guy worked directly for the president. If the White House is part of this thing, whatever this thing is, who knows how far the tentacles go? One thing is for sure—whoever sent him won't hesitate to send a replacement."

"If we don't stay here to tell our side of the story, they will think we murdered them," said Lexy.

"If we stay here, we may end up telling our story to another executioner," he replied, glancing around the room. "Anyway, a good team of homicide investigators should be able to reconstruct what happened here. And they'll have the video."

"But he turned it off before he showed us the photographs and shot Eamon."

"No one looking at those interviews will believe we had murderous intentions."

"How can you trust whoever gets here first not to destroy them?" asked Lexy.

"You're right," he conceded, his exhausted mind reeling. "The only thing we can do at this point is go to ground until we can find out who we can trust."

"Go where?" asked Lexy.

"One burning building at a time," said Macaulay, removing the disk drive from the video recorder and putting it in Langdon's briefcase along with the sheaf of photographs still lying on the conference table and his federal credentials.

Lexy noticed that Langdon's iPad had fallen to the floor. She picked it up.

"We should take this too," she said. "Maybe there's something on it that will explain what's behind this."

While she added it to the briefcase, Macaulay went over to the bodies and pulled out their wallets. Langdon had sixty dollars and the little agent ten. He took the cash and put their wallets back where he found them.

"We'll leave everything else as it is," said Macaulay.

"Our fingerprints are on those guns," said Lexy.

"And everywhere else too," he said, turning out the lights behind them.

When they reached the first floor, Macaulay saw that the staircase kept going down to a subbasement. Following it, they came to two intersecting corridors, one leading to a series of underground offices, and a second that led into darkness.

Macaulay produced the flashlight from his pocket, and they continued along the second corridor for another hundred feet until arriving at another set of concrete stairs that led up to a steel door with a self-locking security bar. Macaulay opened the door and stepped into what appeared to be a small emergency power plant. Two large diesel generators sat in the center of the room.

"These probably provide backup power to the terminal," said Macaulay.

Wind-driven snow was lashing the windows. Looking outside, he couldn't see any sign of the police cordon, but he assumed they still surrounded the general aviation terminal.

The small building backed up to the long-term parking facility, and that gave him an idea. Picking up a flatiron bar from the workbench along the far wall, he said, "Wait here."

Forcing open the exterior door, he stepped outside and let it slam shut behind him. Walking quickly across the parking lot, he scanned the first row of cars and trucks. All of them were buried by more than a foot of snow.

A Ford Ranger pickup in the second row had less than three inches on it. Macaulay assumed that if the owner had just left the vehicle in the long-term lot, there was a good chance he wasn't coming back right away.

Using the bar, he smashed a small hole in the rear window on the driver's side and reached inside to unlock the door. Climbing in, he shined his flashlight on the ignition switch.

It was no challenge to hot-wire the ignition. Long before he fell in love with fighter jets, Macaulay's passion had been working on fast cars. Using his jackknife, he pried the plastic cover panel off the ignition tumbler.

It was a standard assembly with five wires clipped to the rear of the tumbler. He pulled loose the red power wire and the brown starter wire. As soon as he connected them, the engine surged to life.

Macaulay turned the heat up to maximum and headed back for Lexy. Five minutes later, they were driving toward the exit. No one was working the tollbooth, and the security barrier was raised to the open position to allow access for the snowplows. Macaulay saw that the surveillance camera on the roof of the kiosk was covered with snow.

"We're lucky," he said. "At least they won't know how or when we left. We have a good chance to cover a lot of ground before daylight."

He turned the truck onto Route 95, and they headed south into the storm.

THIRTY-TWO

1 December
The Bowers
Catoctin Mountain
Leesburg, Virginia

Lieutenant Colonel Thomas Everett Somervell IV (ret.) sat dozing in the leather recliner in his walnut-paneled study. Waking up, he glanced through the window at the snowy landscape. In the pale light of dawn, he saw the three-legged doe and her new fawn munching acorns under the white oak tree.

It gave him pleasure to know that she had survived another year in the realm of the weekend gunslingers. These days, anything that moved on the mountain during open season was at risk of being shot down.

He no longer slept through the night. He rarely enjoyed anything approaching real slumber at any time of the day or night. He needed just a few hours of dozing to function.

Picking up his personal iPad, he resumed his perusal of

the Web site. It was quite amazing to him how much new material was added to it in each twenty-four-hour cycle, literally hundreds of new leads to research and explore.

His cell phone began to ring and he picked it up.

"This is Meg."

He could hear the irritation in her voice.

"The deputy director would like to see you in his office at ten o'clock."

"I'll be there," he said, hanging up.

He was grateful to still have his hand in after the wholesale housecleaning of the covert-operations branch in the previous year. Old and venerable went out. Young and bold came in. Although he was now relegated to a tiny basement office in the CIA library annex, a week rarely went by that he wasn't consulted on an intelligence matter that required someone with an institutional memory.

The thirty-something Meg had replaced him in his seat at covert operations. Overly ambitious to make her mark, she was obviously irked that he still had access to those at the top.

His fingers moved smoothly over the iPad keys like darting extensions of his nervous system. He usually spent at least an hour on the same site, punching the familiar icons of the search engine, hunting for an ideal candidate.

The wainscoted wall of his study was covered with photographs that documented his long journey from Exeter to Yale, his years as an air force fighter pilot, five more in the Pentagon, a decade of service at the agency, and the final ascendancy to wise man status.

At sixty-four, he looked like a rugged version of Tennessee Williams, with a shock of white hair, a long narrow nose, and a sprinkling of liver spots on his cheeks from exposure to the desert and tropical sun. He still wore the same seersucker suits that were his personal trademark, regardless of the season or the continent.

Over the years, he had served at some of the agency's angriest hot spots—Beirut, Athens, Moscow, Baghdad, and Beijing. Along the way, he had had one lung removed after a three-pack-a-day habit, and absorbed a dozen shards of shrapnel from a bombing attack in Libya. Now he was in the proverbial pasture.

It gave him plenty of time for his favorite pastime of savoring the Internet smorgasbord of beautiful young men from all over the world. After two broken marriages and countless liaisons across the globe, he found that the Internet provided all the excitement he needed in his personal life. It was so much better than the sweaty reality and residual guilt from incidents like the sordid mess in Beirut that had almost cost him his career. Now he could have his pleasure through the virtual reality of the computer screen.

The cell phone began to ring again. He picked it up.

"Tommy?"

He had an ear for voices. This one was air force; the first, Gulf War.

"Dear boy, I told you to never call me here," said Somervell, chuckling. "People will talk."

"They have been for the last twenty years," said Steve Macaulay, "which is why I'm amazed you're still there."

"The agency is well aware of my proclivities," said Somervell. "They've put them to good use in the name of God and country."

"I never asked. You didn't tell," said Macaulay.

"You were a stalwart in those days," said Somervell, "even if you didn't return my feelings of genuine passionate love."

Macaulay glanced up from the pay phone at the rest stop on the Maine Turnpike as a burly young man in a Patriots NFL jersey came through the entrance door, carrying a toddler in his arms. He went into the men's room without glancing at him.

"I need your help, Tommy," said Macaulay.

"Name it," said Somervell.

"I'm probably being hunted for two murders," said Macaulay. "At least that would be the cover story. It was self-defense."

"Who is after you?"

"Half of spook land."

"What have you done, dear boy?"

"We . . . I killed a senior agent on the president's domestic antiterrorism task force. An FBI field agent was also shot."

"That's not good."

"The senior agent was about to kill me, and he was clearly following orders that came from somebody higher up the food chain."

"How high?"

"There's got to be a mole in the White House national security team," said Macaulay, "and maybe more than one. Somebody needs to find out. I don't know who else to call. Are you still in covert operations?"

Somervell glanced down at the iPad screen. A slender young Pakistani was busy entertaining a fellow student at an English university.

"More or less," he answered.

"This rogue agent's name was James Langdon—ex-army if that helps. He was after a photo memory card I brought back from Greenland with an old Viking inscription that might contain the location of Leif Eriksson's burial tomb."

"You're losing me, Steven."

"I know it sounds crazy. Langdon was part of a Norse religion called the Ancient Way. Apparently they look at Leif Eriksson as some kind of god."

"I crossed paths with a few of them in Paris some years ago . . . tough boys . . . serious about their work."

"They wiped out our whole expedition up in Greenland. John Lee is dead too."

Lexy came out of the ladies' room and walked over to him.

"Oh my," said Somervell sadly. "I always saw him as indestructible."

"One more thing. I believe they have a warship of some kind. A serious warship."

"How serious?"

"Serious enough to be equipped with attack helicopters."

Macaulay turned around again as a state police officer wearing a SMOKEY THE BEAR hat entered the rest stop and walked over to a vending machine. Inserting a dollar bill, he waited for the coffee to pour.

"I've got to go," said Macaulay.

"With regard to our mole, do you have any insights into gender, background, whatever?"

"No idea," said Macaulay, cupping his hand over the

phone. "Whoever it is has a pass into the White House basement."

"I will try to help," said Somervell. "Discreetly, of course. How can I reach you?"

"No idea for now."

"Call me back tonight if you can," said Somervell. "I'll give you a rundown on what I find out."

"Who was that?" asked Lexy when they were back in the stolen truck.

"A friend at Langley who can help us find out who is involved in the White House," said Macaulay. "I worked with him in the Pentagon. He knows the turf down there. Right now we need a place to hole up for a while."

"I've been thinking about it," said Lexy. "I know where we can go."

Tommy Somervell reluctantly terminated the page on the Web site he had been surfing and took the time to erase his recent browsing history. Picking up his secure phone, he placed a call.

"This is Tommy," he said. "Are you awake, dear girl?"

"What do you think?" came back the irritated voice.

"Are you still tracking violent religious organizations?"

THIRTY-THREE

30 November
Brattle Street
Harvard Square
Cambridge, Massachusetts

Barnaby Finchem came up out of the depths and parted one eyelid.

Towanda, the female cat bestowed on him by his second wife, was curled up on the bed between him and Delia Glantz, one of the doctoral candidates in archaeology he was mentoring at the university.

The now twenty-two-year-old Towanda was the last in the menagerie of animals that had passed through his life since he had emigrated from England to join the faculty at Harvard. All three of his wives had been fond of pets, including horses, dogs, cats, turtles, clams, exotic fish, potbellied pigs, Hereford calves, and one llama.

Towanda had won a place in his cynical heart after she and her sister had been tied inside a canvas bag and tossed by their former owner into the deep tidal pond near his summer cottage on Cape Cod.

Barnaby and his second wife, Barbara, had been returning home across the dunes from a dinner party, when she heard them crying in distress. A moment later, she was diving into the water in her cocktail dress to save them.

Upon bringing the kittens home, Barbara had promptly named them Idgie and Towanda after two characters in her then-favorite novel, *Fried Green Tomatoes at the Whistle Stop Cafe*. Some years later, Idgie had disappeared on her nightly walkabout. Towanda was still going strong.

Across the bedcovers, Barnaby contemplated the exquisite symmetry of Delia's naked breasts. She was an incredibly ardent lover, even if her half-written thesis on the nomadic pastoralists in the Sumerian city of Eridu during the Uruk period suffered from a distinct lack of imagination or original research. She more than made up for it in bed.

Barnaby had ceased to care whether his students bedded him for his brains or his marking pen. At the age of sixty-eight, he was just grateful to wake up next to a comely young woman like this and not have to worry about paying her alimony. He was never meant for the holy sacrament of marriage.

He had always adhered to a strict policy of never attempting to seduce any of his students. On the other hand, if one of them attempted to seduce him, and she was appealing enough, his defenses could be rapidly breached.

Even approaching seventy, Barnaby found his juices were still flowing in every way, although his recent heart bypass surgery had put a dent in his robust libido. Regardless, he vowed to never indulge in the potency pills so many of his colleagues resorted to in order to satisfy their wives and girlfriends.

He turned onto his back and stretched his massive six-and-a-half-foot-long frame. It was an unalloyed joy to again be able to wake in the morning without feeling any pain. The stroke had shaken him to the core. After a previous physical, the doctor had told him that his good cholesterol level was the highest he had ever seen, and that his death wouldn't be from heart disease. Barnaby had the stroke two weeks later, followed by open-heart surgery.

He now taught only one course at Harvard, the Origins of Civilization lecture series, and the waiting list to take it was hundreds long. The class required only three hours of his time every Monday morning, allowing him the rest of the week to concentrate on his other passion in life besides sex, the study of the rune language.

After achieving first class honors at Cambridge, the Englishman had spent nearly four decades crisscrossing Europe in an obsessive hunt to track down buried, stolen, and lost rune stones and etchings to add to his fund of knowledge, and he was now close to completing the thousand-page manuscript that comprehensively catalogued the language's evolution through the centuries.

Although he knew that early morning had arrived, it was still dark outside. He could hear rain hammering the windows, and it felt good to be there with Delia, warm and sexually spent under the goose down comforter.

The telephone in his study began to ring.

Barnaby always kept its volume on the minimum setting. Delia probably couldn't hear it over the rain, but the relentless ringing began to irritate him. There was no message machine on the line because the number was known to only a handful of people. After two minutes, he sensed that whoever was calling would not be deterred.

Planning to verbally flay whoever it was, he climbed out of the bed and walked naked to his paneled study. As he picked up the receiver, he looked out the window overlooking Harvard Square. Under the force of the sleeting rain, the sidewalks and streets were empty.

The voice on the other end of the line was excited and upset. He thought it might be his third ex-wife, Bonita, calling about his missing alimony payments, until the voice said, "Barnaby, it's Alexandra."

He knew only one Alexandra. The Alexandra.

"Are you there?" she demanded in the same smoky voice he remembered so well.

"Alexandra, it's barely morning," he growled, "and I'm still recovering from the stroke from hell."

"I need your help, Barnaby," she said. "I'm on the run."

"On the run," he said caustically. "I seem to recall that line from *High Sierra*—Ida Lupino says . . ."

"It has to do with the Greenland expedition you recommended me for," she said. "They're all dead."

Barnaby remembered now.

"Where are you?" he asked.

"We're in front of the yogurt bar down the block from you."

So she wasn't alone. He could see the café's lights from the study window.

"Give me ten minutes," he said.

Barnaby went back to the bedroom and gently woke Delia Glantz.

"Something's come up," he said. "An old friend of mine is in trouble."

He could tell she was upset because she kept staring at him stone-faced while she put on her clothes. He had faced similar scenes many times. There was no point in telling her it was simply a matter of friendship and responsibility. He waited for her to tell him he was a heartless son of a bitch.

Instead, she stood at the door with tears in her eyes and said, "You're the most wonderful teacher I've ever known, Dr. Finchem."

He was immediately tempted to tell her to take her clothes off again and get back in bed, but it was too late. When she left, he went over to the window to look down at the street.

Two figures were walking quickly up Brattle from the corner of Church Street. One was Alexandra. The other was a man. He had one arm around her in a protective way. In his other hand, he was carrying a briefcase. Barnaby padded to the bathroom and began running hot water into his oversized enamel tub.

As the tub filled, his mind traveled back to the time he had mentored Alexandra. From the start, he had known she was a remarkable student, deeply motivated and eager to make her mark in Norse studies, a field most people in the archaeological world viewed as a dead end.

She eventually became the finest runologist he had ever trained, with a natural, almost instinctive gift for translating the dead language from every period. Almost as good as he was. He had called her the code breaker.

His only disappointment with her stemmed from the fact that in the years she studied under him, she showed no interest in him sexually. At one point, he considered straying from his policy of never pursuing a student, but in the end restrained himself, sure she would rebuff him if he tried.

Their relationship had remained one of maestro and acolyte.

Barnaby waited by the study window until they arrived at the stone staircase of his brownstone and stepped under the portico to push the intercom button over his mailbox.

He pressed the button that delivered an electronic signal to unlock the front door. A few moments later, he heard them climbing past the second-floor landing on their way to the top floor. He opened the apartment door as they arrived. In the light of the stairwell lamp, the man's eyes were wary and distrustful.

Even drenched to the skin, Alexandra was as lovely as he remembered, more beautiful now that she was in her thirties and her active lifestyle had added character lines to her face. At the same time, she was much thinner than he remembered, and skin was peeling from her nose as she came into his welcoming arms.

As he watched them embrace, Macaulay took an immediate dislike to the man.

Barnaby led them into the living room and the cheerful fire he had set in the grate the night before. After he had stoked it with another log, Alexandra introduced the man as Steven Macaulay.

To Barnaby, he looked ex-military but not unintelligent, probably in his late forties, with the rugged, angular handsomeness of the old generation of Hollywood's leading men like Gregory Peck. It was clear that Macaulay had the love light in his eyes each time he looked at Alexandra.

"How did you get here?" Barnaby asked.

"I stole a truck in the long-term parking lot at Bangor Airport, and we left it at the long-term lot at Logan," said Macaulay. "We took a taxi from there to Harvard Square."

"Very resourceful," said Barnaby.

Macaulay wasn't prepared for the sheer magnitude of the older man. Macaulay was six feet tall, and the man towered over him. Broad and deep-chested, he had a leonine pelt of gray hair that ran halfway down his back. His high-crowned nose looked like it had been broken more than once, and it was crisscrossed with fine, reddish veins. He was dressed in a tentlike flannel nightshirt.

Barnaby walked to a walnut cupboard and pulled out a bottle. Uncorking it, he poured stiff drinks into two water glasses and said, "Drink this."

Lexy drank hers in one long swallow, remembering the fiery warmth of it from past ceremonial occasions with Barnaby.

"Calvados," she said to Macaulay. "Apple brandy from Normandy."

"You need to get out of those wet clothes," said Barnaby. "I'm running a hot bath and will try to find some spare things for you while yours are in the dryer."

After all his years in the air force, Macaulay had a good feel for accents. The old man's voice was intrinsically English and highborn. He heard the faint echo of the arrogant ruling class.

Fifteen minutes later, they joined Barnaby back in the galley kitchen. Lexy was wrapped in a gargantuan terry cloth bathrobe, and Macaulay was swimming inside one of his nightshirts.

Barnaby had already brewed a pot of coffee, and he was now scrambling a half dozen eggs in a large skillet. The smell of the food reminded Macaulay that they hadn't eaten anything since the FBI agent had given them the lobster rolls.

"So why are you on the run?" asked Barnaby, pouring the coffee.

Macaulay started with what happened to them after their arrival at the Bangor airport. When he finished the brief account, Barnaby said, "And you're sure this man Langdon was an agent of the White House antiterrorism task force?"

Macaulay retrieved Langdon's briefcase from the living room and opened it.

"Here are his credentials," said Macaulay, "and here are the photographs he showed us. This disc is a recording of our statements in which we told him everything that happened to the Hancock expedition up on the ice cap."

Macaulay held off telling the old man about Falconer's memory card.

"Instead of repeating the story again, just give me the disc and the photographs," said Barnaby. "While you're having breakfast, I'll watch the interview."

Taking his coffee, Barnaby went into his study and shut the door behind him.

"Why didn't you tell him about the memory card?" asked Lexy.

"Because I no longer know who we can trust," said Macaulay.

"You can trust Barnaby," she said fervently. "And we're going to need him to translate the markings that are hopefully recorded on the card."

"We'll see," he said.

Finishing his meal, Macaulay strolled around the apartment, trying to get a better sense of the man. Obviously, Lexy believed in him blindly, but that could simply be a product of past hero worship. Or maybe even more.

The apartment felt like a bachelor's lair with its blond Scandinavian furniture, interior window shutters instead of curtains, oil paintings of sailing ships. Books filled the floor-to-ceiling shelves in the living room. After scanning the titles, he found it odd that none of them related to the study of the Norsemen, which was supposedly the old man's livelihood.

Wandering back into the kitchen, he opened the refrigerator and saw it was loaded with red meat, brown eggs, wine, Cuban cigars, and imported beer; this also seemed strange for a man supposedly recovering from open-heart surgery.

Barnaby reentered the kitchen to see Macaulay examining the contents of his refrigerator. There was a look of detached amusement in his eyes as he divined the younger man's thoughts.

"We only go through this existence once," he said, "and I don't plan to spend mine eating seaweed and low-fat granola."

Barnaby led them back into the living room and

stretched out on the sofa. Lexy and Macaulay took seats in the club chairs facing him.

"We're dealing with the ancient curse," said Barnaby, his slate gray eyes looking to Macaulay like great nail heads in the reflected glow of the fire.

THIRTY-FOUR

30 November
Brattle Street
Harvard Square
Cambridge, Massachusetts

"The ancient curse?" asked Lexy.

"It has taken many forms over the aeons," said Barnaby, "but there is one word for it, and that is religion, the attempt by man to resolve the cause, nature, and purpose of the universe by giving his existence a divine foundation."

"I'm not sure I follow you," said Macaulay.

"You look like an ex-military man," said Barnaby. "I'm sure I don't have to enlighten you about all the meaningless wars fought through the millennia under the banner of the great religions. My favorite is that of Sir Godfrey de Bouillon, who captured Jerusalem under the flag of Christendom during the First Crusade in 1099. Unable to determine with any certainty which members of the populace were Christians and which ones might be Muslims or Jews, he ordered them all to be slaughtered, after which he knelt in supplication to his savior Jesus Christ with his bloody crusader sword and prayed in gratitude for allowing him to deliver the holy city from the infidels."

"What does that have to do with what happened in Greenland?" demanded Macaulay, now sure the old man was just another Harvard blowhard.

Barnaby picked up the sheaf of photographs, peeled off the top one, and held it up in front of them.

"Hjalmar Jensen," said Lexy.

"Hjalmar has been a true believer as long as I've known him," said Barnaby, "and that goes back a long way."

"A true believer in what?" asked Lexy.

"The Order of the Ancient Way . . . the divine revelation of the Norse gods," said Barnaby. "Today it is derided as paganism by Christianity, but the Norse religion is almost as old as man itself. And you should know that worshippers of the Norse faith do not share the message of gentle love preached by the carpenter from Galilee. They believe in . . ."

"The Hammer of Thor," said Lexy.

"Yes," said Barnaby. "Thor . . . the ancient deity responsible for thunder, lightning, and storms, but also imbued with the sacred power to protect mankind. He was worshipped as a god throughout all recorded history, including the Roman occupation of Germania long before the birth of Jesus. Of course, he is only one of the Norse gods."

"Sorry, but it sounds totally ridiculous," said Macaulay.

"Oh really," replied Barnaby. "Are you a religious man, Mr. Macaulay?"

"I'm not," said Macaulay.

"Well, I don't ride with God's cavalry either," said Barnaby, his voice tinged with sarcasm, "but a third of the American people reject the theory of evolution, the fundamental underpinning of the science of biology. They believe that God created humans within the last ten thousand years. You don't think the Norse gods sound plausible? Let's look at the other so-called plausible religions."

Barnaby got up from the couch and stood over Macaulay, almost dwarfing him.

"Fifteen million people currently embrace a faith created just two hundred years ago by a New York polygamist who made his living as a treasure hunter, selling shares in his venture by claiming he had found a magic stone that allowed him to see underground, which he then used to find two golden plates buried in upstate New York. Of course, only he could translate the words on the plates, which no one else ever saw, and the manuscript was published as the Book of Mormon. When he was shot to death in 1844 by an armed mob while in prison for treason and polygamy, Joseph Smith's last words were, 'Oh Lord my God.' Not quite as powerful as 'Father, forgive them for they know not what they do,' but Smith had five bullets in him at the time."

"I think I get your point," said Macaulay, but Barnaby wasn't finished.

"Or how about this idea for a religion," he went on, his eyes boring into Macaulay's. "It was created after the Second World War by a mentally unstable man who had undergone a nervous breakdown after being relieved of command of his navy patrol boat, and was later arrested and convicted of larceny while indulging in what he called sex magic rituals with his spaced-out friends. After writing several science fiction stories in his trailer home, he told his friends that writing for a penny a word was a waste of time and that he could make a million by starting his own religion. After taking the time to marry his second wife without divorcing his first wife, he started a religion based on the premise that seventy-five million years ago, an intergalactic dictator sent billions of human beings here to Earth in spacecraft, after which they were all murdered with hydrogen bombs and became theta beings, the source of life. Of course, this was only to be revealed to church members who donated large amounts of money." Barnaby paused for a moment before adding, "Scientology has eight million believers."

"Okay . . . I get it," said Macaulay, sounding almost chastened.

"There's something I haven't told either of you," said Lexy. "Langdon had a small tattoo on his wrist. It was the Mjolnir. And the Mjolnir emblem was stitched onto the chests of the uniforms of the men who attacked us on the ice cap."

"What is the Mjolnir?" asked Macaulay.

"Thor's hammer," said Barnaby. "In Norse mythology, it is a fearsome weapon, sometimes described as an axe, and one that can never fail, that will never miss its target."

"It is obviously their amulet," said Lexy to Macaulay, "their equivalent of the crucifix or the Egyptian Tarveret."

"Evidently," said Barnaby before walking back into the kitchen to pour another drink. Glancing out the darkened window, he saw that a car was parked across the street in the no-standing zone that ran the length of the block. The tiny glow of a cigarette momentarily came to life behind the windshield.

"What do these people actually believe?" asked Macaulay when Barnaby returned to stand in front of the fire. "What do they want?"

"Like the Jews, Christians, and Muslims, Hjalmar's faithful believe they are the chosen people, charged with the responsibility of saving humanity by preserving the Nordic race as the stewards of the world. Their catechism is that the Norse gods began their existence as mortals, humans who through their extraordinary accomplishments reached eventual veneration as gods, called upon in prayer by successor generations in the face of famine, flood, and war."

"Not only is God on their side," said Lexy, "but they could actually become one."

"Exactly," said Barnaby. "To these people, Leif Eriksson is a deity. If they find his final resting place, it will become the Norse religion's equivalent of the Church of the Holy Sepulchre in Jerusalem. To men like Hjalmar, your friend Hancock was a desecrator. Imagine how Islamic fundamentalists would react to an infidel digging up Muhammad's tomb in Medina."

"How many believers are there?" asked Macaulay.

"Who can say?" responded Barnaby. "Back in the early 1990s, Hjalmar and I were on a dig together at a place called Skjak where one of the first Norse churches was built. We were snowed in there for more than a week. In those days I wasn't quite as cynical as I am now, and Hjalmar thought he could help to save my eternal soul. He confided that he was a practicing believer of the Forn Sior, or the Ancient Way, and that his congregation in Oslo numbered in the thousands. He assured me that great men of wealth and prestige of his faith had begun to penetrate the highest circles of power in Europe, and that the message of the church was spreading to America and even Russia."

"The master race again?" asked Macaulay.

"No," said Barnaby. "They're different . . . smarter. I'm sure they see their aims as benign, even as they commit ruthless acts to achieve them. They are looking to save a world they see descending ever closer to chaos. He told me the church had a brilliant team of Scandinavian geneticists working for them. Frankly, it sounded like *The Boys from Brazil*."

Macaulay had heard enough.

"You should know that we have the memory card from Rob Falconer's camera," said Macaulay. "Lexy thinks he photographed the rune stone in the Viking cave before Jensen killed him, and that the markings might hold the secret of Leif Eriksson's burial place."

Barnaby's eyes reflected true amazement.

"I've been waiting for this all my life," he said as the lights went out.

"It's probably just another outage," he said, going into the kitchen to check the circuit breaker panel. After seeing that none of the circuits were tripped, he was about to head back, when he glanced out the window and saw the lights in the apartment across the way.

He looked down at the street. The car he had seen in the no-standing zone was no longer there. It had been replaced by two others. He could see the indistinct shapes of men in the front seats. Mildly curious, he walked to the back bedroom that faced out over the alley behind his brownstone.

The car that had originally been parked on Brattle Street was now blocking the mew gate that led from his building into the alley. A man in a raincoat was standing next to the car, looking up at his apartment. A second man was approaching the rear entrance, carrying a short rifle.

Barnaby walked back into the living room and stood by the fire.

"It would appear we are surrounded," he said.

THIRTY-FIVE

30 November
Brattle Street
Harvard Square
Cambridge, Massachusetts

A woman began to scream on one of the lower floors of the apartment building. Her frantic cries ended ten seconds later.

"Do you have a gun?" asked Macaulay.

"Why would I have a gun?" said Barnaby.

Running to the dryer in the laundry room, Lexy retrieved their clothes and hurriedly put hers on. They were still clammy, and she momentarily wondered if she would ever be truly warm again. In the kitchen, Macaulay stuffed the contents of Langdon's briefcase, including Falconer's memory card, the photographs, and Langdon's iPad, into his pockets.

Throwing on a belted raincoat over his red flannel nightshirt, Barnaby picked up a flashlight in the kitchen and led them to one of the bedrooms. Opening a closet, he removed a wooden stepladder and placed it under a rectangular access panel in the ceiling. Climbing the ladder, Barnaby shoved up the access panel and disappeared through the opening into a crawl space above the crossbeams.

After following Lexy up, Macaulay pulled the stepladder up after him and replaced the access panel. Farther along the crawl space, Barnaby had already unhooked the reinforced wooden hatch that opened onto the roof.

"Damn," said Macaulay.

"What is it?" asked Lexy, alarmed.

"I forgot the disc drive of our recorded statement in Bangor."

"I've got it," said Barnaby, shoving the roof hatch away from the opening.

"Let me go first," said Macaulay.

"Gladly," said Barnaby.

Macaulay slowly raised his head above the opening and glanced around him. No one was moving on the other roofs. He saw that all the brownstones on Barnaby's side of the block were approximately the same height and appeared to abut one another.

In one direction, the line of buildings ended at the edge of a tree-filled park. In the other, the last brownstone was flanked by a larger structure that was still indistinct in the gloom. He decided to head that way.

Helping Lexy and Barnaby up through the opening, Macaulay snugged the hatch down over the crawl space and guided them over the low brick wall that separated Barnaby's building from the next in line. Two steps across the roof, he nearly fell into a shallow lap pool, its greasy-looking surface clogged with moldering leaves.

He went quickly across to the next roof with Barnaby bringing up the rear. This one had a miniature mansion constructed on it with columns in front. Macaulay could hear the cooing of birds inside and realized it was a high-end pigeon roost.

The next one had a terraced garden, and the one after was covered with staging equipment and new roofing shingles. Stepping across the construction material, Macaulay glanced back at Barnaby's building. There was no movement yet above the roof hatch.

As he reached the last brownstone in the block, he gritted his teeth. There was no fire escape on the side of the building and the larger one beyond it was at least ten feet away.

A long board was lying at the roof edge, but even if it could have reached the windowsill of the next building, Macaulay knew it would never support Barnaby's weight.

"Have you ever done any rappelling?" asked Macaulay as the others came up to him.

"We're archaeologists," said Barnaby as if the answer were self-evident.

Macaulay jogged back the way they had come until he reached the construction materials. Picking up a coiled bundle of rope, he looked around for work gloves, settling for the strips of canvas that had been used to anchor shingles to the pallets.

"There's no time to make a friction hitch," he said, uncoiling the rope at the edge of the roof. "Wrap these canvas strips around your hands before you slide down. It looks to be about forty feet."

Barnaby didn't hesitate. As soon as Macaulay had anchored one end of the rope around the chimney, he was over the side with his feet braced against the wall of the building. For all of his immense bulk, he was surprisingly agile on the rope line, reaching the ground in only four backward jumps.

Lexy went next. Macaulay waited for her to touch ground before grabbing the line and slipping over the edge of the roof. As he went over, he heard the sound of shattering glass. Across the dead space between the two buildings, he saw one of the windows disintegrate from the force of an exploding bullet.

Glancing back toward Barnaby's brownstone, he saw a man poised above the roof hatch with a suppressed rifle. Macaulay dropped below the roofline before he could fire another round.

Hitting the ground, he ran after Barnaby and Lexy, who had almost reached the next block. A taxi was coming slowly up the street toward Brattle. Barnaby stepped in front of it to flag it down. He could see fear in the turbaned driver's eyes as he took in the sight of him, but he stopped short, giving Lexy the time to reach the door and swing it open.

A few moments later, they were inside the cab and Barnaby was exhorting the terrified driver to make a U-turn away from Brattle Street. As they accelerated away, Macaulay looked back and saw three men converging from both sides of the street. One of them raised his rifle, but by then they were in the busy traffic pattern on JFK Street.

"State Street metro station," said Barnaby to the driver, who continued to stare ahead as if not wanting to accept the reality of the enormous figure stuffed into the passenger seat next to him.

Barnaby told him to pull over to the curb in front of the subway station. He turned to Macaulay and said, "You have any money?"

"About twenty bucks," said Macaulay, handing it up to him.

"That's enough," replied Barnaby. "I have plenty where we're going."

Barnaby watched the cab disappear into traffic.

"It struck me that if our erstwhile driver is picked up any time soon, he should have as little information as possible," said Barnaby.

"Wise assumption," agreed Macaulay. "You're learning."

Barnaby bought their tickets and they boarded a blue line train. None of the other commuters appeared to take notice of him in his nightshirt, slippers, and raincoat. It was Boston.

When they arrived at the New England Aquarium station, Barnaby got up from his seat and led them off the train. Lexy noted that one of the exit signs read CHRISTOPHER COLUMBUS PARK. She had to smile at the irony of it.

A hundred feet away from the station, they came to a pedestrian promenade that appeared to connect the old wharves along the harbor. Barnaby led the way, keeping up a brisk pace.

They passed a tourist restaurant, then the Boston Marriott Long Wharf hotel, then more restaurants. Up ahead, Boston Harbor was a dark, gunmetal gray. Lexy noticed a boat marina off to the left. With December approaching, most of the slips were empty. She could smell a rank fish odor.

"John Singleton Copley grew up here," said Barnaby as they passed the Custom House.

Increasingly nervous, Macaulay just wanted to get off the street to plan their next move. They were walking past a granite-and-brick building that looked like a small warehouse, when Barnaby suddenly turned toward it and descended a set of stone steps.

A solid steel door met them at the bottom. It had no knob or handle. Barnaby pulled a set of keys from within the folds of his nightshirt and inserted one of them into the tumbler of a dead bolt. Unlocked, the door swung open and he led them inside.

A stone staircase rose up through an arched brick corridor to the next level. Barnaby kept going to the third floor and then headed down a windowless passageway until he arrived at another steel door and inserted a second key.

"My personal lair," said Barnaby as he stepped through the opening.

Inside, it was black as a crypt until he turned on a series of overhead lights, bathing the enormous brick-walled chamber in bright light. About fifty feet by fifty feet in area, it had a twenty-foot ceiling and rough-hewn oak beams that arched across the whole expanse. Window openings that once looked out over the harbor were clad with iron shutters.

"This location must have cost a fortune," said Lexy.

"My second wife was a Carnegie," said Barnaby. "She breathed money from the womb. It had no importance to her. When she asked me for a divorce, this place was a parting gift."

"If your name is on the deed, the people who tracked

us to your apartment will track us here," said Macaulay. "They're securing all of your personal information as we speak. With the resources of the White House security apparatus behind them, we probably have less than ten minutes to get out of here."

"Relax," said Barnaby. "It's still in her name, one of a hundred properties owned by her trust. I never bothered to change it, and no other soul has been within these walls in ten years. It is solely a place for me to work without distraction. There isn't even a telephone here. They won't find us."

One quarter of the loft was living space. The kitchen area was equipped with commercial appliances and a granite-surfaced island with sinks and work spaces. Copper pots and pans hung from an iron rack. Nearby, an elevated sleeping loft constructed from raw timbers stretched along the outer wall, adorned with sheepskin coverlets. Beneath it, a doorway led into a small guest bedroom.

"A Viking sleeping pallet," said Lexy admiringly. It was not only a man cave, she thought. In many respects, it could have been the lair of a Norseman of old.

The next section looked like the joint laboratories of a scientist and a pathologist, with traditional Bunsen burners, vats of acid, and jars full of chemicals interspersed with forceps, clamps, bone drills, and chisels on a long workbench.

The third quarter consisted of a digital photography and computer lab, with printers, cameras, recorders, and other equipment sitting under a seventy-two-inch flat-screen television monitor.

Macaulay now understood why there was nothing related to the Norsemen in Barnaby's Brattle Street apartment. It was all here. The last section was Barnaby's Norse library, with documents, books, diaries, and letter folders stacked almost floor to ceiling. A carved trestle table was covered with old vellum manuscripts and rune tablets. Mounted on the wall was an assemblage of Viking swords, tools, shields, knives, and other equipment.

Lexy began examining one of the vellum manuscripts as Barnaby took Macaulay back to the kitchen and filled a teapot with cold water. Going over to the deep freezer, he pulled out a large stoneware tureen and set it on the granite countertop to thaw.

"We could live here comfortably for a month without leaving," said Barnaby. Raising his voice to be heard across the room, he called out, "Let's get to work, Dr. Vaughan."

THIRTY-SIX

30 November
SB-18
U.S. Capitol
Washington, DC

When Jessica Birdwell's cell phone began vibrating on her belt clip, the deputy Homeland Security adviser was giving a top secret briefing to the chairman of the Senate Intelligence Committee in his hideaway office in the depths of the U.S. Capitol building.

"It's Ira Dusenberry, Senator," she said. "I need to take the call."

"Jess," she said into the phone.

"Where are you?" Dusenberry demanded. "All hell has broken loose."

"I'm up on the hill," she said.

"So am I," growled Dusenberry, "and Ad Kingship is on his way up here from the FBI building. Meet me in the senate majority leader's conference room as soon as you can get here."

"Check," she said, ending the call.

She apologized for having to cut the briefing short and headed upstairs through the labyrinth of underground corridors. Dusenberry and Kingship were waiting for her in the majority leader's office.

"Jim Langdon has been shot and killed," said Dusenberry without any preliminaries.

"My God," said Kingship.

"How did it . . . What . . . ?" blurted Jessica.

"Jim and a young FBI field agent from the Portland office flew up to Bangor to meet the plane carrying Macaulay and an archaeologist named Alexandra Vaughan," said Dusenberry. "In response to Jim's request for a protective cordon, the county sheriff's office ringed the private aviation terminal with deputies. The four of them then went up to a conference room to get statements. From there on, it's all conjecture. Two hours after they went up, the senior deputy sheriff knocked on the door of the conference room and no one answered."

"Why did it take him so long?" asked Jess.

"The private terminal had been shut down by a snowstorm and was deserted. Jim had told the deputy to wait until the statements were completed, which he said could take quite a while. When the deputy finally decided something might be wrong and entered the room, Jim and this agent, Gallagher, were lying dead on the floor. Macaulay and Vaughan were missing. We don't have ballistics yet, but it looks like Jim was shot twice with Gallagher's pistol and Gallagher was killed with Jim's gun."

"That doesn't mean they fired the bullets," said Kingship, his voice rising.

"No," agreed Dusenberry.

"What else do we have?" asked Jess.

"A video camera was set up on the table to record their statements, but there was no disc drive in it," said Dusenberry. "Also Jim's credentials and his iPad were missing. Whoever killed him presumably took them."

"Who is handling the investigation at this point?" asked Jess.

"The bureau," said Kingship. "We'll take it over as a national security matter, and our forensic team can be there in a couple hours. We should have a plausible reconstruction of what took place by tomorrow."

"We need an immediate and comprehensive background check on Macaulay and the archaeologist," said Jessica. "I know he's a retired air force brigadier, but he could be suffering from some post-traumatic stress condition; he could be psychopathic; he could be anything, including a mass murderer."

"What motive would he have had to kill our agents?" asked Dusenberry. "He was seeking federal protection from the people who wiped out Hancock's team in Greenland."

"All we have to go on so far is the story Macaulay told Mark Devlin at Anschutz in Dallas," said Kingship. "What if it's all a lie?"

"So we can't rule out anything at this point," said Dusenberry. "It's also possible that the people who did this somehow got word of Macaulay's and Vaughan's arrival in Bangor and went after them, killing Jim and the FBI agent in the process. Macaulay could be dead by now too."

"There's one more piece of information that may be relevant to what we're dealing with," said Kingship. "Our

Boston office reported that early this morning a group of men armed with suppressed assault rifles entered an apartment house near Harvard Square in Cambridge and terrorized several of the residents. Their apparent target was a Harvard professor who lived on the top floor."

"Half the street gangs in the country are armed with assault rifles and machine guns," said Jessica.

"The professor was identified as an English expat named Barnaby Finchem, and he is apparently a leading authority on Viking archaeology. Alexandra Vaughan received her doctorate in Norse archaeology from Harvard."

Dusenberry took it in.

"Where is Finchem now?" asked Jessica.

"None of the victims knows what happened to him. The armed men were inside less than ten minutes, just long enough to search his apartment and carry out a computer and several boxes of unidentified material."

"Any description of the men?"

"They wore masks. According to one witness, two of the men had European accents."

"That's a big help."

"So . . . what does all this tell us?" said Dusenberry.

"One possibility is that they're kidnapping or murdering renowned archaeologists who have expertise in Norse history," said Jessica, "which brings us back to what happened on the Greenland ice cap."

"We have a team in place up there right now," said Dusenberry. "They reached the coordinates supplied by Anschutz and have discovered traces of an encampment at the site. They're working in total darkness and have requested more staging equipment to broaden the search.

I informed the president and he authorized me to do whatever it takes to locate Hancock and his party."

"Here's another possibility," said Kingship. "Macaulay and Vaughan escaped from whatever occurred up there in Bangor. Not knowing whom they could trust, they drove to Boston to seek refuge from her mentor, Finchem."

"Or maybe they went to Boston to eliminate Finchem," said Jessica.

"That's possible too," agreed Dusenberry.

"It could be just a dispute over an archaeological discovery," said Jessica. "I know John Lee Hancock was a friend of the president's, but that shouldn't trigger the same response as tracking down a suicide bomber with a nuclear bomb in his suitcase."

"Either way, we need to find them," said Dusenberry. "Suggestions?"

Kingship scrolled down his iPad.

"I can put out an APB for both Macaulay and Vaughan as persons of interest to all the law enforcement agencies in New England," he said. "The bureau can also compile a list of Macaulay's and Vaughan's family members, friends, and business associates in case they try to reach out to them. We'll also gather the data on their credit card records, cell phone numbers, and bank information."

"If they're on the run, they're not likely to use their credit cards to help us track them," said Jessica.

"Who knows where they'll slip up?" responded Kingship. "With all the surveillance technology at our disposal, it isn't easy to disappear these days."

"As soon as we're finished here," said Dusenberry, "I'll order the NSA to demand video from the TSA of every transit facility in New England for the last twenty-four hours, and then place NSA agents with the subjects' photographs in positions to monitor airports, concourses, train stations, and bus and metro terminals going forward. All those facilities are now equipped with cameras that provide sequential overlapping fields of vision. Incidentally, did anyone bother to ask for video from the Bangor private terminal or its parking lot? Unless the snow blotted out the coverage, we might be able to get the license plate number of the vehicle they used to leave the airport. Anything else?"

"If Macaulay and Vaughan have gone to ground in the Boston area, Finchem could be the key to their whereabouts," said Kingship. I would recommend we identify and track all of his family, friends, and colleagues . . . all of his students too, or at least the current ones."

"He probably has hundreds of them," said Jessica. "That would shift an enormous amount of manpower from other priorities."

"We have the manpower if you don't," said Kingship, "and a lot of them are sitting on their ass. If nothing else, this will be good practice. Once we have the names, we'll monitor their cell phones, e-mails, Facebook postings, and everything else they do."

"You're talking about hundreds of people who have no connection to this," said Jessica. "What about First Amendment rights?"

"We're covered under Section 215 of the Patriot Act," said Dusenberry. "For our purposes, our three subjects of interest have triggered the tangibility requirement relevant to a terrorism investigation. Let's get going."

THIRTY-SEVEN

Barnaby flipped the switch that turned on a bank of television monitors in his computer lab. After inserting Falconer's memory card into the port of a digital reading device, he downloaded the material on the card onto two laptop computers on the console table.

Lexy sat down in front of one of them as he began projecting the photographs onto the seventy-two-inch flat-screen television monitor mounted above the table on the brick wall.

She had expected to see a succession of photographs of the Viking cave, but the first set of images consisted of a video sequence apparently filmed in a hotel room in which a red-headed woman was performing sex on the man holding the camera.

"Our late young Casanova, Dr. Falconer, I presume," said Barnaby.

"Let's move on," said Lexy.

The next set of images included still shots taken by Falconer aboard the helicopter on his way to the Greenland base camp. There were candid views of Sir Dorian and Hjalmar Jensen, followed by several of Hancock and Macaulay. The final series of shots began with a view of the ice-covered entrance to the deep cave.

"Here's what we're looking for," said Lexy.

Falconer had filmed close-ups of the faces of all the Viking corpses, followed by shots of their equipment and clothing, and then more than a dozen photographs of the rune tablet from different angles.

"He obviously wanted to make sure he had it all," said Barnaby.

To Macaulay, the crude rune markings looked like nothing but little stick figures intersected with horizontal dashes and circles. There were twelve separate lines of them, each one full of the incomprehensible symbols.

Barnaby joined Lexy at the console table in front of the television monitors and began furiously typing on his laptop. A moment later, the larger television monitor above them lit up with a brilliantly clear image of the complete text of the stonecutter's inscription.

Three smaller flat-screen television monitors were mounted beneath the big one. As Barnaby continued typing, a spate of English words began to appear on the small screen to the left.

"I'll use this one for my first take at a translation of each passage," said Barnaby to Lexy. "You'll have the middle screen for your interpretation. Once we're agreed on the exact wording of a passage, we'll project the final cut onto the third screen."

Macaulay looked on with fascination as they began trading thoughts on possible definitions and meanings for the first row of symbols. To Macaulay, they might as well have been hoofprints around a muddy water hole in west Texas.

"Definitely early eleventh century," said Barnaby. "The ancient futhork with a few added wrinkles."

"Wrinkles?" asked Macaulay.

"Each early stonecutter had his own personal style, unique to his training and experience," said Barnaby, "just like the early telegraphers when they were mastering the Morse code."

"These first lines are his impressions of Vinland," said Lexy.

"Agreed," said Barnaby as they both continued typing their translations.

The wild beasts feared us were the first words to make it to the third screen.

"Why would he have written that?" asked Macaulay.

"It means that the animals in Vinland had already been hunted and were afraid of man," said Barnaby, "which means that other hunters had already been there. In Greenland, wild animals were unafraid when the Norsemen first arrived. Until recently, that same phenomenon was true in the Galápagos."

Every few minutes, Lexy or Barnaby would get up from the computer console to go over to his library to consult one of the vellum manuscripts on the big walnut refectory table.

"He begins the saga of the voyage home on the third line," said Barnaby after about half an hour.

We have come through the tempest and survived, wrote Barnaby on his screen.

"Not quite," said Lexy. "*Tempest* is from Vulgar Latin *tempesta*, an alteration of the Latin *tempestas*, season. It's thirteenth century."

We have come through the storm and survived, wrote Lexy on her screen.

"Agreed," said Barnaby.

Seas like mountains . . . hull damaged, next made it to the final screen, followed by *landed small island*.

Klief, wrote Lexy at that point.

"Old Norse," agreed Barnaby. "A rugged shoreline with cliffs."

Macaulay was watching both screens when he felt the floor beneath his feet begin to tremble, and a thunderous noise penetrated the thick fortresslike outer walls of the building.

"A helicopter," said Macaulay, "flying very low along the wharf."

"What time is it?" asked Barnaby.

Macaulay gave him the time.

"Could be anything from our erstwhile mayor giving a tour to prospective Chinese hotel developers to a TV news helicopter," said Barnaby.

"It could also be our friends," said Macaulay as the clamorous din ebbed away.

We battled a strange being of great force and strength, Lexy wrote on her screen.

"I would almost say that *strange* translates to *alien being*," she added.

"Perhaps," came back Barnaby.

"It's definitely something that none of them had ever seen before," said Lexy.

"An extraterrestrial?" suggested Macaulay.

Barnaby gave him a look of derision.

"A being different in its fundamental nature of immense force and strength," he said. "Perhaps a large wild quadruped."

Leifr lies in the hallowed place with his vanquished, wrote Lexy next.

"A grizzly bear?" offered Macaulay.

"Why don't you make yourself useful in the kitchen?" said Barnaby. "There is a large stoneware tureen of coq au vin I've already prepared in the kitchen. And decant two of the bottles of Banfi Centine you'll find in the wine closet."

"By your command, my liege," said Macaulay with an exaggerated bow before heading toward the kitchen.

"You told me he's a retired general," said Barnaby in his clipped English accent. "Now I see why."

THIRTY-EIGHT

1 December
RV *Leitstern*
North Atlantic Ocean
Nova Scotia

Hjalmar Jensen turned away from the two young women in white lab coats when the compartment door of the computer lab slid open behind them. He inwardly shuddered when he saw who it was.

"It is a great pleasure to see you again, Professor Jensen," said von Falkenberg as he entered on Steiger's arm.

Jensen felt the same stab of unreasoned apprehension he always did when in his presence, as if death were coming to visit. He was startled to see the physical change in him since their last meeting only a few months before in Stockholm. The prince's shoulders were now as scrawny as turkey wings. There was still great force in his eyes, however, and they were focused on Jensen.

"Your recent discovery in Greenland was the greatest

gift I have received since the birth of my first daughter in 1927," said von Falkenberg.

Jensen tried to smile. "It was a great gift to me too, Your Grace."

He remembered someone once telling him what the Russians had done to von Falkenberg's wife and three daughters at the end of the Second World War.

"Have you deciphered the rune stone yet?" asked the prince, joining them in front of the computer screens.

One of the large screens displayed the complete text of the stonecutter's saga, and another the passages that had been translated.

"We are making good progress," replied Jensen, "although some parts remain elusive, as you can well imagine after a thousand years."

"Which parts?" asked von Falkenberg.

Jensen deferred to the two young women.

"Let me introduce Dr. Krusa and Fraulein Johannson," said Jensen. "Both are experts in the field of runology."

Dr. Krusa briefly bowed her head.

"The first inscriptions in the saga were relatively simple," she said nervously as the prince trained his hooded blue eyes on her. "They recount that the expedition was returning from Vinland to Greenland, when a sudden storm carried them off course to a small rocky island. While their ship was being repaired, the men were attacked by something strange and very powerful. In the ensuing battle, Leifr Eriksson was mortally wounded and buried there with his vanquished enemy. Then the rest of the men departed for Greenland. There, an even greater storm carried them to their final resting place in the cave where they were found."

"And the rest of the inscriptions?"

"They provide the signposts for a future expedition to find the exact location of Eriksson's burial tomb," said Fraulein Johannson, "but those signposts existed a thousand years ago, so it will be very difficult to pinpoint them. We are now in the process of downloading topographical maps of the islands along the northeast coast of America to help in the search. Unfortunately, there are thousands of them."

It lies under shadow from the dawn, read the prince silently on one of the screens.

"You say he fought something strange and powerful?" he asked.

"Yes," added Fraulein Johannson, "an alien form of life, at least as they saw it at the time."

"The term *alien being* could well be the correct interpretation," agreed Dr. Krusa. "Possibly something from another world."

The prince laughed out loud, a tinny emanation that died a few seconds later. He motioned to Jensen to follow him a short distance across the room, out of earshot of the two women.

"I have lived ninety-five years on this earth, Herr Jensen, and have traveled to every continent in the world," he said with an attempt at a smile. "The only alien beings I have ever encountered were Zhukov's Siberians outside Moscow in December 1941. Otherwise I don't believe in aliens."

His voice was as cold as the Russian winter.

"You must do better," he went on gravely. "I have put great faith in you as someone who can help us to restore the Ancient Way to its exalted glory, to bring about the new dawn of our common heritage. With this discovery, you now carry a great weight on your shoulders. In Leifr's DNA lies the true God particle."

"I understand, Your Grace," said Jensen.

"I only hope my confidence is not misplaced," said the prince.

Jensen noted the subtle change in his eyes as the prince implied that his services might no longer be needed at some point.

"I am also aware that others may share the same knowledge we do," said von Falkenberg. "We cannot allow someone else to get there first."

"As you know, runology is not my field of specialization," said the Norwegian haltingly. "Dr. Krusa and Fraulein Johannson have been very helpful, but . . ."

He paused as if unsure whether to continue.

"Say it," demanded von Falkenberg.

"I must say that we might enjoy quicker success if Dr. Finchem or Dr. Vaughan could be convinced to work with us," said Jensen. "They are the best in the world in this field."

"Our friends are searching for them now to bring them to you," said the prince. "In the meantime, you will have to do your best. Time is not on our side."

He suddenly pitched over as if his stomach had cramped. Steiger moved to steady him.

"I will do my best, Your Grace," said Jensen, watching the old man's face turn ashen white.

THIRTY-NINE

Barnaby pushed his massive bulk back from the kitchen table.

"You heated that coq au vin very well, General," he said, heading over to his cigar humidor. "I think I can trust you with washing the dishes."

"I'll try to prove worthy, my lord," said Macaulay.

Barnaby's lair had proved to be a temporary sanctuary, but Macaulay knew it was only a matter of time before they were traced. Hundreds of people with sophisticated surveillance and intelligence-gathering equipment were searching for them by now, and they would soon find the lead they needed.

"We now know that Eriksson and his men fought something strange and powerful on the small island," said Lexy, "and that Eriksson was buried there in an underground tomb."

"Where is 'there'?" asked Macaulay.

"That's the heart of it. We have to make sense of those ancient clues in a modern context," Lexy said. "But we'll do it."

"That's why Langdon had orders not to kill you," said Macaulay. "They want your help in deciphering the tablet."

"Which also explains why they came for Barnaby before they could have known we were even there," she said. "If we can find the answers before they do, we have a chance to stop them."

"What now?" asked Macaulay.

"There are ten thousand islands from Massachusetts to Maine," said Barnaby. "In order to narrow the hunt, we must first divine the starting point of their return voyage from Vinland. The stonecutter wrote that they sailed for a full day and part of one night before encountering the storm. That suggests they were at sea for at least eighteen hours before the storm drove them onto the island. Knowing where they started from would greatly narrow the possibilities."

"In Greenland, Sir Dorian made the case to Mr. Hancock that Vinland was somewhere along the Massachusetts coast," said Lexy. "I don't think he was convinced."

"I'm not either," said Macaulay. "So grapes grew there in abundance and cattle were able to find food all winter long because the grass didn't die. That could be anyplace in the northeast. Why not New Hampshire or Maine as the starting point?"

"The oldest surviving record of Vinland's location can be found in the *Descriptio insularum Aquilonis*, which was written by Adam of Bremen seventy-five years after

Eriksson discovered it," said Barnaby, "but his descriptions obviously haven't convinced you."

"Or most other archaeologists, from what I gather," said Macaulay. "There's a lot riding on these questions, not the least being our lives."

"The most convincing evidence of Vinland's location is totally scientific," said Barnaby. "I was planning to deliver a paper on my findings next month to the British Archaeological Society."

"Go ahead."

"*Sol hafdi par dagmalastad ok eyktarstad um skamdegi,*" he said.

Macaulay looked back at him blankly.

"Those are the exact words from the saga of Eriksson's first voyage to Vinland and they roughly translate into this: On the shortest day in the winter, the sun was already up when they ate their *dagmalastad*, or breakfast meal, and the sun hadn't yet set when they were eating their *eyktarstad*, or supper."

"How the hell do you know when the goddamn Vikings ate their supper a thousand years ago?" said an exasperated Macaulay. "Maybe the old ones ate the early-bird special at five o'clock sharp."

"Not very amusing, but it's a fair question," said Barnaby. "The Norsemen had no clocks, so they constructed cairns of stone that could accurately reflect the times of the day. There were specific markers for the *dagmalastad* and the *eyktarstad*. In the earliest Icelandic ecclesiastical code, it was *eykt* when *utsudrs-ett* was divided into three and the sun had passed through two divisions and still had one to go."

"We all knew that," said Macaulay with sarcasm.

"There is a point to this," said Barnaby, "and it's worth trying to explain it to you."

Lexy attempted to ease Macaulay's confusion.

"The Norsemen divided the horizon into eight parts, each having an arc of forty-five degrees," she went on. "*Utsudr-ett* was the octant of the horizon that has south-west in the middle, the arc being between south twenty-two and a half degrees west to sixty-seven and a half degrees west. *Eyktarstad* is at the azimuth when the sun has passed through two-thirds of this octant and has one to go. Now do you understand?"

"Just like the Rosetta stone," he said, shaking his head.

Lexy held up one of the vellum manuscripts from the library.

"The astronomer Geelmuyden calculated that in the first part of the eleventh century, the latitude where the sun would set at *eyketarstad* on the shortest day of the year would be forty-nine degrees fifty-five minutes."

"Maybe it's beginning to make sense," said Macaulay.

"In the first saga, Eriksson wrote that the sun had not set at *eyktarstad*, but rather was still shining," said Barnaby, taking over again, "which means that the actual setting of the sun took place several degrees beyond his *eyktarstad*. Assuming a five-degree difference in the azimuth, a very conservative estimate, the latitude at which the sun set in Vinland in 1005 would be about forty-two degrees. Do you know what lies along the forty-second parallel?"

"Japan," said Macaulay. "I was stationed there for two years."

"Very good, General. In that hemisphere it would be the island of Hokkaido. What about this hemisphere?"

"Massachusetts?" said Macaulay.

"Excellent. Cape Cod, to be specific," said Barnaby.

"Okay, I give up," said Macaulay. "Leif and his boys sailed from Cape Cod. I can see them now."

"We now have to dissect the rest of the clues," said Barnaby.

"I'll focus on something equally important like doing the dishes," said Macaulay.

"Each to our own talents," said Barnaby.

Ten minutes later, Macaulay could hear them working again.

"*Hvalr*, I believe," said Lexy.

"I agree," said Barnaby. "I make it *beneath the hump*. . . . No . . . *under the tail*," said Barnaby.

"Could he have died fighting a whale?" asked Lexy.

"The Norsemen saw plenty of whales at sea," said Barnaby. "They would not have seen one as a strange being. Let's try the next passage."

Five by five squared, wrote Lexy on her screen.

"Would they have been familiar with the square root formula?" Barnaby asked.

Lexy nodded.

"The knowledge is at least as old as the *Sulba Sutras* in ancient India," she said. "The Egyptians were extracting square roots four thousand years ago."

Macaulay put the clean dishes on the drain board and dried his hands. Checking the time on his wristwatch, he went to the walk-in closet under the Viking sleeping loft and pulled out a hooded snorkel coat. Macaulay couldn't wait much longer or the streets would empty out, and he wanted to mix in with a crowd.

The safest option for the call to Tommy Somervell was

to steal a cell phone on the street, but there was always the risk of being caught or even photographed by a bystander with another cell phone. With Christmas coming, a shopping mall would give him the most cover. He decided to look for a pay phone some distance from the lair.

He debated whether to tell them he was leaving and decided it would only lead to serious anxiety on Lexy's part. She had enough to focus on with the rune tablet. Picking up Barnaby's keys, he silently slipped out through the steel entrance door.

FORTY

1 December
Benjamin Franklin Mall
Boston, Massachusetts

Macaulay quickly scanned the brightly lit interior promenade. The mall was decorated for Christmas and packed
with shoppers, mostly women and children, surging along
in both directions, packages and shopping bags in hand.
The mall's sound system pounded out a rap version of
"Jingle Bell Rock."

He had walked more than forty blocks from the Long
Wharf, and no one had given him a second look. Aside
from a street person begging for a handout while he was
changing a ten-dollar bill into quarters at a self-service car
wash, Macaulay had spoken to no one. With the fur-lined
hood of the snorkel coat covering most of his face, there
was no way a surveillance camera could identify him.

Once inside the mall, he had joined the heaving mass
until he came to a small bank of pay phones opposite a
North Face outlet. After punching in Tommy Somervell's

cell phone number, he inserted the money demanded by the recorded voice.

Somervell was at his desk in his small office in the CIA library annex in Langley, reading the latest intelligence summary and waiting for the call. Putting down his mug of coffee, he answered on the second ring.

"It's me," said Macaulay.

"You have certainly poked your stick into the wasp's nest, dear boy."

"How bad is it?"

"They have invoked the Patriot Act on you," said Somervell. "Along with Dr. Vaughan and Professor Finchem, you're being sought as part of an international terrorism investigation. They've gone all in . . . FBI, Homeland Security, local law enforcement, even private contract operatives. And that doesn't include the other side."

"Anything else?"

"Most of their assets are focused in the Boston area," said Somervell. "They're monitoring airports, parking lots, train stations, bus and metro terminals. If you're still there, find secure transportation and get out before they find you."

Macaulay turned to glance back down the promenade.

In the blur of the crowd, a tall, well-built man with silvery hair in a camel overcoat was standing in a line of shoppers waiting to get into a Victoria's Secret outlet. The man appeared to be looking in his direction before his gaze moved away.

"Have you found out who ordered Langdon to meet us in Bangor?"

"The decision came from a hybrid national security

team in the White House. Ira Dusenberry chairs it. . . .
Word is he will be the next national security adviser to the
president. The other two are Addison Kingship and Jessica Birdwell. Kingship is senior FBI. Langdon worked
under him at one time. Birdwell is a rising star at Homeland Security. If there is a mole, it's likely to be one of
them."

"Try to find out," said Macaulay.

"I will, dear boy. I would offer you a safe house, but I
can't tip my hand while looking up their skirts."

"I understand," said Macaulay.

"You should know that one of my covert contacts in
Paris suggests that the Ancient Way people might have
something big planned," said Somervell. "No idea what
at this point. I'm working on that too."

Macaulay looked down the promenade again. The line
of shoppers had disappeared into the Victoria's Secret
store. The man in the brown suit was still there, talking
into a cell phone.

"I think somebody made me, Tommy," said Macaulay,
hanging up.

He joined the slowly moving tide of shoppers on the
promenade and headed away from the brown suit. Stepping up the pace, he passed two young women pushing
baby strollers and looked back. The tall man was coming,
his head craning above the rest.

Macaulay turned into a Patagonia outlet, walking toward the rear of the store. He glanced back as he neared
a bank of changing rooms. The man was moving quickly
to close the gap.

Beyond the changing rooms was a steel door with a
red sign above it reading EMERGENCY EXIT ONLY. When

he shoved it open, an exterior alarm went off. He looked down at an iron-railed concrete staircase that led to a loading dock.

Shutting the door again, he ducked into the last changing booth and closed the curtain. A few moments later, the sound of the alarm became louder again as someone else opened the emergency door.

Macaulay slipped out of the changing booth. The tall man's back was framed in the open doorway. He was holding a silenced semiautomatic pistol in his right hand and looking down the staircase.

Macaulay chopped down on the wrist of his gun hand while driving his shoulder into the man's back. The pistol fell as he went headfirst down the staircase. Macaulay picked up the gun and shoved it inside his belt before closing the steel door. As he headed back past the changing area, the store manager confronted him in the hallway.

"What's going on here?" she angrily demanded. "I've already called the police."

"There's a man out on the loading dock with a gun," he said, watching her anger turn to alarm. "Don't open it until the police get here."

Once on the promenade again, he examined all the faces surging past him, looking for another one that didn't belong, offering everyone a grim smile to show he was feeling the Christmas spirit.

FORTY-ONE

The prince lay huddled in his berth as Steiger administered a dose of morphine into his bloodstream. It was uncomfortably warm in the stateroom, but von Falkenberg still felt chilled.

The cancer that had been held in check for three years was now ravaging his vital organs, his once-impregnable vitality ebbing away to little more than a flickering candle. Getting up from the berth, he pulled the purple and red satin dressing gown tighter around his chest.

There was a light knock at the door and Steiger went to answer it. A tall man wearing a white lab coat was standing in the passageway next to the Lynx, who was guarding the compartment.

"May I have a few minutes with His Grace?" asked the man.

"Please come in, Per," said von Falkenberg, sitting up and beckoning him forward. "It is always a pleasure to see you."

In truth, the church owed the greatest debt to Dr. Per Larsen and his research team of Jurgens, Klaus, and young Ainslie, the Britisher whose parents had been murdered by Hezbollah gunmen in Beirut. It would not have been possible to launch Operation Tjikko without Larsen's undeniable genius.

The prince remembered his first meeting with the penniless young geneticist in his unheated laboratory over the auto repair shop in Oslo fifteen years earlier. The visit had been arranged by a hereditary biologist who followed the Order, after Per's initial breakthrough while experimenting with rhesus monkeys. Thanks to his subsequent research, they now had the tools to shape the future destiny of mankind.

Even taking into account his own physical disintegration, the prince was surprised at Per's physical condition. Since their last meeting six months ago, his hair had gone gray and there were wrinkled pouches under his eyes.

"I think you have been working too hard, Doctor," said the prince. "You must make time for adequate rest and relaxation. We are counting on you as we move forward with Tjikko."

"I am here to ask you to grant me a great favor, Your Grace," said Larsen.

"Of course," said the old man. "We are all in your debt. Please sit down. Would you like some coffee? A stronger stimulant?"

"No, Your Grace," he said, sitting down at the stateroom table. "I am here to ask you to stop the Tjikko operation."

"But why?" asked von Falkenberg. "Is it a question of the soundness of your science?"

"No, Your Grace," he said, pausing to collect his thoughts. "It is the . . . magnitude of what we are about to do."

"Your conscience?" asked the prince.

Larsen nodded. Von Falkenberg watched the scientist's eyes fill.

"I am haunted by its being the end of millions of unborn children . . . and its being my work that will bring this about."

The prince deliberated on how to respond. Per Larsen was a good man, a thoroughly decent man. How could he explain to him that goodness alone could not bring an end to man's depravity and brutality? He thought of the commando named Joachim who was guarding the door. The one they called the Lynx. That one is of the beast, he thought. In him there is no goodness at all. But both types of men would be needed in the coming battle for the human race.

"Do you know why we have called it Operation Tjikko?" asked von Falkenberg.

The scientist shook his head.

"Tjikko is the name of a Norway spruce tree in the mountains of Sweden that is believed to be the oldest tree in the world."

"I don't think I understand, Your Grace," said Larsen.

"Have you ever seen the results of a ravaging forest fire?" said von Falkenberg, "the burned-out devastation that replaces a green and seemingly healthy forest? It is as ugly as anything one could imagine, but all forests reach a point where they need revitalization, and the only natural path to provide this is through an all-engulfing fire. At first the landscape is hideous, but soon new, healthy seedlings give it life again, and the forest is on its way to again becoming strong and vibrant. We are bringing that same purging fire to a depraved world."

"It is my research that will be used to bring the fire, Your Grace," said Larsen. "I never anticipated this when I unlocked the key to genetically breaching the autoimmune system by race."

Von Falkenberg knew he hadn't reached him. Perhaps it would be impossible.

"How old are you, Doctor?" he asked.

"Thirty-seven."

"And you are married, I believe."

"Yes, Your Grace. We have three daughters."

"As I once did," said the prince. "What kind of world do you want your daughters to grow up in?"

"A safe world," said the scientist. "A peaceful world."

"As do I and all of us who follow the path of the Ancient Way," said von Falkenberg. "Our goal is to build that world for your daughters as well as the generations of the Larsen family to come. That is what is at stake, Per, the world itself."

"I can't help feeling guilt at what we are about to do," he came back.

"This is to be expected," said von Falkenberg. "You are experiencing the same feelings as many of the scientists who first released energy from the atom. Nothing so important comes without responsibility."

"It is a responsibility I do not wish to have," said

Larsen. "I can only ask you to prevent this from happening."

"How can I convince you to be proud of this achievement?" said the prince. "You have accomplished something that will guarantee a turning point in the history of man. Like you, I regret that lives will be lost, but our one and true purpose, Per, is to save humankind from its own destruction. We are not fanatics. . . . We are fighting to save the human race."

For the first time, Larsen nodded at him in possible understanding.

"Look around you, Per. In Europe, we have watched the exponential growth of teeming slums in the great cities like Berlin, Paris, Stockholm, and London, along with growing lawlessness, street violence, suicide bombings, and anarchy. Across Europe and the United States, Islamist fanatics continue to carry out massacres of innocent people such as those who died in the World Trade Center attacks. And these same fanatics are at work to build nuclear weapons that will destroy the so-called infidel nations."

"I agree that they must be stopped," said Larsen. "But . . ."

"And what about Equatorial Africa? For hundreds of years it has run red with the blood of millions of innocent people from ongoing tribal warfare, their embrace of genocide, the systematic rape of millions of women, ignorance, slavery, and greed. Tell me. What has changed? Nothing. It is exactly the same today, except that the African race is spreading its depravity to the rest of the world."

The scientist appeared to be looking at him with some degree of understanding.

"A long winter is coming, Per, a winter that portends potential disaster for the world as we have known it," said von Falkenberg. "Just as we all must die, so too can planets die. On any clear night, we can watch the falling of stars that are billions of years old. Nothing is permanent except our place in Valhalla."

The prince felt a sudden stab of pain in his abdomen, but it was important that he finish.

"It is natural for you to fear what is coming, but it is by no means without precedent. The plague of Justinian killed twenty-five million people in the sixth century. In 1347, the Black Death, carried by fleas on rats, killed a third of the world population. Smallpox and tuberculosis have led to millions of deaths since then."

"But none of them were genetically engineered to eliminate specific target groups," said Larsen.

"That is true, but typically they took the weak and infirm along with the parasites who have always fed on the corpus of humanity. This will simply be the latest in a line of diseases and viruses that provide a course correction for civilization."

"You make it all sound so noble, Your Grace," said Larsen.

"Tjikko will be focused on those who would hinder human progress, rather than enhance it," said von Falkenberg. "Our goal isn't mass extermination, but instead to take measured but significant steps to affect the birthrates of those races that would destroy us, while providing our own people with a chance to survive in the future."

The scientist nodded again, this time with less uncertainty.

"You must continue to have faith in the Ancient Way,

Per, the faith to know that we work for the deliverance of humankind from cataclysmic destruction, and for building a future world for your children until the day in the future when we reach out to the stars the same way Leif Eriksson once explored the unknown here on Earth. It is our destiny," said the prince as another wave of excruciating pain flowed through him.

"The Nordic race," said the scientist.

"Of which you are a vital part, Per," concluded von Falkenberg. "Thanks to you, the human race will emerge ever stronger."

The scientist looked momentarily invigorated, but only time would tell.

"We will talk again after this evening's briefing by the Tjikko operational team," said the prince, standing up from the table.

"Yes, Your Grace. Thank you for giving me this time," said Larsen before bowing to the old man and leaving.

"Bring me brandy," said von Falkenberg as soon as he was gone.

FORTY-TWO

1 December
The Long Wharf
Boston, Massachusetts

It was almost midnight when Macaulay got back to the wharf. No one was lingering near the downstairs entrance to Barnaby's building or on the stone staircase leading up to the third-floor corridor. He was inserting the key into Barnaby's dead bolt when the lock was suddenly released from inside and the door swung open.

Lexy stood there, a mixture of outrage and fear in her violet eyes. Barnaby was looming behind her, wielding a Viking axe in his right hand, his Medusa thatch of gray hair erupting in all directions. They had obviously seen him through the peephole in the door.

"Where did you go?" Barnaby demanded.

Macaulay was forced to smile at the sight of the huge old man with his axe.

"We were low on dish soap," he said.

Macaulay thought Lexy was about to hit him. A moment later she was in his arms.

"You're an idiot," she said.

While she made coffee, Macaulay told them what had happened at the mall.

"Well, now they know we're still in Boston," said Barnaby when he was finished. "I hope it was worth it."

"We have to get out in the morning anyway," said Macaulay. "Have you made progress with the translation?"

"The short answer is that we are looking for an island off the midcoast of Maine," said Lexy. "Leif Eriksson lies in a burial vault there sealed with beeswax in an underground island cavern."

"Beeswax?" repeated Macaulay.

"Yes, beeswax," said Barnaby. "Undisturbed, it is as good a sealant as lead or cement. They recently discovered a six-thousand-year-old cracked tooth from a Neolithic man filled with beeswax. It's very durable."

"Where would the Vikings have found beeswax?" asked Macaulay.

"They were probably bringing it back to Greenland along with the casks of honey they had collected in Vinland," said Lexy.

"Amazing," said Macaulay.

"The Norsemen were resourceful," said Barnaby, "and they had the time to construct a secure crypt. If Eriksson's body was exsanguinated from his wounds, he might well be in a state of mummified preservation to this day."

"Drained of blood," added Lexy before Macaulay asked what it meant.

"How did you narrow the island to midcoast Maine?" asked Macaulay.

Barnaby led him back to the computer lab where a nautical map of the New England coast from Massachusetts to Nova Scotia was projected on the seventy-two-inch television monitor.

"Eriksson and his men had to have sailed about a hundred fifty miles before the storm hit," said Barnaby. "It's one hundred forty miles from Cape Cod to Portland, Maine. We're presuming the storm was a nor'easter. Typically, they drive up the coast along the Gulf Stream, so it's likely the storm would have taken them to an island somewhere along here," he said, pointing to the midcoast of Maine.

"So you've made real progress," said Macaulay.

"There are forty-six hundred islands in Maine," said Lexy, hitting several keys simultaneously on her laptop.

The nautical map was replaced by dozens of contoured images of coastal islands.

"We downloaded a set of LiDAR maps integrated with three-D profiles and panchromatic imagery," she said. "We then created a computer program to generate a cross-referenced analysis of the things we know about this island, which dramatically reduced the number of targets."

Lexy brought up the list of search criteria.

"The stonecutter described it as a *small island*," said Lexy. "We decided it had to be small enough for them to take it all in visually from the sea, no longer than a mile or so in length. We know the Norsemen *filled their casks* before they left the island, which suggests it had a potable water supply. It also referenced cliffs, so we included a minimum elevation of one hundred feet."

Barnaby suddenly felt the same fluttering tremor around his heart that presaged his first attack. Light-headed, he breathed deeply several times before it slowly disappeared.

"Are you all right?" asked Lexy.

"Just tired," he said.

"Those criteria brought us down to just twenty possibilities," said Lexy, bringing up another set of island images that showed dark clefts in otherwise-solid rock walls. "And finally we know the island had to have a natural cavern of some kind, a place that would keep the body safe until their next expedition returned to bring him home. So, the last criterion was that our island have at least one or more natural caves."

Macaulay watched as three contoured shapes filled the screen, each with its latitude and longitude.

"These three are especially good possibilities," said Lexy. "The one on the left is Ragged Island, and it's in Casco Bay south of Harpswell. It meets all our programmed criteria. The one in the center is called Monhegan Island. It is twelve miles out to sea off Boothbay Harbor and reportedly has the highest cliffs on the East Coast. Captain John Smith put a settlement there in 1614 due in part to its natural aquifer. The third and last one is Great Duck, which is farther north, near Frenchman's Bay. It also has sheer cliffs and abundant water."

"I would suggest we start with Ragged," said Barnaby. "It's the closest one."

"What do we do when we get there?" asked Macaulay.

"We use our collective two and a half brains to ponder the landscape and interpret the rest of the clues," responded Barnaby.

"We'll need a car," said Macaulay ignoring the sarcasm, "and obviously a boat."

"I don't own a car," said Barnaby proudly, "but I do have ample cash to meet any contingency."

"The vehicle can't be traced to us," said Macaulay.

"What about another one from the airport?" asked Lexy.

"There are cameras everywhere at Logan and they're all being monitored. We would be identified before we ever got out of the parking lot."

"I know someone who can help us with a car," said Barnaby. "No one is aware of our . . . friendship."

"If we're leaving in the morning, I think we should all get some rest," said Lexy, glancing anxiously at the old man.

"Good idea," agreed Macaulay.

As Barnaby lumbered up the stairs to his sleeping loft, Macaulay turned off the lights in the computer area and walked back to the kitchen. Lexy was pouring herself a glass of milk.

"You're hitting the hard stuff again," he said.

"You've learned another one of my secrets," she said, downing the whole glass. "I'm addicted to milk."

"I'm addicted to you," he said, taking her in his arms.

He wondered nervously whether she would turn her mouth away when he attempted to kiss her. She didn't. The kiss lasted a long time.

"There are good addictions and bad addictions," she said, smiling up at him. "You've chosen well. Now let's get some sleep."

By the time he had finished turning off the rest of the lights and came into the bedroom, Lexy was already lying under the covers in the bed, her eyes luminous in the lamplight.

"In light of your addiction and in the pursuit of science, I think we might need more skin-to-skin contact," she said.

"I thought we needed to get some sleep," he whispered, already aroused.

"You can't turn your back on science," she said.

She watched as he removed his clothes.

"Come over here," she said, her voice hoarse with urgency.

When Lexy raised the blankets, he saw she was naked. She opened her arms to embrace him. A few moments later, her lips were covering his mouth.

FORTY-THREE

2 December
RV *Leitstern*
North Atlantic Ocean
Off Bar Harbor, Maine

"Starboard twenty! Midships! Steady!" called out Captain Peter Bjorklund to the ship's coxswain as a helicopter lifted off from the ship's forward landing deck. Bjorklund glanced up to see the next chopper waiting a hundred feet above them to land.

A steady stream of important visitors had continued to arrive, and Bjorklund was grateful that the capricious North Atlantic had moderated to a whisper of its usual shrieking self.

He stared down from the bridge at the landing pad as a man in a French military uniform emerged from the newly landed helicopter and quickly crossed the landing deck to the main hatchway.

Bjorklund had found his personal salvation through the Ancient Way after losing his wife and children in an airliner crash. He had resigned his commission in the Norwegian navy after the prince personally asked him to take command of RV *Leitstern*.

He wondered what had spurred the gathering that was taking place in the ship's medical amphitheater two decks below the bridge, but he knew better than to ask. It had been made clear to him that his sole responsibility was commanding the ship.

He glanced up at the charcoal sky. It was almost one with the horizon.

A messenger called out, "Signal, sir."

Bjorklund took the message and quickly read it.

"A storm of major intensity is on its way," he said to the others on the bridge.

In his mind's eye, he could see it coming with murderous winds and possibly snow or sleet. He hoped the new arrivals gathered below would all be gone by the time it hit.

Two decks below him, the Marquess Antoinette Celeste de Villiers, the secretary-general of health of the European Union, felt a thrill of anticipation as she gazed up at the faces of the men and women surrounding her in the amphitheater.

She had become terribly seasick the previous day, but the newly calmed seas had restored both her sense of well-being and her enthusiasm for everything about to unfold.

"Welcome to you all," she said with an expansive smile.

De Villiers had met most of them during her decades of service within the international diplomatic community, but she had been stunned to discover just how many were followers of the Ancient Way.

In the first four rows, she recognized five ambassadors, three senior officials of the United Nations World Health Organization, several European generals and admirals, and a number of high-ranking ministers.

Projected on the wall-length screen behind him were the words:

OPERATION TJIKKO

"For those of you hearing the details of our operation for the first time," said de Villiers, "our goal is nothing less than restoring the stability of this earth."

Sitting alone in the top row, Johannes Prinz Karl Erich Maria von Falkenberg wondered how long he could endure the pain now raging through his intestines without crying out in agony. He sat hunched over his cane, his fingers desperately clutching its carved lion's head.

"Phase one of Operation Tjikko will begin in two days, and its impact will be felt almost everywhere in the world," said the Marquess de Villiers, pressing a button on her remote-control device.

Behind her, a high-resolution digital map of the world was projected on the massive screen, encompassing all the continents, countries, and major cities.

"You will note that the cities and regions included in phase one are offset in red," she said. "Phase two areas are identified in blue, and phase three in yellow."

"In the first round of cities, waterborne viral agents prepared by our research team will be introduced into the principal reservoirs providing their drinking water supplies. In those regions in which the population is more dispersed, such as the Middle East and China, airborne agents will be disseminated by aircraft."

Von Falkenberg knew he wouldn't live to witness the fruits of his sacred contribution to the future generations of his race. He didn't want to die. In spite of everything he had suffered during the Second World War, including the loss of his wife and daughters, the life force was still strong within him. He could still savor the joy of spontaneous laughter, the pleasure of a good book, the serenity of spring along the Rhine.

He thought of the vast fortune he had raised to make Operation Tjikko a reality. It hadn't been easy, particularly in the early years when he had made the case to donors that the future belonged to the genome. Few believed it possible, telling him it sounded like a science fiction story.

"Let us take a look at what will happen in Germany," said de Villiers, using her remote control again.

A detailed thematic map of Germany, showing population densities by regions and cities, as well as racial and ethnic concentrations, took the place of the map of the world.

"As you will note, Germany's current population is characterized by declining birthrates among Caucasians and soaring fertility rates among non-Caucasians. Although Germany is the sixteenth largest nation in the world, it has the third highest number of international migrants, nearly twenty million persons. In 1965, one of every seventy-five children in Germany was on the welfare rolls. Today it is nearly one in four. The vast majority of these are non-Caucasian peoples, with Africans being the fastest growing group, along with Turks, Arabs, Kurds, Chinese, and Latin Americans. You'll see in the following chart that the percentage of perpetrators of violent crime mirrors the same proportion of non-Caucasian peoples, principally in Berlin. It is unsustainable."

Von Falkenberg managed a weak smile as he contemplated a future in which the Fatherland would regain its rightful place as leader in the community of nations, a beacon of promise to the world.

"Simply put, the viral agents we will introduce in Germany and the other phase one regions are designed to break through the genetic defenses in non-Caucasian mothers. Although the calibration of the potential impact cannot be precise, our estimate is that approximately half of all non-Caucasian women will be unable to conceive a child after being exposed to the agents. Those already pregnant will face a significant chance of miscarriage. In a few cases, the very young may succumb as well."

A chart showing future birthrates was projected on the screen.

"In cities like Berlin, Paris, London, and New York, the result will be a dramatic reduction in the birthrates of non-Caucasian women," said de Villiers. "We anticipate a mass migration from our targeted cities of the non-Caucasian populations within two years."

One of the United Nations health officials raised his hand.

"How is Caucasian defined? Who will actually be immune from the virus?" he asked.

"Utilizing the genetic building blocks isolated by Dr. Larsen and his team, we have defined the Caucasian race for the purposes of Operation Tjikko to be made up of four subcategories—the Nordic race, the Dinaric or Epirotic race, the Alpine race, and the Mediterranean race, or any mixture of men and women within these categories," said de Villiers. "No one else will inherently possess the genetic immunity to combat the viral agents we are employing."

"What about those Caucasians whose blood was mixed with non-Caucasians, perhaps in the long-distant past?" said an ambassador.

"As I have stated, only those prospective mothers whose genetic makeup is derived entirely from those four categories will be immune," said de Villiers.

"Why won't it affect non-Caucasian adults?" asked one of the ministers.

"You'll have to ask Dr. Larsen that question," said de Villiers. "He was the man who unlocked the key to genetically breaching the autoimmune system by race, and he and his team have calibrated the formulas to accomplish the task that was laid out for them. We are not mass murderers. We are hoping to minimize any loss of life."

Von Falkenberg would not be alive to see it, but he knew he was leaving the world a better place. And when his mortal life ended, the halls of Valhalla were waiting. And Ingrid would be there along with their three daughters. He yearned to see her face again, as she had been when he last saw her, before the Russian animals had violated her.

He prayed once more that he would live long enough to kneel before the immortal remains of Leifr Eriksson, his personal divinity in the pantheon of heroes from Bjarki to

Hagbard, Ragnar, Lodbrok, and Sigurd Ring, and to know that, in the future, Leifr's DNA would complete the genetic map of his beneficiaries.

The marquess stepped toward the assembled leaders.

"When the impact of phase one is first felt, it will appear to be the latest in the long line of perplexing viruses that have always afflicted mankind, the latest being AIDS," she said. "Historically, horrific and epidemic diseases and viruses have struck with great ferocity, taking millions of lives before they are brought under control. Today, what were once cataclysmic diseases such as measles and smallpox are little more than minor afflictions. However, we are about to introduce an entity from which there is no antidote, no accommodation. Where did this affliction come from? the world will ask. We are preparing an evidentiary chain that will make the case it emanates from a spoor carried within an asteroid shower that recently landed in many parts of the world."

"Why was the Congo chosen as one of the first targets?" asked De Ruyter of the UNWHO as he looked again at the original map. "They are successfully destroying one another on their own without the use of viral agents."

"The Congo was a personal request of Prince von Falkenberg, who is so responsible for bringing about this day," said de Villiers.

Many of the dignitaries turned to look at the old man in the top row.

"We consider it to be a merciful blessing," went on the Marquess de Villiers. "As you know, the magnitude of the continuing tribal slaughter there is simply horrendous. Hundreds of thousands of women were raped there just in the last year. How many nights of sleep I have personally lost to the evil being perpetrated there, I cannot tell you. Yes, it will be a blessing."

"Will this not sow a war between the races?" asked the Swiss foreign minister. "If Caucasian mothers are not affected by the virus, won't it set off a firestorm of rage against us?"

"An excellent question," responded de Villiers. "The answer is that it will simply serve to confirm the superiority of the Caucasian race. None of us will be cheering from the sidelines as the non-Caucasian population begins to shrink across the world. To the contrary, we will publicly pledge to commit all our resources to help. After sufficient time has passed, we will introduce what in essence will be the antidote. By then, non-Caucasians who are still uncontaminated will be desperate to embrace a cure that will enable them to have a healthy baby immune from the disease. In the face of this modern plague, we will provide a cure at no cost. Of course, it will no longer matter what the genes of the parents are. We will inject a gene sequence into the embryo that will deliver a Caucasian baby."

"The genetic remapping of the world," said one of the generals with a tone of awe.

"Precisely," agreed de Villiers. "Before we break up into smaller groups to go over individual assignments, I would like to take this moment to offer our heartfelt gratitude to the man most responsible for what we are about to accomplish. I am speaking of course of Dr. Per Larsen."

The scientist was sitting in a seat at the end of the first row. When they rose as one to give him a standing ovation, he stood for a moment to gaze up at the cheering disciples. Ashen, he turned on his heel and strode out the door of the amphitheater.

When von Falkenberg tried to stand up to follow him, he found he was unable to raise himself from his seat. Even worse, he was disgusted to realize he had soiled himself in the process.

FORTY-FOUR

2 December
The Long Wharf
Boston, Massachusetts

Barnaby counted up the cash he had on hand. It came to almost fifteen thousand dollars. He divided it into three stacks and passed one to Lexy and another to Macaulay.

"In case we get split up along the way," he said.

Ten minutes later, Macaulay was standing in his hooded snorkel coat outside the basement entrance to Barnaby's lair when Delia Glantz pulled up in her cherry red Lexus LX SUV. Barnaby and Lexy were waiting just inside the door, their gear stacked behind them on the stone staircase.

Lexy had gently asked Barnaby to make himself a little less noticeable when he was dressing for the trip. After brooding for several minutes, he had reluctantly hidden some of his hair under a plaid Balmoral bonnet. Then he had put on a one-piece fleece-lined navy blue boiler suit.

"The car is almost as inconspicuous as Barnaby," said

Macaulay as he directed Delia to park the SUV between the building's four Dumpsters. While Barnaby led her aside, Lexy and Macaulay began stowing the gear in the SUV's luggage bay.

"Are you sure I can't come with you, Dr. Finchem?" said Delia.

"I'm sorry."

"I know you're in danger," she said. "I heard on the radio that your home was invaded and you were reported missing."

"You can see that's not true," he said.

Lexy climbed into the driver's seat and Macaulay joined her on the passenger side. Starting the car again, she noted that fewer than a hundred miles were registered on the odometer.

"Delia, I need you to do something very important for me," said Barnaby. "Promise me you won't tell anyone that you have lent me your car. Absolutely no one . . . You mustn't call or e-mail your parents, your friends, or any of your fellow students about me. Do you understand?"

"I understand," she said, standing on her toes to kiss him good-bye.

Barnaby began to feel his resolve weakening when Macaulay pressed the button to roll down his window and said, "We need to leave before the world comes to an end, Dr. Finchem."

Barnaby climbed sulkily into the backseat and shut the door. Delia stood watching him as Lexy put the car in gear and they headed down the wharf.

"Is that what they call mentoring one's students?" said Macaulay.

"Why don't you just shut up?" said Lexy.

Macaulay found himself wondering if she and Barnaby had once shared the same kind of relationship. He tried to rule it out of his mind as they worked their way through a small traffic jam on North Washington Street and merged onto Route 95 heading north. She kept the speed to a steady seventy-five, and an hour later they crossed the Piscataqua River Bridge at Portsmouth, New Hampshire, and headed into Maine.

"Our first objective is Ragged Island," said Barnaby, reading a collection of data from his iPad. "It's located on the edge of Eastern Casco Bay about three miles due east of Bailey Island, and its size is seventy-seven acres. It was once owned by the poet Edna St. Vincent Millay and is a traditional nesting place for eider ducks. It has potable water, orchards, pastures, some caves, and rocky elevations."

"Edna St. Vincent Millay," repeated Macaulay. "That could be a clue."

"According to my search, the closest place to charter a boat is at the southern tip of the Harpswell Peninsula," said Barnaby. "Potts Harbor Marine and Fishing Charters, it's called. 'Captain Mike Grubb at your pleasure.'"

He told Macaulay the address and asked him to plug it into the GPS system.

"I'll buy a map when we get into Maine," said Macaulay. "A GPS system is potentially traceable. Anyway, I doubt he's doing business this time of year. How many fishing charters do you think people book in December?"

"Leave that to me," said Barnaby.

Barnaby fell asleep as they drove through Brunswick. The modern amenities of Chinese restaurants, John

Deere dealerships, gas stations, and motels quickly gave way to fallow fields and pastures cloaked in the dim winter light when they turned south onto a country road. There was no traffic in either direction.

Lexy gazed at a succession of well-kept saltboxes and capes, their garden patches covered with seaweed for the winter. Some had boats lying in the driveways, draped with canvas tarps. Smoke rose from a few of the chimneys. Many were summer cottages closed up until the summer season.

Barnaby was still asleep, and his breathing was becoming increasingly labored. Lexy turned around to look at him. His color was very pale and there were dark shadows under his eyes.

"I don't think we should let him go with us," she whispered to Macaulay. "What if he has another heart attack?"

"Can you find the tomb without him?" asked Macaulay.

While pondering the question, she smelled the tang of the sea. A moment later, Barnaby stirred in the backseat.

"Alexandra," he said, "I've been pondering a few of the clues."

Macaulay was about to suggest it sounded more like snoring, but he desisted as Barnaby retrieved the translation of the rune inscription.

"It lies under shadow from the dawn," he read aloud. "At daybreak on the island we're looking for, one part of it is lit by the sun while another remains in shadow. In those first few seconds, I believe the area where the cavern entrance is located will be in shadows. Of course, the light falls differently in the winter than in spring when the storm wrecked them there, but it can't be all that different."

"Assuming the sun comes out at this time of year," said Macaulay.

"Don't be a pessimist, General," said Barnaby.

"What about *five by five squared* and *over and under?*" asked Lexy.

"I've given that thought too. I think the surviving Norsemen sealed the entrance to the cavern with slabs of rock, each of them cut roughly to five feet square. 'Over and under' suggests that there are two layers of them, one on top of the other for additional protection."

"Vertical or horizontal?" asked Lexy.

"They are lying flat," said Barnaby, his eyes closed in concentration. "If they were vertical, the evenly seamed formation would have attracted serious curiosity at some point in the last thousand years. By now the slabs would be almost interconnected with the surrounding rock formation, or possibly buried under standing water, or under soil or scrub growth. Exposed to light, however, the seams in the rock slabs will still be roughly parallel."

"I think we've arrived," said Macaulay.

The spit of land had gradually narrowed until the shoreline closed in on both sides of the car. Ahead of them, the southern tip of the peninsula ended with a long rocky ledge.

A harsh wind buffeted the SUV as Macaulay slowed down and stopped next to a wooden sign at the edge of the road that read POTTS HARBOR MARINE. Another handmade sign tacked over it read CLOSED FOR THE SEASON.

"What did I tell you?" said Macaulay.

"A minor impediment, oh ye of little faith," said Barnaby.

A two-story, cedar-shingled cottage sat by the edge of the sea at the end of the brown lawn. Barnaby could see the glow of a bare bulb shining through one of the downstairs windows.

"Wait here," he said, stepping out of the car and stretching for a few moments as a curtain of wind-driven salt spray peppered his face and boiler suit. Fully revived, he strode toward the front entrance.

Beyond the cottage, he could see a wooden pier extending into a small cove protected by a rocky ledge. Tethered to the pier was a traditional down east trawler, about thirty feet long with a wide beam and deep hull. Its superstructure was wrapped in a white canvas cocoon.

Above the front door of the cottage, a red banner proclaimed PROUD TO BE A CITIZEN OF THE RED SOX NATION. Before Barnaby could knock, the door was opened by a man in overalls. He waved him inside and shut the door.

"No need to heat the state of Maine," he said. "I saw you pull up. Who are you looking for?"

"Captain Mike Grubb," said Barnaby.

"You've found him," said the man.

Barnaby guessed he was about fifty. Short and wiry, he had narrow-set small eyes and a walrus mustache that covered most of his mouth. He led Barnaby over to a wood-burning stove in the living room and sat down in one of the sprung easy chairs, motioning Barnaby into the other. There was a bad smell in the room.

"The place isn't for sale," said Mike Grubb. "I'm doing just fine."

A coffee table near the stove was littered with the remains of a huge lobster and six empty cans of Canadian ale. A fake Christmas tree was tipped over along the rear wall.

"I'm not looking for real estate, Captain Grubb," said Barnaby. "I would like to charter your boat for a quick run out to Ragged Island."

"My ex-wife, Greta, handles all the reservations," he said. "She'll be back up here from Florida in April."

"I meant right now," said Barnaby. "This minute."

"The *Dorothy B.* is put to bed for the winter," said the little charter captain, cracking open another can of ale. He didn't offer any to Barnaby.

"I'm asking you to wake her up," said Barnaby. "I'll pay you well."

Grubb took a deep swallow and focused his bleary eyes on Barnaby.

"You with the circus or somethin'?" he asked.

"Actually, I'm a retired gynecologist," said Barnaby, "and if you don't have anything important on at the moment, I would like you to take me and my friends out to that island."

"You ain't wanted by the police?"

"Do I look like I'm wanted by the police?" responded Barnaby, removing his Balmoral bonnet. "I'll tell you the truth. Have you ever watched the new reality show *Incredible Race to Getaway Island*?"

"I think so," said Grubb, scratching his crew-cut hair.

"We're one of the teams," said Barnaby, "and there's a big prize for the winner. I'll give you two thousand dollars in cash to get us out there."

Grubb stoked the fire with an iron poker, glancing out the back window of the living room at the surging black sea. Reaching to a wall switch next to his chair, he turned on a dock light that bathed his trawler in light.

"The *Dorothy B.*'s your classic down east design, wide-beamed and stable in a rough sea like we got now. She'll do sixteen knots in a heartbeat and . . ."

"I don't need to buy the boat, Captain Grubb," interrupted Barnaby. "I want to pay you a king's ransom to rent it for the afternoon. Time is of the essence. There's a rival group on the show trying to beat us out there right now. Are you a man of action or not?"

The wily charter captain kept shaking his head.

"It's a good five miles out there," he said. "I'd have to swing all the way south around Bailey Island before heading out into the open sea. I wouldn't do it for less than three thousand."

"Fifteen hundred now and the rest upon our return," said Barnaby, pulling a wad of cash out of the breast pocket of the boiler suit.

"Be a bit wicked going out, but we'd have a following sea coming back," said Grubb, counting the money.

Barnaby was walking across the yard to the car, when he felt a searing bolt of pain in his chest, as if someone had suddenly strapped it in a vise. Lexy was standing by the edge of the road, watching him come. He saw the terrified look on her face as he began to fall.

He came awake again to find himself sitting in Captain Grubb's easy chair by the fire, a blanket wrapped around his shoulders. He felt like he had just run ten miles. His mouth was dry and tasted like bitter almonds. It was a challenge to keep his eyes open.

Macaulay held a small glass of amber liquid to his lips,

and he swallowed it, feeling the heat of the whiskey rush through him. Through the window, he could see Captain Grubb removing the white canvas cocoon from his trawler.

"We need to get you to a hospital," said Lexy.

Barnaby shook his head.

"Just leave me here," he said. "Bring me the medication I have out in my travel bag and I'll be fine."

When Macaulay opened the door to go out to get the bag, Lexy heard the sound of the boat's engines starting. Barnaby motioned her to sit down next to him.

"When you get to the island, try to imagine Eriksson and his men being wrecked there in the storm. Imagine the sun rising in your mind. Use your instincts. You have something close to a sixth sense in these matters. If it looks promising, come back and pick me up, and we'll search it together."

Captain Grubb came back in through the patio door.

"When are the TV people getting here?" he asked.

FORTY-FIVE

3 December
The White House
Washington, DC

Turning to face the battery of television cameras arrayed across the side wall of the East Room, the president pressed the switch to light the eighteen-foot-tall Douglas fir tree, now decorated with hundreds of handmade ornaments and colorful decorations from schoolchildren all over the country.

"As we enter this joyous season," began the president solemnly, "let us show appreciation to all our troops who will be spending the upcoming holiday overseas, risking their lives every day to defend the freedoms we hold dear."

Standing behind him beneath the Gilbert Stuart oil painting of President George Washington, Jessica Birdwell led the applause. Ira Dusenberry, on the other side of the East Room near the buffet table, was gazing longingly at the small mountain of iced jumbo shrimp and the pewter platters piled with smoked salmon. They would have to wait. He was on a mission.

When the president finished his remarks, Dusenberry worked his way through the throng of applauding guests until he reached Jessica's side.

"Jess, I need to talk to you if Senator Fowler can spare us two minutes," he said.

In the Red Room, he led her over to one of the Empire couches and sat down.

"As of yesterday evening, General Macaulay was still in Boston," he said, "which means that Dr. Vaughan is there too. The manager of a Patagonia outlet at a downtown mall reported to police that a man who fit Macaulay's description was involved in an altercation there late last night. A male shopper in one of the changing rooms saw the other man in the altercation carrying what appeared to be an automatic pistol. By the time police arrived, both men were gone. The witnesses were shown a photograph of Macaulay and they both confirmed it was him."

"Any ID on the other man?" asked Jess.

"He disappeared before the police got there and presumably is not one of ours," said Dusenberry as an elderly man came into the Red Room and sat down on an Empire chair. The man had a beefy face with a thin mustache and vaguely reminded him of someone.

"We sent a team into the mall," went on Dusenberry. "There was a small bank of pay phones opposite the North Face outlet, and they ran a trace on all outgoing calls from those phones during the time frame Macaulay had been there."

Two white-coated waiters came by, one carrying a silver tray full of canapés, and the other wine and champagne. Dusenberry selected three puff pastries stuffed with chanterelle mushrooms, pancetta, and garlic.

"And?" demanded Jessica as he consumed one of the pastries in a single bite.

"And one of the calls was of possible interest," he said, washing down the canapé with a swallow of red wine. "It went to a CIA-connected cell phone. Identity restricted."

"Even to us?"

"We would have to ask the CIA officially. It would take days and probably lead nowhere."

"What's your take?" asked Jessica.

Ira glanced again at the beefy man, who now appeared to be gazing at the painting of John Jay Audubon hanging over their couch. Tennessee Williams. He looked like Tennessee Williams at the end of his life.

"Macaulay has a friend at the CIA," said Dusenberry. "Not a problem for us. Maybe the agency will help track him down."

"Do you know that man?" she whispered as Dusenberry finished his third canapé.

"A seersucker suit in December," he whispered back. "He's probably one of the president's campaign guys. They're all flaky."

Getting up from the couch, he led her back to the East Room.

"Keep me posted from your end," he said, heading toward the buffet table.

Jessica had just received her overcoat from a handsome young marine in the foyer when she felt her cell phone begin to tremble against the inside of her thigh. She took the call in a small private bathroom down the corridor.

"Jess, this is Marc," came the disembodied voice.

"What have you got?" she said, lowering her voice an octave.

She had met Marc Goodrich shortly after her posting to Homeland Security. He was already a fair-haired boy in the bureau and was now overseeing the joint surveillance task force looking for Macaulay, Finchem, and Vaughan.

"So we've been monitoring about three hundred people who had even the remotest level of contact with this Harvard professor Finchem," said Goodrich.

"Right," she came back. "We're the ones who initiated the interagency request."

"Okay. Well, I've hit pay dirt."

"Tell me," she said, her eyes coming alive.

"One of the thousand bits of raw data logged by my teams was the fact that a PhD candidate named Delia Glantz, who is one of Finchem's graduate students, registered a brand-new Lexus SUV earlier this week at the Massachusetts DMV office in Boston."

"What's so unusual about that?"

"Nothing," he said. "But this afternoon she went to a Hertz agency in Cambridge and rented a car. When the hit came in, there was nothing else happening. On a hunch, I paid her a visit three hours ago, showed her a fake police ID, and told her I was investigating an accidental death. Gorgeous girl by the way . . ."

"Just tell me what happened," interrupted Jessica.

"All right," he said, stung by her tone. "I could tell she was nervous, so I said that her SUV had been in a terrible accident and we were attempting to identify the victims. She broke down and began sobbing that she should have been with him. 'Who?' I asked. 'Dr. Finchem,' she said."

"That's great work, Marc," said Jessica.

"Here is the other piece of good news," said Goodrich. "Her brand-new Lexus is equipped with a theft-prevention tracking device."

"Fantastic. Where is the car now?"

"South Harpswell, Maine. The GPS coordinates put it at a boat charter outfit. The tracking platform delivers real-time updates every ten seconds. The vehicle hasn't moved in two hours."

"Send me all the data on the car to my secure computer address."

"Will do."

"I need to confide something to you that is vitally important," said Jessica, her voice going even lower. "There is a security breach here in the White House. We know whoever it is must be tied to the foreign organization responsible for the murder of Jim Langdon. This information must be closely held in case it gets into the wrong hands. I have to insert a clean operational unit."

"Understood," said Goodrich. "You and Ad Kingship are giving the orders. Just remember who broke the lead when the awards are handed out."

"Don't worry," said Jessica, ending the connection.

Her next call was to a secure automated reception line.

"This is Freya. I will be sending further information electronically, but I have pinpointed the location of Finchem and Vaughan."

FORTY-SIX

4 December
RV _Leitstern_
North Atlantic Ocean
Off Rockland, Maine

"We have made good progress, Your Grace," said Hjalmar Jensen.

Von Falkenberg had made another unannounced visit to ask for an update from Jensen's translation team. He had brought Per Larsen with him. The faithful Steiger helped the prince to settle into a cushioned chair.

"Please specify that," said von Falkenberg.

"Thanks to the excellent work of Dr. Krusa and Fraulein Johannson, we have narrowed our search to just twenty-five small islands off the Maine coast," said Jensen. "It will now be necessary to assemble search teams to visit each of these islands to garner the additional information that can narrow the search further."

The prince's face clouded.

"That is unacceptable," he said bluntly. "I need your solution to this question immediately."

Jensen fought to control his nerves.

"We will continue to do our best, Your Grace," he said.

Von Falkenberg turned to Per Larsen. He was glad to see that the scientist appeared to have regained some of his vigor.

"Once we have located the tomb, do you see any reason why it would not be possible to extract the divinity's DNA?"

"Paleogenetics isn't my field, Your Grace," said Larsen, "but I have studied the current science with respect to ancient DNA and morphological preservation. My colleagues have already replicated the DNA of mummified human samples that were several thousand years old. Professor Jensen has stated that the tomb is in an underground cavern. Assuming it has not been compromised by the sea, between mummified tissue, bone, hair, paleofeces, and teeth, we should have no difficulty accomplishing the task."

Von Falkenberg could see the sacred burial place in his imagination. It was so close. Once more he silently prayed for the chance to gaze on his personal divinity before entering the halls of Valhalla. He thought about the chosen ones, those who would be imbued with Eriksson's DNA to become progenitors of a new race founded on a bloodline now hidden behind the veil of antiquity. His reverie was interrupted by one of Bjorklund's junior officers who arrived with a printed message. He read it quickly and smiled at Jensen.

"It would appear that we are much closer to locating our island," he said, getting to his feet and walking with Steiger's help toward the compartment door. "Have the Lynx meet me in my stateroom."

The commando leader arrived after von Falkenberg received another morphine injection.

"You will have the honor of assembling the party to capture the two American archaeologists who have apparently located our objective."

The Lynx read the printed message.

"Professor Jensen and I will be following behind you to wait at a secure destination," said the prince. "You are to bring me the archaeologists unharmed, both mentally and physically. Do you understand?"

"Yes, Your Grace," said the Lynx, remembering the woman who had escaped them on the ice cap. "Unharmed."

"If necessary, you are to eliminate anyone who stands in the way of the success of your mission. But you must remember that Maine is not Greenland," added the prince. "You cannot move about with impunity or without fear of exposure."

"I understand, Your Grace."

"One of the ship's transport helicopters will deliver you, your men, and two vehicles to a location within a few miles of your destination. From there you are on your own."

"Yes, Your Grace."

"No one is to know you were ever there."

"Yes, Your Grace."

"Do not fail me," said the prince.

"I will not fail, Your Grace," said the Lynx.

FORTY-SEVEN

4 December
The *Dorothy B.*
North Atlantic Ocean
Off Bailey Island, Maine

God, the North Atlantic was bleak in the winter, thought Macaulay as the boat plunged through a deep trough and rose to meet the next precipitous wave. In the initial run across Merriconeag Sound, the water had been relatively calm, but as soon as they rounded the tip of Bailey Island and headed out into the ocean, they ran straight into six-foot seas.

Behind them, Bailey had long ago disappeared into the mist. Ahead of them was a dense bank of unbroken fog. They hadn't seen another boat during the entire course of the trip.

"It should clear up some when we get closer to the island," Grubb shouted over the noise of the engines.

They had been at sea for nearly an hour. After they entered the fog bank, Captain Grubb had turned on the boat's Furuno radar system and navigated the boat electronically.

The *Dorothy B.* was not rigged for winter. Even with the protection of the overhanging roof above the wheelhouse, they were exposed to the bitter wind, and it cut through the still-weakened Lexy. She kept her gloved hands gripped around the warm exhaust funnel from the engine compartment as she stared forward into the thick haze.

Her mind was still focused on Barnaby, and she hoped he was resting comfortably back at the cottage. They would need to get him to a doctor at some point, with luck after they had found the tomb.

A few minutes later, the shoreline of the island began to appear out of the gloom. Although it was still only late afternoon, light was already failing as Grubb began steering the *Dorothy B.* toward a pebbly beach on the island's western shore.

"Please take us all the way around," said Lexy.

"I thought you needed to go ashore to find the prize," he came back.

"I'll let you know if and where I want to land," she said, looking down at the leaping wave crests.

First she wanted to get a feel for its entirety, particularly the eastern side, where Eriksson and his men would presumably have been driven ashore. Grubb turned north, staying about twenty-five yards out from the shoreline.

Lexy used a handkerchief to wipe the mist off her binoculars and began to survey the unfolding landscape. The western edge of the island was low to the sea, mostly rock ledge crowned by patches of green spruce trees. Along the northern edge, the rocky escarpment grew higher as if the island itself had long ago erected its own defensive barrier against the worst of the North Atlantic storms.

Through the binoculars, she observed a line of black-backed gulls, quietly perched like sentinels above the sharp clefts. Along the steep-faced wall of rock, the sea seemed to sigh, like some great hibernating beast.

The *Dorothy B.* began to pitch more violently as they ran down along the eastern edge. Another line of mature spruce trees crowned the striations of ancient rock formations. Beyond the shoreline, she could see what looked like a small grove of gnarly fruit trees and what might have been traces of a settlement.

"What are you looking for?" asked Macaulay when they were about halfway around.

"I don't know," said Lexy.

In truth she was waiting for that familiar subliminal signal from somewhere within, the intuitive recognition of something in the landscape that would comport with what she had imagined after deciphering the rune markings, the moment when her nerve endings would come alive with excitement.

Macaulay watched as a lone seagull began to follow the boat, flying in their wake about fifteen feet above them. The bird was obviously hoping for a handout. They swung around past the southern tip and began closing in on the pebbly beach where Grubb had started the run.

Lexy put down her binoculars.

"There is no point in landing," she said to Grubb. "Let's go back."

"I still get my money, right?" he said.

"Of course," she answered.

The Norsemen had never been there. It wasn't the place. She was sure of it. She would have felt it inside.

"I'm going to lie down in the cabin," she said, heading below.

"So what's with her?" asked Grubb as he turned the *Dorothy B.* to the southwest and headed back to South Harpswell. "Sore loser?"

Macaulay just shook his head and stared forward.

Barnaby sat asleep in Mike Grubb's easy chair in the growing darkness of the cottage. He was sailing in a Viking longship through a greenish yellow fog. The smell around him was dank and repulsive, reeking of corruption. Over the side of the ship, men were floating on a sea of blood, the corpses of men long drowned. Below the dense surface lay something horrible, unutterable, rising steadily toward him.

A voice intruded on the feverish dream.

"Where are the others?" asked the Lynx.

Barnaby awoke and took in the coarse-grained blond hair and piercing blue eyes.

"It is useless to lie to me, Herr Finchem," he said. "I know they were here with you."

He was just as Lexy had described him, the cool, merciless commando leader who had wiped out Hancock's expedition team in Greenland. He was no longer dressed in the one-piece thermal winter suit she had described with the Mjolnir crest emblazoned over the breast. He now looked like a model from an L.L. Bean catalogue. Only the automatic in his belt and the submachine gun in his right hand confirmed his lethality.

Barnaby glanced out the window into the fading light

and saw two more armed men in the glow of the dock lamps. One was entering the small fish house that housed Captain Grubb's gear, while the second disappeared down a ladder at the end of the dock.

"They've gone on," said Barnaby.

"And left you here?"

He nodded.

"We will wait for them to return," said the Lynx.

The fire had gone out in the woodstove, and it was very cold in the room. Barnaby wrapped the blanket tighter around his shoulders as the blond man went to the windows, staring out at the water.

Barnaby checked his pulse. In spite of all the hard mileage he had subjected his heart to for almost seventy years, the beat was steady and reassuring, and he felt no residual pain or discomfort from the most recent incident. Good to go, he decided, whatever comes.

Barnaby's ears pricked up at the distant sound of an engine. At first he thought it might be a car, but it was coming from beyond the window, somewhere out at sea. The sound grew increasingly louder.

It was almost certainly Captain Grubb's boat returning from the island, and if they weren't warned, they would all fall into the same net. Barnaby had little doubt what would happen to them once their usefulness in finding the tomb was ended.

The Lynx remained at the window, gazing out to sea. He had deployed his men at every edge of the property with two waiting at the dock. He slid a shell into the chamber of the Czech-made Skorpion Evo III submachine gun.

Barnaby surveyed the bare living room for some means

to warn them, taking in the sagging Christmas tree, the array of empty beer cans, two overstuffed trash baskets, and several fishing rods leaning against the wall. He was wondering how he might employ the fishing rods as a weapon, when his eyes landed on the light switches above Grubb's chair. He had used one of them to turn the dock lights on.

Barnaby could hear the boat engine begin to slow down as it approached the dock from the misty sea. He threw off the blanket and noisily attempted to get out of the sprung chair.

"What are you doing?" demanded the Lynx, training the automatic on him.

"Water," said Barnaby, seemingly choking as he held up the pill bottle. "My heart."

"Stay in your chair or I'll kill you," he said, stepping quickly through the open door into the kitchen.

Barnaby could hear the sink running as he reached over and pulled the switch, throwing the dock area into darkness. The Lynx was back a moment later, handing him the water glass. It took him only a few seconds to notice that the dock lights were out.

"What have you done, you miserable old swine?" he demanded, knocking the water glass out of Barnaby's hand and jamming the barrel of his automatic into his ear.

"I don't like it," said Mike Grubb from the steering console of the *Dorothy B*.

"What is it?" asked Macaulay.

"Someone just turned off my dock lights—probably that English circus freak."

"It could be an outage," said Macaulay.

"There are still lights up at my house," said Grubb. "I want to know what's going on."

"Stop your engines," demanded Macaulay.

He had to assume the worst. Somehow they had tracked them all the way from Boston to Maine. Barnaby was either dead or their prisoner. Either way, he and Lexy had to try to escape.

"I'm heading on in," said Grubb. "You pay me what you owe me and we'll call it even."

"I said stop the engines," repeated Macaulay.

"Fuck you," said Grubb, continuing to steer toward the darkened dock.

Macaulay pulled out the silenced semiautomatic pistol and leveled it at him.

Grubb hauled back on the two power throttles, and the boat slowed to a crawl.

"I never seen a reality show like this one," said Grubb.

"I want you to drop us off farther up the coast," said Macaulay. "After that you're free to go where you want. Now turn it around."

Grubb swung the bow around.

"Open it up," demanded Macaulay, and the captain obliged.

FORTY-EIGHT

4 December
Eagles' Cleft
Seal Harbor
Mount Desert Island, Maine

Barnaby rode in the backseat of the Jeep, his massive head enclosed in a black cloth hood that had breathing holes for his nose and mouth. Men sat on both sides of him to block access to a passenger door.

He was astonished to still be alive, sure that the commando leader was about to kill him at the cottage when Grubb's boat had turned around and disappeared into the night. His right ear was still bleeding from the blunt force of the pistol barrel.

Barnaby had watched the Norwegian's facial muscles quiver as he fought to control himself. Finally stepping away, he had made a call on his cell phone, requesting in Norwegian that a helicopter be dispatched immediately to track the path of Grubb's boat. The request was apparently denied, after which he smashed everything within reach, including the living room window.

Sitting in the silence of the SUV, Barnaby pondered how they could have been tracked down so quickly, concluding that Delia must have revealed the information, almost certainly unwillingly.

Still weak from the fainting episode, he found himself dozing off, coming awake again when the car began bumping heavily over a road surface studded with potholes. One of them elevated him off the seat.

"Langsamer du Narr," spat a voice in German, breaking the silence.

A few minutes later, the car rolled to a stop.

It was raining again when they hustled him out of the car and into an open field. His shoes sank into soft, marshy ground and his clothes were soaked by the time they made it across. He heard the low whine of an idling helicopter engine. Someone helped him inside the machine and strapped a safety harness over his chest.

The jet engine surged to life and he felt the helicopter leave the ground. About thirty minutes later, he sensed they were descending again. After another short run in a car, he heard the soft crunch of the tires on a gravel driveway; then it came to a stop.

Outside, the rainy air was scented with pine needles. The men on each side of him walked him into another building and up two sets of stairs. He could smell wood smoke as he heard a door close behind him. The hood was removed.

A young red-haired woman in a scarlet pantsuit welcomed him with a convivial smile. They were alone in a high-ceilinged bedroom decorated with fine old English pine furniture, wide plank floors, and a stone fireplace. A log fire crackled in the grate as rain pelted the windows.

"The prince thought you might like a hot bath and a refreshing libation after your difficult journey," she said.

"You don't know how difficult, my dear," he replied. "Tell the prince, whoever he is, that both ideas sound bloody marvelous. And feel free to join me."

She blushed furiously before leaving him alone with a snifter of brandy. He went to the windows and looked out into the rainy night. In the distance, he could see the revolving beacon of a lighthouse. Heavy rollers hammered into a rocky shoreline.

It was finally starting to make sense, the reason he had not been liquidated. Hjalmar Jensen hadn't been able to decipher the rune inscription or effectively interpret its clues. Apparently, their only hope for a quick discovery lay with him or Lexy. What was the urgency? he wondered. And who was the prince?

When he climbed out of the Jacuzzi, Barnaby found a pair of silk pajamas waiting for him on the bed, along with a thick flannel dressing gown and padded slippers. There had to be a secret video camera in the room, because as soon as he was dressed, there was a knock at the door.

A butler in white tie and tails led him down a mahogany staircase and into a vast great room in which another log fire was roaring. Two of the commandos he had seen at Grubb's cottage flanked the entrance. A blond woman in a black cocktail dress stood in front of the fire with an elderly man in a blue suit.

As he drew closer, he saw that she was at least sixty. Nature or plastic surgery had kept her face unnaturally taut, with wide cheekbones and full lips. Her figure was still slender and athletic.

The man was much older, with a thin, long-nosed, aristocratic face. His face was seamed with lines of trouble or pain and his skin looked like delicate parchment. They were both holding cocktail glasses.

"Welcome to Eagles' Cleft," said the woman without formally introducing herself or the old man. Barnaby was sure he had never met him, but there was something familiar about the woman. The butler asked Barnaby if he wanted refreshment, and he asked for another brandy.

"I'm told that you were forcibly blindfolded before being brought here, Dr. Finchem," said the old man. "That was the grievous mistake of an overzealous subordinate."

His accent was unmistakably German, cultured, and aristocratic.

"I assumed it meant I had a better chance of surviving the night," said Barnaby.

An oil painting of the mansion towered over the mantelpiece. It was the kind of house the Astors and Rockefellers once called a summer cottage, ten thousand square feet of oceanfront elegance, fifteen-foot-high ceilings, fireplaces suitable for human sacrifice, and walls of glass facing the sea.

Barnaby remembered who the woman was. She had been one of the television successors to Julia Child, who had ridden her intelligence and magnetic smile into a personal empire of branded housewares, clothing, furnishings, and decorator items. For many years, it had been hard to turn on a television set without seeing her face. Then she had dropped out of sight.

"I am told you are a renowned Norse archaeologist, Dr. Finchem," she said with the radiant smile he remembered. "Do you follow the Order of the Ancient Way?"

"I'm in full retreat from all organized religion," said Barnaby.

"I pity you," she said. "You will never know the salvation of Valhalla."

"You're very perceptive," he replied.

"Dr. Finchem is a true skeptic," said von Falkenberg. "But he and I have much in common, I believe."

"Really," said Barnaby.

"We both share a deep and abiding love of Norse culture, its gods, and its noblemen who shaped our world."

"The Norse culture, yes," said Barnaby as the butler returned with his brandy.

"Let me be direct," said the prince. "I would be deeply grateful for your assistance in finding the final resting place of my personal divinity, Leifr Eriksson."

"I'm sure you would," said Barnaby. "My colleague Hjalmar Jensen has apparently failed to interpret the clues."

"Dr. Jensen is indeed one of us."

"He told me quite a bit about your church," said Barnaby. "At the time, it sounded like you were worshipping at the holy grail of Josef Mengele."

"We are trying to save the world from destroying itself," said von Falkenberg.

"Not the world, just the chosen ones," said Barnaby. "I met one of your acolytes a few hours ago. He reminded me of a boy I knew growing up who used to pet kittens with one hand while dousing them in gasoline with the other, and then lighting them up to enjoy their agony."

"I'm afraid you do our cause an injustice," said von Falkenberg, his pallid face showing the first trace of color. "And he is not one of our leaders."

"You look like you've probably led a privileged life," said Barnaby. "As far as I'm concerned, you just benefited from the luck of the draw. A microsecond later you might have been born into a beggar's family in Calcutta. Those are my views on racial superiority."

"To the contrary," said the prince. "That was my destiny. As for racial superiority, your adopted country of the United States led the way in fostering it. Your founding fathers saw the threat of the indigenous subspecies right from the beginning, and addressed the challenge by selling the Native Americans blankets diseased with smallpox. They eradicated eighty-five percent of the tribes of North America in less than a hundred years."

"I do not condone that evil," said Barnaby.

"And America also led the way in eugenics in the last century," said the old man. "Have you never read of the Human Betterment League and its national campaign to sterilize millions of minority Americans? Mr. Gamble of Procter and Gamble was one of the proud sponsors."

"The world has made a lot of progress since then," said Barnaby, "including stamping out Hitler and National Socialism in your country."

"How do you define progress, Dr. Finchem? At this moment, millions of young African predators languish in your prisons, at ten times the rate of the rest of the world. And they are there for celebrating the same culture their forebearers brought with them from Africa, murdering those in authority and turning their women into whores. That is progress?"

"You've obviously never read Shakespeare," replied Barnaby. "He summed it up four hundred years ago. With all our human flaws, we are all of us about possibilities, every one of us, for better or worse. No race is immune or superior."

"Thank you for enlightening me," said von Falkenberg, his scarred and heavily wrinkled hand beginning to tremble as it held the glass.

"You don't have much time, do you? I can see it in your face," said Barnaby. "That's why you need my help."

"If you choose not to cooperate with us, I will be forced to ask Dr. Larsen to extract the information," he said, trying to maintain a tone of civility. "It would be a pity to do that, because after he is finished, I doubt you will ever remember who you are."

"That's more like it," said Barnaby. "I won't help you."

Von Falkenberg motioned to one of the guards, who immediately left the room.

A moment later, the prince seemed to stagger forward. From the shadows on the other side of the fireplace, a badly scarred, old, white-haired man rushed toward the prince with a pronounced limp.

The blond socialite turned her cold blue eyes on Barnaby.

"I pray that you die," she said.

FORTY-NINE

4 December
Off Orr's Island
Maine

"I'll give you another two thousand dollars to take us farther up the coast," said Lexy, careful not to reveal their ultimate destination.

Mike Grubb pointed to the boat's gas gauges, both of which were approaching empty.

"There's no marina to buy gas between here and Thomas Bay," he said. "I don't think there's enough to even get me home."

"Take my advice," said Macaulay. "Don't go home tonight."

"Why not?" asked Grubb.

Macaulay debated how much to tell him.

"All I can tell you is your life would be in danger. Trust me."

"Trust you?" repeated Grubb, glancing at the pistol in Macaulay's belt. "I'd sooner trust my ex-wife, Greta."

"Where are we now?" asked Lexy.

Grubb checked the GPS monitor.

"About halfway up the back side of Orr's," he said.

"Do you have a map of these waters?" asked Lexy.

"In the chart locker," said Grubb.

Down below, Lexy spread a water-stained nautical chart on the galley countertop.

"The closest place from here to reach Monhegan Island is Boothbay Harbor," she said, pointing to a seaside village farther up the coast. "It looks to be about ten miles farther north."

Macaulay gave the chart a closer look.

"This dotted line from Boothbay to Monhegan indicates there is a ferry service going out there," said Macaulay, speaking loudly enough to be heard over the engines, "but it probably isn't running this time of year."

Lexy glanced up through the open hatch of the cabin and saw that Mike Grubb had placed himself in a position to observe them while he continued to navigate the boat from the wheelhouse. She moved to block his view of the chart.

"Even if we had the gas, it would take us too long to get to Boothbay by boat," said Macaulay. "We need to find another car. From Orr's Island, it shouldn't take us more than an hour to get there."

Returning to the deck, Macaulay told Grubb to put them ashore right away. Slowing the engines, he turned on a searchlight, and trained it on the shoreline. In the distance, Macaulay could make out a long finger-shaped pier jutting out from one of the oceanfront homes. Grubb steered toward it.

As they were approaching the dock, Macaulay pulled

out the boat's Motorola CM200 marine transmitter from its cradle above the steering console and clipped the power cord with his knife.

"Sorry but there's a lot at stake," he said.

"Goddamn reality shows," said Mike Grubb, glowering at him. As soon as they were on the pier, Grubb gunned the *Dorothy B.* in reverse and headed back into the murky night.

It was spitting rain as they crossed the grounds of the shuttered estate. Macaulay was about to search the garage, when a dog started barking stridently from the porch of the neighboring home. They kept on going to the front edge of the property and began walking north along a two-lane road.

Macaulay tried to think through their next possible steps. He had no idea how many agents were on their trail, but a few had obviously managed to track them to Harpswell with no apparent difficulty. There had probably been a global tracking device in the SUV, he concluded, angry with himself for not foreseeing the possibility.

They needed to find transportation that was untraceable. If he stole another car or truck from one of the occupied homes along the road, it would almost certainly be reported to the police right away. It had to be a vehicle that wouldn't be missed, which meant no more human interaction.

They had walked half a mile when the outline of another darkened summer cottage loomed up off to the side of the road. Macaulay crept to the window of the attached garage and flashed a light inside. It was empty.

He checked out four more seasonal cottages along the country road with the same result before he spied a long, tree-lined driveway leading off the road. A sodden newspaper was sticking out of an overstuffed mailbox with the name GROVER CONNELL painted on it. Using his flashlight, Macaulay pulled out the newspaper and checked the date: August 31.

At the end of the driveway, an old Victorian manor house with wraparound porches faced the sea. Approaching the kitchen door, Macaulay began looking for the wiring components to its electronic security system.

"This is Maine," said Lexy. "They don't need security systems up here."

Smiling, she turned the knob of the unlocked door and stepped inside. It felt colder in the kitchen than it had outside. Macaulay found the family liquor supply in the butler's pantry, along with two glasses, and poured them each a stiff shot of Laphroaig scotch.

"We need dry clothes," said Macaulay as they walked through a family room adorned with photographs of four generations of Connells, the family that owned the home.

"I feel like we're trespassing," said Lexy.

"We are," said Macaulay as they climbed the center staircase to the second-floor bedrooms. Ten minutes later, he was dressed in a cargo shirt, work pants, and an Irish wool sweater. Lexy found two insulated ponchos in the mudroom. They joined each other again in front of the wall of family photographs. Lexy gazed admiringly at the new crop of Connell grandchildren.

"I don't want to destroy their illusions about this place being a safe refuge," she said.

"If we survive this thing, I promise that we'll come

back and make full restitution," said Macaulay, carrying the bottle of Laphroaig.

The garage was a separate building, a two-story affair that matched the colored trim of the main house. Macaulay's heart sank as he surveyed the interior. There was no car, truck, or any other four-wheeled transportation. A polished mahogany Chris-Craft speedboat sat on a car trailer in one bay. Several bicycles hung from hooks on the wall, along with water skis and sea kayaks.

He briefly considered the idea of launching the speedboat, but it probably ate gas. He flashed the light into a shadowy corner and saw a large object wrapped in a tarp. Tugging it open, he uncovered an ancient motorbike, already a relic when Calvin Coolidge was president. It had a wire basket in front of the handlebars and a small sidecar.

The controls were antiquated, but someone had lovingly restored it. The high-gloss paint job looked fresh. Amazingly, the tiny engine roared to life on the first pull of the starter wheel. Macaulay was wheeling it out of the garage when his Suunto wristwatch began throbbing. Its storm-warning sensor was registering another incoming storm in the next six hours.

He met Lexy in the driveway after shutting the garage door.

"Please assume your new throne, milady," he said, pointing to the sidecar.

"And you said Barnaby was conspicuous," she said, climbing into it and tucking the leather wind protector around her.

"It's a black night," answered Macaulay as they headed down the driveway.

*   *   *

A weary Mike Grubb tied off the bow and stern lines of the *Dorothy B.* at the dock below his cottage. He had been lucky to make it back. He had nursed both engines at their lowest rpm in order to conserve fuel; one of them ran out of gas just as he was approaching the pier.

All he wanted to do now was crack open a Sam Adams twelve-pack and order an eighteen-inch pizza from the Domino's in Brunswick. He was sitting on thirty-two hundred dollars, not bad for an afternoon's work even if he had to replace the power cord to his radio. If he didn't go crazy again at the high-stakes bingo game in Falmouth, the money would carry him until Greta got back.

It had been a wild day, starting with the visit of the circus freak and then the idiotic run out to Ragged Island. He couldn't wait to tell Greta that the contestants were now using guns on reality TV. She watched them all.

Leaving the dock after buttoning up the boat, he saw that the SUV they had arrived in was gone from the front yard. Just in case the guy hadn't been bullshitting him about some danger, he took the boat hook with him. Its tip was sharpened like the point of a stiletto.

As he approached the house, he saw the smashed picture window in his living room. Only jagged edges of the glass remained in the wooden frame, with the rest littering his yard in front of it.

He pushed the back door open and stormed inside with the tip of the boat hook held out in front of him like a lance. In the shadowy light from the single bulb in the kitchen, he could see that someone had trashed his place.

The furniture was overturned and his most prized possession, the huge swordfish he had caught off St. George's Bank, was broken in several pieces on the floor. Leaning the boat hook against the wall, he went over to pick it up.

"Welcome home," said the Lynx, sitting in Grubb's favorite chair near the woodstove.

Grubb tried to make him out in the gloom. The guy had a foreign accent.

"Are you with the rival team?" he asked.

"Rival team?"

"From the TV show," said Grubb.

Instead of answering, the Lynx pulled out his automatic.

"You people all use guns on the show. Is that the deal?"

"You have one chance to save your life," said the Lynx, picking up the boat hook. "Tell me where they are going."

"Where who are going?" said Grubb.

"The man and woman you took out in your boat."

"Do I get to use my lifeline?" asked Grubb with a knowing grin.

"What are you talking about?" demanded the Lynx.

"They always give you a lifeline."

"All right, I'm your lifeline."

"That's not the way it works. It's gotta be somebody I choose."

"I'm your deathline," said the Lynx. "If you don't answer my next question correctly, I will shoot you in the knee."

If the other contestants were willing to give him three grand for running them out to the island, Grubb decided, who knew how much this question was worth?

"Five thousand," said Grubb, "and that's my final answer."

The silenced bullet exploded in his knee and he collapsed to the floor.

In his agony of pain, Grubb gazed in horror at his ruined leg. The Lynx got up out of the chair and stood over him with the boat hook.

"I have no more time," he said quietly.

"How do I know . . . you won't kill me anyway?" he asked.

"You will have to take my word. You have five seconds."

"Boothbay," said Mike Grubb. "I heard the guy say Boothbay Harbor."

"Thank you," said the Lynx, driving the boat hook through his heart.

FIFTY

4 December
Boothbay Harbor
Maine

Macaulay kept the throttle of the motorbike shoved all
the way forward. Its maximum speed was just thirty-five
miles an hour. Fortunately, there was no traffic on the
small country road and very little after they turned onto
Coastal Route 1. They slowly puttered past ice-rimmed
harbors, aromatic mudflats, and darkened coastal villages.

A strong wind began gusting off the sea, occasionally
threatening to blow the bike into the oncoming traffic
lane. When the rain turned to sleet, Macaulay was forced
to lower his hooded head against the stinging flakes of
ice.

They stopped once to refill the bike's small tank at an
all-night gas station. The manager of the station, an old
man wearing a Hawaiian shirt, watched them through the
window with open curiosity.

They had passed through the village of Wiscasset and

were crossing a low bridge across tidal mudflats, when Macaulay heard a growing roar behind him and looked back to see an eighteen-wheeler overtaking them. The guardrail hemmed the bike into the roadway, but he moved to the right as far as possible without wrecking them.

The truck driver was going at least seventy miles an hour and didn't see the motorbike's small headlamp and tail reflectors until he was right on top of them, swerving to the left at the last moment and almost jackknifing his rig before bringing it under control. As he disappeared ahead of them, he let out a long angry blast of his air horn to make clear there was no place on a highway for them.

Past Wiscasset, they saw a sign for Boothbay Harbor and turned onto another secondary road. Fifteen minutes later, they rolled into the village's tiny commercial district, which was dotted with art galleries, boutiques, antiques shops, and restaurants, all closed for the winter.

A side street took them down to a deserted wharf. Beyond it, through the sleet, Lexy could make out a smattering of fishing and pleasure boats lying at moorings in the wind-roiled harbor.

"We have to get rid of the bike in case anyone saw us," said Macaulay, "and then we have to find a boat to take us out to the island."

His fingers were almost frozen into a curled position from gripping the handles, and his hands felt like blocks of ice. Wheeling the bike to the end of the unlit wharf, he glanced in every direction before shoving it over the edge. It dropped ten feet into the harbor with a loud splash, disappearing a few moments later.

The sleet turned to driving snow as they walked two

blocks back into the village. Passing another side street, Lexy saw a signboard swinging in the wind under a single lamp. It read THE BARNACLE, C. 1782.

Inside, a scarred walnut bar extended along one of the exposed brick walls. Oak booths were clustered along the other. There was an open kitchen at the end. The room had a low ceiling and hand-hewn, smoke-blackened beams. It was blessedly warm, and Lexy smelled the aromas of baked bread and freshly brewed coffee. An unseen radio was tuned to a jazz station.

"A dirty night it is," said the female bartender as they sat down at the bar. "Welcome to the Barnacle."

She was in her fifties, with a long ponytail and a pleasant, wrinkled face. Two men in jeans and dungaree jackets sat farther down the bar, nursing bottled beer. Otherwise the tavern was empty.

Lexy looked at the clock behind the bartender and saw it was past ten.

"Are you still serving food?" she asked.

"This is the Barnacle," she said. "If we're open, we're serving, but right now I'm down to what's left from the dinner crowd. . . . All I have for you is a lobster pot au feu with garlic, herbs, carrots, leeks, and onions. There's also my sour cream biscuits and apple brown betty. That's it, I'm afraid."

"We came to the right place," said Macaulay, ordering a double whiskey.

She headed back to the kitchen.

It was eleven by the time they had finished their main course. By then, the other two men at the bar had come over to join them. Both worked as crewmen on local fishing trawlers. Macaulay bought them a round of drinks.

"How long does it take to get out to Monhegan on the regular ferry?" he asked casually.

"About an hour, but the *Balmy Days* stopped running on Columbus Day," said one of the fishermen. "She won't be back running until Memorial Day."

"We were hoping to charter a boat as soon as possible to take us out there," said Lexy. "Like tonight."

The others laughed.

"Only a crazy fool would take a chance going out there with a nor'easter on the way," said the first fisherman.

There was a moment's silence before the bartender and the other fisherman said, "Chris," in perfect unison. "And he ought to be along before too long."

"Who is Chris?" asked Macaulay.

"Chris Pakkala . . . He lives on Monhegan," said Sue. "He's . . . a little different."

"Not the only one," said one of the fishermen.

Lexy was finishing her dessert when the entrance door swung open again. The man coming toward her seemed almost as broad as he was tall, with heavy shoulders and a broad neck. In his late thirties, he had shoulder-length blond hair and weathered blue eyes. Unshaven, he was dressed in shabby oilskins and had a white hand towel tucked around his neck.

"Chris, these folks could use a hand from you," said Sue as he joined them at the bar.

Lexy smelled pipe smoke on him along with a pleasant natural musky odor as he stood close to her. A moment later she felt his hand on her lower back, a brief subtle pressure and then it was gone. Looking down, she saw that he was barefoot.

"A dark Guinness," he said.

"Are you heading out to Monhegan?" she asked.

He grinned at her and nodded.

She saw that two of his lower-front teeth were missing. Then his hand was on her lower back again. It stayed there until she turned away from him.

"It's going to be a fun ride tonight," he said, "but don't worry about the storm. There won't be anything too rugged until late tomorrow morning."

"He's not always quite accurate in his predictions," said Sue. "You should know he's lost two boats in the last three years."

"That was beyond my control," said Chris, downing the Guinness in one long swallow.

"You'll take us then?"

"I have to go anyway," he replied. "Vic Lord has a roofing job for me."

"There will be a lot more roofing jobs after this storm blows through," said one of the fishermen as he paid their bill and left. Through the open door, Lexy heard the moan of the wind rise to a loud keening cry before it was shut again.

"Why do you want to go?" asked Chris, ordering another Guinness.

Lexy pondered her answer. There was something elemental about him, primal and strong. A lot of women were probably attracted to the hint of danger. At the same time, she sensed something decent in him, an adherence to whatever principles he held dear. She decided to tell him the truth, or at least part of it.

"I'm an archaeologist," she said. "I'm hoping to find evidence of an ancient settlement out there."

"You mean the Vikings?" he asked.

The surprise registered on her face.

"Sure, they were there," he said with another toothless smile.

"How do you know?" she asked.

"There are markings out there," he said. "Cut in the stone. I've seen them."

"How do you know they're Norse markings?" she persisted.

"It's in books," he said. "John Cabot wrote about them in sixteen hundred something. Ray Phillips wrote about them too. Besides, I'm Finnish. The Vikings were my people."

"Who is Ray Phillips?" she asked.

"The island hermit," said Chris. "He was famous up and down this coast."

"But I thought Monhegan was a settlement."

"It is," said Chris. "Old Ray didn't live on Monhegan. He was on Manana. That's where the Viking markings are."

"Where is Manana?" asked Lexy as Macaulay looked on.

"It's the little island just south of Monhegan—the tail of the whale."

Her heart began to speed up.

"What whale?"

"The northern end of Monhegan is shaped like the head of a humpback," said Chris. "Captain John Smith described it as looking like a whale when he got there in 1614. It's had a lot of names since."

A thrill coursed through her.

"And Ray Phillips?"

"He lived on Manana for about forty years along with a flock of sheep and his pet gander. He built a bunch of little shacks out of driftwood for them all to live together. He always claimed the Vikings were there first."

"Did he ever write about finding any traces of them?" asked Macaulay.

Chris took him in for the first time. He didn't like what he saw.

"He knew how to read and write if that's what you're asking," he said with a touch of malice. "Ray was no dummy. They say the First World War screwed him up. His pictures and stuff are up at the Monhegan museum on Lighthouse Hill."

Macaulay heard the entrance door open again and turned to see two men standing there in camel overcoats, their eyes roaming the interior. He slipped his hand under the edge of his sweater and grasped the automatic as they stepped forward.

He relaxed when they came into the light. Both were rotund, in their fifties, and wearing bow ties. One of them asked for the wine list and Sue brought it over. Lawyers, he decided.

"We would be happy to pay you to take us out there," said Macaulay.

"I don't need your money," he said, as if insulted.

"I can't help but notice you're not wearing shoes," said Macaulay.

Chris gave him a superior grin and said, "I don't ever feel cold."

"I wish I shared your powers," said Lexy.

"I was abducted when I was a boy," said Chris, as if that explained it.

"I'm so sorry," said Lexy as the bartender looked on, rolling her eyes.

"They didn't hurt me," he said, finishing his third Guinness. "They took me to perform experiments on . . . you know, sexual experiments. They brought me back in their ship when they were finished."

"Were they ever caught?" she asked.

"They were aliens," he said quietly, his blue eyes locked onto hers, daring her to mock him.

She had no idea if he was joking. If he wasn't joking, what did it say for the accuracy of everything else he had said to her? What had been growing excitement inside her began quickly ebbing away.

"I see."

One of the lawyers down the bar raised his voice. "You can have your saltwater fishing. I'll take lakes and streams."

"What do you go after?" asked the second one.

"Bass, they're good fighters. The big ones can run six pounds, great eating," said the first one.

"What do you use for bait?"

"Frogs . . . I always use frogs."

Chris's blue eyes turned to ice. He slowly walked down the bar, stopping in front of the first man, who gazed up at him uncertainly from his bar stool, almost visibly melting as the big man glared down at him.

"Don't ever use frogs for bait," he said.

The man seemed mesmerized, unable to respond.

"Why?" asked the second man.

"Have you ever looked at frogs after you hooked them to the line?"

Both men shook their heads no.

"They grab onto the line with their hands," said Chris. "Do you understand now? They have hands."

The first man still couldn't respond.

"You understand now, don't you, Norv?" offered the second one helpfully.

The first man slowly nodded, his mouth slack.

Chris came back down the bar.

"Are you ready to go?"

FIFTY-ONE

5 December
Central Intelligence Agency
McNamara Library Annex
Langley, Virginia

Tommy Somervell looked across his office desk at Roger Crowell and June Corcoran. None of them had slept for two nights. June's septuagenarian face had begun to remind him of a wrinkled boot. The pouches under Roger's eyes resembled wasps' nests.

Tommy had taken two amphetamine pills since morning, and had gone through the familiar pattern of euphoria and increased energy followed by sluggish torpor. He longed for the ministrations of his favorite house in Bangkok.

Like him, the other two agents had been relegated to the basement of the library annex. Tommy's office was no larger than his butler's pantry in Leesburg, and it was the largest of the three. Officially, they were the golden agers, an affectionate term designed by the director to reward them for the contributions they had made over the years. To everyone else, they were the has-beens, agents who had long ago outlived their usefulness and didn't have the good sense to leave.

For the last forty-eight hours, at least, he had removed them from the scrap pile and restored them to temporary relevance. The chain-smoking June had been a premier paper hauler for almost forty years. If a record existed, she could find it. Now sixty-seven, Roger had once been a top penetration agent, an expert at installing visual- and audio-monitoring equipment that was virtually impossible to detect. His technical prowess had helped to convict the traitor Aldrich Ames.

Tommy could count on them both for absolute secrecy, but they were no closer to solving the riddle of the White House mole or what the Ancient Way was planning. He had learned enough from his contacts in Europe to believe that something significant was about to happen on an international scale, but he had no idea what it was. Time was running out.

June had assembled the individual paper trails of Jessica Birdwell, Ira Dusenberry, and Addison Kingship, including birth records, academic records, military records, fitness reports, and job evaluations. She had pored over them for sixteen hours and followed up on every possible lead.

"There's nothing there," she said. "They're kosher."

"Nothing that would have made one of them vulnerable?" asked Somervell.

"In his sophomore year at Yale, Dusenberry stole a

fully dressed turkey from his eating house," said June. "Someone witnessed it and he made full restitution."

"That's it?" asked Somervell.

She nodded.

"What about surveillance?" asked Somervell.

"Birdwell hasn't been back to her apartment since I inserted the micro camera platform two days ago," said Crowell. "I also put a mini eavesdrop into her purse. She spent the last two nights at the White House."

"Kingship?" asked Tommy.

"He is married to the kind of shrew who would have turned Billy Graham into an atheist. He finds his solace in the arms of a fiftyish lawyer who works in international law at the Justice Department."

"Male or female?" asked Somervell.

"Sorry," said Crowell. "Female."

"What about Dusenberry?"

"I inserted the camera platform in his Watergate apartment. The man only sleeps three hours a night. Otherwise he's working. The only odd thing is that when he gets home, he grills two dozen hot dogs in a big frying pan and eats them in one sitting while watching that old BBC series *Poldark*."

Somervell's mind was wandering. With no compelling evidence, he was still sure that one of them was dirty. After being immersed in the sweet cesspool for so many years, he just knew. One of the three was a White House mole with access to almost every secret the country possessed.

"This isn't about money," he said. "It's about faith."

"I assume that eliminates the hot dogs," said June.

"Perhaps," said Tommy. "It's got to be something in

the past. We haven't dug deep enough. Let's go back farther."

"A previous life?" said June with sarcasm through a cloud of cigarette smoke.

Somervell took it in and nodded.

"Exactly," he said.

FIFTY-TWO

5 December
RV *Leitstern*
North Atlantic Ocean
Off Maine

The darkness was absolute. The unfathomable blackness of the tomb.

He couldn't be dead. His throbbing headache was real and so was the cold air that enveloped him; so was the constant rocking motion that was making him nauseated.

He was lying on his back. He tried to move his hands and legs, but they seemed anchored in position. When he attempted to raise his head, it slammed into a hard surface less than a foot above him. Had they buried him alive?

He swore aloud, but the tinny reverberation of his voice suggested he was encased in steel. One moment he was sweating and the next he was shivering. He tried to remember everything that had happened.

He had been in the ornate living room of the mansion with the old German, and had then been taken to another room and given an injection. Then he had dropped into oblivion.

How long had he been unconscious? he wondered. He had lost all sense of time. The drug they had given him could have wiped out minutes, hours, even weeks. He remembered the German talking about a truth serum.

He knew the so-called truth drugs, scopolamine, amobarbital sodium, and sodium pentothal. They had been around for ages. Maybe these bastards had improved on the cocktail. Had the serum worked? Did they own his mind? Had he already betrayed the information about the two remaining islands? The German had said the drug might erase his memory.

He tried to remember a few incidents from his childhood. They all seemed to be there. He decided to run through the catalogue of women he had slept with in his life, starting with the Nepalese girl in the tiny sleeping crib above Katmandu. They all were there, including the first wife he had vowed to forget.

The drug they had given felt more like a powerful sedative, something that had temporarily cauterized his brain. He drifted in and out of sleep, coming awake again to the changing pitch of the engines.

He attempted to decipher the rocking sensation. It was a forward-and-back motion, compounded by a sickening roll from side to side. So he was aboard a boat, maybe a ship. The dull heaviness of the engine noise suggested a ship.

Whatever it was, it was tossing wildly enough for him to be seasick. He fought to control it and gradually succeeded. He found he was very thirsty and wondered if and when someone would come to check on him.

Why was he still alive? There had to be a reason. If he had given them all they had wanted, he would be dead. He was alive because they still needed him.

He heard the sound of metal on metal, and a bright piercing light filled the space, forcing him to shut his eyes for a few moments. He opened them to see a man standing above him in a white lab coat.

Barnaby was on his back in a small cabin with a steel bulkhead. Broad canvas belts had been strapped across his chest, midsection, thighs, and feet. The man slid the door to the berth shut behind him.

"I am Dr. Per Larsen," he said.

For a doctor, he projected ill health, with prematurely gray hair and wrinkled pouches under his eyes. His left hand was trembling.

"You do not know me, Dr. Finchem, but your books on my Nordic ancestors were an inspiration to me as a boy," he said. "I wanted very much to meet you."

Barnaby's throat was too dry to respond.

"Water," he croaked.

Larsen went to a small steel basin mounted on the interior wall and ran cold water into a plastic cup. Gently lifting Barnaby's head, he patiently helped him to swallow it all.

"I regret that I have no authority to release you," he said. "I can only pray that you enjoy good fortune in the days ahead."

"Where am I?"

"Aboard the research vessel *Leitstern*," said Larsen. "You should know that the prince was able to locate the island that may hold the tomb of Leifr Eriksson without your assistance."

"Then why am I still alive?" asked Barnaby.

"The prince believes you could still be helpful to him after they penetrate the tomb in the event they meet unanticipated challenges," said Larsen. "At least that is what I told him."

"Thank you."

"It is of little consequence compared to the magnitude of what I have done," said Larsen.

Tears began silently coursing down his cheeks.

"The *Leitstern* is the command center for Operation Tjikko, which is scheduled to be launched twelve hours from now."

"The Tjikko tree in Sweden?"

"Yes. The operation is named for the oldest tree in the world," said Larsen. "In case something happens to me, I wish to tell you what is about to happen across the world."

FIFTY-THREE

"The wind is coming from the southeast and we should have a good following sea heading out there," said Chris as his boat cleared the harbor. "The full force of the nor'easter won't hit Monhegan until tomorrow morning when the wind swings around to the north."

As soon as they were out of the sheltered lee of the harbor, Macaulay was sure the Finn had gotten the forecast wrong. They were pitching about so wildly, it was hard to believe it could get any worse.

Along with the mammoth waves that crashed over the bow every fifteen seconds, the wind was coming in fierce, slashing gusts, driving the snow sideways and penetrating the canvas curtain behind the small wheelhouse. Macaulay was grateful for the foul-weather gear that Chris had given him before they left.

He hadn't been impressed with the boat when they

first boarded it in Boothbay. The name *Different Drummer* had been freshly painted on its stern. That was the only evidence of new paint on the whole boat.

It was a steel fishing trawler that had obviously seen hard use. The window fittings were grimy and corroded. One of the plate glass windshields was cracked, its riveted hull was streaked with rust, and there were numerous scrapes and divots in the wooden trim of the superstructure.

"I just bought her," Chris growled, after noting Macaulay's dour expression. "By next spring she'll be a honey."

When he started the engine, Macaulay felt a bit reassured. It sounded smooth and powerful. He decided to remain with Chris in the wheelhouse while Lexy went below to the forward cabin.

The cabin, which reeked of fish and motor oil, was a dismaying jumble of half-open drawers stuffed with gear, five-gallon buckets filled with engine parts and tools, blankets, life jackets, buoys, and rope. She found a place next to the small heating unit mounted on the bulkhead, and pulled a blanket around her.

Once they were out into open sea, the savage roar of the waves crashing above her head almost drowned out the low steady snarl of the engine, but she felt no hint of seasickness. After everything she and Macaulay had already endured, it seemed almost trivial.

She remembered being on a bucking horse as a teenager and the subsequent wild ride across rough, hilly terrain. This was no different, really. It only added to her excitement at the potential discovery awaiting her.

Her mind was drawn back to Barnaby. Where was he

on this night of all nights? She prayed that he was safe and unharmed and could somehow be there with them when they entered the tomb.

After a thousand years, she wondered, would the discovery change the course of archaeological history? She pulled out the notes she had written while the two of them were deciphering the rune inscription back at the Long Wharf.

Five by five squared.

She tried to visualize it, just as Barnaby had taught her. She imagined the Norsemen sealing the entrance to the cavern with a thick slab of rock cut roughly to five feet square. What would that slab look like after a thousand years? How would she be able to identify it from the surrounding rock formations? What if it lay under standing water or under a bed of scrub growth?

It lies under shadow from the dawn.

With a nor'easter coming, it was unlikely there would be any definitively visible sunrise over Monhegan in a few hours. Would there even be a hint of shadowy light? Perhaps there would be something helpful in Ray Phillips's papers at the museum on Lighthouse Hill that Chris had mentioned. That would be her first destination. Her mind turned to Barnaby again before she fell into a restless sleep.

Macaulay stared ahead through the cracked windshield into the stormy night.

"Are you and the lady going steady?" Chris asked almost harshly.

Macaulay hadn't heard that expression since he was in high school and smiled at the recollection. Chris took it as an insult, concluding that Macaulay was laughing at him.

"I could knock that goddamn smile right off your face," he said.

"Listen, I know you probably eat crowbars for lunch," said Macaulay, "and you would prefer to have the lady all to yourself, but yes, we're going steady and yes, we sleep together. Is that a problem for you?"

Chris thought about it for a while as he gazed forward into the darkness, puffing on his pipe.

"No," he said finally, his feelings seemingly assuaged. "I never poach another man's woman."

"Let's drink to the fine ones," said Macaulay, uncapping the bottle of Laphroaig he had stolen along with the motorbike and handing it to him. Chris knocked back a long swallow. Macaulay did the same.

"This stuff is good," he said. "Thanks."

When Macaulay went below, he was amazed to find Lexy asleep in the pounding din. He spent five minutes rummaging through the five-gallon buckets until he found a can of charcoal lighter fluid and some clean rags. Pulling out the automatic pistol, he removed the silencer and the magazine and gave the gun a thorough cleaning.

Lexy came awake to a careening wave that almost hurled her from the bunk.

"It was probably a night like this that Eriksson and his men were driven ashore," said Macaulay.

"Chris would tell you this is nothing," she said, returning his smile. "We're going to need to trust him."

"Why?" asked Macaulay.

"I've been thinking it through," she said. "If we find the stone slab, we won't be able to raise it by ourselves. I know he seems quirky in some ways, but he looks very strong and able. We have no other choice at this point."

One of the locker doors suddenly banged open and Macaulay's eyes were drawn to a slim object standing about two feet high behind a gaff hook. To Lexy, it looked like a toy weapon.

"What's that?" she asked as he extended its metal collapsible stock.

"It's a Sten gun," said Macaulay, "a British-made 9 mm submachine gun. . . . Second World War vintage . . . simple design, very reliable, and very illegal these days."

"Do you think it still works?"

Macaulay pulled three fully loaded magazines out of the locker.

"I would imagine so," he said. "It looks like it's in perfect condition."

He left the machine gun on the bunk as they went topside together. On deck, Lexy saw that a two-inch white blanket of newly fallen snow covered the stern and wheelhouse.

"As if the storm weren't enough," said Lexy, "we won't be able to see anything if this keeps up."

A moment later, she heard the dull clang of a weather buoy.

"That's Manana, almost dead ahead," called out Chris as the boat skewed crazily again. "That flashing white light you see every fifteen seconds is from the Monhegan lighthouse just beyond it."

The turbulence of the waves abated as they drew closer to the first dark land mass.

"Do you know how to use that Sten gun down in the cabin?" asked Macaulay.

Chris turned to him, his eyes suspicious at first, and then nodded.

"My grandfather carried it when he fought with the Finnish resistance," he said. "He taught me how to use it during the Monhegan lobster wars, but I've only used it on tomato juice cans."

"We might need it against some tomato juice cans that shoot back," said Macaulay.

"Chris, I want you to know how we got here," began Lexy, telling him that they were on the run from an organization that had murdered dozens of innocent people in their quest to learn a vital secret that was apparently part of a shadowy plan to achieve world domination, and that somehow part of this secret could be buried in an underground cavern on Manana Island.

Even as she spoke, she realized the whole thing sounded totally ludicrous. Only a fool would believe her. Chris kept staring forward, smoking his pipe, as she told him that she hoped to find the clues to its exact location in Ray Phillips's papers at the museum. When she was finished, he didn't even ask what the secret was. He turned his head to look at her, his weathered blue eyes already infused with excitement.

"I was expecting something like this," he said, as if he had known about the Ancient Way all along. "Just tell me we're on the right side."

"We're on the right side," said Macaulay, "and a lot is at stake—maybe the world as we know it."

"I think a large stone slab covers the entrance to the cavern," said Lexy. "It's probably rectangular in shape and about five feet square. We're going to need your help removing it."

Chris smiled again.

"I've moved ten tons of stone a day building rock

walls on Monhegan," said Chris. "With my iron bars and the right fulcrum, I can lever up just about anything."

"You should know that the people we're talking about won't hesitate to kill us," said Macaulay.

"The lady already said it was dangerous," said Chris as the dark mass of Manana Island emerged out of the darkness ahead of them.

"Monhegan is just past the southern edge," said Chris. "I'm going to put you ashore there at the wharf," said Chris. "While you're up at the museum, I'll batten down my boat. We can meet back at my fish house on the beach."

The landscape of Manana somehow looked sinister to Lexy as it rose starkly out of the surging black sea, denuded of trees and very primeval.

"Old Ray's little shacks were right up there," said Chris, pointing to a cluster of rubble and debris on its nearest slope. "Most of them burned down about twenty years ago."

He was turning into the small harbor beyond Manana when they entered what appeared to be a dense gray cloud lying low against the water. Standing on the open deck, Lexy felt as if a thicket of nettles were stinging her face as they passed through the foglike mist. The air inside the cloud was bitterly cold.

"Sea smoke," said Chris. "It forms over the sea when really cold air connects with warmer water."

The icy presence swirling around her felt mysterious and timeless, as ancient as the thousand-year-old mystery she hoped to solve.

It felt like coming home.

FIFTY-FOUR

6 December
Monhegan Island
Maine

Macaulay stared up at the dark, windswept bluff above the Monhegan wharf.

After dropping them ashore, Chris had called out, "The museum is at the top of Lighthouse Hill. Turn left on Main Street."

An unpaved rock-strewn path rose steeply from the wharf. It led past a phalanx of boarded-up summer cottages. At the crest of the bluff, they passed a three-story building with wraparound porches facing the sea. It was closed for the winter. A sign next to it read ISLAND INN, C. 1816.

A hundred yards farther along the road, they came to Main Street. It had to be Main Street because the road ended there, but there were no sidewalks or lights. It was another fifteen-foot-wide dirt path studded with a buried rock ledge that wound up toward another hill.

"We have to hurry, Steve," said Lexy as they passed a succession of cedar-shake cottages and stacks of neatly piled lobster traps. "Dawn is almost here."

An even steeper hill pointed the way to the lighthouse and a fog light that swept over them every fifteen seconds. They were nearly exhausted by the time they hiked up the final yards of the ice-covered path.

From the summit, Macaulay looked back down and saw a fenced graveyard dotted with ancient markers on a small plateau. Below it, the island settlement led to the harbor. He could see Chris's boat chugging slowly toward a protected anchorage, but it was too far away to hear the engine.

The houses in the settlement were all dark. Wood smoke was rising lazily into the snowy sky from a few of the chimneys. Macaulay envied the islanders sleeping snug in their beds on such a raw night.

Two clapboard buildings flanked the gray stone lighthouse at the summit. In the beam of his flashlight, Macaulay read the sign identifying the first one as the Monhegan museum.

Its stout entrance door was locked with a dead bolt, and he walked over to one of the side windows, hoping the museum didn't have an alarm system to protect its valuable exhibits. Using the base of the flashlight, he broke a small windowpane, the opening giving him access to the latch.

Inside, he found himself standing in a narrow corridor that connected the museum to the base of the lighthouse. After blundering into a brass binnacle mounted on a pedestal along the wall, he walked back to the entrance and let Lexy inside.

Together, they went through the building, room by room. There were more than a dozen of them on the two floors, each containing relics, photographs, paintings, and exhibits related to different aspects of the island's four-hundred-year-old history.

In one room, the faces of long-dead students who had once attended the island school peered out from black-and-white photographs. Another room was devoted to the lighthouse keepers and another to Captain John Smith of Pocahontas fame. The largest room was filled with early-American fishing and lobster gear, and also included relics of the ships that had been wrecked on its rocky shores.

On the second floor, Lexy found the tiny room dedicated to Ray Phillips.

With his long white hair and flowing beard, the man was strikingly photogenic. In one of the photographs on the walls, he was smoking a pipe while holding a baby lamb in front of the complex of driftwood shacks he had built on Manana. The next one showed a view of his sleeping room, with a straw-filled mattress and beside it a handmade table, which held an old battery-powered radio and a kerosene lamp. The last photograph showed the charred ruins of the shacks after the fire swept through them, long after his death.

"But where are your papers, Mr. Phillips?" demanded Lexy loudly as she searched unsuccessfully through the drawers of a pine washstand.

In the next twenty minutes, they went through the rest of the rooms in the museum, methodically hunting for the papers Chris had told them were there and finally coming up empty.

"He must have been wrong," said Macaulay. "Maybe they've moved them."

It was Lexy who found the museum's archives in a set of oak drawers that had been cleverly built into the stairwell leading up to the second floor. The folders in the drawers were alphabetized and she quickly found the Ray Phillips material. The folder was disappointingly thin and largely made up of press clippings reporting his death.

Among the handful of original documents was a letter from the Veterans Administration informing him of an increase in the monthly pension from his active service in World War I. There was also a bill of sale for the purchase of his property on Manana Island for the sum of seventy-five dollars.

"Listen to this account of his death," said Lexy, reading one of the clippings aloud. " 'According to Kole Gannon, an island resident, the night he died was bitterly cold. He reported looking out of his cottage window to see that the lantern in Phillips's shack had gone out, which was unusual. The following morning, Donald, the hermit's pet gander, was observed swimming across the harbor to Monhegan, apparently seeking help. When Gannon rowed across to Manana, he found Phillips dead on the bed in his shack.' "

"I don't see how any of this helps us," said Macaulay.

"It doesn't," agreed Lexy.

Macaulay checked his wristwatch.

"Chris said that dawn arrives this morning at seven fourteen," he said. "That's four minutes from now. Where do we need to be?"

"There was no lighthouse here a thousand years ago, and we are already at the highest point on the island," said Lexy. "We can watch it from these front windows."

As the minutes passed, they both gazed toward the smaller island, expectantly waiting for the first shards of light to illuminate its surface. Manana slowly emerged out of the gloom, but there was no perceptible shadow cast over its dark mass.

"It's no good," said Lexy as she prepared to leave. "We'll have to wait until tomorrow."

Feeble dawn light had slowly crept through the room near the front entrance, which held an assemblage of exhibits and relics that offered a broad overview of the island's history and its people.

"Maybe not," said Macaulay, leading her to an oil painting on the far wall.

The work was hanging above a glass case displaying an array of arrowheads from the Native American tribes that had lived on the island a millennium ago. Painted by an artist named Alison Hill, it was a contemporary landscape.

"Oh my Lord," said Lexy, taking in its title, *Sunrise*.

The painter had been standing on Lighthouse Hill when she captured a burst of glorious sunlight breaking over Monhegan. The settlement still remained in shadow, as did the harbor beyond it. The top two-thirds of Manana was bathed in sunlight.

"Look there," said Lexy, pointing to the area in shadow.

Her voice was tinged with disappointment. The shadowed section filled the entire lower end of the slope from north to south, and virtually all of it was blanketed with dense scrub growth.

"We're going to need a little divine assistance," said Macaulay.

FIFTY-FIVE

6 December
RV *Leitstern*
North Atlantic Ocean
Off Maine

Standing on the open wing of the bridge, Captain Peter Bjorklund ordered his ship turned into the wind before giving permission for the AgustaWestland AW139 helicopter revving its engines on the rear landing pad to take off.

Thirty seconds later, a second helicopter was launched from the forward pad. Hovering high above the *Leitstern*, two more Agustas waited to land after their arrival. Their mission was to pick up the remaining phase one team members and deliver them to the mainland.

Bjorklund was grateful that the capricious North Atlantic weather had cooperated for the launch. The nor'easter would reach its peak intensity in a few hours. According to the radio accounts, it was going to be a bear.

Out of the wind's fury, in the shelter of the covered bridge, the Marquess Antoinette Celeste de Villiers said a silent prayer of thanksgiving for the first successful stage of phase one.

In spite of the black leather coat she was wearing and the multiple layers of clothing underneath, she couldn't stop shivering. She envied the heartiness of Bjorklund, who had gone out to the open section of the bridge dressed only in his uniform jacket and a light woolen sweater.

"Congratulations, Captain. You and your crew have done superbly once again," she said upon his return. "They are on their way."

"Where are they going, if I might ask?" said Bjorklund.

"To do God's work," replied de Villiers.

Bjorklund knew better than to press her further.

A steward carrying mugs of hot cocoa arrived on the bridge, and de Villiers sipped hers while gazing out at the dark horizon. Her seventy-two exemplars were heading to every continent, from China to the Middle East, Europe to the United States. As soon as they completed the first phase, the teams would reassemble in Oslo to prepare for phase two.

She had taken the time to meet each of the two-man teams for a few minutes in her private cabin, telling them they should feel honored and humbled to have been chosen for the sacred mission.

"The serum you are carrying in these canisters will forever change the world. Guard it with your lives, and follow your orders to the letter when you arrive at your destination," she told them, her voice almost choked with passion.

Standing on the lower deck near the landing pad, Per Larsen watched the last helicopter disappear into the gloom before stepping back inside and following the passageway to the maintenance section and the compartment of the supervisor.

He found him sitting in his office chair, massaging his swollen ankles. Petty Officer Van Loon was in his fifties and had come out of retirement from the Dutch navy to join the crew. Seeing Dr. Larsen, he immediately stood to attention.

"Please sit," said Larsen, forcing a smile. "Attend to your ankles."

"What can I do for you, Doctor?" he asked.

"I need to do a few personal chores," said Larsen.

"We would be honored to help you," he said.

"I would simply ask for the loan of one of your toolboxes."

"A toolbox?" he asked, confused.

"The ones your men carry," said Larsen, "equipped with basic tools."

"Allow me to send one of my technicians to assist you," said Van Loon. "Any one of them would be grateful for the opportunity."

"My own work has been accomplished for the time being, and I would enjoy the chance to putter with my hands on a small project," said Larsen. "Do you understand?"

"I think so," said Van Loon.

Putting his shoes back on, he led the scientist into the supply section and pulled out one of the red stainless steel toolboxes from a storage cabinet. He placed it on the countertop and opened it.

"Is this everything you need?" he asked.

The top two trays held screwdrivers, pliers, spanners, and assorted screws and nails. The remaining space contained a cordless drill motor, pipe wrenches, sealers, glues, glazing compound, and lubricants.

"It will do perfectly," said Larsen, replacing the trays and fastening the top.

When he had left, Van Loon went back to his office, still pondering the visit. The scientists he had met aboard the ship all struck him as peculiar to say the least, but if Dr. Larsen needed a repair in the lab complex, he was supposed to request it through him.

Every action aboard the *Leitstern* was undertaken within a strict set of procedures. Orders were orders. He pulled out his hand transceiver and punched in the number for the third officer.

FIFTY-SIX

6 December
Monhegan Island
Maine

From the grimy windows of Chris's fish shack, Macaulay and Lexy looked out at the raging surf hammering the tip of Manana. Although it was well past dawn, the sky was still murky. The air temperature had risen above the freezing point as the storm drew nearer, and the snow had turned back to driving rain.

"At least we'll be able to see what's on the ground over there," said Lexy.

"Yeah, but if the wind grows much stronger, it will be impossible to row over," he said.

Chris had pointed his fish shack out to them before dropping them at the wharf. Located along a shingle of beach, it was the size of a large garden shed and had a peaked roof and cedar-shake siding. Inside, it was furnished with a bed, an eating table, and two chairs. There was no bathroom and the shack was unheated. It was very cold.

A few photographs were pinned to the walls, one showing Chris in early boyhood, standing with a woman who might have been his mother. Otherwise, the space was crammed with fishing gear and landscaping tools.

To get warm, Lexy had removed her boots, gotten into the bed, and pulled his two quilts over her. Looking up at the decaying wood under the shingled roof, she counted a dozen separate leaks. Under the larger ones, Chris had arranged pots and bowls to collect the rainwater.

A brindle cat emerged from the piles of gear and jumped up on the bed.

"Do you think he actually lives here, Steve?"

"If he does, he must really love this island," said Macaulay, removing his boots and joining her under the quilts.

"Why wouldn't he allow us to pay him?"

"Money obviously isn't important to him."

He slid his arm around her back and pulled her close to him. The cat slowly curled up in the hollow between their legs.

"In the summer, this place probably rents for a thousand dollars a week," he said as the cat lifted its head and began cleaning its front paws.

When Chris came in a few minutes later, the booming wind slammed the door shut behind him. Taking them in, he grinned apologetically and said, "Sorry, but we have to go. The wind has swung around to the north."

They put their foul-weather gear back on and joined

him outside. Chris had hauled his skiff up to the edge of the beach and waves were crashing into it. He told Lexy to sit in the bow and Macaulay to take the stern. Grabbing the oars, he launched the skiff and climbed into the center seat.

On the bottom of the boat lay a coiled rope ladder, a pick, shovel, coils of rope, and two long iron bars, along with several waterproof lanterns. Chris handed Macaulay a zipped watertight satchel that contained the Sten gun and extra magazines.

"I'm going to need you both to bail," he shouted. "It's going to be wicked out there."

Once past the stone breakwater, the skiff began bobbing like a cork. The sea rose to less than six inches below the gunwales, and it sloshed in from both sides as the skiff pitched and rolled.

Lexy and Macaulay kept filling their bailing buckets and heaving the water over the side, but the sea appeared to be winning the contest. As the icy water reached her ankles, Lexy kept her head down, not wanting to look ahead at what still awaited them.

Staring forward from the stern, Macaulay doubted they would make it across without capsizing. It was testament to the big man's strength and rowing prowess that he was maintaining any headway at all against the wind and waves, literally dragging them through the water.

A small wooden pier at the northern tip of Manana slowly materialized out of the shadows as Chris pulled closer. With the roiling sea lashing the shoreline, the pier jetty was barely out of the water.

As the bow of the skiff drew near the first pilings, Macaulay saw they were dangerously close to being driven straight into the seaweed-covered rock precipice that surrounded it.

At the last moment, Chris reversed direction with one of the oars and turned the skiff broadside to the end of the pier. With amazing agility for a big man, he leaped onto the pier and hauled the skiff out of the sea with them still inside.

After tying off the painter to one of the wooden stanchions, Chris began unloading. Dividing the tools and equipment between the three of them, he began climbing the cross members of a narrow-gauge cable car track that he said had once connected the dock with the abandoned coast guard station at the southern end of the island.

A hundred yards up the steep slope, they came to a utility shed that housed an old rotating drum of rusty cable once used to power the car. The shed door was missing, but they were able to gain temporary shelter from the driving rain by kneeling inside.

"We're almost directly above the remains of Ray's shacks," said Chris. "There's nothing left down there but a few piles of debris."

"What we're searching for is probably covered by all this undergrowth," said Lexy, looking at the low-growing scrub.

"It's trailing yew," said Chris. "Very tough . . . Grows everywhere on the island."

Remembering the shaded area in the sunrise painting up at the museum, Macaulay proposed that they start at the bottom of the slope near the southern tip of the island and work their way back across the slope to the north end.

He and Chris would stand four feet apart and use the iron bars as probes to penetrate the undergrowth along the search line. Lexy would go ahead of them, looking for any hint in the oncoming terrain of a horizontal slab of rock.

"If the slab is about five feet square, we should hit it with one of the pole ends," said Macaulay.

They moved out across the slope on the first search pattern, driving the poles into the earth at five-foot intervals and moving on. There was bedrock just below the surface almost everywhere. In some places it was two feet down; in others less than a foot. At no point did they find any bedrock that was horizontal.

They finished the first pass.

After moving higher up the slope, they headed back along the next pattern. At one point, Macaulay looked down at the pewter sea. It was now crashing into the north face of Manana with ten-foot-high waves. There would be no chance to row back now. They were stuck there for the duration of the storm.

The craggy ridge of the slope was steep and forbidding. It was also treacherous, with small fissures in the rock ledge from which thickets of gorse grew out of the dirt-filled crevasses and hid the sharp edges underneath.

Lexy fell more than once as she led the way. Macaulay found it tough going even in his hiking boots, and he wondered how Chris was able to manage barefoot, but the Finn navigated the uneven terrain like a mountain goat.

An hour later, they halted the search and took shelter

again inside the abandoned utility shed. Chris had brought along a pint of Southern Comfort and they each downed a restorative.

"I think we've covered about half the shaded area," said Macaulay.

"It could be anywhere," said a discouraged Lexy. "Maybe it isn't even here."

The rain and wind came harder as they resumed the search higher up the slope. Halfway across the fourth search line, they came to three large mounds of debris, the ruins of Ray Phillips's small complex. One of the mounds was considerably larger than the other two.

"That was the one he lived in," said Chris.

Evidence of the fire that destroyed them could be seen in several charred roofing timbers. All of it had been exposed to the elements ever since. Sheets of corrugated tin lay alongside the timbers, along with a rusting woodstove and various bits of furniture.

They continued on until they reached the southern end of the search sector, and then climbed the slope to begin working their way back again.

"Only two more passes," Macaulay called out to Lexy as she scanned the ground ahead of her.

They were halfway across the seventh and final pass, when Lexy glanced down the slope and again noticed the rubble piles from the hermit's shacks. She suddenly remembered the photograph she had seen up in the museum of its interior, with the straw mattress, the side table, the radio, and the kerosene lamp.

"The hermit's bed," she called out, as if experiencing a revelation.

"What about it?" asked Chris.

"I saw a photograph of it in the museum," she said, striding back to him. "It was a straw mattress. What did it rest on?"

He shared the same revelation.

"It was on a pedestal," he said as the rain ran in rivulets down his smiling face. "A flat stone pedestal."

FIFTY-SEVEN

6 December
Manana Island
Maine

It took fifteen minutes to clear the rubble from the largest mound. Underneath the debris pile, there was solid bedrock. The driving rain helped to sluice away the remaining waste fragments from the pedestal of the hermit's bed.

Lexy began a closer examination of it on her hands and knees. The first seam she followed ran horizontally and was barely detectable from the natural rock formation above it. It followed a generally straight course and was almost as long as she was tall, maybe six inches over five feet.

It then met a cross seam that also ran in a generally straight, but slightly bowed line perpendicular to the first one. She concluded that the bowed section could have resulted from trimming by the Norse stonecutters to meld it to the surrounding declivity.

Her excitement gradually increased as she followed the third seam. It ran parallel to the first one. By now she was sure that the veins could not have been formed naturally.

"Well?" asked Macaulay as she stood up.

"I think we've found it," said Lexy, trying to remain calm.

While she continued studying the rest of the slab, Chris began gathering small boulders and flat rocks from the other debris piles. He dumped them near the upper edge of the pedestal.

"What are you doing?" asked Macaulay.

"Finding shelter from the storm," he answered cryptically.

Kneeling halfway along the top edge of the slab, he located the seam with his fingers and inserted a three-inch-wide steel chisel into the tiny fissure. Picking up an iron mallet, he pounded the head of the chisel, sending stone chips flying into the air. The loud clunking noise was carried away on the wind.

Without pause, the big Finn kept raising the mallet and slamming it down until a noticeable gap began to appear between the edge of the slab and the surrounding natural formation. He stopped when he reached a depth of four inches and crouched down for a closer look.

"Not there yet," he said, resuming his work.

At a depth of six inches, he pounded the head of the chisel once more and it disappeared into a void. He stood up and went over to retrieve one of the iron bars. After positioning a large flat rock next to the gap, he inserted the flat end of the bar into the crevasse below it.

"I could use a hand here," he said to Macaulay, who joined him at the other end of the bar.

Together, they bore their weight down on the bar. The top end of the slab rose slowly but steadily until it cleared the surrounding formation by several inches. By then the bar was almost parallel to the ground.

"Slide a rock under each end of the slab," said Chris to Lexy.

She found two rocks that matched the height of the opening and slid them under the edges. When Chris removed the iron bar from the gap, the slab remained clear.

Chris picked up an even-larger flat stone to use as a new fulcrum. In successive stages, they raised the slab six inches, then a foot, and finally two. Macaulay shined his flashlight into the black opening.

"I can't see the bottom," he said, "but it seems to slope downward."

Chris grabbed one of the coils of rope and anchored one end of it to the slab. He dropped the rest down the opening.

"Who goes first?" he asked.

"I will," said Lexy, but first giving Chris a brisk kiss on the mouth. "Thank you," she said into his rain-soaked face.

He smiled at Macaulay as if he had just won the Nobel Prize.

Chris handed her one of the yellow battery-powered lanterns before she slid off the edge of the slab and into the tunnel. As Macaulay had thought, it descended in a steep sloping direction.

Once inside, she saw it was a natural fissure in the rock formation, with an irregular opening of roughly three by four feet. She lowered herself carefully along the jagged

edges. After about twelve feet, the trajectory of the tunnel leveled off and then began to rise slightly.

She crawled forward with the lantern held high ahead
of her.

The passageway continued on for another ten feet before it headed downward again, the opening growing
gradually larger. Her heart began to race as she saw the
narrow black void slowly expand into what appeared to
be a large catacomb.

"Are you all right?" shouted Macaulay. "We can't see
your light."

"Yes, it's here," she shouted back. "Bring the other
lanterns and the tools."

Almost too excited to breathe, she stood up and took
a step forward. The floor of the catacomb felt spongy
under her boots, and there was a rank smell of decomposition in the air as she raised the lantern to further illuminate the chamber.

Suddenly, something slashed wildly into her hair, and
the darkness around her was choked with a dense multi-
tude of fluttering wings. She ripped away the membra-
nous creature trapped near her ear and saw it was a brown
bat.

As the furious flapping threatened to overwhelm her,
she dropped the lantern and raised her hands to protect
her eyes and face. Falling forward, she lay on the stone
floor, their wild cries ringing in her ears.

The horrible flapping noise slowly faded away. She realized there had to be another aperture into the catacomb
because they had disappeared without ever entering the
passage she had taken to reach it.

Macaulay found her lying on the floor, the dead bat

lying beside her. A few remnants of the colony were still affixed to their perches in the crevasses of the walls, pulsing silently in the light of the new lanterns.

Macaulay helped Lexy to her feet. She was trembling all over.

"Were you bitten?" he asked.

She shook her head and picked up her lantern. Even with three lanterns, the cavern was too large to illuminate completely, but what she could see of its expanse confirmed that the stonecutter on the Greenland ice cap had told no lie.

Along the nearest wall was an intricately carved, hand-tooled chest, similar to the one she had seen in the Viking ship. The top had fallen in. Whatever its contents had once been, they had long since disappeared into dust. Another wooden chest, as large as a sarcophagus and studded with metal rivets, rested in the center of the catacomb.

"Do you suppose . . . ?" began Macaulay as Chris walked over to it, leaving a clear set of footprints in the carpet of bat guano that covered the cavern floor.

She was about to tell him not to touch it, when he gently placed his hand on the pewter-edged lid. A second later, the entire front section disintegrated into tiny shards of wood and dust, bringing the top section down with it.

"Jesus Christ," said Chris.

They directed their lantern beams inside the massive chest.

The first thing Lexy saw was an ornately decorated hilt of a Viking broadsword. Alongside it was an iron helmet. Lexy saw it was an early Spangenhelm pattern and equipped with a spectacle guard. The chest also held two battle-axes, both inlaid with an intricate silver design. A circular shield rested along the back wall along with an iron-mail chest protector. Two bone-handled daggers and several spear points lay at the base of it, the wooden shafts having fallen to pieces centuries ago.

"An ancient armory?" asked Chris.

"There would be no point in putting one down here," said Lexy. "These are the weapons and battle armor of a Viking leader. The axes are inlaid with silver. The sword hilt is unlike anything I have ever seen. This level of craftsmanship was an emblem of great prestige."

The thought that it might have been Eriksson's was left unsaid.

Lexy poked the lantern beam into every corner of the cavern. She found nothing else of possible interest except a mound of what looked like irregular-sized chunks of black stone. They had originally been contained in a basket or a vessel of some kind, but it too had long since rotted away.

Beside it was something coated in feces, and she stooped to examine it more closely. It looked like two large strips of either animal hide or tanned leather. Metal hinges were attached to each strip. Connected to the hinges was a fragment of worm-eaten wood.

Her rising sense of excitement was almost palpable.

Chris was standing at the entrance to the catacomb.

"Did you hear that?" he said, leaning farther out into the passageway. "It sounds like an engine."

"Helicopter?" asked Macaulay.

Chris shook his head.

"No . . . a boat, I think."

"In the middle of a nor'easter?" asked Macaulay.

The two of them stared at each other.

"Chris and I will check it out," said Macaulay.

Chris picked up the satchel holding the Sten gun and headed up the passageway. Macaulay went over to the armaments chest and pulled out one of the three daggers. It had scrollwork engraved on the foot-long blade.

"It's called a seax," said Lexy, as if the knowledge might help him in battle.

He moved toward the passageway to follow Chris.

"Steve," she said.

He stopped and she rushed into his arms.

"Come back to me," she whispered.

"I'm bulletproof," he said.

FIFTY-EIGHT

6 December
Manana Island
Maine

Chris felt the full force of the wind on his face as he came out of the tunnel and glanced across the harbor toward Monhegan. Licking the salt spray from his lips, he saw that all the boats in the island's fishing fleet were snug at their moorings. Nothing was moving in the harbor, but he could still hear the faint sound of a boat engine.

It could only be coming from the far side of Manana.

He unzipped the watertight bag and inserted a full magazine into his Sten gun. Pulling back the cocking bolt, he fed the first round into the chamber. Macaulay emerged from under the stone slab and removed the Glock semiautomatic from under his belt. He checked the magazine.

"I've only got five rounds left," he said. "Let's hope it's Santa Claus over there."

Together they headed up the slope toward the crown

of the ridge. The leaden sky hung low above them as they crawled the last few feet on their bellies. Macaulay carefully parted the thick yew vines at the crest and looked over to the other side.

Standing offshore was a crash rescue boat. Macaulay had seen several of them during the air war in Desert Storm. About seventy feet long, they looked like PT boats and were designed to rescue pilots and air crews that had crashed into the sea.

Although the crash boat was bucking wildly, the massive bulk of Manana protected it from the even more mountainous waves in the open sea. Macaulay realized that the island also masked what the boat's occupants were doing from anyone on Monhegan.

The boat crew had already managed to put six men ashore in rubber Zodiac boats. Macaulay recognized their uniforms from the Kulusuk airfield in Greenland. They were wearing the same white thermal winter suits and carrying suppressed submachine guns. Three of them were halfway up the slope and heading toward the crest, slowly swinging their weapons from side to side as they looked for targets along the rim.

At least there was no way for the men to outflank them, thought Macaulay, scanning the ridge in both directions. There was no high vegetation to mask any movement. They had to come up the slope on open ground to the ambush position.

"Just so you know," said Macaulay, "these guys take no prisoners."

Chris nodded, his hands gripping the trigger housing and the end of the barrel as he placed it in a camouflaged firing position inside the thick shrubbery.

"They're also wearing upper-body armor," added Macaulay. "Aim for their legs."

As the three commandos came on, a crewman on the forward deck of the crash boat fired a small rocket toward the shoreline. It was trailing a thin cable and buried itself in the turf about fifty feet up the slope. One of the commandos went to work securing the cable to bedrock.

"I think they're rigging a breeches buoy to bring something ashore," said Chris, raising his head for a second as the three others closed to fifteen yards of the crest. One of them detected his movement and cut loose with a spray of bullets that tore into the gorse above him.

Macaulay motioned for Chris to scramble farther down the ridgeline while he moved in the opposite direction.

"Now!" he shouted when they were set in the new positions.

They both rose up just far enough to fire through the thick ground cover. Ignoring Macaulay's advice, Chris aimed for their heads and fired three short bursts, killing the two men in front of him.

Squinting to keep the rain out of his eyes, Macaulay aimed the Glock with both hands and fired at the third commando's right leg, hitting him in the thigh. He spun around and fell backward. Chris stood up to get a clear shot and fired another burst at him before dropping back down. The commando didn't move again.

"Remind me to practice on tomato juice cans," shouted Macaulay, motioning for him to move to a new position along the ridgeline.

Two more commandos were coming up the slope, spread out wide. Macaulay heard the harsh guttural snaps of Chris's Sten gun again as he cut loose with the rest of the magazine. The commando in front of Chris began rolling back down the slope. Macaulay fired at the other one, bringing him down too. Chris stood again for a few seconds to finish him.

The only one left standing was still working to anchor the breeches buoy to the bedrock. As Macaulay watched, another Zodiac was launched from the crash boat and began working its way through the pounding waves toward the shoreline. It held four more commandos.

Lying prone behind the ridge, Chris waited until they had crawled up from the rocky sea ledge to the base of the slope and began fanning out for the next assault. They were still bunched together when he cut loose at them with a long burst. Only one went down, but a second commando fell back into the sea. The other two began zigzagging wildly as they ran full tilt up the slope.

When they drew to within thirty feet of the crest, Macaulay emptied his last three rounds at the one in the lead, but the commando was almost hugging the ground, and it was impossible to get a clear shot. Chris rose to his knees to gain a better angle, but when he pulled the trigger, the Sten gun didn't fire.

Both commandos stopped in their tracks, took aim, and fired at him. Three rounds slammed into his upper body almost simultaneously, knocking him over onto his back as Macaulay scrambled toward him behind the crest.

The Sten gun was still clutched in his outflung right hand when Macaulay came up. He had been hit twice in the stomach and once in the lungs, and was trying to stanch the flow of blood over his abdomen with his left hand.

"It jammed," he said, his face creased with pain.

Macaulay picked up the Sten. Pulling back the bolt lever, he cleared the misshapen bullet from the chamber and inserted a new round. Aiming it through the ground cover, he fired a short burst down the slope without aiming.

The return fire shredded the yew branches above them. Macaulay raised his head just far enough to see that the commandos were holding on the other side of the crest, apparently waiting for him to show himself.

Macaulay helped Chris to sit up. In moments, his hands were covered with warm blood from the exit wounds in his back.

"If you can still move, get back down to the dock," said Macaulay. "I'll cover you from here."

Chris gave him a harsh laugh and a thin stream of blood came out of his mouth. His pain-narrowed eyes took in the Viking dagger wedged inside Macaulay's belt on his left hip.

"You need that?" he asked.

Macaulay pulled it out and handed it to him.

"Cool," he said, coughing out a gout of blood.

Macaulay carefully parted the yew vines and glanced over the crest. Both commandos were slowly crawling toward them on their bellies, their gun barrels pointed up the slope.

"They're coming," he said.

Chris rolled over onto his knees and rose to a crouch.

"Fire another burst," he said.

Macaulay slid the barrel of the Sten through the vines and cut loose again. A moment later, Chris launched himself over the crest. It looked to Macaulay like he was moving in slow motion as he reeled down the opposite slope.

Both commandos rose to their feet and opened fire at him as he staggered toward them, brandishing the short sword. The diversion allowed Macaulay to open fire unmolested, and he dropped the first one with a long burst.

Chris was hit again and again, but he wouldn't go down. The second commando had dropped his empty machine gun and was pulling his sidearm from its holster when Chris slammed into him, plunging the short sword into the man's groin.

Macaulay heard his bellowing shriek of pain over the roar of the wind as Chris ripped upward with the blade. The two men hit the ground together. Neither one moved again.

Macaulay dropped back behind the crest as the last commando by the breeches buoy opened fire on him. He sat breathing deeply as the hard rain washed away the blood on his hands.

He checked the magazine in the Sten gun. It was empty. Raising his head to take another look down the slope, he watched as another Zodiac departed from the crash boat. It held only one more commando. One more was enough, he concluded. He had no more ammunition.

At least he had time to go back to the cavern and bring out Lexy. They could hopefully make it down to the dock and row the skiff back across the harbor. He would convince someone over there to help them.

"Turn around," said a voice behind him. "Slowly."

Macaulay turned to face him, his back to the ridge.

The Lynx was drenched with seawater after falling into the sea, but the turbulent wave action had carried him as if he were on a carnival ride around the island to the opposite side. He had climbed the northern slope without difficulty.

Macaulay started to get up as the blond man pointed the Glock down at him.

"Do not bother," said the Lynx, shooting Macaulay in the head.

Above the island, a cloud of seagulls had gathered, all circling wildly overhead, screeching and cawing. The Lynx wondered if they were drawn by the sound of human activity or the smell of blood.

FIFTY-NINE

6 December
Manana Island
Maine

Barnaby came ashore in the leather sling of the breeches buoy, his massive body dangling over the roiling sea as the motorized zip line hauled him along the cable from the crash boat to the anchored position onshore.

He had heard the sounds of sporadic gunfire in his cabin, but its porthole was sealed. He had no conception of the carnage that had taken place until the zip line carried him past the line of dead men in white thermal suits waiting to be ferried back.

When the leather sling had returned to the crash boat, Johannes Prinz Karl Erich Maria von Falkenberg emerged from his stateroom dressed in hooded arctic-weather gear. The faithful Steiger helped him into the breeches buoy.

Only his ashen face peered out from the warm protective clothing as he rode in the sling over to the island. On the next trip, Steiger joined him ashore, followed by Hjalmar Jensen.

Aside from the Lynx, only two commandos were still alive from the contingent that had boarded the crash boat from the *Leitstern* the previous evening. Barnaby watched as they carried another white-uniformed corpse down the slope from the crest of the ridge.

The Lynx had rigged a canvas sedan chair with two short poles. After settling the prince in the chair, he and Steiger hoisted the poles and began to slowly make their way up the slope. Barnaby followed along behind them with Jensen. The two remaining commandos came last, their weapons trained forward.

As they neared the ridgeline, Barnaby passed the first body that wasn't wearing a white thermal suit. He was lying facedown on the gorse, the man's shoulder-length blond hair matted with blood and at least a dozen bullet wounds stitched across his broad back. Barnaby didn't recognize him.

A short sword lay next to the man's body. Barnaby felt a jolt of excitement when he saw the inlaid carvings on its hilt and blade. It would have been carried a millennium ago by an exalted leader.

As they crossed the crown of the ridge, he visibly grimaced at the next corpse. Lying on its side, the body was unmarked, but Barnaby recognized him from his clothing and boots. Beneath the rain-soaked hair, a mask of congealed blood covered what had once been Steve Macaulay.

Farther down the opposite slope, Barnaby saw the partially elevated stone slab rising above the surrounding formation of bedrock. It was exactly as he had pictured it, roughly five feet square and fitted into position by the Norse stonecutters a thousand years ago with astonishing precision.

He could only assume that Macaulay and the other man had found Eriksson's tomb and died protecting it. But where was Alexandra? The thought she might have been killed in the gun battle made him sick with anguish. He took momentary comfort in there being no more bodies along the opposite slope.

"Die Wikinger waren hier," said the prince to Steiger as he arrived at the stone slab. The Vikings were here. Von Falkenberg stood facing the knife edge of the wind and surveyed the barren landscape around him. It was almost unchanged after a thousand years. It would be the last time he would ever gaze at the earth's austere beauty.

The Lynx ordered one of the commandos to descend first; then Steiger helped the prince to climb under the brow of the slab and into the narrow passageway. Jensen went down next, his agitated eyes full of eagerness at what lay below. With a flick of his pistol, the Lynx motioned Barnaby to go down after Jensen.

He ordered the last commando to remain on guard at the opening.

"Vaer arvaken," he said before following Jensen down. Be vigilant.

At the end of the passageway, two battery-powered tungsten-halogen lights had been erected in the catacomb for the prince's arrival. Von Falkenberg slowly stepped into the brilliantly lit chamber with the same joy of anticipation as a priest entering the Holy See.

Steiger assisted him in removing his arctic-weather gear. Underneath it, he was dressed for the most important occasion of his life in a formal black grosgain silk tailcoat over striped trousers, a white waistcoat and shirt, and a white pique bow tie.

Two rows of ribbons and medals adorned his right breast, all of them bestowed by the elders of the Ancient Way for his services to the church. A large golden Mjolnir pendant hung from a red silk sash in the center of his chest.

When Barnaby reached the opening, the first thing he saw was Alexandra on the other side of the chamber, standing alone and unharmed near an enormous riveted chest, her hands bound behind her back. When she looked up and saw him, a smile of relief lit up her face.

She had felt so powerless after the sounds of gunfire ended. There had been no place for her to hide. When she finally heard someone coming, she prayed it would be Steve.

It wasn't. She recognized him right away, the blond commando leader who had murdered Thorwald and Dr. Callaghan in cold blood before destroying their base camp on the Greenland ice cap.

She shuddered involuntarily, recalling the pleasure he had taken in searching her in the catacomb before binding her hands. Then Barnaby was embracing her. He held her close.

"Where are Steve and Chris?" she asked urgently.

"I'm sorry, Alexandra," he whispered.

When he stepped away from her, silent tears were running down her cheeks.

"Is it necessary for Dr. Vaughan to be bound like a slave?" he called out to the prince, amazed at seeing him in white tie and tails.

"Release her at once," said von Falkenberg. He turned

to glare sternly at the Lynx as one of the commandos released her.

Oblivious to the centuries-old carpet of guano covering the cavern floor, Jensen knelt in front of the riveted chest containing the Norse armor and weapons, gazing in awe at its contents.

"These were his own," said Jensen. "Like the Egyptian custom, Norse tradition was that the greatest warriors' weapons were buried with them to be carried into the next life."

He picked up the broadsword and watched the inlaid carvings dance in the light.

"Leifr is here then," he said.

"Where?" replied Barnaby.

"Yes, where, Professor Jensen?" demanded the prince.

"I do not yet know, Your Grace," replied a nervous Jensen, immediately getting up to search for clues along the jagged rock ceiling and walls.

"His tomb is here," said the prince. "He is here. . . . I can feel his presence in my soul."

"I'm surprised to learn you have one," said Barnaby.

Von Falkenberg tottered toward him. Barnaby could see the old man's end was very near. He had visually shrunk in just the hours since he had first met him in the socialite's mansion.

"How can I convince you and Dr. Vaughan to help me?" he said, clearly doubting Jensen's ability to solve the mystery.

"You can give me your solemn oath that Dr. Vaughan will be spared when this is over," said Barnaby.

"I pledge to you upon my sacred faith that this will be

so," he said, his voice barely audible. "And I offer you the same dispensation."

"You will allow us to live?"

"Certainly," he replied. "Others who choose not to subscribe to our faith are allowed to live and work in our facilities."

"As prisoners you mean," said Lexy, "for life."

"The day is coming when there will be no reason not to release you," said von Falkenberg, "and sooner than you think."

Barnaby looked at her, waiting for a signal.

"Must I demonstrate the alternative if you do not assist us?" said the prince.

Lexy had no doubt that he would follow through on the implied threat. The man had only hours to live and would stop at nothing to realize his dream. And there was something else. All her adult life, she had nurtured the chimerical hope that she might someday prove that the Norsemen had arrived in America first.

"I accept your pledge," she said.

Each picking up a lantern, she and Barnaby ignored the two riveted chests and spent fifteen minutes systematically scouring the walls of the voluminous catacomb, and then every foot of the jagged roof.

"Metamorphic," he said while examining the rock striations in the center. "Look here."

Her eyes followed his to the small carved rings in the jagged stone ceiling before she led Barnaby to the small mound of irregular-sized chunks of black stone she had noticed during her own search. He trained the lantern on the two strips of animal hide lying next to it, along with its small metal hinges and the nearby fragment of worm-eaten wood.

He picked up one of the black stones and turned it over in his hands.

"What do you make of this, Hjalmar?" he said, handing it to Jensen.

"Charcoal?" he said, and Barnaby nodded.

"One of the most ancient of man-made fuels," he said. He turned to von Falkenberg.

"Charcoal was used by the Norsemen as their principal heating source during their travels. It was nearly as efficient as wood with only twenty-five percent of the weight."

"But why here?" asked Jensen. "To what purpose?"

"That is indeed the question," said Barnaby, grinning almost cruelly at him. "I'm surprised you would not know the answer, Hjalmar. Prince von Falkenberg deserves better from his pet archaeologist."

Jensen stared at him with open hatred before throwing a wary glance at the prince and then at the Lynx. When Lexy began studying the tanned leather object, Barnaby came over to join her.

"What is a flexible bag comprising two boards with handles enclosing an airtight cavity with a valve to allow the expending of forced air?" she asked.

"A bellows or a blast bag as it was once known," said Barnaby, "employed to fast-start a fire."

"To what purpose?" repeated Jensen, unable to restrain himself.

Lexy went over and picked up a shovel along with the satchel of digging tools that Chris and Macaulay had carried down to the cavern earlier. Returning to the area near the disintegrated bellows, she carefully scraped away the coating of bat feces from two square feet of the stone floor. Kneeling, she began probing the cleared area with her fingers, poking and rubbing the uneven striations in the veined bedrock.

"Here it is," she said finally.

It looked like nothing more than a tiny circular discoloration in the rock. She used Chris's chisel to scrape up a small chunk of it. She held it close to her nose and began kneading it with her fingers.

Picking up Chris's mallet, she set a small chisel above the discolored material and gave it one hard blow. The material disappeared below, leaving a circular hole about two inches in diameter.

"A beeswax plug," she said, smelling the rush of cold dead air from below. "They used the bellows to start a fire in the chamber below this one. Then they cemented the edges of the tomb with beeswax and used this hole to evacuate most of the remaining air with a hand pump. When the fire consumed all the oxygen in the lower chamber, they had an airtight seal around the remains of the man buried below us."

"But how can we enter the tomb?" asked the prince as he sagged wearily against Steiger.

He could feel himself going, his will to live and his strength nearly depleted. Standing in this hallowed place, he could only pray that he would live long enough to cast his eyes on the exalted being below him.

"Remove the riveted chest from the center of the catacomb," she ordered.

When the two commandos attempted to move it, the chest disintegrated. Jensen helped them to remove its contents from the pile of debris before they swept away the thick layer of guano.

In the center of the catacomb was another stone slab, almost exactly the same size as the one that covered the outer passageway.

Over and under, remembered Lexy from the rune inscription.

SIXTY

The Norsemen had carved two small depressions at the far corners of the slab, each with a shallow stone bridge to permit a rope purchase. Lexy pointed at the cavern roof directly above them.

"You will find matching stone rings directly above those," she said. "We will need two coils of heavy rope."

The Lynx and the commando secured the ends of two lines to the carved bridges on the slab and then ran the other ends through the rings in the roof. When they pulled together on the ropes, the end of the slab slowly separated from the surrounding cavern floor. Lexy heard a sustained crackling sound as the solid seal of hardened beeswax parted from the stone.

When the slab was elevated to a height of four feet, the Lynx and the commando anchored the ends of the lines to the rings on the roof. Barnaby called for the lanterns to be trained into the crypt.

The prince issued a loud groan when he saw that it was empty.

The stone floor of the lower chamber was at least nine feet below them. Lexy went over to the pile of tools that Chris and Steve had carried down earlier and uncoiled the rope ladder.

The Lynx anchored one pair of rope ends of the ladder to the edges of the slab and dropped the rest into the lower crypt. Lexy slid over the edge and slowly descended to the stone floor.

"The chamber extends farther in this direction," she said, pointing the lantern ahead of her and disappearing from view.

"I must go down," said von Falkenberg.

The Lynx descended first, assisting the prince after he arrived at the bottom. Von Falkenberg walked off into the darkness after Lexy, who had finally reached the far wall of the crypt. Lifting her lantern, she trained it on something that extended well out from the end of it.

"Mein Gott," said von Falkenberg as he took it in.

The stone sarcophagus had been constructed out of smooth gray shale. It was about six feet long and two and a half feet wide. The head section lay against the end wall, the rest perpendicular to it. Lying on the stone floor at the foot of the sarcophagus was something equally massive and wrapped in what looked like cured leather.

Steiger, Jensen, Barnaby, and the Lynx came up in single file, each carrying a lantern. In the radiant glow, Lexy saw that the lid of the sarcophagus was two inches thick and rested on top of the side panels. Like the slab above, it was sealed with hardened beeswax.

There was an engraved head of a Viking warrior on the lid, surrounded by smaller engravings of Odin's horn, the Mjolnir symbol, and the wolf's cross. The Viking image had a helmet of dense hair and a short beard.

"You may recall the reference in the rune inscription to the strange and powerful being that was fought and vanquished by Eriksson," said Lexy. "We can assume that it is wrapped in those cured animal hides at his feet."

"I wish to see it," said the prince.

Jensen located the outer seam of the leather panels and used a knife to slit one end of it open. The Lynx started at the other end. When they came together in the middle, Barnaby carefully tugged the cured skins apart.

The skeleton was black and powdery with age but surprisingly intact after a thousand years. The first thought that ran through Lexy's mind when she saw it was the giant in *Jack and the Beanstalk*.

Based on the skeletal structure, the man had been nearly seven feet tall.

Lying alongside his body were the remains of the warrior's longbow and some arrowheads inside what had once been a leather quiver. Lexy was reminded of the ancient arrowheads she had seen at the Monhegan museum.

"He was a Skraeling," she said.

"A Skraeling?" repeated the prince, confused.

"That's what the Norsemen called the indigenous people who were here a thousand years ago," said Barnaby. "To the Norsemen, his size and strength would have made him both strange and powerful."

"And buried like a dog at the feet of the victor," said Jensen with an arrogant grin.

"Please remove the lid covering our exalted one," said von Falkenberg. "I must see him—without further delay."

The Lynx and Jensen used their knives to slit the beeswax seal around the rim. They then stood at one end of the sarcophagus while Steiger and Barnaby assumed positions at the other end. Very slowly, each lifted his respective corner. When the slab was clear, they walked it across the floor of the crypt and set it down along the stone wall.

Returning to the sarcophagus with their lanterns, they trained them inside the slate coffin. Von Falkenberg gazed down at the mortal body of Leif Eriksson and gasped aloud.

Macaulay came up out of the blackness to a searing bolt of pure agony. His head was a white-hot furnace of pain and he was blind. His breath came in short irregular gasps and someone nearby was moaning.

He realized it was his own voice.

He remembered where he was, or at least his last memory. It was on the yew-covered ridge above the stone slab. He had been trying to get up when the blond commando had shot him in the head.

But how could he still be alive? He willed his left hand to move and it headed clumsily toward his head like the hand of a mechanical toy. He felt for his pulse on his carotid artery. Its steady beat convinced him he had to be alive.

He moved his fingers to his face and tried to find his eyes in the viscous mess that was already there. His eyes were covered with a congealed mass of blood. He wiped some of it away.

A ghostly presence slowly came into focus as a single tendril of a yew bush just inches away from his nose. It was drenched with the harsh smell of the salt sea. When he slowly turned onto his back, he felt the pitiless rain on his face. He raised his head from the ground and felt the warmth of new blood flowing over his eyes.

The bullet had hit him at a rising angle in his forehead, but instead of penetrating his brain, it had creased the skull. He gently probed the area above his eyes and discovered that a large flap of his scalp was hanging loose.

He found the side pocket of the snorkel coat and managed to remove the cotton rag he had used to clean his pistol on Chris's boat. After resting for a few moments, he rolled the rag into a bandanna and then reached up to tie it around his head. It held the flap of skin in place and halted the flow of blood into his eyes.

He had to find Lexy. The last time he had seen her had been in the cavern. When he tried to turn over onto his stomach, he fainted. The wind and rain brought him around again. He had no idea how much time had passed. He knew he needed to get going.

He began crawling on his hands and knees down the slope toward the stone slab, keeping his head down in order to see what was right ahead of him, creeping inch by inch over the gorse and rocks, moving left or right to avoid the deep crevasses that loomed up along the way.

When he looked up again, it seemed he was no closer to the stone slab than when he had started. Even worse, he was starting to tire. The cold rain continued to sap what little reserves of strength he had left.

He paused to rest as a rolling clap of thunder filled the air. It was followed ten seconds later by a bolt of jagged lightning that momentarily lit up the leaden sky. He felt the insane urge to laugh. As if the wind and snow hadn't been enough. He briefly considered the bizarre notion that the Norse gods were truly angry.

The stark image of Lexy waiting for him in the cavern spurred him to move on again. Scuttling slowly along, he saw that the distance to the underground passageway was finally decreasing. He thought how good it would feel to be under the slab and out of the weather.

When he was no more than twenty feet away from it, he smelled a wisp of cigarette smoke. It was only a hint on the wind, but he was sure of it. He stopped and stared at the dark opening under the slab. As he watched, a brief curl of smoke rose out of the hole and disappeared in the wind, followed a few moments later by a helmeted head.

The commando was facing away from Macaulay and looking down the slope, his Skorpion submachine gun resting beside him on the rock ledge. If he turned around to look up the slope, Macaulay would be easy prey.

Macaulay began crawling toward him, desperately looking around for something to use as a weapon. He picked up one of the stones that Chris had collected to use as stops for the slab. Silently praying that the commando would remain in his shelter, Macaulay closed the remaining distance and crawled onto the base of the slab, slowly inching his way to the top.

When the commando poked his head out again to survey the landscape below, Macaulay was ready. As the man's helmet reached the top of the slab, he slammed the rock as hard as he could into the back of the man's neck.

He dropped out of sight, and Macaulay crawled around the side of the slab and slid down into the opening of the passageway. The commando was dead, his head dangling at a hideous angle from his shoulders. Macaulay was too weak to even lift the machine gun. He started down the tunnel headfirst.

"You must know better than anyone outside our faith, Dr. Finchem," said von Falkenberg, "why this secret cannot be shared with the world."

"You have plans for his DNA," said Barnaby, "and you probably don't want this place to become another hideous version of Disney World."

"Correct on both counts," said the prince.

Lexy was still gazing down into the sarcophagus, stunned to see how remarkably preserved Leif Eriksson was after a millennium in the airtight chamber. He had lost most if not all of his blood in the battle with the Skraeling, but his condition was also a testament to the steps taken by his men to protect his remains.

His face looked as if it had been fashioned from brown leather, but it was still quite handsome, with an aquiline nose, full lips, blond hair and beard. It must have been a David-and-Goliath battle, she thought. Leif Eriksson wasn't more than five feet seven inches tall.

"In the centuries to come, this will become the most sacred place of our faith," said the prince, "set aside for pilgrimages of those who are worthy, and those who share his blood."

"And where will you be?" asked Barnaby.

"Right here beside him," said von Falkenberg. "I will not be going back with you. . . . I will remain here always."

"I wish to be with you," said Steiger, stepping forward, his eyes moist with tears.

"So be it," agreed von Falkenberg. "Dr. Vaughan, I would be grateful if you and Dr. Finchem might leave us now."

Barnaby and Lexy walked back toward the rope ladder as the prince motioned to Jensen to join him next to the sarcophagus.

"You will inform Dr. Larsen upon your return to the *Leitstern* that we have accomplished our task," he said softly. "When it is safe to return, he is to oversee the DNA extraction. He already has my instructions on how it is to be employed in the future. I have also made arrangements with regard to the small cairn that will house my own remains and those of Korporal Steiger."

"Yes, Your Grace."

"God be with you," he said. "Now we wish to be alone."

"But what about them?" asked Jensen, pointing to Barnaby and Lexy.

"I gave them my personal oath," he said. "Perhaps they could be useful in our underground facility at Tromso. See to it."

"Yes, Your Grace," he said.

The prince suddenly hunched forward as if he had a terrible stomach cramp, and collapsed to the stone floor. Steiger rushed to assist him to his knees. Together they began to pray.

Von Falkenberg could finally let himself go. The vision

of Einherjar came to him, pure and glorious, the heavenly resting place of Valhalla. He had accomplished everything he had set out to do.

Jensen joined the others at the rope ladder.

The Lynx was already planning what to do with the two archaeologists after they resealed the tomb. Especially the woman. Unlike the prince, he had made no pledge and Jensen would not care. Jensen was a coward.

The Lynx sent the commando up the rope ladder first. When he disappeared into the cavern above, he turned to Barnaby. This one wouldn't get out of the upper cavern, he decided, motioning him to go.

Barnaby looked into the blond man's eyes. He knew with certainty what was going to happen to them once the prince was sealed into his tomb. He slowly began to climb up the rope ladder.

"You next," said the Lynx, placing his hand on Lexy's hip as she waited for Barnaby to clear the ladder.

The Lynx removed his short-range pocket transceiver from his belt.

"Horst, we are coming up," he radioed to the commando he had left standing guard at the outside entrance to the tunnel. Jensen stood beside him, waiting for his turn to go up next.

The Lynx waited for the radioed acknowledgment as Lexy made her way up the rope ladder. There was only silence. Something had gone wrong. As always, he could sense it.

"Halt!" he shouted to Lexy as she approached the top of the nine-foot ladder.

Launching himself from the stone floor, he leaped to the fourth rung; from there he reached up and grabbed her left ankle. She screamed as he pulled his Glock from its holster and vaulted up the rest of the way.

As the Lynx climbed over the edge, he saw the commando lying on his side, his dead eyes staring back at him. The man the Lynx thought he had killed on the ridgeline was kneeling on the stone floor with a blood-soaked bandage around his head, holding on to the woman's arms and dragging her away from the opening to the crypt.

Still clutching the woman's ankle, the Lynx leveled his pistol at the man's head for a second time and smiled. He would not miss again.

Standing behind the inverted stone slab, Barnaby swung Leif Eriksson's broadaxe in a wide arc and slashed the two lines that held it suspended four feet above the opening.

The four-thousand-pound slab slammed home.

Sobbing with joy at the discovery that Macaulay was still alive, Lexy folded herself into his waiting arms as the Lynx's severed head rolled across the cavern floor and came to a stop, his vacant blue eyes staring into oblivion.

SIXTY-ONE

8 December
The White House
Washington, DC

Jessica Birdwell swept through the anteroom of the Oval Office, her elation impossible to mask. The president had just offered her Ira Dusenberry's job, now that Ira was moving up to become national security adviser.

As she headed downstairs to the intelligence management center to share the news of her promotion, she almost ran headlong into a man who stepped out of one of the offices along the second-floor corridor.

"I was hoping you might have a few moments to talk to me, dear girl," he said.

Her first reaction was that he looked like a seedy undertaker from Mississippi. There were liver spots on his cheeks and he was wearing a rumpled seersucker suit with a yellow bow tie. She had no idea who he was or why he would want to engage her.

"I'm sorry, but I'm in something of a hurry right

now," she said brusquely as she brushed past him. "Call my secretary for an appointment."

He kept right up with her as she continued along the corridor. There was something vaguely familiar about him, but she couldn't remember why. He certainly didn't look like he belonged in the White House.

"Now would be a very good chance to talk, my dear," he said with a grandfatherly smile.

For the first time, she noticed the two other men trailing behind him. There was nothing seedy about them. They looked military, or possibly ex-military, both about thirty-five and very fit.

"Do you recognize this, my dear?" said the man, holding up a golden pendant.

She stopped to look at it. The locket was hanging from a thin gold chain. She had one similar to it in the secret compartment in her bedroom floor. In a moment of sickening realization, she realized it was hers.

It was the Mjolnir.

"It's all over, Freya," he said.

Only the highest echelon of the Ancient Way knew her real name. After so many years, was it possible they had uncovered the truth? Almost frozen with apprehension, she kept her poise.

"I'm not sure who you are looking for, but my name is Jessica Birdwell," she said, her voice steady, "and I'm late for an appointment."

"Jessica Birdwell disappeared at the age of seven when a tornado destroyed her home in Topeka, Kansas," he said. "She was never found—until you assumed her identity thirty-one years ago. It wasn't easy unraveling the trail, but you can give us a fuller picture of it in the days ahead."

"I must talk to the president," she said, pivoting in the crowded corridor.

"The president is being informed of your true identity right now," said Tommy Somervell. "You will never be seeing him again."

He motioned to the two men behind them, and they moved up on each side of her.

"We have a car waiting by the south entrance," he said.

"Where are you taking me?" she demanded.

"To a place where you will be able to appreciate the simpler pleasures," responded Somervell. "Have you ever enjoyed a sunset over Guantanamo Bay? They are truly quite lovely, dear girl. And you will be in such good company."

8 December
RV *Leitstern*
North Atlantic Ocean

The nor'easter had finally lost its ferocious menace and the deck was no longer vibrating to the towering waves that had exploded over the steel bridge rails, buckling them in several places before sluicing away.

Although the wind had died to little more than a whisper, winter had set in with a vengeance and the ship's superstructure was gleaming with ice. Crewmen with hammers and fire hoses braved the cold to clear it away.

"Aircraft bearing south southwest," called out one of the bridge lookouts.

Captain Peter Bjorklund glanced down at the search radar scanner and saw what appeared to be an entire armada of aircraft converging on his ship. For a moment, he wondered if they might have stumbled into a major military exercise.

In the next few minutes, his plotters in the ship's combat information center registered the arrival of a full strike fighter squadron of American F/A-18 Super Hornets, followed by four EA-6B Prowler electronic warfare aircraft.

In the wake of the Prowlers came a swarm of MH-60 Seahawk helicopters, the bridge lookouts reporting that they were equipped with air-launched torpedoes and Hellfire missiles. Twenty minutes later, a Los Angeles–class nuclear attack submarine was detected on the sonar scanner.

Standing next to Bjorklund on the bridge, the Marquess Antoinette Celeste de Villiers knew precisely why it was happening. Two hours earlier, she had received a coded message from Matthiessen, the commander of the crash boat that had carried Prince von Falkenberg and his party to the small island of Manana off the coast of Maine.

Matthiessen had radioed that he was about to be boarded by a heavily armed United States Coast Guard cutter. Before communications were cut off, he reported that he had received no word from von Falkenberg after he was transported to the island, and that all the commandos assigned to the mission had either been killed or were missing, including their commander, Major Joachim Halvorsen. Hjalmar Jensen, the archaeologist who had accompanied the prince, and the prince's valet, Steiger, were also missing.

After reading the message, de Villiers ordered Captain Bjorklund to set a course for Fredrikstad, Norway, at the ship's maximum speed. The *Leitstern* was already well beyond the twelve-mile limit of United States territorial waters as defined by the United Nations Convention on the Law of the Sea, but de Villiers was taking no chances.

While the warplanes and helicopters continued to circle menacingly overhead, two United States Coast Guard frigates materialized out of the murk ahead, blocking their path of escape.

The officer of the deck handed Captain Bjorklund a radio message that had just been sent in the clear from the American Commander, Naval Surface Force, U.S. Atlantic Fleet. The message ordered the captain of the RV *Leitstern* to stop its engines and prepare to be boarded.

"They have no legal right to board this ship," said the Marquess de Villiers to Bjorklund. "We are no longer in U.S. territorial waters. Ignore the message."

De Villiers had already signaled key advocates in the European governments that the *Leitstern* might soon be pursued by U.S. naval forces, and they were already sending official communiqués of protest to Washington.

Over the ship's PA system, Bjorklund warned his crew that an attack could come at any time. Without deviating from his course, he headed for the coast guard ships blocking his path. When a collision seemed almost imminent, the other two ships turned away, allowing them to pass.

"As I thought," said de Villiers in a jubilant tone. "They do not wish to force an international incident."

Per Larsen sat at his desk in his private compartment two decks below the bridge and finished writing a letter to his wife. If all went well, she would never receive it, but it gave him the chance to express all his tortured thoughts. Their next meeting would be in Valhalla.

Removing his white lab coat, he put on the set of green overalls worn by the maintenance crew that he had taken from the laundry earlier that morning. Since the ship was on full alert, every member of the crew was required to wear a Spectra battle helmet and inflatable life vest. The helmet served to further conceal his face.

Picking up the red toolbox, he left his compartment in the laboratory suite. Crewmen were rushing past in both directions as he walked purposefully along the passageways and stairwells that led to the lower decks.

No one gave him a second look as he turned the circular door wheel to open the watertight hatch that led into the compartment containing the ship's main propulsion engines.

The *Leitstern* was powered by two new General Electric LM2500 gas turbines, which generated forty-one thousand shaft horsepower and rested side by side in the center of the compartment. They each weighed twelve tons and were bolted to a steel platform eighteen inches above the deck.

Once inside the compartment, Larsen spun the door wheel to seal the hatch behind him and walked across the catwalk suspended above the two gigantic turbines. It was very hot and the blast of sound was overpowering. At the other end of the catwalk, he descended to the deck.

Two ratings wearing ear-protection muffs under their helmets were checking one of the right turbine's fuel nozzles as he walked to the back corner. They took no notice of him either.

Between the engine room and the sea were only the bottom shell plating, the keel frame, and the steel hull itself. Momentarily out of view, he knelt down and opened the red toolbox. After removing a can of lubricating oil, he set the battery-powered, digital alarm clock inside the box to ring in five minutes.

Shutting it, he shoved the box as far as he could reach under the steel grating beneath the turbine. Standing up, he spilled the lubricating oil on the deck. When one of the engineer ratings came around the back corner of the turbine, he saw a maintenance man on his knees mopping up a small spill with a cleaning rag.

Standing on the bridge, Captain Bjorklund watched the strike squadron of F/A 18 Super Hornets head off to the southwest, followed by the fleet of attack helicopters and the EA 6-B Prowlers. Only a Grumman E-2 Hawkeye surveillance plane remained above them.

"It will be clear sailing from here to Fredrikstad," said the Marquess de Villiers as the sun poked through the parting cloud layer above them.

Bjorklund had just ordered a stand-down from full alert, when the fitted charge of plastic explosives constructed by Per Larsen with laboratory chemicals and glazing putty exploded under the *Leitstern*'s right gas turbine.

The upward thrust of the explosion blew the twelve-ton engine fifteen feet up into the deck above. Its downward thrust ripped a gaping twenty-foot hole in the steel hull.

Twelve minutes later, the RV *Leitstern* was gone. Captain Bjorklund was the only officer among the twelve crew members pulled from the frigid water by the American nuclear submarine USS *Timberville*.

8 December
Maine Medical Center
Portland, Maine

"Call me Ira," said the president's new national security adviser as he walked across the room to Macaulay's hospital bed and shook his hand.

"The president asked me to fly up to express his personal gratitude for the important service you have carried out on behalf of your country," he said, as if delivering a State of the Union address, "and to extend his best wishes for your full recovery."

Macaulay's head was swathed in a white bandage that covered the thirty-two stitches in his scalp, and he still felt woozy from everything he had gone through in the previous week. Life before Greenland seemed a distant memory.

Dusenberry's smile was quickly replaced by a look of sorrow.

"Of course, the president was deeply saddened to hear of the death of his friend John Lee Hancock, which was confirmed by our recovery team in Greenland. He will be buried with full military honors at Arlington."

Looking on, Barnaby thought Dusenberry seemed more like a Turkish wrestler gone to seed than a senior presidential adviser. Although the room was almost chilly, he was sweating profusely and the fastener of his trousers was unbuttoned, as if he had just come off an eating binge.

Ira turned to Barnaby.

"And thanks to you, Dr. Finchem, we've arrested fourteen of the couriers who were carrying the canisters of viral agents to the phase one targets. Some of them had already emptied them into the water supplies, but based on your assurance that Dr. Larsen had replaced the viral agents with a harmless substitute, we decided to let them think they disbursed the real thing. When nothing happens, their superiors will assume the viral agents didn't work."

"Brilliant," said Barnaby.

"My national security team wanted me to ask you about any lab notes and clinical data you think Dr. Larsen may have saved on those genetic formulas," said Dusenberry. "We wouldn't want those secrets to get into the wrong hands again."

Just into the hands of your own scientists, thought Barnaby.

"Larsen was a true groundbreaker," said Barnaby, "but even more important, he was a decent and caring man. He hated what they had done with his scientific breakthroughs and said that they were too important for any group or government to have. He told me that he had destroyed his formulas."

Dusenberry couldn't disguise his disappointment.

"You're saying all his scientific discoveries died with him?"

"That's correct, but since we're speaking of important scientific discoveries," said Barnaby, "Dr. Vaughan and I are preparing to make an announcement of our own with the discovery of the burial tomb of Leif Eriksson, along with the undeniable proof that he came to the shores of Massachusetts no later than 1016."

Dusenberry removed a vial of antacids from his jacket

and popped four into his mouth. A moment later, his soulful look reappeared.

"I regret to tell you, Dr. Finchem," he said, "that we have had to invoke a complete blackout on anything related to your discovery of that tomb."

"And why?" demanded Barnaby.

"Because of important national security concerns," said Ira.

"National security?" said Barnaby, his voice rising. "He's been dead for a thousand years."

"Everything related to the Order of the Ancient Way and its worldwide agenda has to be put under wraps. Right now, we're attempting to discover which leaders among our European allies might be complicit. Even one of my own White House colleagues was found to be part of it."

Ira remembered the last time he had seen Jessica as she was being escorted out of the White House in handcuffs. Serenely composed, she had never looked more beautiful to him. This female archaeologist was of that same mold, he thought, glancing over at Lexy again.

"By now, you know that the Ancient Way has a network of powerful believers all over the world," he went on. "They believe Eriksson is a god. For you to sanctify him as the man who discovered our country would give them even greater power and influence."

"You must be joking," said Barnaby.

"To the contrary," said Ira. "Just this morning, the secretary of Homeland Security expressed his strong concern that releasing this information would create a serious upheaval across the country."

"Are we talking about Secretary Annunzio?" asked Barnaby.

"Yes, of course."

"In other words, the president doesn't want to lose the Italian American vote in the next election."

"That's an outrageous assertion," said Dusenberry. "I hope you are prepared to apologize."

"Another measure of courage along the Potomac," added Macaulay from his hospital bed.

"Please thank the president for us," said Lexy, leading him to the door.

"As soon as you're better, General Macaulay, we would like to schedule a visit for you to the Oval Office so the president can express his appreciation personally," said Ira.

"In between the Rose Bowl queen and a Four-H prizewinning hog," said Barnaby.

"Have a safe trip," said Lexy, herding Ira through the door and closing it behind him.

"Well, that's that," said Macaulay, sipping water through a straw.

"Instead of sharing the greatest archaeological discovery of the modern age, we are given a gag order," said Barnaby.

"It won't last forever," said Lexy.

Macaulay smiled up at Barnaby.

"In the meantime, you have your mentoring work," he said.

"Yes, there is that," agreed Barnaby. "Have you heard from your CIA friend Somervell since we got you back to Monhegan?"

Macaulay nodded.

"His cleanup team arrived before the storm fully abated," said Macaulay. "Tommy said they covered all our tracks. Everything is as it was when we arrived there."

"What about Chris?" asked Lexy.

"The cover story is that he was lost in the storm," said Macaulay. "He'll be buried this week in a service at the island cemetery."

"I'm going," said Lexy.

"Me too," said Macaulay.

"So the crypt is sealed again, over and under," said Barnaby.

"Yes," said Lexy.

"For another thousand years?" asked Macaulay.

"We'll see," said Barnaby.

25 December
Camp Delta
Guantanamo Bay Detention Center
Guantanamo Bay, Cuba

After her arrival at Camp Delta in the Guantanamo Bay Detention Center on December 8, Freya was processed by a team of joint task force female personnel, issued her complement of prison clothing, and placed in a cell in the maximum security section. The small single room was visually monitored twenty-four hours a day.

Her initial interrogation began the next morning. It included two three-hour sessions divided by a thirty-minute break for lunch in her room. Two seasoned female interrogators conducted the interview. At no time during the first six hours did Freya utter a word.

In the days that followed, a range of interrogation techniques was employed in the interview sessions, all designed to engage and elicit either intellectual or emotional responses from the client. Freya still refused to speak.

The interrogation sessions were halted after ten days. A young male agent who had enjoyed success in establishing emotional and romantic relationships with several hardened Al Qaeda operatives was introduced to the client in an attempt to establish rapport with her. When his efforts proved unsuccessful, a female agent with proficiency in psychological intimidation was given several days to break through the shell of resistance.

Unlike other new detainees at the facility, whose emotions ranged from expressing hatred toward the United States to general belligerence and mental depression, the client Freya maintained a consistent refusal to display any emotion at all, regardless of the provocation.

In the third week of her incarceration, it was decided to employ additional interrogation techniques approved by the Department of Justice, including sleep derivation and the inclusion of small doses of midazolam, 3-quinuclidinyl benzilate, and temazepam in her food and drink. This was followed with extra-loud rap music in her room, temperature manipulation, and twelve-hour uninterrupted interrogations.

None of the techniques made a difference. She continued to refuse to speak. According to the interrogators, her only visible emotions were variously described as "tranquil, composed, almost serene."

At Langley, the agency began a comprehensive investigation to determine who she was and how she had come to assume the identity of a child killed in a Kansas tornado in 1982. Agents were able to trace the individuals who had assumed the roles of her parents when she was growing up in Merced, California. They had allegedly been killed in a boating accident while Freya was attending Cornell, but their bodies had never been found, and the agents suspected an elaborate ruse. The investigation was ongoing.

With no imminent threat to the nation's national security from the Order of the Ancient Way, it was decided that the client would not be subjected to enhanced interrogation techniques at the facility's Camp No, including waterboarding, hypothermia, and stress positions. She was not allowed to fraternize with other detainees and remained in solitary confinement.

On Christmas Eve, Tommy Somervell was sitting alone in his study in Leesburg, Virginia, when the call came through from the deputy director asking him to fly down to Guantanamo.

"We've run out of options at this point," he said.

On Christmas morning, Somervell left Andrews Air Force Base, arriving at Guantanamo two and a half hours later. He asked to meet with the client Freya in a less-forbidding environment than her prison cell.

An hour later, they met for lunch in the Guantanamo officers' club. A sign in the foyer proclaimed that officers wearing academy rings would receive A FREE SHOT OF LEADERSHIP. Freya was accompanied by two guards, who remained standing ten feet from their table. She wore a one-piece denim pantsuit that had been starched and pressed.

Through the large picture windows overlooking the

sea, Tommy could see gentle waves caressing a white sandy beach. Directly beneath them, off-duty personnel were swimming in the club's Olympic-sized pool. A black waiter arrived at the damask-covered table, bearing a silver platter containing a broiled medley of fresh shrimp, tuna, and scallops.

"So, how are you enjoying your time here, dear girl?" Somervell asked.

The wide-set blue eyes were almost feverishly bright, her face reminding him of oil paintings by Pierre-Auguste Renoir he had once seen in Paris. She had lost a good deal of weight, as if all the sumptuous Georgetown dinners had melted off her frame, leaving her lean and sculpted.

She didn't respond to his question. He made several more attempts to initiate a conversation as they ate the meal together. Mostly she looked out at the sea. When she finished her last sip of coffee, the guards stepped forward to escort her back to her cell.

"Good-bye, dear girl," said Somervell. "I'm so sorry."

She smiled down at him after standing up to leave.

"Why?" she said.

ACKNOWLEDGMENTS

Researching this book was a journey of discovery for me in learning about the indomitable Norsemen who explored the continent of North America hundreds of years before Columbus first sighted the Bahamas Archipelago in 1492.

It is highly unlikely that incontrovertible evidence will ever be found to prove the actual location of the temperate land Leif Eriksson chose to name Vinland after wintering there with his men as early as 1003, but one can make a good circumstantial case that it was west of Cape Cod, Massachusetts.

For anyone interested in exploring these theories further, as well as the even stronger evidence of Norse explorations as far west as Minnesota in the 1300s, I would recommend a book published in 1940 by Hjalmar R. Holand called *Westward from Vinland: An Account of Norse Explorations and Discoveries in America, 982–1362.* It provides many of the clues and data utilized in constructing the factual basis for this novel.

As always, I am grateful to my literary agent, David Halpern, for his sagacious advice on the story and characters. I also wish to thank my fine editor, Brent Howard, for his belief in the book. Finally, I would like to thank my longtime friend and mentor, Martin Andrews, to whom the book is dedicated, and who landed his own B-17 safely in Greenland on his way to join the 8th Air Force in England in 1943.